Praise for ~~T~~

"I devoured *The Lost Daught...* ... makes complex history so accessible. So real. . . . It was truly exceptional."

"Another brilliant read from G... ...twine and kept me captivated ... ...forward to getting back to it each evening."

—Tracy Rees, author of *Darling Blue*

"With *The Lost Daughter*, [Gill] has returned to the tragic Romanovs, creating another fascinating story that asks the haunting question: 'What if one of them escaped?' A pleasure to dive into."

—Kate Riordan, author of *The Stranger*

"Fascinating Gill captures this family and this period of history so vividly. Such a wonderful book."

—Hazel Gaynor, *New York Times* bestselling
author of *The Lighthouse Keeper's Daughter*

"A wonderful sweeping tale that totally captivated me and had me on the edge of my seat, clutching my hanky. The story is bold and powerful, filled with emotion, tension and vivid characters in a setting that is rich in historical detail. . . . And the love story? Intense and passionate, it will grip your heart. I loved it."

—Kate Furnivall, *New York Times*
bestselling author of *The Italian Wife*

"An enthralling story: the heartbreak genuine, the research brilliant. I love the way the present narrative throws light on the past story."

—Dinah Jefferies, *Sunday Times*
bestselling author of *The Missing Sister*

The Lost Daughter

By Gill Paul

Women and Children First
The Affair
No Place for a Lady
The Secret Wife
Another Woman's Husband

The Lost Daughter

GILL PAUL

WILLIAM MORROW
An Imprint of HarperCollins*Publishers*

P.S.™ is a trademark of HarperCollins Publishers.

THE LOST DAUGHTER. Copyright © 2018 by Gill Paul. All rights reserved. Printed in the United States of America. No part of this book may be used or reproduced in any manner whatsoever without written permission except in the case of brief quotations embodied in critical articles and reviews. For information, address Harper-Collins Publishers, 195 Broadway, New York, NY 10007.

HarperCollins books may be purchased for educational, business, or sales promotional use. For information, please email the Special Markets Department at SPsales@harpercollins.com.

Originally published as *The Lost Daughter* in Great Britain in 2018 by Headline Review.

FIRST U.S. EDITION

Designed by Diahann Sturge

Chapter opening flower © deisey / Shutterstock, Inc.

Library of Congress Cataloging-in-Publication Data

Names: Paul, Gill, 1960– author.
Title: The Lost Daughter : a novel / Gill Paul.
Description: New York, NY : William Morrow Paperbacks, 2019.
Identifiers: LCCN 2018059051| ISBN 9780062843272 (paperback) | ISBN 0062843273 (trade paperback)
Subjects: LCSH: María Nikolaevna, Grand Duchess, daughter of Nicholas II, Emperor of Russia, 1899–1918—Fiction. | Princesses—Russia—Fiction. | BISAC: FICTION / Historical. | FICTION / Family Life. | FICTION / Biographical. | GSAFD: Historical fiction. | Biographical fiction.
Classification: LCC PR6116.A863 L67 2019 | DDC 823/.92—dc23
LC record available at https://lccn.loc.gov/2018059051

ISBN 978-0-06-284327-2

19 20 21 22 23 LSC 10 9 8 7 6 5 4 3 2 1

To my oldest friend, my aunt Anne,
who remains inspirational in her nineties;
and my youngest friends, Hope (aged nine) and Marshall (six),
who are incredibly brave and very good at making me laugh

~

She packed a bag of items she did not want to be without: her photo album, her sketch pad and pencils, a couple of favorite icons, and the gold Fabergé box, then she put her camera beside it.

She pulled on the undergarments and skirt into which she had sewn jewels, and saw her sisters doing the same.

She pulled on her boots and laced them, then picked up her camera and her travel bag. When they were all ready, they walked out to the drawing room.

As they passed the stuffed black bear at the top of the stairs, her mother crossed herself.

~

PROLOGUE

Ekaterinburg, July 16, 1918

YUROVSKY SURVEYED THE GUNS SPREAD ACROSS THE table: six pistols and eight revolvers. They seemed out of place in this gentleman's study, with its expensive purple wallpaper decorated with gold palm leaves, lavish silver chandelier, stained-glass art nouveau lamps, and wooden gramophone. Two rooms away, the Romanov family was eating dinner along with its four retainers. Omelette; there was a surfeit of eggs that day.

The office door opened and the men sloped in, glancing first at the guns and then at him, before shuffling into a semicircle. Ermakov stood directly beneath a stag's head mounted on the wall, his dark hair unruly and his face shiny with perspiration. Yurovsky wasn't close enough to smell the alcohol on his breath but knew it was there, although it was only eight in the evening and still light outside.

"Tonight," he began, "the Presidium of the Ural Regional Soviet has been charged with a great mission: to rid our country of the enemies of Bolshevism." His stomach knotted; there had still been no telegram from Moscow confirming it, yet all the same it was clear what was required of him. This was his moment; his place in the history books beckoned.

He continued in a businesslike tone: "I want eleven men, one for each of the party, so the deaths are simultaneous. You will be allocated a target and I will give the order to fire. Shoot to kill, so they do not have the unnecessary suffering of seeing each other die."

As he spoke, he looked from face to face, watching for signs of hesitation, or fear, or nerves. He needed steady men, who would obey without question. This bunch were militants from the Verkh-Isetsk metallurgy plant, probably less intelligent than average. That was good; he didn't want any questions about the whys and wherefores, just mute obedience. Most had not met the family yet, so there had been no chance to form attachments. They were young, though, the youngest only seventeen. Would they stay calm when the firing started?

Ermakov was eager. "I'll take a Mauser," he said, reaching for one of the most powerful guns on the table.

Adolf Lepa, commander of this new set of guards, surprised Yurovsky. "I don't think I could shoot the girls," he mumbled, looking at his feet.

Yurovsky glared. Lepa had been at the meeting at the Hotel Amerika when the decision had been made that very afternoon. He knew they couldn't risk the Romanovs falling into the hands of counterrevolutionaries who might even try to reinstate them on the throne, with the backing of foreign governments.

"Me neither," said Verhas, a Hungarian man.

Yurovsky opened his mouth to chastise them, to reiterate the case for the execution, but realized there was no point. He had thought Lepa reliable at least, but you never knew how people would react when they were put on the spot. "Go back to the Popov House, both of you," he ordered. "And don't breathe a word of this. The rest of the guard will not be told till the last minute."

He waited until they had shuffled out before addressing the others. "If there is a gun you prefer, choose now."

They stepped forward, eyeing the remaining Mauser, the Colts, the Nagants, the Smith & Wesson, the Browning, picking them up to test the grip, the weight. One man's hand was shaking so violently he almost knocked a Nagant to the floor. Another smelled strongly of homemade vodka, his breath foul with it, and Yurovsky winced.

"You two." He motioned at them, then pointed to the door. "You are relieved."

That left ten, including him. One man would have to shoot two people. He glanced at Ermakov, nursing the Mauser, his eyes sparkling with revolutionary fervor.

"I'll take two," the wild man volunteered, preempting him.

Ermakov had murdered before; he'd spent six years in a prison camp for decapitating the nightwatchman at a factory he was raiding, but had been released after the Revolution. Now he was a Cheka officer of great renown in the region. Yurovsky knew he would get the job done.

"That's it, then," he said, looking around the men one last time. "Nothing must go wrong. Our leaders have put great trust in us, and I am putting my trust in you. Take your weapons and await orders."

One of them tripped over a rug as he left the room and his pistol fell to the floor with a clunk. Yurovsky sighed. It was going to be a long night.

CHAPTER 1

Ekaterinburg, April 1918

Citizen Romanov, citizen Romanova. I am commissar Avdeyev." The man spoke in Russian and wore a Red Army uniform. He did not even remove his cap with its red badge as he addressed them.

Maria watched her mother bristle. Until March the previous year her title had been Tsarina Alexandra, Empress of All Russias, and she had not come to terms with the change in their circumstances.

"Who does he think he is?" Alexandra remarked in English to Maria's father, the former Tsar Nicholas.

"From now on, you will speak only Russian, the language of our great nation," the commissar reprimanded, and her mother tutted loudly and muttered something under her breath.

Their servants were still hauling trunks up the hill from the station. Maria wanted to stay outside in the bright spring sunshine rather than step into the squat-looking house surrounded by a tall palisade fence. From where they stood, only the curved dormer windows set in a green metal roof could be seen above the fence posts. Avdeyev was beckoning them up the steps, and her heart filled with a gloom that matched the shadowy interior as she followed her parents.

Inside, a flight of stone stairs led up from the foyer. Avdeyev explained that they would spend their days on the upper floor, except when they were permitted out into the yard to exercise. On the landing there was a stuffed black bear with two cubs, and Maria winced; she had never liked taxidermy and it seemed a bad omen to have these dead creatures in their midst.

Her mind wandered as Avdeyev gave them a guided tour, his tone curt. He led them into a drawing room with carved oak furniture and a piano, then through an arch to a further sitting room with a writing desk and bookshelves, and a dining room with a dark, heavy table and chairs. The furnishings were clearly expensive but lacked comfort, as if designed for show rather than use. The bedroom was brighter, with pale yellow wallpaper, but Maria must share it with her parents, while their servants would camp in the living and dining rooms. There was electricity, a bathroom and a lavatory with toilet, and she supposed they should be grateful, but she yearned for the spacious elegance of their rooms in the Alexander Palace.

She walked to the bedroom window and watched an electric streetcar glide up the hill. Men and women strolled past, scarcely glancing at the house. *They* weren't prisoners. They could do as they pleased. Maria wished she had been born an ordinary citizen rather than a daughter of the Tsar. She was only eighteen years old and wanted to have fun, but since the uprising in February the previous year, her family had been under house arrest. Almost fourteen months a prisoner. How wonderful it would be to wake in the morning, open the curtains, and decide to hike in the countryside, or drive to the coast to see the ocean—preferably with a handsome beau. Maria had not yet had a beau and she longed for one. Girls her age usually had beaus; some were married at eighteen, so why not her?

Her mother lay on the daybed complaining of a headache and covered her eyes with a cloth, while her father paced up and down, sucking on a pipe, his cheeks hollowed and his brow creased in worry. Maria went through to the sitting room to help Demidova, her mother's maid, search for some headache powders. Their luggage had been tossed around during the weeklong journey from Tobolsk and a perfume bottle had smashed, its scent cloying and no longer pleasant. She found the powders and took them to her mother with a glass of water, then wandered idly around their accommodation, looking out of windows at the yard and the city beyond: tree-lined boulevards, leafy parks, and, in the distance, factory chimneys belching smoke. Several doors were locked on their floor of the house, which was annoying as they could have used the extra space.

If only her sisters had come with them. Maria missed them terribly, especially Anastasia, two years her junior, who would no doubt be up to some mischief or other were she here. But her siblings had stayed behind at the Governor's House in Tobolsk to look after her little brother, Alexei, who was poorly after a fall had caused bleeding in his groin. Maria had been chosen to accompany her parents to this, their next prison. Why must they be here? Ekaterinburg seemed a strange destination if they were to be shipped into exile, as they hoped, because it was in the landlocked dead center of the country.

There was a guard standing by the top of a second staircase near the bathroom, and Maria said good afternoon before recognizing his face and squealing with delight.

"I know you! You used to work at Livadia. How wonderful to see you here!" The Livadia Palace in Crimea had been the Romanovs' spring retreat. Although it was still winter in St. Petersburg at the end of March, flowers and fruit trees were already in bloom in Crimea, and the sun was warm.

They all loved Livadia. "Forgive me," she added, "for I have forgotten your name."

He bowed his head. "Ukraintsev, ma'am. Konstantin Ukraintsev."

"You were the beater at Uncle Michael's hunts, were you not? And I remember you playing croquet with us on the lawn. You always let me win." Maria wanted to dance with joy at coming upon a friendly face.

"Indeed, ma'am."

"Tell me, how is your family? Did they come here with you?"

"I married an Ekaterinburg woman and have been working in the city for some years past."

"Do you have children?"

He told her of his wife, his two children—a boy and a girl—and she asked about their characters, their interests, drinking in the information. She would embroider a cushion for them, she decided. As an Easter gift.

"Whose house is this?" she asked. "I find myself looking at the furniture and wondering whose hand chose it."

"A merchant called Ipatiev," he replied. "I believe he was asked to vacate it only recently in order to accommodate your family."

"I hope it did not inconvenience him." She frowned, peering down the staircase. "It does not seem an especially large house. Are there many guards here?"

"A few dozen," he told her. "Some sleep on the ground floor and others in a house across the street." He paused. "I'm sorry, ma'am. I took the job because it was much better money than I earned in the factory."

"I completely understand," she cried. "Please don't worry about that. I am just so happy to see you. You must come and say hello to Mama and Papa later."

Another guard ascended the staircase toward them. He

stopped and seemed uncertain when he saw Maria talking to his colleague.

"This is Peter Vasnetsov," Ukraintsev told her.

When she smiled and held out her hand, he hesitated and did not seem to know whether to shake it, so she grasped his fingers and gave them a quick squeeze. He was a tall man, probably around twenty years old. His sandy-blond hair had an unruly tuft at the front, what they called a cowlick. "Charmed to meet you," she said. "I'm Maria."

He nodded without meeting her eye, looking instead at Ukraintsev. "I was sent to relieve you," he told him.

Ukraintsev patted his shoulder, then told Maria, "I shall knock on the door after dinner to give my regards to your parents."

"Please do." She beamed. "They'll be overjoyed."

Ukraintsev turned to go downstairs and she regarded his replacement. "Are you a local man, Mr. Vasnetsov? Do you have family here?"

"My mother and sister," he said. "My father died in the war."

Sympathetic tears pricked Maria's eyes. "Oh, no. I'm sorry. Which front was he on?"

He looked surprised, but answered, "He was killed in Augustow Forest, along with most of the Tenth Army."

"That was February 1915, was it not?" He nodded, and Maria continued, "My father said every last man there was a hero. They held up the German armies for long enough to reorganize the other divisions and thus we were able to hold the line. But I imagine this is no comfort to you. Tell me, what kind of a man was your father?"

"The best. I've never met his like, before or since." Peter spoke with conviction.

"Did he spend much time with you when you were younger? Some men have such busy jobs that they enjoy little family life." She was thinking of her own father, who had frequently been detained on affairs of state when she was young. And now that they were confined together all hours of the day, he seemed sunk within himself and rarely spoke beyond formalities.

Peter smiled, and his gray eyes crinkled at the corners. "I was his shadow. He was the gamekeeper on a big estate and he took me out with him, rain or shine, and taught me all about animals, trees, plants, and weather. It was a happy childhood."

"You didn't go to school?"

"A bit. In our world, there's not much call for book learning, every call for understanding the land."

He was clearly not ashamed of his lack of education, and Maria liked that. "How does your mother manage now?"

He shrugged. "She is a capable woman, so she gets by, but she is somehow . . ." He searched for the right word. "Somehow less."

With the edge of her finger Maria wiped away a tear that threatened to spill over. The poor woman. "Do you live with her?"

"I live here," he said, "in a house across the road. Mother stays with my sister, who is married and has a baby on the way."

Maria smiled. "You must let me know when it arrives and I will send a gift. I *love* babies."

Peter coughed, seeming embarrassed again. "I don't think that would be right somehow . . ."

"I don't see why not. You mean because you are our guard? My sisters and I were very friendly with the guards at the Governor's House in Tobolsk and I hope you and I can be friends here. Otherwise life gets so tedious. You are fortunate that when you finish your shift you can go outside and do whatever you wish. I am stuck with my parents and neither of them is in a particularly gregarious frame of mind."

He frowned, and she sensed he did not understand the word "gregarious," so she continued, "In fact, their company is rather dull. So would you mind if I slip out to chat to you sometimes? To help us both pass the hours?"

He thought about this for a moment. "I'm not sure what the commissar will say, but it's fine with me."

"Good. That's agreed then."

As he had promised, Konstantin Ukraintsev came to their drawing room later to give his regards to her parents. They invited him to sit and chat, which was most unusual for them. Before he left, he promised to send a cable to Maria's sisters in Tobolsk to let them know where they were and that they had arrived safely. Her mother and father seemed much cheered by his visit and spoke for some time about how wonderful it was to see him, then about their memories of Livadia.

No bed had been supplied for Maria, so she lay on a pile of coats in the corner of her parents' room, thinking about Konstantin and Peter as she waited for sleep. They were both nice men, although she supposed they must be Bolsheviks. She was glad she would have some company until her sisters arrived, but decided it would be wise to steer their conversations away from politics.

CHAPTER 2

Next morning, Peter Vasnetsov was once again guarding the top of the second staircase and Maria greeted him as she passed on her way to bathe.

"Have you been there all night? I do hope they let you sleep sometimes."

He gave a shy smile. "I was off duty from midnight till eight, but now I will be here till two."

"Oh, good. After breakfast, might I come and take your photograph? It is a particular hobby of mine. I love to collect portraits and you have a strong face."

His cheeks colored. "I don't know about that."

"You don't know that you have a strong face? Or are you worried that it's not allowed? Personally, I can't see any harm."

He bit his lip before answering. "What would I have to do?"

She almost laughed, but stopped herself. He had clearly never had his photograph taken before. "Just what you are doing anyway: stand still. I'll come back in an hour and explain more."

In fact, it was slightly longer than an hour because her father read to them from the scriptures after breakfast, but when Maria skipped out to the hallway carrying her leather photograph album and her precious Kodak Autographic, Peter was there, standing very erect.

"Do you want to look through my pictures while I set up the camera?" she asked.

He glanced at his hands before accepting the book, and she guessed he was checking that they were clean. He flicked to the first page. "Is this your little brother?" he asked.

She nodded. "Alexei, yes. He was the most *adorable* baby. We all doted on him. Mama and Papa had long given up hope of an heir, so they were beside themselves with joy." She didn't tell him how disappointed her father had been when *she* was born. One daughter was delightful, two was still acceptable—and Tatiana quickly became his favorite—but he did not attempt to hide his despair when a third turned up. As a child, Maria had noticed it in the way he avoided looking at her and seldom made any personal comment to her. By the time Anastasia arrived, he seemed resigned to only siring girls.

Peter turned the page. "And these are your sisters?"

"We call ourselves OTMA," she explained. "From our names: Olga, Tatiana, Maria, and Anastasia."

"You must miss them."

"I do, very much! I can't wait till they join us. You'll like them." She set the camera aperture to the indoors setting and looked through the lens, sliding the bellows in and out to focus. Her sisters had Box Brownies, which were simple to operate, but Maria preferred the sharper results she got with her more sophisticated model.

Peter seemed uncomfortable, clutching the album tightly as if afraid he might drop it, hunching his shoulders and leaning toward the lens.

"Why don't you put the album on that side table?" she suggested. "Then try to stand naturally, as you would if I were not here. Look directly at the camera."

He still appeared stiff, but his gaze was direct and unwavering as she pulled down the lever and took the picture. It would come out dark, but the light spilling from the window illuminated the right side of his face in a way that she hoped would seem artistic.

"Thank you." She smiled, winding on the film. "I will let you see the picture once I am able to get it developed." She wondered when that might be. Perhaps they would be overseas by then; in Great Britain, maybe. She knew that George V, her father's cousin, had invited them a year ago and couldn't understand why they had not left yet. "There are protocols and procedures," was all her father would say.

Commissar Avdeyev came out of his office and scowled at them. "What are you doing? Citizen Romanova, go back to the family rooms immediately."

She picked up her camera and album and obeyed, hoping that Peter would not be chastised for talking to her.

In the sitting room, her mother was sewing, her father was reading, and the air was thick with dust and dullness. They had not been there twenty-four hours, but already she felt the confinement weighing on her soul. She picked up a pen to write to her sisters, to tell them about Konstantin Ukraintsev and Peter Vasnetsov and the house that was nothing like a home.

~

There was a clock on the mantel in the drawing room and Maria rationed herself: she would only look at it again when she had finished writing one page of her diary, or sewing a hem of her petticoat, or reading a chapter of a book to her mother. Inevitably, when she did look, the hour was less advanced than she had expected. The minutes crawled interminably, so slow she suspected the clock had been tampered with in order to torture them.

Their days were punctuated by meals, scripture readings, exercise sessions in the cramped yard where the tall fence blocked much of the sunlight, card games, and then bed. There was little to look forward to, and yet she counted the minutes until Sednev, their footman, announced luncheon, or a guard came to accompany her and her father downstairs to the yard. Her mother seldom went with them as her sciatica was crippling and her headaches frequently left her bedridden. Leaving the house was forbidden; they were not even allowed to attend services at the local church.

Maria's only distraction was chatting to the guards whenever she could make an excuse to slip out of the family's rooms. She befriended several of them and learned about their childhoods, their interests, their ambitions, even their sweethearts. She asked about the countryside around Ekaterinburg, and heard that they were close to the Ural Mountains, the great chain that divided Russia into two halves, where brown bears, wolves, and elks roamed and there was dense forest up to the snowline. She asked about the jobs they had done before coming to the Ipatiev House and learned of the Zlokazov brewery, the Makarov cloth factory, and the steam mills that ground wheat, steel, or gunpowder. Most of the guards were friendly, with only Commissar Avdeyev remaining aloof.

Maria had always enjoyed male company. As a child, she'd had several friends among the officers who crewed the royal yacht, the *Shtandart*, and she'd enjoyed playing billiards, quoits, or deck tennis with them. During the war, she'd befriended the staff at Stavka, her father's headquarters, and had spent many evenings in Tsarskoe Selo visiting wounded soldiers in the hospital. It was there she developed a particular fondness for an officer called Kolya Demenkov. *Oh, Kolya.* She still

sighed to think of him. She used to describe herself in letters
to friends as "Mrs. Demenkov" and go to sleep every night
dreaming of him, imagining what it would be like to be his
wife. Where was he now? She had no idea. She couldn't remember his face clearly anymore; it had all been so long ago.

She had always prided herself on her ability to make friends,
and worked hard to make people feel at ease in her company.
In part it grew out of a feeling that she was an outsider in
the family. Olga and Tatiana were the big pair, and they were
usually inseparable, whispering secrets they could never be
persuaded to share. Anastasia and Alexei were babies, still
happiest when giggling and playing the fool. Maria was neither her father's nor her mother's favorite; she was stuck in
the middle, the odd one out in family affiliations. She had
once written to her mother, all teenage seriousness, saying
that she felt she wasn't loved. Her mother had replied that
she was "just as dear as the other four," but it was difficult
to believe. Actions spoke louder than words.

Why had she been the one chosen to accompany her parents to Ekaterinburg while her other siblings stayed behind?
Her mother only wanted her because she was willing to run
errands; she had overheard her telling her father, "Maria is
my legs." She was not there for her scintillating conversation
or ready wit or adorable nature, but because she was obedient.
And clearly she was the one her siblings felt they could most
readily manage without.

Maria's dream was to fall in love and marry. Her husband
need not be a foreign prince, although a couple had shown an
interest. She would be perfectly happy with a dashing Russian
officer who would sweep her off her feet. Often when she lay
in bed at night she would picture the scene. He'd bring a gift:
perhaps her favorite Lilas perfume or some pretty *bijou*. She
would smile and extend her hand, letting him press his lips

to it. He would fall to his knees, swearing he could not live without her, then begging permission to ask her father for her hand in marriage. She would hesitate for a few moments, so overcome with emotion that she could not at first speak, then she would blurt out, "Yes, oh yes, my dear!" And he would stand and take her in his arms, and kiss her so passionately that she would almost swoon.

This future husband did not at present have a face, but Maria dreamed he would be strong and true, and most important that she would be his great, enduring love, the one and only woman he could not possibly live without.

CHAPTER 3

Ekaterinburg, May 1918

Two weeks after the Romanovs' arrival in Ekaterinburg, Commissar Avdeyev informed Maria's father that Konstantin Ukraintsev had been dismissed due to "lapses in security." He told them that from now on the regime would be tightened up. They must hand over all their money to him for safekeeping; there would be a roll call every morning at ten; and their exercise breaks in the yard would be reduced to thirty minutes, twice a day. Worst of all, as far as Maria was concerned, workmen erected ladders and painted over the outsides of the windows with white paint so they could no longer see out to the street and the interior was even gloomier than before.

She found this terribly upsetting, and complained to Peter in the hallway. "It is as if Avdeyev wants us to disappear. He is trying to wipe us out as if we never existed."

"It's not that," Peter assured her. "He wants to stop the townspeople gawping at you. Groups of them have been trying to peer in through the windows."

"I would prefer being gawped at to living in this faceless prison cell," Maria said, close to tears. "It is hard not to sink into despair. Sometimes I fear that we will be killed in this house. It has a cruel air."

Peter was shocked. "Don't say such things!"

She lowered her voice to a whisper. "Do you know what will happen to us? Have you heard anything?"

He hesitated. "I heard this is just a stopping place before you go to Moscow, where the new government wants to question your father, and then you will all be sent into exile."

She felt relief flood her. "Do you know where the exile will be?"

Peter shook his head, sympathy in his expression.

"I wish they would hurry up. I have such a longing to be free. I don't even care where we go, so long as we are together."

Peter bit his lip. She had noticed he often did that when he was choosing his words, and waited for him to speak.

"Please don't tell anyone—I shouldn't tell you this—but I have heard that your brother and sisters have already left Tobolsk and will be joining you soon. We have orders to open the other rooms on this floor to accommodate the party."

Maria clasped her hands over her mouth so she did not cry out in joy, and stood still to compose herself before replying in a whisper, "I am so grateful for this news. You can have no idea how much it has lifted my spirits."

Peter nodded, and gave her his shy smile.

~

On May 22 there was a late snowstorm that gusted against the whitewashed windows and left the family huddling around the stove for warmth, blankets tight around their shoulders. The following morning, Maria ventured out into the yard, hoping the snow would not delay the arrival of her siblings. It was already melting, but the ground was slippery and the sky was gray and threatening. Soon rain began to fall in large, slushy drops, driving her indoors.

Avdeyev came to the drawing room at eleven to tell them that "the party" was on their way from the station. Maria looked wistfully at the whitewashed windows, wishing she could have watched out for them. What would her sisters make of this grim, faceless house?

Half an hour later, she heard a commotion in the hallway and rushed out to see Tatiana trudging up the stairs, her French bulldog Ortipo under one arm and a suitcase in her other hand. Next came Alexei, who was being carried by his carer, followed by the others and two more family dogs, Joy and Jemmy. They had all gotten soaked in the rain and looked bedraggled and bone-weary, but Maria embraced them one by one with great excitement.

"I'm thrilled to see you. Come in! It's this way. You poor dears, you look half perished. I'll have Sednev brew some tea."

They greeted their parents, then slumped into chairs. Dr. Botkin, the family doctor, who had arrived with the party, crouched to examine Alexei, who looked pale and exhausted.

"What an appalling journey!" Tatiana sighed. "Four long days in a rusty steamship then a filthy third-class train carriage. At moments I felt sure we would not survive—but here we are."

"This room is very dark," Anastasia commented. "Where is our bedroom?"

"I'll show you. Come with me." Maria led her by the hand through the dining room to the newly opened up bedroom that the girls were to share. It had a parquet floor and floral wallpaper but did not as yet have any beds.

Once they were alone, Anastasia whispered, "Last night was awful. The guards were drunk and so disrespectful we did not get a wink of sleep. Such things they called to us . . . I hope never to hear the like again. Thank goodness Papa and Mama were not there or they would have caused an enormous fuss and who knows what would have happened?"

Maria hugged her. "It is safe here. Deadly boring, but safe. Now you've arrived I hope we can have some fun."

"Where are we to sleep?" Anastasia looked around, her nose wrinkled. "And why are the windows whitewashed? It doesn't seem like a place where we can have fun; it's more like a mausoleum in which we have been interred."

Maria sighed. Her sentiments exactly.

~

The number of prisoners increased to fourteen after Maria's siblings arrived. As well as the seven family members, there was Dr. Botkin; Anna Demidova, her mother's maid; Alexei Trupp, her father's valet; Ivan Kharitonov, the cook; Klementy Nagorny, Alexei's carer; Ivan Sednev, the footman; and his thirteen-year-old nephew, Leonid, who was the kitchen boy and a playmate of Alexei's. There were only three bedrooms, so Alexei must share with his parents and Maria shared with her sisters, while Anna Demidova had her own room (a small, newly opened one) and Trupp, the two Sednevs, Botkin, Nagorny, and Kharitonov slept in cots in the hallway. The family's three dogs ran freely around the upper floor, contributing to the crush by getting under everyone's feet.

There was no space to store all their possessions in the rooms at their disposal, so Avdeyev ordered them to be put in a storeroom in the yard, but when Nicholas went to look for a fresh pipe, he found their trunks had been opened and several items pilfered.

"I must insist our possessions are returned immediately," Maria heard him telling Avdeyev.

The commissar did not seem concerned, replying only, "I will look into it."

Nagorny went to remonstrate with him, and the next thing

they knew, both he and Sednev were removed from duty and dismissed from the house.

"It seems to me they are not necessary," Avdeyev said to Nicholas, and none of their arguments could sway him.

Maria was glad that her mother and sisters had hidden their best jewels within the seams of their clothing, or else the Bolsheviks might have tried to steal them too. There were pearls in the boning of their bodices, jewels secreted between the lining and exterior of their hats, and diamonds covered with black silk and refashioned as buttons on gowns. Some garments were double-layered, with whole necklaces encased in wadding between the layers. It made them very heavy to wear, but if it helped to smuggle their jewelry out of Russia, to support them in exile, it was well worth the discomfort.

Within days of arriving, Tatiana had taken over as "boss" of the family. She was the one who went to Avdeyev's office to complain that the camp beds for the girls had still not arrived, or that there was not enough hot water for their baths, or not enough cutlery to go around so they must share knives and spoons. She was fearless and her requests generally got results. Olga, the eldest, seemed sunk in depression and barely communicated with anyone, while Anastasia and Alexei lost themselves in childish games like dominoes, which Maria found dull. It was nice to have her family there, of course, but it did not relieve the boredom as much as she had hoped.

She still chatted to the guards in the hallway and was delighted when a new batch of men arrived on June 7, including one particularly handsome one with black hair and bright blue eyes. Tatiana had told her it was unseemly to consort with the guards, and Avdeyev had expressly forbidden it, so Maria waited until the coast was clear before introducing herself.

"Hello, welcome to the house," she greeted him. "I'm Maria Romanova."

"Ivan Skorokhodov," he said. "Charmed to meet you."

"Are you a factory worker?" she asked. "It seems all our guards come from the local factories."

"The Zlokazov brewery," he replied. "But I am much happier here. It smells more pleasant, and the view is infinitely superior." He looked her up and down with a cheeky grin.

Maria smiled back, enjoying the flirtation. "My goodness, what would your mother say if she heard you talking like that?"

"I think she would say I have extremely good taste," he replied.

Maria continued to her room, a grin on her face. She knew she shouldn't encourage him, but what harm could it do? She had always enjoyed chatting to men.

The next time she saw Ivan was the following afternoon. Kharitonov had just made an urn of tea, and she asked the guard if she could get a cup for him.

Ivan's eyes widened in surprise, but he replied, "Thank you. It is thirsty work standing here all day."

Maria fetched some tea and brought her own cup so they could stand by the top of the stairs and drink it together. She glanced nervously at the door of Commissar Avdeyev's office.

"He's out today," Ivan said. "Or else I would not dare accept this tea."

Maria asked about his interests when he was not working, and he told her he liked to play cards.

"Bezique is my favorite," he said. "I enjoy planning tactical moves."

Maria wondered if he was flirting again; there always seemed to be a hint of mischief in his eyes. "I enjoy bezique too. Perhaps we might have a game sometime. The days here are so long . . ." She paused. "But I have a feeling my parents would forbid it. Pray, tell me, is the countryside pretty around here?"

"It's all right, I guess. There are mountains, forests, and rivers, like anywhere."

"Do you have brothers and sisters?"

"Two older brothers, but no sisters. That's why I find women such a mystery," he told her. "I have no idea what makes them giggle so much. I never know if they are laughing at me, because they refuse to share the joke."

"I expect you will find they are laughing over something entirely inconsequential. Anastasia and I giggle at the most childish things: a mispronounced word, or the silly behavior of the dogs. It is not worth wasting time over."

"I wish you would explain women to me," he said, gazing at her directly. "A great beauty like you must surely have insights that would help me to find a sweetheart."

Maria snorted. "A great beauty indeed! Do you know what my family call me? Fat little bow-wow. I can have no illusions about my appearance with such a nickname."

"But you have eyes as big as saucers, hair that gleams like sunshine, and skin like finest porcelain.". He shook his head, glancing down at her figure. "And you are not even slightly plump. Families are cruel. My brother calls me Teeny because I am the shortest of the three of us."

"I think you are the perfect height," Maria exclaimed. "I'm sure you will have no trouble capturing the heart of a woman— when you meet the right one." She blushed, then continued. "You are lucky to have the opportunity. I will be nineteen years old on the twenty-seventh of June and have not yet had a beau. At this rate, I will die an old maid."

Ivan shook his head. "That will never happen. All men must find you irresistible. As soon as your family's situation is settled, I'm sure you will find happiness."

Maria pursed her lips and gave him a sad look.

~

Little Alexei was still in terrible pain, with acute swellings in his joints after being bumped around so much on the journey. The girls took turns to entertain him, trying to distract him from his suffering. Maria drew pencil portraits of their captors and tried to amuse her little brother with humorous descriptions of their characters: "as pompous as a walrus on a beach," she said of Avdeyev; "a slippery ferret in a rabbit hole" of his deputy, Medvedev. The girls took turns to read to him from any books they could find, and they revived *Three Sisters*, the Chekhov play they had performed at Tobolsk. Sometimes Alexei was well enough for a game of halma, and they moved a table close to allow him to join in.

One sunny day in June, Maria carried him down to the yard to get some fresh air. She had always been physically the strongest of the four girls and did her best to carry him smoothly, without jarring, but she could tell from the frequent intakes of breath that the movement was hurting.

She placed him in a bath chair, from where he surveyed the shadowy yard. Turrets were being built in the corners of the tall fence, and the men's hammering mingled with the clanging bells of streetcars in the road outside.

"Why are we here?" he asked in a small, sad voice. "What do they want from us?"

Maria watched a blue butterfly flit past. "I suppose they want to keep us safe so we can be delivered overseas in due course. It is taking an interminable time, though."

"Why would we not be safe? I don't understand."

Maria shook her head. "Me neither. But I am sure it will not be much longer before we are in our new home. Where would you like to go?"

He considered this. "Perhaps Africa, where I could hunt lions, or India, where we could ride on elephants and shoot tigers."

Maria laughed. "I hope your wishes will be taken into consideration."

He was so pale and thin, with his gangly limbs, that it was impossible to picture him as a big-game hunter. The hemophilia he had inherited from their mother's side of the family ruled out any activities in which he might risk injury. He would never ride a horse or a bicycle, would never ski, and even running was risky. Yet he could still have his dreams; no one could deny him that.

~

On the day of Maria's nineteenth birthday, the family gave her little gifts: a hand-painted bookmark, a volume of Russian poetry, and a precious Fabergé box studded with diamonds and a topaz that had been given to her mother by her sister Ella the year before the war. The box was pretty and Maria knew she should be grateful, but all the same it was hard not to think of previous birthdays: even a year before, they had still been in the Alexander Palace, albeit under house arrest. Her parents had given her a handsome gold bracelet and dozens of other presents before holding a special birthday tea with pretty cakes and her favorite almond toffee. Here, the meal was a single course of stewed meat and boiled potatoes with no desserts. They were dependent on provisions brought each morning by the nuns from a local convent and there was not a lot of variety.

That evening, as they sat in the drawing room after dinner, there was a knock on the door and her father called, "Come in."

Ivan popped his head inside, then walked in holding a cake on a plain white plate.

"Good evening." He bowed his head to the company. "I hear there is a birthday today and thought you might enjoy some *medovik*." He seemed nervous in front of her parents. "I wish I could say I baked it myself, but it was my mother. I bring it with her compliments." He smiled at Maria, who jumped up to take the plate from him.

"You're unbelievably kind," she said. "Truly. Please give my warmest thanks to your mother and tell her how very touched I am by the gesture."

The family looked at each other, eyebrows raised, as Ivan backed out of the room. Leonid Sednev brought plates and all had a slice of the multilayered honey cake. It was the first such confection they had enjoyed for many months, and even Nicholas was moved to say that it was very kind of the guard and his mother. It lifted the mood of the entire party and the girls sang a popular song together, "Shine, Shine, My Star."

Once they had finished, Maria excused herself and slipped out to the hall to thank Ivan in person. He was standing at his post by the top of the second staircase.

"You are very clever for remembering my birthday," she said. "You've made this day special, something I never dreamed would be possible here. I thank you from the bottom of my heart."

Ivan took her hand and pressed it to his lips. Maria glanced over her shoulder to make sure none of the family had followed, but all the doors were closed and there was no sound from Avdeyev's office.

Ivan was still holding her hand and suddenly he pulled her in a swift movement toward a tiny alcove by the kitchen doorway. They huddled inside, bodies pressed together, and Maria trembled. Ivan looped one arm around her waist then stroked her cheek with his finger before leaning forward to touch his lips to hers.

"A birthday kiss," he whispered, "for the most beautiful girl I have ever seen."

Maria gazed at the soft lips that had brushed hers, and couldn't help tilting her head for more. Ivan held her tightly now, his lips exploring hers, and she closed her eyes feeling giddy with excitement. It was the most delicious sensation she had ever experienced, quite different from a parent's kiss, and she wanted it to go on forever.

"Skorokhodov!" a harsh voice barked, and suddenly he was yanked away. Avdeyev and Medvedev were glaring at them.

"Go to your room!" Avdeyev snapped at Maria, and she scurried into the kitchen, terrified by his tone. She glanced back just before the door swung closed and saw Ivan being frog-marched down the stairs, one arm pulled up behind his back.

CHAPTER 4

Ekaterinburg, June 1918

MARIA LAY IN BED, HER HEART POUNDING. WHAT would happen to Ivan? It wasn't fair if he was punished. No harm had been done, and it was as much her fault as his. She hoped Avdeyev would not tell her parents about the scene he had witnessed. They would be horrified by her lack of modesty. Perhaps she would visit his office in the morning and beseech him to excuse their behavior, promising it would not happen again. But she was scared of the commissar and knew she would not have the courage. Besides, she very much wished it *would* happen again.

Avdeyev came into the dining room while the family was eating breakfast next morning. Maria blushed scarlet as he glared around the table.

"I thought I had made it clear there must be no consorting with the guards. It is a blatant breach of the rules and there will be consequences. The guard known as Ivan Skorokhodov has been relieved of his duty. Meanwhile, we will be watching you more closely, and no further breaches will be tolerated."

He turned on his heel, and as soon as the door clicked shut, Tatiana turned to Maria and hissed, "What on earth happened last night? You were gone for ages. What did you and Ivan get up to?"

Maria burst into tears. "Nothing! I just went to thank him for the cake."

"Really, Mashka," her mother reproached. "You mustn't talk to the guards. They are not our friends, and it's not seemly."

"Are you all right?" Olga asked kindly, placing a hand over Maria's. "Did he take liberties?"

"No," she sobbed. "He made my birthday special by bringing that cake, and now it is ruined." She scraped her chair back and stood up. "I wish we could leave here. I'm so fed up with everything."

"Sit down, Maria," Tatiana ordered, but she ran from the room. Instead of turning toward the girls' bedroom, she headed for the lavatory, wondering which guard was on duty that day. When she saw it was Peter Vasnetsov, she checked the hall was empty before whispering through her tears, "What has happened to Ivan?"

"He's in jail," Peter replied, looking solemn.

Maria choked on a sob and ran into the bathroom, burying her face in a towel and crying till her eyes were raw and her chest ached.

~

After breakfast and morning scriptures, Tatiana took Maria to the dining room, where they could talk in peace.

"What happened in the hall last night?" she demanded. "I could tell from your face when you came back to the bedroom that you were distressed, then you were flushed when Avdeyev came in this morning . . ."

Maria stared at her lap, fidgeting. "I just said thank you to Ivan for the cake."

Tatiana scrutinized her. "Do you have a crush on him? I know what you're like with your silly crushes. We all remember Kolya Demenkov." She rolled her eyes.

Maria was cross. "If I like someone, you call it a silly crush. But you like Dmitri Malama. Isn't that a crush too?" Maria was referring to a cavalry officer from home, a man Tatiana was very keen on. They had corresponded throughout the war, and Maria knew he was finding secret ways to keep in touch now they were in captivity, although Tatiana never spoke of it.

Tatiana bristled. "It's completely different. Dmitri and I plan to marry someday, and we are old enough to know our own minds, but you change your crushes with the prevailing wind. You really must stay away from the guards, Mashka. If Avdeyev gets riled, you put us all in danger."

Maria was defiant. "On the contrary, my friendships with the guards could save us. None of them would hurt a hair on our heads. They are kind, gentle souls and I think it is only right to be civil to them."

Tatiana placed a hand over hers. "Mashka, this has to stop. You heard Avdeyev. He is tightening the rules as a result of your flirtation, and no doubt we will all suffer."

Maria pulled her hand away, pouting. "I think your only interest is in spoiling other people's pleasure," she accused. "All I was doing was trying to pass the time."

"Find some other way," Tatiana finished curtly.

~

On July 4, a week after Ivan's arrest, the family was surprised when there was no roll call after breakfast. Instead, while they were having lunch, a group of men came into the dining room and announced that Avdeyev had been replaced by a new commander, Yakov Yurovsky. A man with bushy hair and a dark beard and moustache stepped forward. He looked humorless, Maria thought, and had dead eyes, like the stuffed black bear in the hall.

"I have orders from the Ural Soviet to take all of your jewelry," he announced. "Please gather it and turn it over."

"Is this truly necessary?" Nicholas objected.

Yurovsky insisted it was. "I am told you claim your belongings have been pilfered, so I would like to catalog them. Please produce the jewelry within the hour."

They collected the pieces they were wearing and the ones still in their jewelry boxes but did not own up to the jewels hidden inside their clothing. Everything was piled on the dining-room table and Yurovsky came to collect it personally, wrapping it in a tablecloth to take to his office.

The following day he returned the jewelry in a box, along with a typed list of the contents, which he asked Nicholas to check, item by item.

"At least it seems he plans to be fair," Nicholas remarked, but Maria did not have a good feeling about him. He never looked directly at any of them; it was as if to him they were not human.

∼

Three days later, some new guards appeared, and Maria felt uneasy around them from the start. "Look at the buffers on her!" one remarked as she passed in the hall. He sounded foreign, although he spoke Russian.

Back in their room, Maria whispered to Olga, "What are buffers?" and repeated what she had heard.

"How coarse!" Olga exclaimed. "*Bufera* means breasts. I think you should ask Papa to complain to Commissar Yurovsky." She shuddered. "That is unacceptable."

Maria did not dare to tell her father about the comment,

though. She would have been mortified, and she worried everyone would think she had encouraged the man.

After lunch there was another guard at the top of the second staircase, a young-looking man with a heavy brow and slanting dark eyes, like a wolf. She smiled politely, then tried to walk past.

"You are Maria, are you not?" he said, so she had to stop. "My name is Anatoly Bolotov."

"Pleased to meet you." She nodded.

"Some of the new guards here are Hungarian or Lithuanian; you've probably heard their foreign accents," he said. "But I am a local man, a Russian through and through."

"Where have the other guards gone?" she asked, since he seemed to expect a response. "The ones who were here before?" She hadn't seen Peter Vasnetsov for several days.

"Some of them are guarding the exterior but they are not allowed up to the family quarters anymore. We will be here instead." He gave her a knowing look that made her uncomfortable, and she wondered if he had heard about her being caught with Ivan.

"I hope you will be happy," she said, walking past.

He was still there later when she went to the bathroom to wash before bed. She intended to walk straight past with a nod, but he asked if she had enjoyed her dinner so it seemed only polite to stop.

"There was chicken tonight, and our chef managed to make a very palatable sauce. Have you eaten?"

"We also had chicken in the guards' dining room. How have you and your family spent the evening?"

She didn't like his impertinence, but felt she had no choice but to reply. "I have been trying to draw a honeysuckle flower but I'm not sure I have captured the delicate intricacy of the head and stamens."

"I'm sure it is beautiful," he replied. "I would love to see your drawing sometime."

"I am partial to sketching flowers," she explained, "but there are not many in the yard here. If you ever come across a flower outside, I would be most grateful if you could bring it to me so I have more specimens to draw."

Bolotov colored. "I would be honored," he said with a bow. She hoped he did not attach any great importance to her request.

He fumbled in his pocket and pulled out something gold in color. "I found this on the landing earlier. Perhaps it belongs to one of your family?"

"Goodness! It's my Fabergé box! Mama would have been very cross if I had lost it." She held out her hand for it, but Bolotov wouldn't let go.

"I couldn't work out how to open it. Is there a secret?" he asked.

Maria felt extremely uncomfortable now and wanted to move away, but she felt she had no choice but to show him the clever mechanism. Their heads were so close they were almost touching, and her fingers brushed his palm as she took the box, demonstrated how it opened, then slipped it into her pocket.

"Excuse me. I must wash now," she said, stepping past.

She opened the bathroom door and was about to close it behind her when she felt something blocking it and turned to see Bolotov at her heels.

"What are you doing?" she asked, keeping her voice low lest anyone should hear.

Bolotov closed the door so they were both inside and locked it with the hook.

"Please . . ." Maria begged. "Stop this."

He leaned his face toward her and she pushed him away.

She wanted to scream but the sound stuck in her throat, producing a strangled noise.

"I'll look after you. I'll rescue you from here and we can get married." His eyes burned with an intensity that scared her.

Her throat had closed completely and all she managed was a little squeak of "No!"

"You kissed that other guard, so why not me? I can help you."

Bolotov's hand touched her breast and she froze. What should she do? If she cried out, Yurovsky would hear, her sisters and parents would hear, and they would say she had brought it on herself for being too familiar with the guards. She shoved his hand away and tried to wriggle free, but he planted his arm on the wall beside her so she couldn't escape, then leaned in to kiss her. She gagged at the putrid odor of his breath and the lips that felt cold and rubbery. She couldn't bear the scratch of his chin, the wet tongue that prodded inside her mouth, making her gag yet again.

He had his hands on her skirt now and she struggled harder but could barely move against the weight of him pinning her to the wall. Please let this be over quickly, she prayed. She screwed her eyes tight shut and tried to ignore the feeling of his rough finger touching her most private parts, where no one had touched her before. It was humiliating, awful, by far the worst thing that had ever happened to her. There was a sharp pain and she gasped in agony, the sound muffled by his lips, his tongue in her mouth. She began to murmur the Orthodox prayer to the Mother of God: "Pour the mercy of thy son and our God upon my impassionate soul, and with thine interventions set me unto good deeds, that I may pass the rest of my life without blemish . . ."

At last he stopped and unhooked the door, glancing outside to check the coast was clear before slipping back to his guard post. Maria straightened her skirts, noticing that her petticoat was torn, then looked in the mirror. Her hair was wild, her lips red and chafed around the edges. She splashed her face with cold water and dried it with a towel, rushing in case he decided to return. If only there were another way back to their room. She would have to walk past him again and couldn't bear to see the expression on his face. He was an ugly, loathsome man.

She summoned her courage, opened the door, and ran down the corridor.

"Good night, sweet princess," Bolotov called after her, and she heard mockery in his tone.

She hurried into the bedroom she shared with her sisters. Only Olga was there; the others must be in their parents' room. Olga leaped to her feet.

"What happened, Mashka? Are you hurt?"

Tears flooded Maria's eyes. She longed to confess, but couldn't. Olga would tell Tatiana, and Tatiana would say, "I warned you. It's your own fault since you ignored me."

"Did a guard molest you?" Olga asked, putting an arm around her shoulders and peering into her eyes. "You can tell me and I will understand. I know what these men are like." A shadow crossed her face and suddenly Maria understood that something similar had happened to her sister. She should confess. Olga would comfort her.

But she found she couldn't speak. Her throat was still tight, as it had been at the crucial moment in the bathroom. She shook her head. If she told Olga, that would make it real. There would be consequences. But if she didn't tell, she could pretend it had never happened and that way, eventually, she hoped she would be able to forget.

CHAPTER 5

Ekaterinburg, July 1918

NEXT MORNING, MARIA LAY HUDDLED IN BED. SHE couldn't face getting up for breakfast and told the others she hadn't slept well, which was the truth. It was sore between her legs, her lips were raw, and she felt a deep sense of shame. She saw now that she should have shouted for help; of course she should. Ivan had been jailed for merely kissing her, so this guard would have been jailed too, then she would not have to see him anymore. Instead, she must walk past him every day, because she could not avoid using the bathroom.

She decided to wait until one of her sisters was going and accompany her, so she was never alone in that corridor again. She must not give Bolotov a chance to repeat his assault.

That first day she was relieved to find he was not at his post, but the following morning, when she went to the bathroom with Tatiana, he was there with his sly wolf features. She shuddered, sick to her stomach at the sight of him.

"Good morning, Maria," he called, his voice low.

Tatiana reprimanded him. "How dare you address her with such disrespect! Do that again and I shall report you to Commissar Yurovsky."

She swept past full of scorn. Maria turned to see his response and he winked at her behind Tatiana's back, grinning as if they shared a secret. It was hideous. He was insufferable. She couldn't believe those lips had pressed against hers, his fingers had touched her beneath her skirt, his stubbly chin had rubbed her cheek. Every time she thought of it she wanted to retch.

She had no confidence that Yurovsky would take action if Tatiana reported him. Her father had thought he would treat them more favorably than his predecessor, but every day it seemed new rules were introduced: less time in the yard, even though they were sweltering in their airless rooms; more frequent searches of their possessions; he even decided that they should pull a rope attached to a system of bells whenever they wished to leave their rooms to go to the bathroom. That way, guards throughout the house would know their movements.

"I absolutely refuse," Maria's mother declared. "I will not have my intimate habits scrutinized by a bunch of uneducated commoners. It's absurd."

Maria thought it might help to protect her from Bolotov if bells rang whenever she left the family rooms. She looked away when she was forced to pass him in the hall but could feel his slanting eyes upon her, burning into her flesh. If only they could hurry up and leave this place. She longed to be sent somewhere she would never have to see him or think about him again.

～

They were disturbed one evening by gunfire in the city and Tatiana hurried to Yurovsky's office to ask what was going on.

"He says that some Czech troops are advancing on Ekaterinburg," she told them on her return to the drawing room. "If they come any closer we are to be moved elsewhere for safety."

Nicholas frowned. "It must be the Czech Legion," he said. "Czech and Slovak volunteers who were attached to our Third Army from 1914. They hoped for independence for their country after the war."

"If they are so close that we hear gunfire, perhaps we should leave now?" Alexandra suggested.

Maria hugged her knees to her chest, scared by the thought of these strange soldiers. Who knew what they might be capable of?

Tatiana went to the drawing-room door to check no one was listening outside, then returned to the group. "Papa, you know that rescue plan I told you about?"

Maria frowned. She had not heard of any such thing and worried it would not be safe.

"You mean Dmitri Malama's plan?" he asked.

Tatiana nodded. "I think it will be soon. The Czech soldiers are favorable toward us so it is an ideal opportunity."

"No!" Olga gasped. "It's too risky. The guards in the turrets have machine guns. We would all be killed."

Tatiana hurried to reassure her. "There are several people involved in this plan, including the British consul. Malama wants me to slip out tomorrow evening to hear the details so I can brief you all on what we must do."

Maria's heart lurched. Tatiana's beau was a loyal friend to the family but his plan sounded terrifying. She wasn't brave enough for this kind of intrigue.

"How will you slip out of here without being missed?" Nicholas asked.

Tatiana spoke calmly. "A group of cleaners will come in tomorrow and Malama says one of them is my height and coloring. She and I will swap clothes and she will stay here while I leave with the others. The next morning, when the cleaners return, I will come back, and by then I will know how we are to be rescued. We have no choice, Papa. You know that."

Maria intercepted a look between Tatiana and her father that made her shiver. She had been trying to ignore the tension in the house while she recovered from her ordeal at the hands of Bolotov, but there was no doubt everyone was on edge. The firing in the distance didn't help.

"What must we do?" she asked, her voice faint.

Tatiana replied, "When the cleaner is here in my place, crowd round her so no one gets a close look. Fortunately these new guards scarcely know us. If Yurovsky comes in, shield her from his gaze by some ruse." She looked around at them all. "I'm sure you will manage. It is our best chance."

What did she mean? Maria wondered. Best chance of escape? But why not just remain as Yurovsky wanted them to, while the arrangements for their exile were finalized? She sensed there were things the others knew that they had not told her, Anastasia, or Alexei. Usually she resented being left out of the adult conversation, but this time she was glad not to know. She was anxious enough as it was.

～

The cleaner looked nothing like Tatiana, Maria thought, and she was trembling as they exchanged gowns and shawls. Tatiana left the house with the rest of the cleaning women and the poor girl hid in their bedroom, scarcely saying a word, clearly terrified out of her wits. Maria wondered how Malama had talked her into it. No doubt she was being paid.

All went according to plan that evening, with none of the guards spotting the deception, but next morning when the cleaners returned to continue their work, Tatiana was not with them. She had been supposed to return. What could they do?

"I must leave with the other cleaners," the girl begged Maria's father over breakfast. "My parents are waiting for me."

"Now, now," Nicholas soothed. "You can't leave until Tatiana is back or the guards will notice. If they see one more cleaner leaving than arrived this morning, you would most likely be arrested."

The girl looked pale and kept wringing her hands together, on the verge of all-out panic. "My father made me do this. We need the money. I wish I had said no."

Olga put an arm around her. "Stay calm, dear. Tatiana will be back before you know it."

Maria saw her sister glance across the table at Nicholas and frown. This had not been part of the plan.

When Yurovsky came to take the morning roll call, the cleaning girl leaned her head into her hands so he could not see her face.

"She has a headache, poor soul," Nicholas told him. "She has taken powders but must lie down and rest as soon as you are finished with us."

Yurovsky's gaze traveled around the room before he spoke. "The kitchen boy, Leonid Sednev, is being sent away today. He must visit his family."

Alexei cried out, "But who shall I play with? Please don't make him go."

"I believe there is an emergency," Yurovsky continued. "He will return soon." He left the room abruptly, seeming distracted, as if on urgent business.

Alexei was on the verge of tears, his lip trembling. "I don't want Leonid to go. Tell him not to."

"We'll play with you," Maria said. "Nastya and I will build a den for you. It will be fun."

"It's not the same," he pouted. "Girls don't know how to play."

Everyone was anxious and out of sorts. Maria's mother took to her bed, her father smoked incessantly, and the cleaning girl hid in the bedroom while the rest of them tried to distract Alexei. The minutes ticked by even slower than before.

~

When they went to bed that night, Maria wondered if the rescue might be imminent. That could be why Tatiana had not returned. She packed a bag of items she did not want to be without: her photo album, her sketch pad and pencils, a couple of favorite icons, and the gold Fabergé box, then she put her camera beside it. If anyone came in the night to save them, she could grab her bag and take it with her.

The firing sounded closer now and there seemed to be more traffic in the street. She heard the murmur of men's voices rising through the summer air but could not make out what they said. From the breathing of her sisters and the cleaning girl, she could tell none of them were sleeping, but they did not talk either. Perhaps, like her, they were listening and waiting, trying to work out what might happen next.

Maria woke with a start to a knock on the door and realized she must have nodded off after all. Dr. Botkin turned the handle and looked in.

"You must get dressed. We are being moved elsewhere, for our safety, as the Czechs are approaching. Yurovsky said not to worry about luggage as it will be sent on later."

Maria's spirits sank. When Botkin had started speaking, she had hoped Tatiana and Malama's rescue plan was under way, but instead it seemed they were being moved by Yurovsky. She supposed they were being sent to Moscow, as Peter Vasnetsov had said they would be. But how could they go without Tatiana? The cleaning girl was whimpering like an injured dog.

Maria got up and pulled on the undergarments and skirt into which she had sewn jewels, and saw her sisters doing the same. She rubbed the sleep from her eyes, the weight of the fabric making it harder to fasten the buttons. She pulled on her boots and laced them, then picked up her camera and her travel bag.

When they were all ready, they walked out to the drawing room to meet Maria's parents and Alexei. The four servants—Dr. Botkin, Demidova, Trupp, and Kharitonov—were there too, and Yurovsky was waiting. He bent back his fingers with a loud crack, then opened the door and led them to the hall.

"At least we are getting out of this place," her father remarked, and Maria could tell he was straining to be jovial.

As they passed the stuffed bear, her mother crossed herself, and each of the girls did the same.

CHAPTER 6

Ekaterinburg, July 17, 1918

Yurovsky led them out into the courtyard. Maria looked around and was puzzled to see there were no cars waiting. The sound of gunfire was louder now they were outside, and she shivered. Yurovsky opened another set of doors further along the wall and led them down a short flight of steps, then through a series of guardrooms and hallways until Maria was quite disoriented. They arrived in an empty storeroom with a bare bulb hanging from the ceiling.

"You will wait here until the transport arrives," he said.

The room was about twenty-five by twenty feet, Maria estimated, with a barred window on one wall and double doors behind them.

"How long must we wait here?" Alexandra demanded. "Alexei and I cannot stand for any length of time. Could you bring chairs?"

"Of course. Chairs." Yurovsky turned and gave an order to a guard standing behind him, an ugly man Maria had never seen before.

Two chairs were brought. Her mother and Alexei were seated, then Yurovsky surveyed the group with a frown. Nicholas was standing in front of Alexei, with Alexandra beside him.

"Could you all stand behind the chairs?" he asked, waving the girls and the four servants into a group, almost as if posing them for a photograph. They shuffled into place, and he nodded. "That will do."

He turned and left, closing the door behind him, and they looked at each other, bemused. Maria clung to her bag and her camera, reluctant to put them down. Everyone was uneasy. It hung in the air like fog.

"Why did he bring us downstairs if the transport was not ready?" Olga asked.

"It's most irritating," her mother replied. "They do their utmost to punish us, God knows what for."

"It's in case of shelling by the Czechs," Dr. Botkin said. "We'll be safer in the basement if the house takes a direct hit."

The cleaning girl began to cry quietly and Dr. Botkin put an arm around her, murmuring words of comfort.

"Do you think we are going to Moscow, Papa?" Maria asked. "That's what one of the guards told me."

"Could be," he said, absentmindedly.

"Who will look after the dogs?" Anastasia worried out loud.

There was a long pause before Olga replied. "I expect they will be sent on with our luggage. There's probably no room in the cars."

Most of the time they stayed silent, apart from the cleaning girl's sniffling. Maria was listening for engine noise outside that would signal the arrival of their transport. Why was it taking so long? Where was Tatiana?

There was no mistaking the sound of the truck when it arrived. The engine roared, making the windowpane rattle behind its stout bars.

The door opened and they saw a group of men standing behind Yurovsky. Maria spotted Anatoly Bolotov and her heart sank. Was he traveling with them?

Yurovsky stepped forward, holding a sheet of paper, from which he began to read. "In view of the fact that your relatives in Europe continue their assault on Soviet Russia, the Presidium of the Ural Regional Soviet has sentenced you to be shot . . ."

Maria's mind went blank and she heard a rushing sound in her ears. The men had fanned out around him. Bolotov was staring at her, and she got the impression he was gloating.

"What?" her father asked. "What?"

Dr. Botkin sounded incredulous. "So you're not taking us anywhere?"

"I don't understand. Read it again," Maria's father said.

Yurovsky read from the paper in his hand, his tone level as if he were reciting a shopping list. "Tsar Nicholas Romanov, guilty of countless bloody crimes against the people, should be shot."

They were going to shoot her father. Maria crossed herself, and out of the corner of her eye saw her mother and sisters doing the same. And then it all happened fast. Yurovsky pulled out a gun, the other men did the same, and there were flashes of light and a deafening sound that ricocheted around the room. Nicholas staggered and fell heavily to the floor, but still guns were firing, and that was when Maria realized they were shooting them all. They couldn't be. It made no sense. But they were.

She dived toward the double doors at the back of the room, heart thumping, chest so tight she couldn't breathe. She grabbed the handles and rattled them with all her strength, but they were locked and wouldn't budge. She heard screaming and smelled the acrid tang of gunpowder, recognizing it from her father's hunting trips. She couldn't think straight. The only way out would be to run past the men, get around behind them, but she would never make it. Where was her mother? Where were Olga and Anastasia?

She turned to look for them and felt something hit her leg, as if a sharp stone had been hurled at it. She collapsed, and now she was lying on the concrete floor and the air was thick with caustic smoke, making her eyes stream. She crawled toward a corner where she could hear screaming, feeling wet stickiness beneath her. "Olga!" she screamed. "Mama!"

She felt the edge of a skirt and groped until she could find the body. A tiny waist. Soft hair. "Anastasia?" she whispered, and two arms were flung around her neck. Anastasia was panting with fear and Maria clung to her.

The firing stopped as suddenly as it had started and she heard the men talking in low voices, then they stepped outside the room. Perhaps they had decided to let the women live. Surely they must.

"Are you hurt?" Maria whispered, but Anastasia couldn't speak. As the smoke began to clear a little, Maria realized her sister's eyes were wide with shock. She followed the direction of her gaze and saw their mother on the floor in front of them with part of her skull missing. She retched. There were brains everywhere, white and glistening. Her mother's brains.

She could hear moaning. Women's voices. The others were alive. They had to get out of there. She should crawl toward Olga, ask her what to do, but she couldn't leave Anastasia.

The respite didn't last long. Yurovsky came back into the room alongside a big man with wild dark hair. A long knife glinted in his hand. Maria tried to twist out of the way as he raised it and brought it down toward her, but she felt it slash her middle and she screamed with all her might. Then Yurovsky raised his gun and pointed it at her head, and she looked up into his cold killer's eyes just before she lost consciousness.

CHAPTER 7

THERE WAS COOL NIGHT AIR ON HER FACE. MOVEMENT. Pain. Maria realized she was being carried, slung over someone's shoulder. They were walking. Then they stopped. Other hands were on her. She was lifted and thrown, landing on a surface that was uneven. She was only part-conscious but knew she must keep her eyes shut, stay still.

Someone lifted her wrist, pressed fingers to her pulse. She held her breath. Now they would find out she was alive.

"This one's gone," said a voice that sounded like Yurovsky. The voice of her murderer.

Maybe he was right; perhaps she was dead. But she didn't think so.

There was a thump as something landed beside her and she knew it was another body. She desperately wanted to open her eyes, to reach out, see who it was, but she was frozen in terror. How could they not hear her heart thudding?

Another thump. Were any of the rest of her family alive? At least she knew Tatiana was safe and prayed she would arrive soon with Dmitri Malama to rescue them. Someone must have heard the firing. The noise had been ear-splitting. The whole town must have heard.

There were men's voices around her. It sounded as if there were lots of them, and among the words she could hear the unmistakable sound of vomiting. More than one of the men was throwing up. It must be a grisly sight. The image of her mother's brains flashed into her mind and she swallowed hard.

Someone grabbed at the amulet around her neck and yanked it off, breaking the chain. Another tugged at her gold bracelet, forcing it over her hand.

An engine started and she could feel vibrations beneath her. A cover was thrown over them, then they started to move. Where were they going? She could smell gas fumes; they were making her woozy. And then she drifted into unconsciousness once more.

~

Maria wakened to a rough jolting. It took a few moments before she remembered where she was and a stab of terror took her breath away. The vehicle appeared to be on a track of some kind, because she was being bumped around. She reached out and felt an arm. Whose was it? She couldn't tell, but it was not moving. On the other side she felt a woman's hair, but could detect no sign that anyone else was breathing. There was pain in every part of her but she couldn't think about it, not now.

The vehicle stopped and she heard voices. Men's voices with rough accents. Someone pulled back the tarpaulin over them and she held her breath, rigid with fear.

"We were promised the girls would be alive," a voice complained close by.

"You don't fancy a spot of necrophilia? Personally, it's not my thing."

"They were pretty, but look at all that blood. Fair turns your stomach."

The men had intended to molest them, Maria realized. What would happen if they found she was alive? It would be a fate worse than death. She wished she had died back at the Ipatiev House rather than face this.

"Breakfast is ready," a voice called from some distance away.

"We'll strip them after," one man said. "Bet they've got jewels hidden on them."

"Yeah, I can't wait to see their jewels," another said in a coarse tone, and there was general laughter.

Maria listened as the voices grew fainter. She had to get away before they returned and discovered she was alive. She strained her ears, listening hard for the sound of breathing or footsteps that would indicate there was anyone nearby, but the voices were distant now. Above her she could hear leaves rustling faintly in the breeze. She opened her eyelids just a fraction and saw starry sky through dark branches.

Still there was no sound nearby, and she opened her eyes a little more and turned her head to see where she was, then gasped in terror. Someone was there. It was Peter Vasnetsov, the guard from the house. He was standing right by the truck, his eyes wide in shock to see that she was alive.

"Help me," Maria pleaded in a whisper, her eyes fixed on his.

He glanced over to where the other guards were gathered, as if about to call them. Then he looked at her. In one swift movement he slid her off the back of the truck, pulling her legs from beneath the tarpaulin, then slung her over his shoulder and ran full tilt toward the edge of the forest.

CHAPTER 8

Sydney, October 20, 1973

VAL THREW TOGETHER A CHICKEN AND PINEAPPLE casserole from a recipe in *Women's Weekly*. She'd serve it with boiled rice, and some leftover sponge roll for dessert. Tony always insisted on dessert.

She cleaned the kitchen, careful not to leave any smears on the work surfaces, then glanced at the clock: ten minutes before she planned to leave. Queen Elizabeth II was opening the new Opera House down at Bennelong Point and Val hoped she could push her way to the front of the crowd to see her in the flesh, maybe even shake her hand. She'd been practicing her curtsies just in case.

Val was fascinated by the pretty English queen, just eight years her senior, and her dashing husband, Philip. In photos they looked as if they were madly in love. Val had read in a magazine that Elizabeth had had to fight to be allowed to marry him: her parents felt he was not her equal as he was just a Greek prince in exile, without much money, while she was heir to the British throne. They had been writing to each other since she was thirteen, and finally overcame parental opposition and got married when she was twenty-one, in a glitzy ceremony that was straight out of a fairy tale, with gilded coaches, frock-coated footmen, and a flowing white dress.

Val's father had opposed her marriage to Tony, which meant they'd had to wait till after her eighteenth birthday before they slipped off to tie the knot. He said Tony wasn't ambitious enough, and objected to the fact that his family was Catholic. "They'll expect you to raise twenty kids," he warned, and told her she was too young to know what she was getting into. She should have listened. She'd been so naïve back then, so desperate to escape from the gulag conditions at home with her Russian father, that she hadn't realized the trap she was falling into.

If only she'd had a mom to offer advice, things might have been different, but her Chinese mother had left home five years earlier. She'd just walked out without so much as a goodbye. Val's dad said it was because she didn't love them anymore, but that had never made sense. Val had heaps of memories of a warm, affectionate woman who used to build elaborate sandcastles, who taught her old Chinese songs about tigers and pandas, and made her favorite jam sandwiches cut into butterfly shapes. It had never made sense that she'd left them.

Val's teenage years had been overshadowed by that huge, baffling loss, and when Tony came along calling her "princess," buying her presents and telling her she was beautiful, she fell into his arms. She was lonely and desperate to be loved, and he seemed a catch. He was good at math and planned to work in finance. He played for the rugby team, so he was strong and fit. She was only slight in stature and she liked the fact that he was so much bigger. Why did he pick her out of all the prettier, more confident girls in their year? When she asked, he said he liked being her first boyfriend, because he didn't want a girl who'd been around the block. He could tell she was unhappy and he wanted to be the one to rescue her; she was precious and special and he loved her with all his heart.

Looking back, it was easy to see the moments when she should have walked away. The first time Tony slapped her was the week before their wedding, when she shrank one of his shirts in a hot wash. He tried to make a joke of it, but the slap hurt and left a stinging puce mark on her cheek that she had to cover with pancake makeup. On their beach-resort honeymoon she was sore and bleeding from the roughness of the sex, but still he wanted more and she had to bury her face in the pillows to muffle her cries of pain. But it was around three months into the marriage that she learned the true nature of her Jekyll and Hyde husband.

She'd spent a couple of hours that afternoon sitting in the sunny backyard reading a library book she simply couldn't put down. Dinner was prepared, because she knew Tony liked to eat as soon as he got in the door at five thirty, but she'd forgotten to clean his boots, which had gotten muddy during a weekend hike in the Blue Mountains.

"Hey, baby," he'd said, coming into the kitchen and sitting at the table. "What's cooking?" He grabbed her butt and squeezed as she walked past, then his eyes scanned the room and alighted on the boots still on the mat by the back door.

She opened her mouth to tell him about the meal, but before she could speak, he'd leaped to his feet, gripped the back of her neck, and forced her head around so she was looking at the boots.

"What the bloody hell have you been doing all day?" he asked. "Gallivanting around town? Got yourself a fancy man?"

"I've been in the yard . . ." she replied, her voice trembling.

"In the yard. Relaxing, I suppose. Getting a bit of sun." His voice was soothing, singsong, then it changed abruptly.

"While I've been slaving away earning the money to pay for your bloody idle lifestyle." He yanked her hair back, pulled her face close to his. "Do you think I like my job? Do you?"

He seemed to want an answer, so she shook her head, desperately trying to think of a way to calm him down.

"Don't you think I would rather be home, sitting in the sun in the yard?" A vein was bulging on his forehead and spittle sprayed her face.

"I'm sorry," she whispered. "It won't happen again."

He shook his head, pursing his lips. "You say that, but how can I believe you? Thing is, words are easy and I'm not here all day to keep an eye on you. I think you need something to remind you." He grabbed her left wrist, thumb on one side, fingers wrapped around, and bent her hand backward.

"Please, Tony," she begged, trying to wriggle free of his grip.

He gave a sudden, vicious twist and she heard the bone crack before she felt it, like the sound when you pull apart the joints of a chicken. She screamed in shock and a wave of giddiness washed over her.

Tony pulled her in for a hug, his tone loving now. "You understand why I had to do that, don't you?" He kissed her temple on the hairline, and stroked her long black hair.

It hurt so much that Val was shaking convulsively. "I need to go to the hospital," she stuttered. "You've broken my wrist."

"I'll take you once I've had dinner," he said, gripping her shoulders and turning her toward the oven. "We don't want food going to waste. It's not as if I'm made of money."

Val fashioned a sling from a tea towel, holding a corner between her teeth while she tied the knot. Next, she got an aspirin from the cupboard and swallowed it with some water, her hand shaking so violently the glass clattered against her teeth.

"Hurry up," Tony urged. "Sooner we eat, sooner I'll take you to hospital. We'd better decide what you're going to say." He regarded her with narrowed eyes. "Probably best tell them you tripped over the porch step and fell awkwardly. That'll work."

Val served the dinner with one hand but felt too sick to eat. Vomit rose in her throat, and her wrist throbbed with a sickening pain that radiated up her arm into her neck.

At the hospital, Tony was every inch the loving husband, joking with the nurses about Val's clumsiness. She stayed tight-lipped but couldn't stop shaking for hours afterward.

Her wrist set a little wonky, with a lump protruding, and it would always be weak on that side, unreliable for carrying heavy weights. But the main side-effect was that she became scared of Tony; properly scared. If he could deliberately break her wrist, what else was he capable of?

There had been plenty more slaps and pinches, kicks and shoves in the years since then, but he hadn't broken any more bones; he didn't need to, because the threat hung over her. If she did as he said, he was kind. They had holidays on the Gold Coast, he bought jewelry on her birthday and their wedding anniversary, they liked the same TV programs. It wasn't all bad, but she never knew when some insignificant incident would trigger the reemergence of his angry alter ego. And she was desperate to stop that happening.

~

Val decided to wear her only suit for the opening of the Opera House. It was a Jackie Kennedy–style pencil skirt and box jacket in pale blue seersucker trimmed with white braid. She'd wear a pearl necklace too, so the Queen's aides would consider her the right sort of person for the monarch to approach; they weren't to know the pearls were fake. Of course Tony would never have let her attend the royal event, but in the seventeen years that had passed since he broke her wrist, she had developed ways of rebelling against his control. It wasn't that the fear had lessened; she had simply gotten better at outwitting him.

He made her list all her expenditures in a lined accounts book that he checked every Sunday evening, and woe betide her if he thought she had wasted a cent; but she had found ways of siphoning off small amounts here and there, by shopping in markets that didn't give receipts and inflating the totals. She kept the money hidden in a box on a tiny shelf between the back of her dressing table and the bedroom wall, and smiled to herself each time she was able to add a couple of dollars.

In another bid for independence, she often rushed through the chores so she could slip out for coffee with her friend Peggy. If Tony rang while she was out, she'd act puzzled. "I must have been at the store," she'd say, or "Maybe I had the vacuum cleaner on."

When their daughter was born in 1968, that had restricted her freedom for a while, but now that Nicole had started preschool, Val was determined to make the most of her spare time.

She brushed her hair and smeared on some pale pink lipstick, then grabbed her handbag and car keys ready to hurry out the door, but just at that moment the phone began to ring. It could be Tony checking on her, so she picked up.

"The Doyle residence," she said in her telephone voice.

"Is that Valerie Scott?" a voice asked. A woman's voice. "Daughter of Irwin Scott of Bondi Junction?"

She hesitated, heard the woman's breathing down the line. "Who wants to know?"

"I'm calling from Sandy Bay nursing home in Bondi Junction. Your father has been here for six months. He named you as his next of kin."

Val was surprised. She hadn't realized her father had her phone number. They hadn't spoken since she left home to marry Tony. "My father and I are estranged," she told the woman, "so I can't imagine why he would give my number." Of course, she realized, he probably didn't have anyone else.

The woman exhaled loudly. "I'm afraid your father has dementia. His mind is deteriorating rapidly and he's started saying some very odd things. We're not sure what to do. If they're true, we should call the police, but you never know where dementia patients get their ideas from. That's why we thought we should call you first."

"What kind of things?" Val glanced at her watch and frowned. She didn't have time for this.

"He keeps repeating over and over 'I didn't want to kill her.' Then sometimes he says 'There was so much blood' and wrings his hands."

"Jeez." Val was listening hard now. Could he be talking about her mother? Had her father *killed* her? She shook herself. He was an objectionable character, but not a murderer. Funny that that had been the first thought to enter her head.

"You understand we're in a tricky position," the woman continued. "We wondered if you would come and talk to him, see if you can find out what he's talking about."

Val had always suspected her father knew where her mother had gone, but had never been able to get any information out of him. If he had dementia, there was no time to be lost. "I suppose I'd better come," she said, biting her lip, then wrote the address on the notepad by the phone, carefully ripping out the page and slipping it in her handbag so Tony wouldn't see. "I'll be there as soon as I can. Maybe tomorrow."

She hurried out the door and drove to the harbor, her mind turning over the odd conversation. It didn't make sense; at least, she hoped it didn't.

She had to park miles away from the quayside, and by the time she arrived, the crowd was so dense there was no chance of getting near the front, but by standing on tiptoe she could see a tiny figure at a podium. Like her, the Queen was wearing pale blue: a sleeveless dress and matching hat, with white gloves. She was gripping the sheets of paper on which her speech was written as a brisk wind tried to rip them from her hands. Her refined voice echoed through loudspeakers, muffled by the sound of wind buffeting the microphone. Prince Philip sat behind her with some dignitaries Val didn't recognize.

After the Queen's speech, the royal party disappeared inside the building. Val wondered what she would think of the design. There had been much debate in the Australian press about the strange curved concrete shells protruding from a redbrick base, and the budget, which had soared way beyond estimates, but Val liked it. To her it was like a sailing ship about to drift out to sea on the next tide.

The Queen and her husband appeared on a balcony halfway up to watch as, out in the bay, hundreds of boats, large and small, sounded their horns in a cacophony of noise. Reels of pinky-red streamers were released, then a host of balloons—"Sixty thousand of them," the woman beside Val said in awed tones. The sky filled with pink, blue, green, purple, and yellow spheres, like a swarm of beautiful insects rising on the breeze. It was quite magnificent, and Val felt lifted out of herself. Her problems seemed insignificant in the midst of such a large crowd, watching such a beautiful sight. She felt proud to be there, in that moment; proud to be Australian.

CHAPTER 9

Sydney, October 21, 1973

VAL DIDN'T TELL TONY SHE WAS PLANNING TO VISIT her father because she knew he would forbid her. He liked the fact that he and Nicole were her only "proper" family. His parents lived in Perth and they visited once a year, but Tony was always grumpy after they left, his ears ringing with their criticisms. Why hadn't he been promoted at work? Why didn't they have a bigger house? Why did it take Val twelve years to get pregnant with Nicole then nothing since? Why couldn't she produce more grandchildren, as his brothers' wives had done?

Val had no answer to that; it was just the way it was. Until she was thirty years old she'd thought she must be infertile, but then her baby daughter popped out with a beaming smile and a happy nature, like an amazing gift from the universe. Gazing at Nicole's peachy skin, the long eyelashes, the teeny fingernails, she knew that everything had changed in the most fundamental way possible. From now on, for the rest of her life, this little person would come first.

Tony changed too. He cooed over his new daughter and took endless photos to post to his mother. He bought a set of Lego bricks, and Val didn't dare tell him they were dangerous for a newborn, so she just kept a close eye to make sure Nicole didn't stick one in her mouth. They grew closer as they admired their daughter's wobbly first steps and giggled at her made-up toddler words. When Tony swung her in the air or let her clamber over him, his eyes all soft and affectionate, Val could almost love him again the way she used to before they were married. He'd kept his part of the marital bargain, getting a decent if dull job in finance, and buying them a house with a garden and a car apiece. If only it weren't for his temper, and his desire to control her every move, perhaps she could have been content.

Nicole chatted on the way to preschool that morning, asking food questions: "What do you like better? Chips or yogurt?"

"Yogurt," Val said.

"Vegemite or ham sandwiches?"

"Definitely ham. Poo-ee to Vegemite."

Nicole laughed. This was their little joke. Tony liked Vegemite but Val had to hold her nose while spreading it for him because she loathed the smell.

"Apples or 'nanas?" Nicole persisted.

She took the answers very seriously, cataloging them in her brain, and Val knew she would remember months later: "You said you like apples best, Mommy."

It seemed a miracle that Nicole had been born with a talent for happiness when neither of her parents was happy, but so it was. At preschool, she was greeted by a throng of little girls and trotted in after giving Val a quick hug, utterly confident in her own skin.

Val turned the car toward Bondi Junction, and almost immediately hit a traffic snarl-up. It was a stifling day and gas fumes wafted through the open window along with the noise of some idiot leaning on their horn. Only now did she allow herself to think about the prospect of seeing her father after

seventeen years, and it made her shudder. Even with dementia, she was sure time would not have mellowed him. Did he
still drink as much? Did he cry crocodile tears for Mother
Russia when he was drunk?

She could barely remember what he looked like, apart from
the perpetual scowl. He had dark bushy brows, and eyes too
close together, but she couldn't picture his mouth and chin or
put the pieces together to make a whole face. She could remember his voice, though: thickly accented, harsh, tyrannical.
She would never forget his unpredictable temper and the belt
he used to hit her across her bare legs. She remembered him
yelling at her school friends, accusing them of being sluts,
scaring them so they would never come to her house and avoided
inviting her to theirs. He used to embarrass her by using de-
rogatory terms for anyone of a different skin color, especially
Aborigines, whom he called "scroungers" and layabouts. It
seemed personal, since her mother was Chinese and Val had
her thick black hair, buttermilk skin, and almond-shaped eyes.
Were they scroungers too? Did his Russian birth and pale skin
make him superior?

She remembered the tension of mealtimes after her mother
was gone, when her father used to quiz her on general knowledge. What was the capital of Mongolia? How many feet in
a mile? She'd done her best to answer, but seventeen years on,
as she pulled into the nursing home parking lot, she felt her
stomach clench with dread, the way it always used to do as a
teenager.

Why was she visiting him? Would he still be able to ter-
rorize her? She was a married woman with a daughter; she
must stand up for herself. People could only bully you if you
let them.

She walked down the spartan air-conditioned corridor, following a nurse in white uniform. The nurse knocked on a

door and pushed it open, and there he was, in a chair by the window, recognizably him, although the bushy brows were silver and the posture was hunched.

"It's your daughter to see you," the nurse said in a too-bright voice, and Val approached, stopping when she was six feet away.

"Hi, Dad." There was another chair, and she positioned it so she was out of arm's reach before sitting down.

"I'll leave you to it," the nurse said, glancing from one to the other, perhaps surprised that Val hadn't attempted to hug or kiss him.

"How are you keeping?" Val began. Her dad's eyes were vacant, a paler shade of brown than she remembered, with spidery red veins. Hairs sprouted from his nostrils and ears, and the hair on his head was combed flat across a shiny skull. "What's it like here?" she persevered.

"You look tired," he said, his voice croaky. "You've got shadows under your eyes."

Charming, she thought. "My daughter wakes me early and my husband keeps me up late. What can I do?" She tried for a lightness of tone, wondering if he would pick up on the fact that he had a granddaughter. He didn't.

"The food's shocking. Just shocking." He pronounced the *sh* like *ch*. *Chocking.*

"Dad, have you heard from Mom at all? Ha Suran, your wife? Where is she?"

He looked blank. "I don't have a wife."

"You did have a wife. I'm her daughter. Where did she go?"

He shook his head, and a tear trickled out of the corner of his eye. Val wondered if he was crying, but decided it was just his eye watering, because he didn't seem emotional. There was a blanket on his lap and he rubbed the satin binding, back and forth. Val watched his hand with its funny raised scar like a red slug nestled between thumb and forefinger.

"The nurse told me you keep saying 'I didn't want to kill her.' Who did you not want to kill?"

He turned to gaze out the window and mumbled the words. "I had no choice."

"Was it Mom? Is she dead?" She wanted to shake him, force him to tell her what had happened when she was thirteen.

He shook his head. "There was so much blood. So much."

"Whose blood, Dad?"

"I didn't kill her."

"Where is she then?"

"There was so much blood."

"Did you stab her?"

"I had no choice." He shook his head sadly. "I didn't want to kill her."

For a while they went around in circles, but he just repeated the same phrases over and over, without seeming to have any understanding of their meaning. Whatever memories had been in his brain had faded, like a blackboard wiped almost clean, leaving just a few traces of words but no sense of their context. They could have come from a movie he'd seen.

"Do you know who I am?" she tried.

"Of course. You're . . ." He scratched his wrist. "You're a visitor."

"I'm your daughter, Val."

"I don't have a daughter," he said. "You've got the wrong person."

"Do you remember Ha Suran? She had shiny black hair, so long she could sit on it, that she wore piled up on her head." Val demonstrated with her own hair.

There was no sign of comprehension, not a twitch. Anything

he knew about her mother's disappearance was long gone. He was a senile old man, and Val became aware that he smelled of urine. Had he wet himself as they sat there? It hadn't been obvious when she first entered the room.

She tried to find a vestige of affection for the man who had raised her, but felt nothing but distaste. She wasn't going to get any information out of him and suddenly couldn't bear to stay a moment longer. She rose, hesitated. Should she kiss him goodbye? The thought made her feel sick.

"See you, Dad," she said, secretly hoping she wouldn't.

He didn't reply, just gazed out the window, where a dog was crouched, bowlegged, scent-marking a spot on the lawn.

~

"I don't think he's a killer," Val assured the nurse. "He was an obnoxious old goat when he was younger, but it wouldn't have been in his character to commit murder. I think he's just repeating something he heard."

"If you're sure . . ." The nurse was relieved. They didn't want the hassle of a police investigation. "Will you visit again?"

Val made a face. "It's difficult. We live quite far away—Croydon Park—and I've got a nipper at school. But you've got my number . . ."

She had goose bumps on her arms and couldn't wait to get back into the heat of the day. The stink of urine lingered in her nostrils as she drove across town to collect Nicole, feeling shaken by the encounter.

It was difficult to accept that the helpless, pathetic creature sitting in a chair by a window was the same man who had menaced her during her teenage years. The monster had faded but the harm he had done remained, and she couldn't forgive him. She had read enough psychology books, borrowed from the library, to understand why she had walked straight from a violent bully of a father into the arms of a violent husband. Human beings were attracted to what was familiar. The way Tony treated her must have triggered a feeling instilled in childhood that it was all she deserved. Sometimes she still felt that.

During the years of infertility, Tony had called her a failure as a wife, a useless waste of space, and it was hard not to take the criticism on board. What was the point of her life? He wouldn't dream of letting her get a job because it would make him look as though he couldn't afford to support her, so she spent her days cooking and cleaning like a domestic robot. Her friend Peggy repeatedly urged her to leave him, but where would she go? What would she use for money? How would she pay for a roof over her head when she had no qualifications, having left school at Tony's urging without taking her final exams?

Her marriage was unhappy, but wasn't everyone's behind closed doors? Even Peggy moaned about her husband's untidiness. Once Val had Nicole, everything else became bearable. Her daughter gave her all the love she needed.

She pulled up at the preschool just as the staff began releasing the little ones onto the playground, braids flying. Nicole ran to her waving a painting in garish reds and blues, daubed so thickly the paint was still wet and lumpy. Val swept her up and hugged her tight, feeling her daughter's ribs through the cotton T-shirt, smelling the sweet scent of her hair, not caring that she got paint on her blouse. The primal love she felt for this little person was so overwhelming that it made her want to cry out with joy.

CHAPTER 10

'M AFRAID I'M CALLING WITH BAD NEWS," A WOMAN'S
voice said down the line, and Val's heart gave a lurch. Was
it Nicole? Had there been an accident at preschool? Please,
not her.

"Your father died in the early hours of the morning," the
woman continued. "He had a cold that went to his chest, and
he simply stopped breathing during the night. He won't have
felt a thing. I'm sorry we couldn't alert you so you could be
with him at the end."

"No worries," Val said quickly. "I'm glad it was peaceful."
These were just words, the kind of thing you were supposed
to say. In truth, she felt only relief that the phone call wasn't
about Nicole.

"Will you come and collect his belongings? There are various
formalities, and the funeral to arrange. We can advise you."

"Of course," Val agreed. "Thank you." As soon as she hung
up, she rang Tony at the office. He would know what to do.

"Does he still have that big house in Bondi?" Tony asked.
"He must do. And you're the sole heir, right?"

"I suppose so. I don't know what he's been doing since I

left home, but I'm pretty sure he won't have remarried. Who would have him?"

"Give me the address and I'll drop in at the nursing home after work to pick up any paperwork," he volunteered. "You don't want to be bothered at a time like this."

From anyone else she might have thought it a kind gesture, but she knew Tony's motive was greed, pure and simple. He would probably be on the phone to an estate agent to find out what the house was worth as soon as she got off the line.

Suddenly she panicked that the nursing home would let slip she had visited her dad a few weeks earlier. That was the kind of thing that would make Tony fly off the handle. She picked up the phone to call and beg them not to mention it.

~

There were just three of them at the Russian Orthodox funeral: Val, Tony, and the elderly priest, Father Methodius. Three living people, that is: her father lay in an open coffin with a wreath across his forehead, a cross and the Trisagion prayer in his right hand. Val avoided looking at his pale features and thin strands of gray hair as they circled the coffin, while the priest sprinkled holy oil and recited from the Book of Psalms: "Give thanks to the Lord, for he is good; his love endures forever."

The smell of incense caught the back of her throat and the rhythm of the words tugged upon childhood memories that made her feel unbearably sad. As the casket was closed, sealing in her father for time everlasting, grief choked her and she sniffed back tears. Now there was no chance of her questions being answered. She would never understand what had happened to her mother, and what had made him such a bitter, angry man.

If only there were extended family members—a cousin or a sibling, someone to share this with; but there weren't any more blood relatives, not even any close friends. Tony had met her father a couple of times but only briefly, so he was unlikely to shed any light.

After the funeral, the full weight of grief descended upon Val. It felt as if she were wearing a suit of chain mail that made her movements slow and difficult. She was tired all the time and often lay on the sofa while Nicole was at preschool, staring into space, nothing particular in her head.

"You'll have to clear the house," Tony told her. "Make a pile of anything that can be sold and junk the rest. Sooner we can get it on the market, the better."

He didn't notice her depression, wouldn't have understood it if he had. Why should she feel grief for a father she hadn't seen for seventeen years? She couldn't understand it herself. Nicole sensed it, though, and climbed onto her lap for frequent cuddles, twirling Val's jet-black hair around her little fist and offering kisses from her cherry-colored lips.

Val had to steel herself to drive to the house on Penkivil Street, just fifteen minutes' walk from Bondi Beach. It was Edwardian-style, with pillared balconies on the upper floor, stained-glass windows on the lower, and a grand archway at the main entrance. Once it had been smart, but now it reeked of neglect, with peeling paint and a garden wall that was close to collapse. She parked in the drive, walked across the over-grown yard, and turned the key in the door to be met with a smell that made her recoil. It clearly hadn't been cleaned in ages, and the air was stale and sour, with an underlying odor as if some creature had died and was in the advanced stages of decomposition. Holding her breath, she ran from room to room on the ground floor, throwing windows wide and turning on fans.

She quickly saw that nothing had changed in seventeen years. There were the same beige cabinets in the kitchen, sticky to the touch from years of built-up cooking grease; the pantry was buzzing with flies, and a rubbish bin contained something noxious that she quickly threw out the back door. The worn brown sofa and chairs in the living room had suspicious stains on the upholstery. Still there was no TV. As a teenager Val had begged her dad to get one, but he refused, and the only entertainment came from an old phonograph and a pile of sentimental Russian records. The dining room had a burnt-orange patterned carpet and a dusty twelve-seater table that to Val's knowledge had never been used.

Upstairs, she hesitated in the doorway of her old bedroom, which was just as she'd left it. She surveyed the pictures she'd stuck on the walls: a poster for *The African Queen*, starring Humphrey Bogart and Katharine Hepburn, her favorite film at the time; a close-up shot of Bill Haley & His Comets on stage somewhere; an advertisement for Lustre-Creme shampoo, with the caption "Never Dries—it Beautifies." The dusky rose-pink bedspread her mother had bought was still spread on the single bed, coordinating with the curtains and the frill around her dressing table. There was nothing she wanted to keep, no part of that teenage girl she felt nostalgia for.

She popped her head into her father's bedroom but drew back at the intimate smell of his body, still as strong as if he were around the corner in the bathroom, about to emerge in his camel dressing gown, newspaper in hand. She moved on quickly, past the spare room that was never used. There were some faded photographs of her in a niche in the hall, but no trace of her mother anywhere: no clothes, no makeup, no pictures. As far as Val could remember, they had only moved to this house after her mother disappeared.

Her father's office was at the back of the house, and it was his inner sanctum, the place where he kept all his personal items, many of them brought from Russia. She pushed the door wide and surveyed the gloom. If she were going to find a clue to her mother's fate, it would be in the wooden desk her father had always kept locked. After her mom disappeared, Val had snuck in there many times to hunt for the key, checking behind the gold-painted icons in the shrine in one corner, and under the leather-bound tomes on the bookshelves, but she had never found it.

She tried the drawers now: locked, as always. She ran downstairs to the tool closet and selected a hammer and chisel. Back in her father's office, she got to work, hammering the chisel blade into the top right-hand drawer first. The elderly wood splintered easily and she was able to yank the drawer open, but inside there were only some pencils, mathematical instruments, and bottles of ink. She had hoped for an address book with a forwarding address for her mother, or a copy of her parents' divorce certificate, but there was nothing like that.

When she prised open the top left-hand drawer, she gasped at what she saw inside: the unmistakable shape of a pistol wrapped in a white cloth. She sat down on her father's revolving chair before unwrapping it. The barrel was dull black metal and it had a brown handle with a honeycombed grip, a chamber with space for six cartridges, a cocking hammer, and trigger: it was an ugly weapon, nothing elegant about it. Some bullets rolled around the drawer. Why had he owned a pistol?

Suddenly she wondered if he had shot her mother and buried her in the garden. Was that why there had been "so much blood"? Should she get the police to dig it up?

She shook herself. That was ridiculous. There was no evidence. Finding an old pistol in a drawer wouldn't persuade the police a crime had been committed. It had never occurred to her to suspect her father of murder until she heard what he kept repeating in the nursing home, and that was just the ramblings of a senile old man.

She stood and applied the chisel to the lower drawers. On one side she found several years' worth of household bills, while on the other she found her father's tax returns neatly filed in folders with the years marked on the outside. Tony had asked her to set aside any financial documents so he could deal with the tax affairs.

She pulled out the drawers and searched behind them in case anything had fallen down the back, but there was nothing there. She was choked with disappointment not to find any information about her mom. This was the only place she hadn't been able to search during those sad teenage years when she missed her so badly.

She took a deep breath and began to sort everything into piles. She wrapped up the pistol, along with its bullets, and put it by the door to be sent to an antique dealer for valuation. The icons went there as well, along with a silver samovar, a cloisonné cigarette case, and an old-fashioned camera with a concertina-style leather bag behind the lens that she spotted on a bookshelf. All the books were in Russian but Val had never learned the language, and didn't speak a word of her mother's Chinese tongue either. Her father had insisted that she was raised an all-Australian girl. She couldn't think of a use for his Russian books but she would ask the dealer if they had any value.

Next she began transferring the papers from the bottom desk drawers into a cardboard box she'd brought with her. One file slipped from her grasp and fell to the floor, spilling its contents. Val swore and lifted it carefully, trying to push the papers back in the same order, and that was when she spotted an old envelope covered in sums in her father's handwriting. He'd clearly been using it as scrap paper for some calculations. What interested her was that the back of the envelope gave an address in Harbin, Manchuria—and she knew that was where her mother had been born. She took it to the window to look more closely. The envelope was ripped so she couldn't make out a name or any street number, but maybe a letter would still get there and someone would know something. She stuffed it in her handbag.

None of the other documents she found made reference to the fact that her father used to have a Chinese wife. Nothing was in Ha Suran's name. She had been excised from history as cleanly as if she had never existed and Val had merely imagined she once had a mother.

~

Next morning, after Tony left for work, Val wrote to the address in Harbin asking if there was anyone there who had known Ha Suran Scott, who used to live in Australia. She explained that she was her daughter and wanted to get word to her of the death of her ex-husband, Irwin Scott. She gave her Croydon Park address and asked if they would kindly contact her if they had any information about her mother's whereabouts.

For a moment she felt a flicker of hope that something might transpire from this, but then dismissed it as a long shot. The address was incomplete, twenty-two years had passed since her mother disappeared—and the image of that pistol weighed heavy on her mind.

CHAPTER 11

Sydney, December 1973

THE WEEKS AFTER HER FATHER'S DEATH WERE HARD for Val, as she grieved without being sure who or what she was grieving for. She felt stranded and rootless, uncertain who she was and what kind of genetic legacy she had passed to her daughter.

She knew the bare facts of her parents' backgrounds: her father had fled the civil war in Russia around 1920 or 1921 and had arrived in Harbin, just across the border, where he met her mother some years later. She knew they had emigrated to Australia in 1930 and that she had been born in 1938, but everything else was a blank. What kind of families had they come from? Were there any other living relatives, no matter how distant the connection? Why had the mother she remembered as both warm and beautiful married such a cantankerous, unprepossessing man? Now that there was no one left to provide answers, it made Val question her own identity: who was she apart from Tony's wife and Nicole's mother?

She enjoyed being a mom and thought she did a reasonable job, simply by following her instincts. She remembered the games her own mother used to play with her, the fun they had, and tried to emulate them, while rejecting the authoritarian parenting style of her father, who had tried to ban all joy from the household. There were never any jokes; she couldn't remember the sound of her father laughing and suspected she had never heard it. After her mother disappeared, he bought the teenage Val strictly utilitarian clothes, designed to "last a good few years." It was astonishing she had managed to get a boyfriend wearing those long, shapeless skirts and baggy blouses that earned her the nickname "Hillbilly" at secondary school. She'd been pathetically grateful when Tony asked her to be his girl, and there had been no hesitation when he proposed while she was just seventeen.

Now her daughter supplied the only joy in her life, but she faced the prospect that Nicole would leave home one day and have a family of her own. Then Val would be relegated once more to joyless domestic servitude with Tony as her lord and master. Was that what life was about? Did other people settle for that?

Around and around her thoughts swirled. She was kept busy emptying her dad's house and preparing it to go on the market, but that gave her too much time to think, surrounded by the detritus of his existence. Everywhere there were memories of life with him: the worn saucepans she had to scrub clean after meals, the rough, scratchy towels, the leather belts that hung in his bedroom closet and that still made her shiver.

Preschool broke up for the summer holidays and Nicole had to accompany her to the Bondi house, bringing dolls, puzzles, and drawing materials to keep her occupied. Usually they went to the beach in summer, or to the park, or a museum, so they were missing out by being stuck in a stuffy old man's house. Val resented it, for her daughter's sake and her own.

Meanwhile, as if she wasn't busy enough, she had to maintain standards in her own home, and produce an edible evening

meal for Tony. She was constantly occupied but felt discon-
nected. She lost her appetite, because there was a lump in her
throat that made it hard to swallow, and if she did manage a
few mouthfuls, they weighed heavy in her stomach. She
couldn't sleep, but lay awake in the dead of night with Tony
snuffling and grunting beside her.

Although she felt bone-weary, sick with exhaustion, her
mind wouldn't shut down. The same questions came up time
and again. What had happened to her mom? What had her
dad been referring to when he said "I didn't want to kill her"?
And what could she do to make her own life better?

~

"Mrs. Doyle?" the voice on the phone said. "It's Graham from
the antique dealer's."

She felt slow. Who was Graham? "Uh-huh," she said, trying to nudge her brain into action.

"About one of the items you dropped off for valuation? The
camera? It's a Kodak Autographic, a type they started making
around 1914. It's a lovely camera. Very popular at the time."

"Uh-huh," Val repeated. Why was he ringing her?

"I thought you'd want to know there's a roll of film left
inside. Someone forgot to process it."

Val frowned. Who might her father have photographed?
Was her mother on there? Her father's birth family? "Would
it be possible to process the film now?" she asked.

"It will be tricky, but I have a friend who runs a developing
studio and I took the liberty of calling him this morning. He's
willing to give it a try, as an experiment, so long as you realize he might not be able to get any clear images. He says it
depends on all sorts of things. It can be hard if the camera
was kept in a humid climate, for example."

"How much would he charge?" Val asked. She couldn't see Tony consenting to this, so she'd have to fund it herself.

"I think he would do it out of curiosity, but let me give you his number and you two can talk direct."

~

A week later, with Peggy babysitting for Nicole, Val drove to Paddington and parked in a back alley before walking up some metal steps to a first-floor photographic studio. There was no bell, so she knocked on the door and waited. She knocked again, and heard footsteps coming toward her before a man with a sweep of chestnut hair and a shaggy beard appeared.

"Mrs. Doyle? I'm Alan. Come in."

"Call me Val," she said as he led her down a dim corridor, past a bicycle and a stack of cardboard boxes.

"This is my darkroom," he said, indicating a door with a sign that read *Keep Out If You Value Your Life*. "Your prints are hanging up inside. Follow me."

It took a few moments before her eyes grew accustomed to the light, which emanated from a reddish bulb. Bottles of chemicals sat on a shelf along one wall, and a row of prints hung on a string above a sink. The smell was acrid, making her eyes water and her nostrils sting. She fumbled in her bag for a tissue and Alan sympathized.

"It's a mix of vinegar and ammonia. I'm used to it so I barely notice anymore until visitors react as if they're being poisoned."

Val dabbed at her eyes, keen to get out again as soon as possible. "You said on the phone that some of the pictures have come out?"

Alan nodded. "I could see there were images on your film as soon as I took it out of the camera, but I had to leave it in the developer longer than usual to get any clear results, so they're a bit overexposed. There are eight of them. Here!" He indicated the first picture hanging on the line. "This was clearly a group shot. I've enlarged it to pull out all the detail I could."

Val peered at the black-and-white image. It had a patina across the top like a string of ink blots joined together by threads, but behind them she could make out some figures. Girls, she thought, with wide white ankle-length skirts and straw hats, their faces indistinct. The next image showed a seated couple, but there was a smudge across their faces and they were only clear from the waist down. In a third shot she could see a garden but no detail of the figures that appeared to be the subject of the picture. The fourth one showed what appeared to be a little boy lying on a sofa. Could they all be members of her father's birth family? There was a Russian feel to the images, although she couldn't put her finger on what made her think that.

"There were some interesting ones toward the end," Alan said, walking further down the line of prints. "The Kodak Autographic had a curious feature: an aperture in the back where you could use a stylus to write a caption for the picture, perhaps the place or date. Your photographer chose to write the names of three of his subjects."

Val read them out loud, stumbling over the pronunciation: "Konstantin Ukraintsev, Peter Vasnetsov, Ivan Skorokhodov." Russian names. The three images showed men in uniform, staring at the camera without smiling. "They're very solemn."

"Back in the Victorian era, subjects had to stay still because of the long exposure time, and that's why you get those characteristic stiff poses. By 1914, that was no longer necessary, so you'll find some more candid portraits with people smiling and fooling around. But I guess there was still a sense that being photographed was a formal occasion, especially if you weren't used to it." There was no hesitation in his reply; he spoke as an expert.

Val looked at the faces of the three men. The shots were grainy, with one side of the figures brighter than the other, and they all appeared to have been taken in the same room. She could make out a window to the left of them. Were the men friends of her father's before he left Russia? They looked distinctly Russian, with strong bone structure and sturdy figures.

"I wonder why he wrote the names of some but not others?" she mused.

"Easy," Alan replied. "He felt the need to remind himself because he didn't know them so well."

"So you think he knew the girls in the earlier shots . . ."

"I'm just guessing, but it seems a reasonable explanation."

Val went back to the first five pictures and looked at them again. It was like a jigsaw puzzle, with different parts clear in each shot. Two slender figures posing against a tall fence. The exterior of a white-painted house. Girls in white dresses. Here and there she could make out shoulder-length hair, a round face, a high-necked blouse, and she got the impression the girls were pretty. Were they her father's sisters, and therefore her aunts? Were any of them still alive? None of the figures she could make out resembled either her father or her mother, and that was disappointing.

"I'm sorry they're not clearer," Alan said, "but this is pretty good for film that's over fifty years old."

"It's better than I expected," Val said, biting her lip. "I wonder if I might have copies of the prints?"

"Of course," he said, straightaway. "I made a set of six-by-fours, and you can take the enlarged ones as well if you like."

"Are you sure I can't pay you anything?"

"Wouldn't dream of it," he said. "I love a challenge."

When Val got home, she flicked through the prints again but couldn't make out any more than she had in the darkroom. She got a creepy feeling from them, and decided to hide them on the shelf behind her dressing table, where Tony wouldn't find them. It was a safe bet he wouldn't approve.

CHAPTER 12

Sydney, January 1974

Two months after Val's father's death, his house was empty, the rooms looking huge without furniture, the wallpaper marked with ghostly rectangles where pictures used to hang. As soon as Tony put it on the market, it was snapped up by a property developer with plans to renovate and extend it, adding a pool out back. Val was relieved she no longer had to make the daily commute to Bondi, but still her depression wouldn't shift.

"Maybe you should go to the doctor and get a prescription for Valium," Peggy suggested over cream soda drinks in her yard, while Nicole played with her son, Lenny, in their sandbox. "A mate of mine, Lynette, says it worked for her."

Val screwed up her nose. "I don't like the idea of taking pills. Tony says it's mind over matter and I should be able to snap out of it."

Peggy snorted, expressing her opinion of Tony. "Maybe if he gave you a bit more support . . . or took you out for dinner some night instead of expecting a slap-up meal on the table . . . Mind over matter indeed!"

Val shrugged. There was no chance of that. The evening before, Tony had complained that she'd served burgers twice in a week, saying that any fool could grill a burger. He'd also complained about dust on the windowsill in the living room and sticky fingermarks on the TV screen, and she'd braced herself for a slap that didn't come. He hadn't hit her for a while now. Maybe that was the most she could expect after the death of a parent: a temporary cessation of violence.

Nicole ran over in her white sundress with a strawberry print, her skin golden from the sun. "Come see our castle," she urged, holding out her hand. "A fairy princess lives inside and there's a goblin in the moat who is trying to capture her."

Val loved the stories that emerged from her daughter's head—a mixture of characters from the bedtime stories they read every night and her own lively imagination—but the effort it took to respond sometimes felt phenomenal. She willed herself to stand up, take the weight in her legs, and walk to the sandbox, but nothing happened. She couldn't do it. Peggy gave her a puzzled look and went over instead.

"Is that a drawbridge?" she asked, crouching to admire the sandcastle. "You'd better lift it so the goblin can't run across."

"Maybe he can swim," Nicole suggested.

"I reckon your fairy princess will know a good spell to stop him."

Nicole clapped her hands with glee, and she and Lenny began inventing nonsense words that might work as a magic spell.

Peggy returned to where Val was sitting and put a hand on her shoulder, her eyes full of concern. "Want me to keep Nicole for the afternoon so you can go home and get some shut-eye? You look done in."

Val shook her head. She might not be any use as a mom at the moment, but she needed Nicole around. Her daughter's happy chatter and innocent take on the world were the only things keeping her remotely sane.

~

Nicole started at primary school and was immensely proud of her school uniform, with its pleated gray skirt and short-sleeved white blouse. Peggy complained that Lenny never told her what he had done at school during the day, but Nicole always rushed out to the playground in a breathless torrent of words.

"Today the teacher. told us a story from days of yore. Do you know about days of yore, Mommy? It's like the past, when they had knights in armor and unicorns."

She kept up the stream of news on the walk home, requiring little response from Val, pausing only to beg for some popping candy or fizzy cola sweets when they passed the milk bar. Val never had the heart to refuse, even though it was expenditure she would have to hide from Tony when she filled in the accounts book. He didn't approve of sweets.

"We've got a pet rabbit at school, Mommy," Nicole continued, her words thick from the sweet she was chewing. "His nose goes like this . . ." She demonstrated, her tiny nose wiggling up and down in a pretty accurate imitation of a real rabbit.

"What color is it?" Val asked.

"White. And his name's Edward."

"How do you know it's a boy?"

Nicole raised her eyebrows: "Of course he's a boy! He's got a boy's name."

"Silly me." Val smiled, and the movement felt unfamiliar, as if the corners of her mouth might crack.

"He escaped today. Sally was holding him and he jumped out of her arms and ran all over the classroom. Everyone was screaming. Mrs. Cole shut the door and got a piece of carrot and she tried to trap him in the corner but when she got near, he leaped over her arm and escaped again." Nicole giggled from deep in her belly, a sound full of joy. "It was the funniest thing *ever.*"

Her face was so animated, her pleasure so genuine that Val spoke without thinking. "Maybe we should get a pet rabbit at home."

As soon as the words were out, she regretted them. Tony would never agree. He'd worry about the smell, the cost of pet food, the incursion of a rabbit run into his precious yard.

"Oh, *please!*" Nicole begged. "Pretty please."

"We'll see what Daddy says. Maybe he'll want you to wait till you're older so you can look after it yourself." It was hard to backtrack from such a tantalizing offer. "Why don't you leave me to ask him? You don't want to annoy him or he'll definitely say no."

But the seed had been planted, and Nicole's talk all afternoon was of names for rabbits, the different colors of their fur, and the foods she thought they liked best.

At dinner that evening—sausages and mashed potatoes—Nicole told Tony about the school rabbit. He laughed out loud at her imitation of its nose twitching, and encouraged by the response, she told him about Edward escaping and the pandemonium in the classroom as they tried to catch him. Proud that her story was going so well, she waved her arm in the air to demonstrate how Edward had leaped over the teacher's arm, and a lump of potato flew from the fork she was holding and landed on the floor.

Quick as a flash, Tony reached across and rapped her knuckles with the handle of his knife, so hard Val could hear the clunk of metal on bone. "Mind your manners," he said calmly.

Nicole gasped, a deep, long in-breath when time seemed suspended.

Val leaped to her feet and ran around the table before the scream erupted. She knew her daughter's cries intimately: the ones that were for show when she wasn't really hurt; the ones when she was scared rather than injured; but this was a cry of genuine pain. She grabbed Nicole and scooped her into her arms, then yelled at Tony, hysteria in her voice.

"You can't do that! She's only five!"

She could put up with him hitting her, but not her baby. Nicole was screaming, her whole body trembling. Val lifted the reddened knuckle to her lips and kissed it softly, feeling her daughter's pain. Should she run it under a cold tap? Might the bones be broken?

"She's got to learn," Tony said, lifting a forkful of sausage to his mouth. "You know how I feel about table manners."

Val never swore, but a string of expletives filled her head. She wanted Tony to feel her fury, and only the presence of the shrieking Nicole in her arms stopped her from venting it. Instead she hurried to the sink, where she made a cold compress, keeping one arm tightly around her daughter, not letting her go for a second. She sat with Nicole in her lap, holding the compress around her knuckles, rocking her gently as the screams subsided into sobs and then whimpers.

"Daddy didn't mean to hurt you," she whispered. "He didn't know it would hurt so much." But that was a lie. He had meant to inflict pain on their daughter. Severe pain.

In a flash, it came to Val that she had to leave him. If they stayed, he would bully Nicole just as her father had bullied her. History would repeat itself. She couldn't bear to watch that confident, sunny little girl become anxious and withdrawn, the way she herself used to be as a teenager—still was, if truth be told.

"What's for pudding, Val?" Tony demanded, but she ignored him.

Peggy had urged her to leave many times, but Val had always been overwhelmed by the knowledge that Tony would do everything in his power to stop her. She had never stood up to him, just as she had never stood up to her father. But Nicole was so full of happiness that it would be a crime to sit and watch as it was knocked out of her, blow by blow.

She had fallen asleep in Val's arms now. She often fell asleep after hurting herself; it seemed to be her body's physiological response to shock. Val rose to carry her upstairs to bed.

"Where's the bloody dessert?" Tony called after her.

"There's ice-cream sponge in the freezer." She felt like ramming it in his face but restrained herself.

She walked slowly so as not to wake Nicole, and laid her carefully on the bed. She managed to strip off her school skirt and blouse and slipped her under the covers in her undershirt and panties, then sat by the bedside, thinking hard.

Suddenly it came to her that her depression over the last two months hadn't been about her father's death; it had been about her subservience in a loveless marriage. Becoming an orphan had focused her mind on her own mortality and made her assess her life—and she couldn't bear what she saw.

She would have to plan her departure carefully, arranging everything in advance. If she waited till the beginning of March, when Tony gave her the housekeeping money, there should be enough to pay a month's rent somewhere cheap. Peggy would help out with furniture; she had stacks of it in the attic from her great-aunt's house. Better not to let Tony get wind of it. If she presented him with a fait accompli, he would accept it eventually, and when they came to a settlement, she should get the money from the sale of her father's house. It would be a lifesaver.

During the next two weeks, Val often felt terrified about what she was planning, but whenever she looked at her daughter's swollen knuckles, she knew she had no choice. She found a one-bedroom flat not far from the waterside in Balmain—just a box of a place on the first floor of a large, decrepit house, with a stove, fridge, and sink along one wall of the living room and a toilet and shower in a closet off the bedroom. Peggy borrowed her brother's van and drove over with an old bed, table, and chairs to furnish it.

Then one Saturday morning, while Tony was playing golf, Val packed all her and Nicole's possessions into the car and, with shaking hand, wrote a note for him and propped it on the kitchen table.

I'm leaving you, it said, *and taking Nicole*. From pure force of habit, she added a PS: *There's a casserole in the fridge*.

She took Nicole's hand and led her out to the car, feeling lighter than she had in years.

CHAPTER 13

The Ural Mountains, July 17, 1918

THE FOREST WAS SO DENSE THAT LITTLE LIGHT PEN-
etrated. There were just a few slanting shafts as the sun
rose higher in the sky. The air was damp and smelled strongly
of spruce. Maria clung to Peter as he ran with her slung over
his shoulder, jolted by his pounding footsteps. It was clear he
knew the area well, because he didn't once hesitate about the
direction he took. She strained her ears for the sound of guards
pursuing them, but all she could hear was Peter's feet tramp-
ing in the undergrowth, his heavy breathing, and the squawking of birds high above.

"Please stop," she begged. "Leave me here and go back for
the others."

He didn't slow down. "It's no use," he panted. "I'm sorry."

Maria's voice rose. "I'm sure some of them are alive. We
can't leave them behind."

Peter kept running. "If I go back," he explained, "I will be
arrested, then they will find you and kill you."

"You would leave my sisters to their fate at the hands of
those monsters?"

There was panic in her voice. It was imperative he return.
Why could he not understand?

It was a while before Peter replied, and she sensed he was trying to decide what to say. "None of the others were alive," he told her at last. "I'm sorry."

"How do you know? How can you?" She wouldn't believe it. "You didn't know I was alive until I opened my eyes."

He didn't answer, just kept pushing forward. Each step caused a jabbing pain in her belly. She felt light-headed and so profoundly shocked she couldn't think straight. Her brain wouldn't work.

They emerged by the side of a lake, which glowed pink in the morning light, with a mirror image of the tall trees reflected on the surface of the water. Peter stopped and laid her on the bank, and she was grateful to be still. She closed her eyes to stop her head spinning, but opened them when she sensed him nearby. He had some water cupped in his hands.

"Drink," he ordered.

The water was so cold, it jolted her awake. It had a sweetish taste.

"Are you *sure* they're all dead?" she asked again.

He nodded. "I'm afraid so."

"What about little Alexei? Anastasia? How could they kill children?" She couldn't believe it. Refused to.

Peter had no answer. He busied himself making a small fire from some twigs, under the shelter of a rocky alcove.

"Tatiana is alive," she told him. "She wasn't in the house last night. She was with a friend who was trying to rescue us, a man called Malama. We need to find them."

Peter created a spark and blew on it to get his fire burning. After that, he returned to the lakeside and scooped up some mud with his hands, bringing it back to the fire.

"We can't go to Ekaterinburg," he said at last. "We need to get as far from here as we can. We'll worry about finding your sister later."

"But *how* will we find her?"

"I don't know."

She saw he was fashioning a kind of bowl from the mud, shaping it with his curved palms. He held it over the fire, turning it this way and that, jacket sleeves pulled down to protect his hands from the heat. It was pale gray in color and she could see it becoming solid as she watched. It must be clay.

"Tatiana is clever," she told him. "She will know what to do. We just need to find her."

Peter didn't say anything, but after a while, he rose and went back to the lake, where he scooped some water into his makeshift bowl.

"What are you doing?" she asked.

"I'm boiling water to clean your wounds, if you will allow me. We can't risk infection setting in."

He placed his bowl in the fire, fanned the flames around it, then sat watching as the water heated.

"Won't the guards see the smoke?" she panicked.

He shook his head. "The wind is blowing in the other direction and we are sheltered by that rock face." He pointed behind her.

"You won't leave me, will you?" she asked, remembering that not long before, she had begged him to do just that while he went back for the rest of her family.

"I won't," he said, in a tone that made her understand she could trust him.

She lay back and rested for a while, but opened her eyes when she felt him dabbing the side of her head with a hand-kerchief soaked in boiled water.

"I'm sorry to wake you," he apologized. "The bullet only grazed your temple. There's a lot of blood but it should heal quickly. Where are the other wounds?"

She placed a hand on the blood-soaked bodice of her gown, where the pain was throbbing and incessant. "Here. And in my leg." She touched the spot on her outer thigh.

"Do I have your permission to dress them?" he asked, his eyes serious, his tone formal.

"Yes," she said, then added, "Thank you," in a quiet voice.

She closed her eyes as he cut open the front of her gown with a knife and cleaned around the gash in her abdomen. She could feel he was doing his best to protect her modesty, exposing no more than was strictly necessary, but still it felt strange to be touched there by a man she hardly knew.

"There are jewels in your bodice," he said. "It seems they deflected the bayonet thrust. They almost certainly saved your life."

"*You* saved my life," she murmured.

He peeled back the hem of her dress to look at the wound in her thigh, and she shuddered, remembering Bolotov raising her skirt and the ugly fingers that had prodded between her legs. Peter could not have been more different; his touch was gentle and he restricted his attention to the wound site.

"The bullet has emerged through the other side," he reported. "That's good. I won't have to remove it."

All the same, it hurt a lot when he began to clean around the holes in her thigh, and suddenly a wave of darkness descended, carrying her off to unconsciousness.

~

When she came around, Peter was nowhere to be seen. Maria raised herself onto her elbows to look for him, scared that he had left her. The movement caused a wave of sickness. She turned her head and vomited into the grass, then wiped her mouth with the back of her hand. Alerted by the noise, Peter emerged from the woods carrying handfuls of plants. He hurried over, dipped a piece of cloth in the warm water and wiped her mouth clean, then used the remaining water in his bowl to rinse the grass alongside her head.

"This is yarrow," he told her, indicating the plants he'd brought, which had white flowers on feathery-leaved stems. "We call it soldier's woundwort because the army often use it in the field. It stops bleeding and prevents infection. I'm going to make poultices with it to bind your wounds. Then I'll look for some meadowsweet, which will relieve the pain and stop you feeling nauseous. After that, we must be on the move again."

She watched as he peeled the yarrow leaves from the stems and mashed them in his clay bowl. The pain in her wounds was fiercer now and she couldn't help moaning as he laid his poultice across her belly and secured it firmly with strips of cloth. She wondered where the cloth had come from, then noticed that he had cut strips from the bottom of her petticoat. He must have done it while she slept.

Next he bound her leg, and finally her head. She tried to be brave, but there was pain radiating around every part of her: her head, her belly, her leg, but most of all her heart. Her chest was so tight it was an effort to breathe. Tears sprang to her eyes, and he watched without speaking, his own eyes full of compassion, as she tried to blink them back.

"I let them down," she whispered. "I abandoned them."

"You were the only one alive," he said quietly. "I promise you."

That was when she began to cry properly. She didn't want to, because she was scared she might never stop, but the sobs forced themselves out.

"I should have died too," she said. "Then I would have gone to heaven with them. Instead I saved myself and that makes me a bad person. I wish with all my heart I were dead."

Peter picked up an unused strip of petticoat and handed it to her to use as a handkerchief, his eyes downcast. On a tree branch nearby, a tiny bird with brown feathers and a ruby-red throat trilled urgently as if trying to tell them something. Its tone was pure and clear as a flute played by a world-class musician.

CHAPTER 14

Ural Mountains, July 1918

A FTER HER WOUNDS WERE BOUND, PETER LIFTED Maria onto his back, like a soldier's kitbag. The position was immodest since her legs must wrap around him, but he said it would be easier for him to walk without stopping to rest.

"Where are we going?" she asked, as he headed back into the forest.

"West," he said. "Into the mountains."

They walked for many hours, stopping only for short breaks, and when night fell and it grew too dark to see, he laid her on the earth and found leafy branches to place over her blood-stained gown to keep her warm. He curled up nearby, keeping watch, and Maria drifted off to sleep within minutes, overwhelmed with fatigue. She dreamed that she was with Olga and Alexei, Anastasia and her parents, all of them playing with the dogs in the snow, laughing as they slid and fell. And then she opened her eyes to a Siberian forest dawn and the unthinkable truth.

Peter was crouched beside her, offering a handful of wild berries. "You must eat," he said, but she turned her face away. How could she eat when her family were dead? How could she even think of it? What had been done to them felt unreal, like a grotesque nightmare. She couldn't begin to comprehend the enormity of her loss.

For three days they headed west, most of the time in silence. Thoughts of death were never far from Maria's mind. It was hard to understand the finality: that she would never cuddle Alexei or giggle with Anastasia again; that she would not see her parents anymore in this lifetime. Hopes of finding Tatiana seemed unrealistic; she could be anywhere. Maria often contemplated killing herself but worried that it would mean turning her back on God, and if she did so she would not be reunited with her family in heaven. Instead she murmured prayers for them, remembering the words of the memorial *panikhidas* as best she could: "O Lord, set to rest the soul of your servants who have fallen asleep, in a place of light, in a place of green pastures, in a place of rest whence all pain, sorrow and sighing have been driven away."

Peter left her to her own thoughts, asking only if she was warm enough, or if she would like some food or water. She wished she had another gown to change into instead of the one she was wearing with a slash in the bodice. By turning her petticoat back to front she could stop her flesh being exposed, but she felt tainted. Each day Peter checked her wounds, looking for signs of heat or redness or swelling that could indicate infection. When he lowered his head and sniffed them, she asked, "What are you doing?"

"I would be able to smell if an infection was taking hold," he said. "But you are healing well."

She didn't care if she healed or not. It seemed irrelevant. She didn't even ask him where they were heading or if he had a plan. Somehow she couldn't bring herself to care.

During the afternoon of the third day, they arrived at an abandoned half-ruined hut. The roof had collapsed inward and the interior was full of rubble and animal droppings. Peter laid her on a grassy bank nearby and went inside.

"I thought we could stay here till your wounds heal," he called through the doorway. "No one will find us in such a remote spot."

She nodded. All around was silent and still, with only the barest breath of wind ruffling the topmost branches of the trees and a few birds calling from afar. She had never been anywhere so quiet.

White clouds meandered past in the vast blue sky and she lay back to watch. Her brain was awash with emotions: guilt, anger, and sorrow, all mixed together. Sometimes her fury with the assassins came to the forefront, at other times her guilt that she had abandoned her family. Grief always hovered in the background, so immense that she could not let herself give into it for fear of being swallowed up.

Peter occupied himself with clearing the hut, then he used his knife to cut some spruce branches with which to repair the roof. Maria twisted to watch as he arranged the fronds in an overlapping pattern. He jumped down and stood inside the hut, peering upward to check for gaps, then hacked off more branches to fill them. Once he'd finished, he collected armfuls of fallen leaves and moss and arranged them over the top, before bringing further armfuls to create a floor covering inside. It was clear he had done this before.

He vanished for a moment, then appeared by her side with the clay bowl full of water.

"Drink," he said, and she obeyed. The water was icy.

"Do you think I must have committed terrible sins to be so punished?" she asked him. "Perhaps I should have been a better sister and a better daughter. I often argued with Anastasia, and sometimes I hid when Alexei wanted to play with me. Do you think God has cursed me for my selfishness?"

"No." He shook his head vehemently. "I am not a believer in God, but if there is such a thing, I cannot believe he is some tit-for-tat tyrant. Besides, it makes no difference what God wills when you are faced with a band of crazed men intent on murder."

"Why did they want to murder us? I don't understand." She frowned and closed her eyes to hold back the tears.

He hesitated a moment, choosing his words. "The Bolsheviks have a black-and-white message: the old system under your father was corrupt and favored the few, while the new regime will make society fairer. They need to create demons in order to push through their reforms—and sadly they decided your family were those demons."

Maria noticed he said "were." Past tense. They were no more. "Do *you* think we were demons?" she asked.

"Of course not."

"Yet you worked for the Bolsheviks."

"I did. I believed—still believe—that the country's wealth should be more fairly distributed, but I don't think Lenin's men are going about it the right way. It's not necessary to destroy the old in order to bring in the new." He stood up. "But it does no good to dwell on these matters. What's done is done. I am going to find dinner. I will be gone no more than an hour."

Maria opened her mouth to object, but he had vanished into the trees. She peered after him and suddenly remembered one of the guards telling her that there were brown bears and wolves in those woods. What would she do if a wild animal appeared? She couldn't run; her injured leg wouldn't take her weight.

A cloud passed in front of the sun and she shivered in the sudden chill. There was a rustle in the undergrowth behind her, but when she turned her head, there was nothing to be seen. Surely Peter would not leave her if there was any danger?

Fear pricked the back of her neck and suddenly she was back in the basement, her ears ringing with the terrified screams of her sisters, crawling on her hands and knees across a floor that was slippery with their blood, the smell of gunpowder choking her. She saw her mother's brains glistening, Anastasia whimpering by her side, her father falling as the bullets came thick and fast. She saw the hatred on that guard's face as he thrust at her with his bayonet, heard the ugly crowing of the men as they plotted to scavenge their corpses. She covered her face with her hands and moaned but couldn't make the images go away. There was the sound of repeated screams and she realized they were coming from her own lips, bursting out of her in staccato pulses.

"What is it? What happened?" Peter appeared from nowhere and crouched to put an arm around her shoulders.

He placed two fingers on her lips to silence the screams, then sat on the ground and wrapped his arms tight around her, careful not to touch her wounds. His body was warm and sturdy and smelled of earth and spruce. She clung to him as hard as she could, taking comfort in his steadiness.

"It's all right," he murmured. "You're safe." His hands were on her back, his chest pressed against hers, and she felt his warmth flowing into her cold flesh.

She pulled her head back to look at his serious gray eyes. A straggly beard was sprouting on his chin, as he had not shaved for three days; it made him look older. On impulse she leaned forward and kissed his cheek, then his lips, and soon she was kissing all over his face in a frenzy. It wasn't planned; she was just following some instinct she did not understand. She held his face in her hands and planted kisses on his forehead, his chin, his nose, his temples.

He didn't try to stop her but he did not kiss her back either, and after a while she paused. Who was this man who would not take advantage of her, even when they were alone in the mountains and she had more or less invited him? He gave her a wan smile, tilting his head to one side.

Suddenly she realized that in saving her he had risked his own life. If they were caught, they would both be executed. "What have I done to you?" she asked, full of remorse that it had not occurred to her before.

"Nothing. At least, not compared with what they have done to you," he replied.

"I had forgotten that you have lost your family too. Your mother. Your sister. All because of me." He looked sad, and she added, "I hope one day you will find them again."

"I wish you could meet them." He had a distant look in his eyes. "After this war is over, perhaps I will be able to introduce you."

"I would love that," she said. Their faces were close, his arms still around her, but now that she had calmed down, he disengaged and moved away.

Maria watched as he built a fire. If only some other member of her family had been rescued by a man as kind as him. "Tell me . . . You are a Bolshevik, you believe in the Revolution, so why did you decide to save me, knowing that you would lose everything in the process?"

He shrugged. "It was simple. My father taught me there are right things to do in the world and wrong things, and that I must always opt for the right ones. When I saw you were alive in the back of the truck, I knew instantly what was right."

CHAPTER 15

Ural Mountains, August 1918

MARIA'S WOUNDS HEALED WITHOUT BECOMING INfected and her body grew stronger, so that before long she was able to walk short distances using a walking stick Peter had fashioned. It was painful to lift anything or to turn at the waist, but she could wash herself and scrub the worst of the bloodstains from her gown in a freezing spring that gushed from the mountainside. Peter roasted rabbits and birds he had caught in homemade traps, and Maria gnawed the meat from the bones, suddenly ravenous. He made delicious tisanes from mountain herbs and soups from mushrooms he had foraged, and every day he brought bowlfuls of fruits of deep red, blue, and black hues: wild strawberries, cloudberries, and crowberries, he told her, as she devoured them.

While he spent his days gathering food, Maria wandered close to their camp engulfed in a thick fog of grief. She was becoming sick of the continuous crying that left her with no air to breathe, crying that came from a place deeper inside than she had imagined possible, but she couldn't stop herself. The sight of a tiny bird pecking at the grass; a pretty flower nestled in the roots of an ancient tree; everything seemed to spark a memory of her family and set her off again. She tried to keep her tears from Peter now. It wasn't fair for him to witness such misery, hour after hour. He had done his best by rescuing her and it wasn't his fault that she wished she had died along with her sisters.

In the evenings, they talked. He told her he had learned his hunting skills from his gamekeeper father, and his knowledge of herbal medicines had been passed down from his mother's grandmother.

"The estate where I grew up was a wonderful place to spend a childhood," he said, "but I always knew my place. The children of the landowner would turn away when I passed because I was not of their class."

Maria felt ashamed. Had she ever averted her eyes when she saw a child from a poor family? She didn't think so. A memory flashed to mind of a time when they were traveling in their open-topped automobile through the countryside and saw a beggar girl by the roadside. Olga had been playing with a china-faced doll in a lace-trimmed gown but on a whim she threw it out the window to the poor bedraggled girl, who looked bemused as she picked it up. Maria remembered that look of puzzlement. Perhaps the child had never owned a doll before and did not know what to do with it. Perhaps she would have preferred food.

She asked Peter about his sister, and heard that she worked as a seamstress and had two children and a husband who, like Peter, had worked at the Makarov cloth factory.

"Why did you not remain on the estate and follow in your father's footsteps?" she asked.

He hesitated before replying. "I had a growing sense that the old system must change, and I did not want to work for the aristocracy anymore. At the factory we held meetings and talked about owning the plant collectively, each man having a stake . . . It seemed fairer to me than one man taking all the profit of our labors simply because of the family he had been born into."

"I suppose there was a lot of anger stirred up," she mused. "Perhaps that explains why they directed it at my family."

Peter shook his head. "I never blamed the Tsar personally. It was the system that was at fault."

"And yet"—she shuddered—"those guards who formed the execution squad hated us. I could see it in their eyes."

"Those men were animals," he said forcefully. "They were brought in specially from the Verkh-Isetsk metallurgy works, where they had been handpicked for their brutality. At least one was a convicted murderer. None of us regular guards could have done what they did. I was asleep in the house across the road and awoke on hearing the gunfire."

"What will happen to them now?" she asked.

He shrugged. "I hope that when Lenin learns of it, they will be arrested and imprisoned as common murderers."

Maria wished it would be so. She couldn't bear to live in a world where men like that could walk down the street as respected citizens. Whenever she thought about returning to civilization to resume the search for Tatiana, she imagined bumping into one of those killers and froze in terror. She would rather spend the rest of her life in the mountains, far from anyone else. At least there, with Peter, she felt safe.

~

One afternoon, as Maria lay resting beneath a fir tree, Peter returned to the clearing dragging a small deer by the hind legs. Its throat had been cut and blood smeared the undergrowth behind him as he walked. He jumped in front of the creature when he saw Maria watching and apologized.

"I'm sorry. I hope the sight is not distressing for you."

Tears pricked her eyes at his sensitivity. "Not at all," she said, blinking. "I was merely thinking how delicious that deer will be for dinner tonight, and how talented you are to have caught it."

"It is an elk calf. See the spots on its coat? It would have lost these by the end of the summer. This one is around three months old, I reckon. I wouldn't normally kill creatures so young, but with only a small knife I couldn't risk going for the mother, who looked as if she weighed four hundred pounds. Luckily I managed to scare her off."

He pulled the calf to the area where he had dug a fire pit and began to slice the coat from the flesh. She watched his concentration as he worked methodically around the creature, not an ounce of meat going to waste. How clever to have such a skill, she thought. She was lucky to have been rescued by a man who was able to fend for them both, and a gentleman too.

When he finished, he rose. "I'm going to wash," he said, and she saw that he was covered in the animal's blood. "I hope you will forgive me if I wash my clothes. They should dry quickly in the sun and I will take care not to offend you with my nakedness."

She laughed at that. "We are living outside society here and I think we must make our own rules based on pragmatism."

He frowned, and she sensed he didn't understand the word.

"We must live in a manner that is practical. I will not be remotely offended if I see you wandering around in your undergarments." That was what she did when she washed her own clothes.

He strode off toward the spring, and a few minutes later she smiled as she heard the customary yell he gave when he splashed himself with the icy water.

When he returned an hour later, his hair was still wet and

his clothes clearly damp. He shivered as he made the fire, whistling a tune under his breath.

"What is that song?" Maria asked, and he started.

"I hadn't realized I was whistling out loud," he said. "It's a marching song from the war. I seem to remember it was called 'Farewell to Slavianka.' I don't know the words but the tune is catchy."

"You have a tuneful whistle." She smiled and saw he was embarrassed.

"Me? No, you are surely wrong."

He had brought a pile of sticks with him and used them to build two tripods on either side of the fire. He threaded a haunch of the elk calf onto a longer stick and suspended it on the tripods to roast above the heat. It dripped juices, making the flames crackle and spark.

Maria found herself watching the way Peter's hands moved. She liked the contrast between his precision when performing a delicate task and his extraordinary strength. It had not occurred to her at the time, because she was stunned with shock, but somehow he had carried her through the forest for the best part of three days, barely stopping to rest. How had he managed that? His body was strong, with a thick neck and clearly defined muscles on his arms and legs. He was a man who had lived an active life.

The meat was delicious: fresh, with a rich gamy flavor. She huddled close to Peter at the fireside because the evenings grew cold as soon as the sun set. When she finished her first portion of elk, he hacked off another and seemed pleased to see her eat so heartily, a half-smile in his eyes.

Their knees touched as he leaned over to turn the meat on the spit, and he murmured an apology.

"Surely we are no longer strangers since we sleep under the

same roof?" she asked, eyebrow raised. "There is no chaperone here but the moon and the stars."

While he concentrated on arranging the meat over the fire, she placed a hand on his shoulder. "Your tunic is still wet," she said. "Are you sure you would not rather take it off? I would hate for you to catch a chill."

"No, it's fine. Please don't worry."

"It is getting cooler in the evenings, as if summer is coming to an end." She shivered suddenly.

"It is September now. The third."

She watched his face in the firelight as he busied himself with storing the remaining meat among some spruce fronds, and suddenly she felt an overwhelming urge to kiss him again, as she had the day she was overcome with terror. She longed to feel his body pressing against hers, wanted to hear his heartbeat. Was it very wrong of her? She shuffled closer and put her arm around him, turning his face toward hers with a hand, then touched her lips to his. It felt magical. She kissed him some more, rubbing her hand up and down his back, feeling the ridge of his spine. As before, he let her do as she wished but did not kiss her back, and suddenly she was overcome with desire. It wasn't something she thought through, just a physical need.

She kissed his lips more insistently, turning his shoulders so he faced her and running her hands over his chest. He gave a little moan under his breath, so she continued running her hands over him, down his thighs now, to his calves, then back up.

He placed a hand in the small of her back to hold her close and stroked her hair, but pulled his face away. "What are you doing?" he whispered.

"This is what I want," she told her. "Do you not want it too?"

He made an animal noise in his throat. "Of *course*, but I

don't want to hurt you. You would regret this later when you came to marry and could not be honest with your husband on your wedding night."

In answer, Maria kissed him harder. "Please," she said. "I won't regret it. Please."

Peter drew away, stood up, and walked to the edge of the clearing, his arms folded. "You are not in your right mind," he said. "You are half crazed with grief and it would be wrong of me to take advantage."

Maria felt close to tears. "I need this," she said. "I need something good and true to help me replace the awful memories of the last weeks." As she spoke, she was picturing Bolotov's attack on her in the bathroom two months earlier, rather than the massacre. "I know you are a good man, and I am asking—no, *begging* you to make love to me." Her voice quavered.

Peter paced around, without looking at her.

"I think your father would say it was the right thing to do," she added softly.

At last he came and sat by her again, cupping her face in his strong fingers and looking into her eyes. "I will do as you wish, but tell me straightaway if you want me to stop." He began to caress her slowly, his mouth on her neck, the inside of her wrist, the swell of her breast. It was glorious to feel such sensations and soon she was completely caught up in the moment.

Only when he raised the hem of her skirt did she freeze for a second, thinking of the pain of Bolotov's assault. Would this feel the same? Peter sensed her hesitation and stopped immediately, but she urged him on: "No—please. I want you to." She was scared but very sure.

Gently he placed his fingers on her private parts and she gave a sob of joy and wriggled her hips toward him. By the time he entered her, she felt as if her entire body had turned to liquid. It hurt a lot, but was exquisite at the same time. She felt they were bound together, made of one flesh, just as she had always dreamed it would be with a man.

"I love you," she whispered in his ear. When it was finished and she lay in his arms, with tree branches waving against the brilliant, almost-full moon, she repeated the words, then said, "I wish we could be married. I don't want any other man. Just you: Peter Vasnetsov."

He hugged her tighter, kissed her brow, the tip of her nose. "I love you too," he said, his voice cracking with emotion. "You have no idea how much I love you!"

"Really?" She was amazed at this. "Why do you love me?"

He stroked her hair slowly and rhythmically as he replied. "Many of the guards in the house dreamed of marrying one of the Romanov girls, but I never dared to think such thoughts. I just liked you very much. From the newspapers I had expected you to be haughty and conceited, but you were utterly natural and friendly and you won my heart in an instant. It meant so much to me that you had tears in your eyes when I told you of my father dying. And since we have been here, your courage has taken my breath away. I love your intelligence, your beauty, but most of all I love the strength I can feel in you."

Maria blinked. She didn't feel strong at all. "That is sweet of you to say, but I am worried you are only staying with me because you feel a sense of obligation, having rescued me. When we leave here, if you want, you can take me somewhere safe and leave me. You need not feel you have to stay with me because of what has happened between us tonight." She held her breath.

"Never!" he cried with passion. "I would never leave you. Not as long as you want me, at any rate." He paused. "But perhaps you only think you have fallen in love with me because

I saved you? Once you are back in society, I will be a misfit and you will not wish to know me anymore."

Maria wrapped her arms around him and clung to him, her face pressed against his. She could feel his eyelashes brushing her cheek. "I have watched you these last weeks and have grown to know and love your character. I pray with all my heart that we will never be parted again."

She placed her lips on his and kissed him hard, trying to communicate the strength of her love without any further words.

CHAPTER 16

Ural Mountains, September 1918

WHEN MARIA OPENED HER EYES THE NEXT MORNING, she curled her body against the back of the sleeping Peter, all the delicious sensations of the previous night coming back to her. He stirred and she pulled him to face her, ready for more lovemaking.

When at last he rose to light a fire and prepare breakfast, she watched in a reverie, her skin tingling, already planning how she would tempt him to lie down with her again after they had eaten. She loved the way he touched her, the way their bodies fitted together. Was it wrong to do this when they were not wed? She couldn't believe God would condemn them.

The next days passed in a haze. Now that they were lovers, she wanted to make love all the time. She couldn't look at Peter without feeling a tug of lust in her belly. When he went hunting for an hour or two, she hugged herself, feeling bereft without his presence. Lovemaking connected her to life again and distracted her from the rawness of her vast grief, preventing it from rising up and engulfing her. It was still there—she cried every day—but now she had something wonderful to occupy her thoughts as well.

Peter whistled as he worked around their little encampment, and seemed to have a permanent grin on his face. He brought her tiny bouquets of forest flowers and arranged blooms in her hair. He teased her when she slipped into what he called her "grand duchess ways"—correcting his grammar or wiping his beard when specks of food caught in it.

"Look how straight you sit!" He mimicked her position. "As if you are a piece of furniture."

"My mother taught us to sit straight." She smiled. She liked the gentleness of his humor; this man could never be cruel.

"What age are you?" she asked one day, and was surprised when he said, "Nineteen." The same age as her. He seemed so much more mature.

Were they fooling themselves? Could a marriage between them work? He had less education than her but vastly more knowledge of the skills necessary for survival, and that seemed more important now. Was she not in her right mind, as Peter had worried? Perhaps not, but she felt as if she had changed fundamentally and would never be the old Maria again. There was no reason why the new Maria could not be the wife of Peter Vasnetsov. She knew with certainty that she wanted to be with him for the rest of her life.

~

The weather was changeable now, going from warm sunshine to gusty rain then back again, all within the hour. More worryingly, the temperature was plummeting at night. Peter put extra moss and leaves on the roof, creating a thick layer to trap any heat, but still Maria woke shivering in the early hours and had to cling to him for warmth.

"We can't stay here over the winter," Peter told her. "You know that, don't you? I've been waiting as long as possible for your wounds to heal, but we must be on the move soon."

Maria's insides twisted in anxiety. "But where shall we go?"

"I need to find out if the Bolsheviks are still in power and which way the civil war is turning. Rather than head east toward Ekaterinburg, where we might be recognized, I think the western side of the mountains is safest."

Maria felt a lurch of hope. "Aunt Ella, my mother's sister, lives in Perm. Tatiana might be there."

Peter gave her a strange look she could not decipher and seemed about to say something, then stopped. "All right." He nodded. "We will go to Perm. But we will have to disguise ourselves, and we will need new clothes."

"I have the jewels that were hidden in my garments. We could sell those." She had removed them and now kept them in a cloth bag fashioned from one of her bandages.

He shook his head. "Any buyer will ask where they came from. Let's bring them with us but keep them hidden, my love. In civil wars, the safest rule is to trust no one."

They set off one sunny morning and headed toward a mountain pass Peter knew, which cut through the peaks without forcing them to climb too high. Maria felt anxious about leaving their sanctuary, worried about what lay ahead, but comforted herself that all would be well while she had Peter by her side.

Before long her wounded leg ached, and by the end of the first day her feet were covered in painful blisters because her buckled leather shoes were not designed for a mountain trek. Peter found a weed he called plantain and squeezed the sticky juice from its leaves directly onto her poor feet.

"It will soothe and heal the blisters," he said, and she could feel the sting ease straightaway.

Next morning he presented her with some new shoes he had made during the night from birch bark. "They're called *lapti*," he told her. "This is what peasants wear. I've put some plantain leaves inside to protect your feet as you walk."

The *lapti* were comfortable; they gripped the earth firmly yet did not chafe. Was there anything this man couldn't do?

Her grief seemed stronger now they were on the move, but at the same time she pictured her joy if they found Tatiana at her aunt Ella's house. They could all three comfort each other. What would they make of Peter? She remembered Tatiana chastising her for consorting with the guards, but she must change her mind in the face of this courageous man who had carried her on his back for three days. He would be Tatiana's brother-in-law once they wed, and she thought he had many qualities in common with her sister's sweetheart Dmitri Malama, who had been decorated in the war. They might have been born into different classes, but like Malama, Peter was a man of great courage.

The rain grew more persistent as they reached the western side of the mountain range, and Peter explained that moisture was drawn in the atmosphere all the way from the Atlantic Ocean then trapped by these rocky peaks. "That's why it rains more in Perm than in Ekaterinburg," he said. Maria hadn't known that before.

He told her that you could predict the weather by watching the behavior of animals. "If birds are flying high, there is good weather ahead, but when they come in low it's to avoid a storm. Sheep and cattle will get skittish and spiders will leave their webs and seek shelter just before rain arrives."

Maria was enchanted by this folk wisdom, so he told her all the signs he had noticed that indicated it would be a cold winter that year. "The pine trees make larger cones when there's a rough winter ahead, and squirrels build thicker nests."

"How do they know?" she asked, wide-eyed.

"They just do." He shrugged.

Each day he would point to a landmark on the horizon and suggest they try to reach it by sundown, but Maria struggled to keep up with his pace. Sometimes he put her on his back and carried her for a while, as he had when he had rescued her, but the going was steep and he couldn't manage it for more than an hour at a time.

They reached a small hamlet of a few houses, but did not stop because Peter said strangers would be remarked upon there. It was only when they arrived at the outskirts of Perm that he decided they could rest. He spotted an abandoned shed in the remote reaches of a farm and they stayed there for a day, eating strips of dried meat he had brought for nourishment and bathing their feet in a trough full of rainwater.

The next morning, Peter left Maria for an hour to look for some clothes, and she cowered behind an abandoned tractor, startled by every slight noise. She knew she must get used to being alone, because the following day they had agreed that he would travel into the city to call upon her aunt Ella. There might be Bolshevik guards posted around the house, who would no doubt recognize Maria, so he would go alone to see how the land lay.

When he returned, he was carrying armfuls of clothes. "I stole them from a washing line. I feel bad, but at least I chose a house where they seemed reasonably wealthy."

Maria held a skirt against herself. It looked about her size, but when she tried it on she could not get all the buttons to fasten. A blouse would not close across her chest. Even the petticoat was tight.

"I think the excellent food you served in the Ural Mountains has caused me to put on weight," she said, patting her belly. "I have become fat little bow-wow again—that's the name my sisters used to call me." She became aware that Peter was giving her a strange look. "What is it?"

"Don't you know what's happening?" he asked softly. She shook her head, mystified. "You are with child."

Maria sat down, feeling unsteady on her feet. "But how do you know?" she asked, still ignorant of such women's matters. Then, after a moment's thought, she muttered, "Yes, of course. That's exactly the kind of thing you would know."

She placed a hand on her belly, trying to decide how she felt about the news, and was filled to the brim with a wave of protectiveness for the tiny creature growing inside her. She looked up and saw that Peter had tears in his eyes.

~

He returned from Perm the following day with disappointing news: Aunt Ella's house was empty and barricaded. Some neighbors told him she had not been seen since the early weeks of July.

"They know that the Tsar—your father—has been executed but seem to think the rest of the family have been sent elsewhere for safekeeping. If only that were true." Peter looked grim.

Maria felt crushed. She had pinned her hopes on her aunt being there. "Is there no word of Tatiana?" she asked, anxiety bubbling inside.

He shook his head. "I'm sorry, but it seems we have been fleeing in the wrong direction. The White Army of Admiral Kolchak has taken Ekaterinburg from the Bolsheviks and established a new government in Omsk. But here, in Perm, the soviets still rule and we are not safe. All we can do is hunker down for winter and hope the Whites advance across the Urals before too long."

"Where will we live? What will we do?" Sometimes it was hard to contain her panic.

"I will find work without too much trouble. The Red Army has been conscripting farmhands, so many farms are short-staffed. They have also been requisitioning all the grain except what is needed by the farmers' immediate family, but I can find food for us."

Maria nodded. She didn't doubt it.

"I have a question for you," he continued. "I met a man on the road who says he can provide us with false identity papers. There is a brisk trade at the moment among bourgeoisie try-ing to pose as ordinary workers. The man I met will take jewelry as payment without asking any questions. Would you allow me to give him one of your diamonds?"

"False papers?" This was a whole new world for Maria. "What names will we take?"

"I suggest we keep our first names but change our patro-nymics, matronymics, and places of birth. I couldn't learn to call you Ludmilla or Valeriya without tripping myself up some-times." He smiled.

"You said that in times of civil war we should trust no one."

"Yes, but this man has nothing to gain by betraying us. He would lose his business and his profits. I think he can be trusted."

Maria marveled that Peter seemed so calm about this, as if it were an everyday occurrence to change names. "If you're sure," she said. She selected a small diamond from her cloth bag.

Later that night, when she was dressed in the stolen clothes, with a peasant woman's scarf on her head, Peter burned her old ripped gown. It was far too grand for "Citizen Dubova," a farm worker's wife, and the bayonet slash on the bodice would arouse suspicion. She wasn't sorry to see the last of it; it held too many nightmarish memories within its expensive threads.

~

"Have you traveled a long way?" the farmer's wife asked Maria, looking her up and down. "You seem worn out, and your *lapti* are so battered there is scarcely anything left. My name's Svetlana. Here—take some bread. Your baby needs you to eat for two. When is he due, by the way?"

Maria made a quick calculation in her head. "June, I think."

"A June baby is lucky," Svetlana continued. "He will look after you in your old age, or so the saying goes."

"It might be a girl . . ."

Svetlana shook her head. "I can tell it's a boy from the shape of your belly. I'm never wrong about that. You've come to the right place; I can help you through the labor."

Maria paled. She had not given much thought to childbirth and found the prospect terrifying. Her bump was so big already she could not imagine how its contents would ever emerge.

"Don't worry." Svetlana smiled. "I've delivered four of my neighbors' babies, as well as umpteen calves."

That was vaguely reassuring, although Maria wondered if calves were born the same way as humans. She couldn't see how, given that they had four legs not two.

"Do you have children?" she asked, but Svetlana shook her head.

"It never happened for us, sadly. It wasn't God's will."

All the same, she looked as though she had given birth, with a huge sagging bosom and ample hips. Maria guessed her age to be around forty.

Svetlana continued. "I hope you will be able to help me with the tasks the men leave to us women—you know, weaving, milking, feeding the animals, pickling, baking, and so forth. We'll be company for each other."

Maria paled. She had no knowledge of the tasks Svetlana

would expect the wife of an itinerant farm worker to be familiar with.

Her ignorance was soon revealed when they went to the shed to do the afternoon milking and she did not know which part of the cow to grab hold of. She tried to copy Svetlana, but no milk came out. The farmer's wife regarded her thoughtfully.

"You're a *kulak*, aren't you? Makes sense. I had my suspicions from your accent and the fancy way you sit on a chair."

"What's a *kulak*?" Maria wondered if it was something like a Cossack, but it seemed not.

"Bourgeoisie; born to wealthy parents. We shouldn't be hiring *kulaks*, but my husband, Joe, likes your husband and thinks he will be an asset to the farm."

"Peter is not a *kulak*," Maria said quickly. "My parents were bourgeoisie but they are . . ." She couldn't bring herself to say the word "dead" and sought alternatives. "They are gone now." Tears came. They always did when she talked about them.

Svetlana put an arm around her. "Don't cry, my dear," she soothed, rubbing Maria's shoulder. "There, there. Too much grief will infect the child in your womb so he will have a melancholy soul."

Maria thought there was no chance the child could avoid infection because grief filled every cell of her body, even if she was able to control it a little better now than she had a few weeks ago.

Svetlana kissed her cheek and squeezed her shoulders. "I am no lover of the Bolsheviks and their countless rules. We are supposed to abandon religion because it is old-fashioned and anti-Communist, but I still perform *obednyas* every day, in secret. We have a local priest you can trust. Perhaps you would like to worship with me?"

Maria hesitated. "I will ask my husband," she said, for they had told the farmer and his wife that they were already married in order to secure the job and the cramped living quarters in a room above a barn. The words "my husband" had a ring she liked.

~

"Might we ask the priest to marry us?" she asked Peter later. "I want my baby to be born legitimate."

Peter smiled indulgently. "I think you will find that Bolsheviks set little store by such formalities. But let us meet this priest and decide if we trust him, then if you want us to be wed it shall be done."

"You don't want to?" she asked quickly, anxiety in her voice.

He pulled her close for a hug, and kissed her forehead. "In my mind and in my heart we are already husband and wife, but if a priest's blessing will make you happy, then so be it."

Two weeks later, Maria could not stop the tears flowing as the priest intoned the sacred words of the Orthodox wedding ceremony: "O Lord, our God, who hast poured down the blessings of Thy Truth according to Thy Holy Covenant upon Thy chosen servants, our fathers, from generation to generation, bless Thy servants Peter and Maria, and make their troth fast in faith, and union of hearts, and truth, and love . . ."

When the crowns were held above their heads, it was almost too much to bear. The old man stopped and asked, "Are you all right, child? Do you want to continue?" and she nodded and blurted out, "Yes, please." Peter squeezed her hand tightly but still she could not stop sobbing.

All her life since she was tiny, she had dreamed of her

wedding day and of the dashing man she would marry and raise children with. But in those dreams she had always imagined her husband-to-be asking her father's permission for the betrothal, her mother helping to plan her trousseau, and the rest of the family celebrating the happy day. Now she had none of these—just Peter. He was all the family she had left.

CHAPTER 17

Outskirts of Perm, winter 1918–19

THE FIRST SNOW CAME IN NOVEMBER, AND LAY IN A powdery sprinkling on earth that was already hard as flint and glittering with frost. The days grew shorter, so it wasn't light till eleven in the morning and was growing dark again by midafternoon. Soon the snow got heavier so the trees disappeared beneath thick winter coats. Svetlana lent Maria and Peter some blankets, and Peter made sure there was always a fire burning in the grate to keep their room cozy when wintry gales blasted outside.

As well as caring for the farm's livestock, Peter rode into the woods to hunt elk, whose meat could be cured to last the winter months, and he caught fish through holes in the iced-over lake. The farmer and his wife were delighted with his prowess but Maria proved less useful: she never did get the hang of milking cows, though she learned to feed the chickens, to weave baskets from reeds, and to pickle chopped vegetables in Svetlana's kitchen.

One day she borrowed a halma board and pieces from Svetlana, and that evening she taught Peter the rules of the game. It was relatively simple: you had to move all your pieces to the opposite corner by the fastest route possible, leaping over your opponent's pieces on the way.

Peter followed her lead during the first game, but by the second he was winning hands down.

"How can you beat me when you have only just learned?" she asked, baffled.

"You have no strategy," he laughed. "You move your pieces on a whim. I, on the other hand, am thinking several moves ahead. That's the fun of the game."

Maria smiled. "Would it not be more gentlemanly to let a fat pregnant lady win?" She patted her belly. By now the child was moving inside her, kicking out. Sometimes she could see the shape of a tiny foot under her skin.

"You would like me to play badly? Is that the grand duchess talking? Pray, forgive me for being so presumptuous as to beat you, ma'am." He tipped an imaginary hat.

She giggled and grabbed his hand to pull him over for a kiss, then placed his palm on her belly. "I think our son is going to be strong, like you," she said.

He stroked her bump thoughtfully. "Yes, it certainly looks that way," he said, a faraway expression in his eyes.

～

On the night of the second of April, when it was still pitch black and wintry outside, Maria woke to an unfamiliar stabbing sensation. "Peter," she cried, then the pain grew so intense she could only grip the blanket in her fists and moan through gritted teeth.

He leaped to his feet and lit the oil lamp, then bent to examine her. For a moment she felt normal, and then the gripping pain came once more and she screwed up her face, trying not to scream out loud.

"What's happening to me?" she asked when the wave of pain passed.

"The baby is coming," he said. "Don't worry. I'll fetch Svetlana. And I'll be right outside."

It was all very well for him to say "don't worry," but she could see in his eyes that he was worried. The baby was too early. There must be something wrong with it. Her worst fear was that it would have hemophilia, the bleeding disorder that had stunted her little brother Alexei's short life. Peter did not know the disease ran in her family, as the Romanovs had always kept it to themselves and a few trusted advisors, but he must have seen with his own eyes that Alexei was a sickly child.

Another wave of pain came and she stood up to pace around the room. Where was Peter? Where was Svetlana? Suddenly she longed for her mother, for Olga or Tatiana—just one of them. She needed her family more than she had ever thought possible. Tears came and she was sobbing hard when Svetlana bustled in with a pot of boiling water and some fresh towels.

"There, there," she said, placing her hand on Maria's brow. "It's normal to be scared, but I have not lost a baby or a mother yet and I'm not about to start."

～

The pains lasted through the night, waning for a while then coming back stronger than ever. Sometimes Maria screamed for Peter, but Svetlana would not let him enter the room, saying it was bad for a marriage.

"I'm here," he called through the door. "I'm not leaving, not even for a moment."

By the time dawn broke, Maria was overcome with exhaustion. "I can't go on," she panted. "It's too much."

Svetlana was calm. "You can and you will. That child can't stay inside, but he will not be born before he is good and ready."

She lifted Maria's shift to feel the baby's position and suddenly exclaimed, "Good God, what is this?"

Maria looked down. Svetlana had spotted the jagged purple line of the bayonet scar. "An accident," she murmured. "At home. I fell . . ."

"You're lucky to be alive!" Svetlana was aghast. "What on earth did you fall onto?"

Maria struggled to think of something sharp. "The blade of an ice skate," she said, and saw Svetlana frown and touch the scar as if not entirely convinced, but she did not question further.

In the late morning, Maria suddenly felt a huge pressure, as if her internal organs were being expelled from her body and ripping her apart. She could not even try to muffle her screams as Svetlana pulled the baby's head from between her legs. She looked down and saw blood and began to sob hysterically. "I'm dying. Please save me! I don't want to die."

"Silly girl," Svetlana soothed. She pulled the baby clear and held it in the air, where it gave a gasp and then a thin, reedy wail. It was covered in white waxy mucus with streaks of bright blood, its tiny face screwed tight. "It's a boy," she said. "Did I not tell you? I'm never wrong."

She snipped the cord, washed the child in water she had boiled earlier, and swaddled him in a soft white blanket before handing him to his mother. Maria gazed down at this creature who had grown inside her, and all of a sudden the memory came back to her of the first time she saw Alexei. She was five years old and had been led, with her sisters, into her mother's bedchamber, where he lay in a crib by the bed. She remembered her awe at the daintiness of his clenched fists, and the feeble squawking noises he made. This child was making the same noises now—"Mm-wah, mm-wah"—with doggedness, as if demanding something from her.

"Why don't you let him feed?" Svetlana asked, and Maria was momentarily stunned. Her family had used wet nurses to feed their babies, but it dawned on her that they could not afford such a luxury here. She was poor now, and must do as countrywomen did.

Svetlana loosened the neck of Maria's gown and showed her how to position the baby so he could suckle at her nipple. She felt a tickling sensation as she watched his tiny jaws working, and was overwhelmed with such joy it felt as if she was floating.

"Can Peter come in now?" she asked, not wanting him to miss this.

"Wait till I've cleaned you up," Svetlana replied. "Then I will call him. I think the child has his chin, don't you?"

Maria looked down, but to her the baby resembled her little brother, Alexei, with his round features and his sparse wisps of hair. Pray God the resemblance was only superficial and he did not carry the dreaded bleeding disorder. She shuddered, trying to remember how long after Alexei's birth he was diagnosed.

~

Peter was awestruck at the sight of his son. He took the bundle from Maria, and as soon as he cradled him, the boy stopped squawking and peered up, boss-eyed and curious.

"Can we call him Nicholas?" Maria asked. It would be lovely to remember her father that way.

Peter glanced at Svetlana, who was making a bundle of the soiled sheets and towels. "Let's discuss it later," he said. "He can be little No-name for now." He ran a finger along the baby's brow and kissed his button nose. "Everyone says newborns are beautiful, but this one—he is a miracle child. Looking at him, I can tell he will do something very special with his life."

Maria beamed. "Once we find her, I will ask his aunt Tatiana to be godmother."

Peter put a finger to his lips and shook his head slightly, warning her not to say more. The baby had fallen asleep in his arms.

"I'll leave you in peace," Svetlana said, smiling at the vision of father and son. "Keep the room warm, and call if you need anything."

"We will be forever in your debt," Peter told her, and Maria added, "Yes, thank you a million, million times over."

After Svetlana had gone, Peter sat on the bed by Maria, still cradling the baby.

"I think we should avoid giving the boy a Romanov name," he said. "And beware of mentioning your siblings in front of our employers. They are good people, but we cannot expect them to keep our secret, should it come out."

"What do *you* think we should call our son?" Maria asked, unable to take her eyes off his little face, trying to memorize every inch of it.

"A good honest country name. How about Stepan?"

That felt right. She smiled. "Stepan it is."

~

Maria recovered quickly from childbirth and threw herself into caring for her baby. She loved the sensation of breastfeeding, the idea that she was providing vital nourishment for Stepan. She loved bathing him and spent hours lying on the bed watching him sleep. Svetlana showed her how to fashion a sling to carry him next to her body as she went about her work, so she hardly ever had to put him down.

In the early weeks she kept a close eye out for any signs of hemophilia, but his cord healed normally and dropped off, and there were no odd bruises or unexplained marks. Even as a baby Alexei had been sickly, but this boy seemed hale and strong, like his father.

One of the greatest pleasures for Maria was watching Peter with his son. His large, work-roughened hands were tender as he cupped the downy head, his voice low as he whispered to him, his eyes brimming with emotion. It made her love for her husband deepen as she watched him with the child they had created together.

"I hope Stepan will have your cowlick," she mused.

"My what?" He was mystified. "I have been licked by a cow?"

"That tuft of hair at the front." She pointed to his hairline. It was a phrase used in English, but perhaps there was no Russian equivalent.

"You say the oddest things sometimes." He smiled.

It was hard to think that Stepan would never know his Romanov grandparents, and had lost almost all his relatives before he was born. Her grief still lurked, and sometimes the tears fell while she cared for her child. He was a serious soul, who looked up at her as if wondering about the source of her sorrow. Having him to look after helped to distract her, though. Sometimes an hour or two went by when she did not think of Anastasia or Alexei, and then she felt guilty, because it was still less than a year since they were murdered. If only they could have met their miraculous nephew!

"Why was he early?" she asked Peter one day. "I had thought he would be born in June."

"He knew you needed him," Peter replied. "Look how much he has helped you. Before he arrived, I had never heard you laugh."

Maria couldn't help but smile at his words. "Will you write to your mother and tell her of the birth of her grandson?" she asked.

He made a face. "I imagine the authorities will be keeping watch on her mail deliveries. They know that I ran off with you and I'm sure they will be trying to find us."

Maria felt sad at that. "Is there no way we can get word to her?"

"Perhaps I will post a letter from some faraway place, so that if they search for us there, they will not find a clue to our whereabouts." He nodded to himself, mulling it over.

"And you must tell her that we are married. I want her to know that."

"She and my sister will want all the details . . . I will write a letter and mail it next time the farmer sends me to a distant market."

A day later, he showed Maria the letter he had composed. It was the first time she had seen his handwriting, and it was better than she had expected from one who had received little schooling. His spelling was poor, but she had no trouble making out the words. He told his mother that he had fallen in love with Maria while guarding the Romanov family at the Ekaterinburg house. He explained that he had seized the chance to rescue her and that they were now married and had a beautiful son together.

At the end of the letter there were two sentences that moved Maria to tears: *I miss you badly, Mama, and my sister too, but I want you to know that I am happy. If I could turn back time to that July morning when I pulled Maria from the truck and ran into the forest, I would do exactly the same thing again.*

CHAPTER 18

Outskirts of Perm, June 1919

Nmote farm where Peter and Maria lived, but Peter heard snippets when he took farm produce to markets around the region. He and Maria had pinned their hopes on the White Army advancing and driving back the Bolsheviks, and they rejoiced when they heard that Admiral Kolchak's troops had crossed the Urals and captured the strategic town of Tsaritsyn in June that year.

"Surely it must only be a matter of time before we can come out of hiding and search for my sister and my relatives?" Maria asked. "My grandmother must still be alive, and my cousins—and perhaps Tatiana is with them."

She tried to imagine finding Tatiana and introducing her to her little nephew, but the picture refused to come into focus. Was she kidding herself? The entire nation had been ripped in two and hers could not be the only family to be broken apart. That was what civil wars did.

A couple of months later, Peter came back from market with news. "I heard from a British merchant that your grandmother, Maria Feodorovna, was rescued from the Crimea by a ship sent by the British king, George V, and that she is currently his guest in London."

"And Tatiana?" Maria asked immediately, her heart leaping. "Is she in London too?"

He shook his head. "My source didn't mention her. Perhaps she is keeping a low profile in case the Bolsheviks are still intent on wiping out the direct line of inheritance to the throne." He glanced at little Stepan, asleep in a cot he had carved from pine, and Maria followed his gaze. Of course! Her baby son was an heir of the Romanov dynasty. That could put him in danger if anyone were to find out.

"Is there a way we could get to London?" she asked, then answered her own question. "Even if we could reach Murmansk or the Baltic shores, it would not be easy to board a ship sailing for Britain, would it?"

Peter shook his head. "Passenger ships, trains, all forms of transport are operated by militant workers. If we sold some of your jewels to pay for our passage, they would demand to know where the money came from. Besides, I don't think we should take this little man from a safe home and subject him to the hardships of such a journey."

They both looked at the sleeping child. His blond baby curls were darkening and his features becoming more distinctly his own, but he retained an equanimity of character that Maria thought was just like his father's. He seldom cried, but watched the world carefully, drinking it all in.

~

By the end of 1919, all talk of traveling to London was abandoned after Maria found she was pregnant again. Svetlana reacted with irritation to the news.

"It's irresponsible to bring us another mouth to feed at a

time like this. Didn't your mother teach you how to stop yourself falling pregnant?"

"No," Maria replied, wide-eyed. She'd had no idea such a thing was possible.

"You must count the days after the start of your monthly bleed," Svetlana explained. "Avoid lovemaking from the tenth to the seventeenth day."

"A whole week?" Maria was astonished. She and Peter made love several times a week and she couldn't imagine abstaining for such a long time.

"I expect you to keep up with your chores during this pregnancy," Svetlana scolded. "There's a lot to be done bringing in the harvest and preparing for winter. This is no place for idle hands."

"Of course," Maria agreed. "I promise."

~

Maria gave birth to a baby girl in August 1920, by which time Stepan was toddling around the farm. He was enchanted with the newcomer, whom they named Irina, and sat watching patiently while Maria fed and changed her, then entertained her by dangling a rag doll made from scraps of fabric. Irina smiled at anyone who came near, and soon won the heart of the farmer's wife.

"She is a happy soul." Svetlana beamed, giving her a cuddle. "Your little boy is serious, as if he has the world's problems on his shoulders, but this one is full of joy."

Maria felt guilty at that. Stepan had been conceived, carried, and born while she was in the depths of mourning. All those tears she had shed must have infected him, as Svetlana had warned they would.

"Nonsense," Peter said when she told him later. "Irina smiles at us because we smile at her. She is mimicking our expressions. Perhaps we did not smile so much at Stepan because we were still learning how to be parents. I don't think it's done him any harm."

Maria liked the way he always had a logical answer. They were a good match: she was prone to bouts of anxiety and panic, but he quelled them with his calm rationality. As a child, she had feared she was not lovable, certainly not as well loved as her siblings, but Peter made her feel precious and special, as if he couldn't believe how lucky he was to be with her.

Sometimes she woke in the night, stricken with terror that she might lose him one day. She knew she would never manage to look after the children without him. But listening to his breathing helped to soothe her, and if the fear was especially intense, she would snuggle close and pull his arm across her, feeling the heat of his body—he was always much hotter than her—and the steady beat of his heart.

~

A severe drought in 1921 spoiled the grain harvest throughout the region. Peter worked long hours carrying buckets of water from the lake in an attempt to irrigate the crops, but it was not enough to save the wheat and barley; their stalks withered and died in the ground. Not only would they be unable to bake bread to feed themselves then sell their excess produce at market, but there was not going to be enough fodder to see the animals through the winter. Peter and the farmer calculated how many cows they could afford to keep, then Peter set off to sell the rest for the best price he could obtain.

"Now there will be less milk and less beef," he told Maria. "I'll have to do more hunting through the winter."

He began hunting in the early hours of the morning, then

again at dusk after he had finished his chores, but the population of elk, grouse, and rabbits seemed more sparse and his endeavors could not save them from hunger pangs most days that autumn. With the winter fast approaching it was hard to know how they would cope.

"Did you know the Revolution in February 1917 was sparked by women protesting over the shortage of bread?" Peter asked Maria, while they played with their toddlers in the barn one evening. He was pretending to be a big bear and chasing them around so they would be tired enough to sleep despite the hunger knotting their stomachs.

"We girls had measles and were in our sickbeds that month," Maria told him. "The first I knew of the Revolution was when Papa returned from army headquarters and told us he was no longer Tsar. New guards arrived and we were confined to the palace grounds."

"I heard your father ordered his royal guard to open fire on the protesters but they refused," Peter told her. "There were too many women in the crowd—women who simply wanted to be able to feed their children."

"My goodness, I can't believe Papa can have known that. He must have been misinformed."

"Perhaps." Peter was tight-lipped.

Maria felt she had to defend her family. "I know stories were circulating in the newspapers saying that the Romanovs ate caviar at every meal and ordered their clothes from Paris couturiers, but they were quite unfair. We did not buy any new gowns after the start of the 1914 war, and our meals were humble fare. I mean . . ." She thought back. There had been fish and meat at dinner, usually cooked in light sauces, and out-of-season fruits were often imported from southern lands. As she had eaten from delicate dishes served on fine china, with crested solid silver cutlery, she'd had no idea what it was like to play with your children in a barn so that hunger would not keep them awake. Surely if her father had known that those women merely wanted bread, he would have given them some?

Svetlana appeared in the doorway, holding a lantern. "Could you keep the noise down?" she asked, looking at Stepan and Irina, who were shrieking with excitement. "I have a headache."

"Yes, of course," Peter said straightaway. "Be quiet, children."

They stopped obediently, crestfallen that the game was over.

"I hope your head feels better soon," Maria called with concern, as Svetlana turned back toward the farmhouse.

~

The symptoms of starvation crept up slowly, like a wolf circling, waiting to pounce. At first there were painful stomach cramps that left a sensation of light-headedness when they passed. Maria sometimes had to clutch at doorways to stop herself falling over into a faint. Lethargy made it hard to get out of bed in the morning and drag herself over to heat some leftovers to line her children's stomachs. She and Peter each tried to make the other eat, pretending not to be hungry.

"You must have more than me," she insisted. "You have physical work to do while I can sit here conserving my energy."

"I find berries when I am out hunting," Peter argued, but she knew there were few to be had now the snows had come. He looked gray and gaunt, and although they had no mirror in their room, she realized she must look the same.

One evening, Peter arrived home after dark and opened his satchel to show Maria a long fish inside, with a silver belly and gold fins.

"It's grayling," he said, "but I only caught one. I'll fillet it then take half to Joe and Svetlana."

"It is not big enough to share," Maria said quickly, salivating as she imagined the flavor. "I think we should keep it. It's not right they should have half when there are four of us and two of them."

"That's unfair," he objected. "Remember all they have done for us."

Maria was thinking out loud. "Svetlana has a sensitive nose, but if we cook it in the forest, she will not detect the smell. Please, Peter. Your children need to be fed. Look at them!" She pointed to where they sat on the bed, listless, not even attempting to play with each other. Their baby chubbiness had dissolved and their cheeks had hollowed alarmingly. "They need food. Svetlana and her husband are still plump, and it's just one meal. Please."

He was clearly reluctant, but gave way in the face of her determination. They wrapped the children against the biting cold and trudged out in the snow toward the forest, carrying a lamp to light the route. Peter led them to an area where he had dug a fire pit in summer, and Maria hugged the children close while he struggled to light a fire in the bitter damp. At last the flames were flickering and he gutted the fish swiftly and efficiently, then threaded a skewer through and suspended it over the fire, turning it after a few minutes.

As soon as it was cooked, he cut chunks of flesh and doled them onto plates Maria had brought along. The fish was white and delicate flavored, the skin crisp and scented with woodsmoke. Never had Maria savored a meal as much as she did this one, eaten beneath a starry expanse of winter sky.

When they had finished, Peter heaped snow onto the embers and they rose to walk back to the farm. Just at that moment, a beam of light appeared through the trees, coming toward them, and they saw Svetlana standing behind it, her features distorted. Maria tried to kick snow over the fishbone that lay on the ground, but Svetlana saw and bent to pick it up.

"This is the thanks you give us for our hospitality!" she said. "I followed your steps because I thought it odd you should all go out so late, and now I discover your secret."

"I'm sorry," Peter began. "It was for the children. Their health is failing and I only caught one small fish today."

"It's the dishonesty of sneaking out here that I detest. I'm guessing this is a regular outing, and that you have been making fools out of my husband and me." Her fury was increasing as she spoke, and the children cowered against Maria. She scooped them up, balancing one on each hip.

"This is the only time it has happened, I give you my word," Peter said. "Your husband knows me for an honest man. Look how often he has trusted me to get the best price for his stock."

"Perhaps he was mistaken. No doubt he will change his mind when he hears of your betrayal."

Maria hadn't spoken yet, but now she begged Svetlana. "Please forgive us this one mistake. You must understand that it's hard to watch the children suffer. I promise you with all my heart that we won't do it again."

Svetlana rounded on her. "Why should I take your word for anything when you have lied to me all along? I know you're a Romanov. Why don't you go and fetch some of your millions and we can all dine richly tomorrow?"

"What do you mean? I'm not a Romanov," Maria stuttered, at the same time as Peter said, "I think you must be mistaken."

"I'm not mistaken," Svetlana hissed. "I overheard you talking about it some weeks ago. Now, you both know I am no lover of the Bolsheviks, but neither am I a lover of the last Tsar and his wife. I will tell my husband what has happened this evening and we will discuss what should be done. He has a great respect for you, Peter, and I hope that will make him look favorably upon you."

"Please . . ." Peter began. He gestured toward the children in Maria's arms. "Think of the innocents."

Svetlana turned on her heel and marched off through the snow.

~

Peter and Maria hurried back to their room. Her heart was thudding with panic, her brain a muddle of thoughts. They settled the children to sleep, then huddled by the fire, ashen-faced.

"She is not a vindictive woman," Maria said. "She has known for some time without saying anything, so I doubt they will run to the authorities now. But all the same, it is not good . . ."

Peter was rubbing his chin between his fingers. "There is bound to be a reward for our capture. It will be hard for them to resist in these straitened times. Maybe they will not report us tonight, but as the winter continues and food remains scarce, they will weaken."

"I shouldn't have forced you to keep the fish for us. You didn't want to." She should have listened to him; he was a better person than her.

"There's no point regretting what's done," he said, staring into the fire. "It's what we do next that counts." He came to a decision. "We have to leave tonight."

"No!" She was terrified. "We can't! How would we survive?"

"I will take Joe's horse and wagon. We can leave one of your jewels in payment. They will be furious, but by morning I hope we will be many miles away." He stood up. "It's the only way, Maria. You pack our things and I'll harness the horse. We must leave within the hour."

"But where will we go?" she asked, feeling dread deep within her bones.

He shrugged and shook his head. "As yet, I have no idea."

CHAPTER 19

NICOLE WAS THRILLED BY THE TINY FIRST-FLOOR apartment in Balmain, and delighted that she and Val would be sharing a bed. She unpacked her storybooks and colored pencils and put them in the little cabinet on her side of the bed, arranged her dolls along the pillow, then helped Val to put the few pots, pans, and plates she had brought into the kitchen cupboards. When they had finished, they went for a walk down the road in the direction of the bay, which glinted blue between the houses. Three girls, slightly older than Nicole, were skipping on the other side of the road, one jumping while two turned the rope, chanting: "Kookaburra sits in the old gum tree, merry merry king of the woods is he . . ." They turned to watch Nicole passing and she gave a quick smile and a little hop, clearly hoping that one day soon she might be invited to join their game.

Val did not know the area and was charmed by the higgledy-piggledy houses with unique shapes created to fit the odd spaces between pubs and disused factories. The exteriors were decorated with a mismatched jumble of motifs—seashells, grapevines, Dutch tiles, art nouveau panels, stone urns—while the balconies had wrought-iron railings, most in a state of dilapidation. The whole area was set on a slope, with cross-streets linked by twisty flights of steps. Nicole ran up one flight only to jump back down again two steps at a time, and Val marveled at her energy. She herself was exhausted from the move, and kept looking over her shoulder, worried that Tony would somehow find them and drag them back to Croydon Park. At the same time, she felt exhilaration at being free to make her own decisions for the first time in her life. She and Nicole could eat, sleep, watch TV, go out, all to a routine that suited them, and that was a thrilling prospect.

They entered Mort Bay Park, a beautiful green space on the edge of the Balmain peninsula. It used to be a dry dock for shipbuilding, but now it was a tree-circled, concrete-edged waterfront with views all the way to the Harbor Bridge and the city, as well as around the harbor. Val pointed to a ferry chugging into the wharf.

"If we ever want to go to the center, we'll catch the ferry," she told Nicole. "It's much quicker than driving."

Nicole grabbed her hand and tugged on it. "Can't we go now, Mommy? I want to go on the boat. *Please!*"

Money was tight, but it seemed a good way to celebrate their freedom, so Val led Nicole onto the ferry and handed over a dollar, frowning at the few coins she received in change. It was worth it, though, when they started to move out past Goat Island and right across to the north side of the harbor. Diamond lights sparkled on the surface of the water. A sailing boat flitted past and Nicole waved, squeaking with glee when the occupants waved back.

"Are there sharks?" she asked, gazing over the railing as if trying to spot one in the depths.

"Could be," Val teased. "Don't fall in."

She stretched out her bare arms, feeling the sun bake her skin. She never dared to tan at home in case Tony accused her of slacking; she sensed it would be a while before she stopped thinking about what Tony would think or do. She would have to get used to this freedom slowly, like a prisoner released after serving a particularly long sentence.

~

On Monday morning, Val enrolled Nicole at the local primary school, just two streets away. Nicole was clearly daunted, but she gave a brave smile as she said goodbye before a teacher led her toward a classroom. Val caught a glimpse of thirty or so children sitting at low tables and willed her daughter to be happy there. She had seemed popular at her preschool, but it was always hard to be a newcomer.

Nerves tightened in her own stomach as she walked out of the school grounds and onto Darling Street, the main thoroughfare through Balmain. The priority now was to find work, preferably a job that could fit around school hours. She started by asking in all the shops on the nearest five blocks, then she stopped in some small businesses: a print shop, the swimming pool, a metalworks factory. Most said they didn't have any vacancies. A few asked about her experience and references before telling her they didn't have anything suitable.

At the metalworks, a sharp-faced man with a moustache regarded her wedding finger, where she still wore her ring. "Is your husband so poor he has to send his wife out to work?" he asked.

Val blushed and admitted, "My husband and I are recently separated."

He looked at her with a mixture of pity and contempt. "Oh dear. Well, we can't be employing your sort here," he said.

It's not my fault, she wanted to tell him. *I* never broke a single one of Tony's bones. *I* didn't make him a prisoner in his own home. She paused, then turned away at the look in his mean eyes. She'd be wasting her breath.

She didn't want to work in a pub, because the shifts would start after Nicole finished school and she couldn't afford to pay someone to mind her for the evening. But as business after business turned her down, she began to get desperate. She only had enough money in her savings to last a few weeks before they would be destitute. She couldn't ask Peggy to lend her any cash because she and Ken weren't exactly flush, and Tony would be incandescent with rage at her departure so he was hardly going to volunteer to pay alimony.

It was almost time to collect Nicole from school when Val spotted a sign in the window of an office block in the neighboring suburb of Rozelle saying they needed a cleaner. She went inside to inquire and was told there were four floors in which the cleaner had to empty the trash, clean the toilets, and vacuum the carpet; she would start at six in the evening when the staff left and work till she finished. The money was terrible, but they agreed she could bring Nicole with her, so long as she didn't touch anything. It would have to do, to start with at least.

Val worked her first shift the following evening, and Nicole sat contentedly drawing pictures and poring over a book the school had lent her, pretending she could read the words.

"The girl sees the sea," she said, "and wants to go for a swim, but she is afraid there might be sharks."

The noise of the huge industrial vacuum cleaner drowned out her voice as Val heaved it slowly across the flint-colored carpet.

It was almost midnight and Nicole was fast asleep on a sofa when Val finally finished work. She was bone-weary, muscles aching in places she hadn't known they existed, but still she had to lift her five-year-old daughter and carry her for a mile all the way back to their apartment. No matter; at least she was free of Tony.

Why didn't Mom do this? she wondered. When she left her father, why hadn't she taken Val with her? Val would never have dreamed of leaving without Nicole. It was unthinkable. Had her mother not loved her enough? Or had something happened to stop her?

~

Two weeks after she'd left, Val realized that Nicole hadn't once asked after her daddy. She hadn't wondered why they were living in a new apartment or when she would see him again, but seemed perfectly content with their altered living arrangements. She had already made friends at her new school and came home requesting her own skipping ropes to practice with.

"Charlie Chaplin went to France, to teach the ladies how to dance . . ." she chanted, a jump for each syllable, and Val laughed. She knew Nicole didn't have a clue who Charlie Chaplin was.

Peggy came to visit and reported that Tony had been around their house a few times accusing her of aiding and abetting Val's getaway and demanding to know where she was.

"Fortunately I'm a world-class liar"—she grinned—"and Ken can't stand the bloke, so he's backing me up."

"Thanks, Pegs. I'm sorry he's bothering you. I suppose I'll have to call him soon. He has a right to know his daughter is safe."

"He should bloody well pay you some money to look after her, cheap bastard," Peggy said fiercely.

"We're just settling in. I'll deal with that when I have the strength for a battle."

On Saturday afternoon, she took Nicole to a kids' playground near their apartment. Straightaway Nicole called in greeting to a couple of girls who were hurtling down the slide, skirts flying up to reveal skinny tanned legs and white cotton knickers. Although the slide was higher than any Nicole had been on before, she rushed to join them with a shriek of excitement. Val resisted the urge to run and catch her at the bottom. She didn't want to make her look babyish in front of her friends, but held her breath until Nicole slithered to a graceful halt and gave her a triumphant grin.

On the road outside the park there was a phone booth, and Val counted the coins in her purse then made a spur-of-the-moment decision to call Tony. After seventeen years of marriage, she owed him that. Keeping her eyes fixed on Nicole and her friends, she dialed the number, sick with nerves.

"It's me," she said when he answered. "I just wanted to let you know that your daughter and I are safe. I'm sorry I told you I was leaving in a note, but I was worried you would try to stop us."

"Where are you?" he asked, and she couldn't read his tone. Was it concern?

"We're still in Sydney. I've got a flat. Look, I'm sorry, Tony, but we both know that neither of us was happy in our marriage. It was only after Dad died that I took a step back and realized that this is it—you only get one life." She had rehearsed these words so often in her head that now she blurted them out, wanting them all to be said before he began to argue back. "We got married too young and I loved you at the time—I really did—but we married for the wrong reasons and it's not been working for a while. I've been miserable and I'm sure you have too. Thing is, we're both young enough to try again, and I hope we can find happiness next time. When we get

divorced, that is . . ." Her voice trailed off at the long silence
on the other end of the line.

"Divorce?" he said, his voice as cold as steel. "Over my dead
body. You get back to this house right now, you bloody bitch.
You're lucky I haven't called the police to have you arrested
for abducting my daughter. What makes you think you can
get away with this? You've got another man, haven't you? You'd
never be brave enough to do this on your own—"

Val made a snap decision and hung up. The sound of his
voice disappeared midsentence. If only she had been able to
switch it off so effectively before. She pictured his rage. Knowing him, he'd hurl the telephone across the room. That made
her smile, although her hands were shaking. It felt empower-
ing to have that control.

Nicole waved from the top of the slide and let go, her long
hair flowing in a shiny curtain behind her.

~

Just opposite the office block where Val worked there was a
dark-green-painted building with the sign *Henry Trotman &
Son, Family Solicitors*. Underneath, in smaller letters, it said
Divorce, Child Custody, Property, Wills, then *First Consultation
Free*. She stood in the doorway, staring at the smart reception
area with its leather chairs and paintings on the wall. The
receptionist caught her eye and smiled, and that helped make
up her mind. She pushed open the door.

"I'd like to make an appointment for a consultation. The
free one, that is. If I can." She cursed herself for being so
timid.

"Of course. Let me check the diary."

The receptionist had been so warm, and had seemed so

sympathetic, that Val had been expecting the same from the solicitor. Instead, when she arrived for her appointment with Mr. Trotman (the son), his manner was businesslike and formal. He didn't look at her directly but focused his attention on the notes in front of him or the cup of coffee at his elbow, into which he laboriously stirred two sugar cubes.

"Your husband has a right to see his daughter. You must make arrangements for access immediately, or it could make a judge look unfavorably on you," he said after hearing her story. Val's spirits plummeted.

"But Tony is violent. He's been violent toward me for years and he had started to hit our daughter. She's only five." Her voice rose, sounding squeaky and, to her ears, unconvincing.

Mr. Trotman picked up his pen. "Do you have proof of that? Were the police called? Does your family doctor have a record of your injuries?"

Val rubbed her left wrist. "He broke my wrist once, but he told the hospital it was an accident. I've never told the police or our doctor."

"Any relatives who can back up your story? Your daughter's teachers, perhaps?"

Val lowered her head, shook it slowly.

"We can't sue for divorce on grounds of his violence without proof, but we could try to insist that your daughter's access visits are supervised. Is there a family member or friend who would do that?" He narrowed his eyes and she could tell he was assessing her, judging how reliable she seemed.

"I could find someone," she said.

"The problem is that in New South Wales it is well-nigh impossible to get divorced without what we call 'proof of fault' if the other party does not consent. And from what you say, your husband wants you back, so that could be a sticking point." He put his pen down and Val panicked as she sensed him giving up on her.

"Will Tony have to pay maintenance for Nicole even if we're not divorced? I'm struggling to manage."

The solicitor stuck out his lower lip, considering. "Certainly we could try. Is your husband well off?"

"Yes, not bad. We have a three-bed house in Croydon Park." She stopped, hating to use the word "we." "My father died at the end of last year and his house sold for eighty thousand dollars, so surely I am entitled to my inheritance at least?"

At last Mr. Trotman seemed interested. "When did the sale go through?"

"Just last month," Val told him. "I was the sole heir." He made a note and Val guessed he could sniff a way of getting his fees paid.

"Do you have a copy of any of the documentation? In particular, I need what is called a grant of probate. Could you get your hands on it?"

Val knew that Tony kept all the papers to do with the estate in his desk at home. "I could try," she said, biting her lip.

"Must have been a fancy house," the solicitor continued. "Where did your father's money come from? Did he have any other assets—investments, perhaps? It's worth finding out."

Val was stumped. Where *had* her father's money come from? She had always assumed he must have inherited it, because she had never known him to work. She couldn't remember him being interested in anything except the church, his daily Russian newspaper, drinking, and going for solitary walks.

"I guess he came from a wealthy family," she offered. "But I'm not sure."

The solicitor frowned, and she could imagine what he was thinking: organized crime, drug trafficking.

"He filled out tax returns," she said quickly, hoping to dispel this notion.

"But he didn't have any profession?"

Val sat back in the chair, mouth open. It had never occurred to her to ask where her father's money came from. They didn't have the kind of relationship in which she felt she could question him. He always snapped that it was none of her business if she asked anything about his past. It wasn't as if he splashed cash around, but he clearly wasn't short. He must have brought money from Russia with him, but how did he make it there? It was too late to ask now. Perhaps it was just something she would never know.

CHAPTER 20

Sydney, April 1974

VAL ARRANGED TO MEET PEGGY AT A COFFEE SHOP in The Rocks. "Save The Rocks" banners hung on every building, because local residents were struggling to stop developers from moving in on this prime waterfront real estate between the Opera House and Darling Harbor. Val had seen pictures in the papers of stalwart protesters being dragged away by police after they tried to block new building works.

"They'll never win, will they?" Peggy sighed, joining Val at a table near the window. "Big businesses always get what they want."

"I don't know . . . From what I read, the protesters seem to have a lot of public support."

Peggy shook her head. "They're letting it happen by the back door: evicting the public housing tenants then leaving buildings empty so they get run-down and have to be demolished. It's a losing battle if you ask me." She arranged some shopping bags at her feet. "So tell me: what's happening with you?"

Over coffee, Val explained what the solicitor had said, and Peggy huffed her indignation.

"Why should Tony have access to his daughter? He never

paid attention to her when she lived with him, except to yell at her for something or other she'd done wrong."

Val agreed, but said, "I have to be seen to be reasonable in the eyes of the law. He is her father."

Peggy tutted. "Well, I guess I can put up with a couple of hours at his place one Saturday afternoon to supervise a visit. I bet he won't offer me so much as a glass of water. He's convinced I'm to blame for you leaving."

"I know it's a lot to ask, but if you get a moment . . ." Val explained where the probate document was likely to be, in the top left-hand drawer of Tony's desk. "Don't worry if you can't. I don't want to make the afternoon any more awkward for you than it will be already."

Peggy grinned. "It will be my pleasure. I always fancied a life of crime, and I can't think of a better cause."

~

When she was told that she was to visit her father, Nicole protested. "Do I have to, Mom? Cheri is having a tea party in her yard." Cheri was one of the older girls across the road, part of the skipping group.

"He's missing you and is dying to see you," Val urged. "It will be fine. But remember: don't tell him the name of your new school or the road where we live. We need to keep them secret for now. You understand about secrets, don't you?"

Peggy beeped her car horn outside and Val led Nicole downstairs, giving her a tight squeeze before opening the door to help her into the front seat. Nicole moved slowly, obviously reluctant.

"We'll be back at five," Peggy called. "You put your feet up and don't worry. I can handle him."

Val cleaned the bathroom, scrubbing the ancient tiles till

they were a much paler shade of beige than before, then she polished the fronts of the kitchen cupboards and mopped the wooden floor. What if Tony kidnapped Nicole and ran off with her? What if he hurt her? What if Nicole accidentally revealed their address? All kinds of things could go wrong. Her chest felt so tight she could hardly breathe, and she yanked at the neckline of her T-shirt, stretching the fabric. She hated to imagine Nicole in that house. She wasn't safe there. Her daughter had long forgotten the knife rap on her knuckles, but Val knew that she herself never would, because that cracking sound of metal on bone had been the death knell for her marriage.

During the next couple of hours, the physical pain of missing Nicole was so great that it made her wonder yet again how her own mother had left her all those years ago.

Peggy pulled up at five minutes after five, honking cheerfully. Nicole seemed subdued when she emerged from the car, but cheered up immediately when Val said she could run across to Cheri's yard, where she could see the tea party was still under way.

Peggy heaved an oversized shopping bag from the back seat and winked. "Wait till you see what I've got."

"Did you find the probate?" Val breathed, following her upstairs.

"I told him I was going to the loo and sneaked into his study. I didn't dare stop to look through all the papers in the drawer, so I just scooped up everything, then I hid my bag by the front door and grabbed it as we were leaving." She opened the bag and tipped a huge pile onto Val's table. "There you are."

"Christ!" Val exclaimed, eyes wide. "He'll be furious. You'd better warn Ken that he might pay you a visit."

"Ken could take him anytime." Peggy laughed. "Don't worry about us."

Val started to flick through the documents: valuations, legal letters, tax forms . . . It looked dull, but it was exactly what she needed. Several were in Russian. "Scott" was the surname her father had chosen when he moved to Australia, but she didn't know his Russian name, and it was hard to tell from these papers.

"Thank you!" She hugged Peggy with feeling. "I owe you big time. If you ever need me to turn to crime to help *you*, just ask."

After Peggy went home, Val shoved the papers to one side and heated a can of spaghetti for Nicole's supper.

"How was your dad?" she asked as they ate. "Did he play with you?" He never used to, but she hoped that as a weekend dad he would make a bit more effort.

Nicole shook her head. "We watched *Skippy* on TV, then Auntie Peggy played Snap with me. Mom, can we get a TV? Please?"

Val sighed. "One day, sweetie. When Mommy has a bit more cash."

Once Nicole was tucked up in bed, Val returned to the pile of papers. The probate document was near the top, attached by a paper clip to the form Tony had filled out requesting it. She noticed that the grant was in both their names, not just hers. Maybe that was the way it worked when you were a married couple, but it annoyed her all the same. Tony had barely known her father.

She flicked further through the pile: correspondence with the tax office, with the estate agent who had sold the house— and then her eye was caught by a brightly colored Chinese stamp with pictures of smiling workers and a Communist-style logo. It was a letter, addressed to her, that had come all the way from China. The handwriting was neat and the envelope had been opened. Tony had obviously read it and decided not to pass it on.

Val pulled the letter from the envelope and scanned the first few lines: *Can it really be you? After all this time? I am overwhelmed with joy to hear from you.* She clutched her throat and turned the pages over to check the signature: *Your loving mother, Ha Suran.*

She dropped the letter onto the table and covered her face with both hands, so overcome that it was several minutes before she could read the rest: *When your father sent me back to Manchuria, my heart broke in two. He knew I could never raise the fare to return to Australia as I was penniless and my family is very poor. I wrote hundreds of letters but never received a reply, and I guessed he must be keeping them from you.*

Val was stunned at the cruelty of this. What if Tony snatched Nicole and never let Val see or hear from her again? The pain would be unbearable. Why had her father done that to Ha Suran—and to her?

Ha Suran did not explain why she had been sent away, but she did ask dozens of questions about Val's life. Was she married? Did she have children? Where did she live? Could she send a photograph? Was she happy? She longed to know that her little girl was doing well.

Near the end of the letter, she wrote that she did not want to cause alarm, but that her health was poor and she did not expect to live much longer. She wrote that Val should not be sad, because now she could die happy knowing that her daughter was safe.

Coming on top of all the other revelations, this knocked the wind out of Val. Her mother was alive, but might not be for long. What was wrong with her? She tried to calculate how old she must be: much younger than her father, so probably only in her sixties. Far too young to die.

It seemed unlikely that Ha Suran would be able to come to Australia, so Val decided there and then that she and Nicole would have to go to her. She couldn't let her mother die without seeing her again and asking all the questions she had been unable to ask her father. But the only way she could afford it would be by getting her hands on her father's inheritance—money that should be hers by right.

CHAPTER 21

Mr. Trotman looked through the papers Val had brought, his expression giving little away. There was a valuation of the antiques she had taken to the dealer, including the old camera and the Russian icons; statements from three bank accounts containing almost a hundred thousand dollars among them; half a dozen stock certificates; and, among everything else, a receipt for a safe deposit box in a city-center bank.

"Do you know what was kept there?" he asked Val.

She glanced at it and shook her head. "No idea."

"Perhaps you should ask. It doesn't look as though your husband has got around to checking it. Have you been in contact with him?"

"I let him see his daughter for a supervised visit," Val said. "We made the arrangements by phone."

"And he was happy for you to take these documents? These are originals, not copies." He frowned. "He'll need them to finish winding up the estate."

"It's my money, though, isn't it?" Val asked. "My father left his belongings to me, not Tony. He couldn't stand Tony and tried to talk me out of marrying him. I should have listened . . ."

Mr. Trotman was emotionless. "As a married couple, any inheritance is jointly owned."

"Really?" She screwed her mouth to one side defiantly. "So does that mean I own half of the Croydon Park house?"

The solicitor inhaled slowly. "It depends whose name the title deeds are in. Is there a mortgage on the property?"

Val didn't know.

"Did you sign any papers when the house was purchased?"

She couldn't remember. Tony was always putting documents in front of her and demanding a signature. He took care of the finances and she took care of the house. "So what happens now?"

"As I explained last time, you can't divorce your husband without his consent, or without fault being proved. That situation hasn't changed, so I suggest you sit down with him and work out a sensible settlement. I'm sure he won't let his"—he hesitated, checked the paper in front of him before finishing the sentence—"daughter starve."

"You don't know him," Val said bitterly.

Mr. Trotman looked at his watch. "In the meantime, how would you like to settle the bill for this consultation? I made it quite clear that only the first one was free."

Val stared at him. "You know I don't have any money. I can't pay you unless you make Tony give me my inheritance."

He cleared his throat. "My secretary will agree terms with you: a weekly sum until the bill is paid."

Val stood up, alarmed. "But you've done nothing. What am I paying you for?"

Mr. Trotman rang a buzzer on his phone and asked his secretary to escort Val to the door. "My invoice will be in the mail," he said.

She opened her mouth to argue, then decided not to bother. Let him sue! She swept all the papers into her shopping bag and hurried out without another word.

~

After the meeting, Val felt fired up with rage and drove to the city-center bank where her father had held a safe deposit box. She marched up to the counter, showed the letter, and asked the clerk if she could see inside the box.

She was asked to take a seat while the young man made a phone call and went to talk to one of his colleagues. Val glanced at the clock on the wall: two fifteen. She had to collect Nicole from school at three.

After seven long minutes, an older man in glasses and a suit with buttons straining over a potbelly came to talk to her.

"Mrs. Doyle," he began, "I'm afraid your husband emptied the deposit box a few weeks ago. I guess he forgot to tell you." He handed the receipt back to her.

"Are you sure it's the same one? It was in my father's name: Irwin Scott. Not Doyle."

"Exactly. Your husband signed our termination-of-rental form when he took the possessions away. I have a copy here." Val checked the document. He'd emptied it just days after she left him. The bastard. "Do you remember what was in it?"

"I'm afraid not. Even if I did, I wouldn't be at liberty to tell you."

Val was livid. He had been *her* father; it was *her* property now. "Might I use your telephone?" she asked. "I need to check with my husband that it was him who came here and not an impostor. I'm surprised he didn't mention it."

The man hesitated, then agreed. He led her to a side office and showed her how to press the button on the phone for an outside line, then hovered in the doorway as she called Tony's office.

When he answered, she launched straight in. "Tony, what was in my dad's safe deposit box? I have a right to know."

"You've got no rights at all. None. Why the hell should I tell you anything? You left me and stole my daughter, then you got your ugly cow of a mate to steal the papers from my desk. I owe you nothing. Sweet nothing."

Val clenched the receiver, trying hard not to lose her temper. "Can't you just tell me what was in the box? He was my dad, after all."

Tony gave a harsh laugh. "A dad you didn't speak to for seventeen years. Give me back my papers and I might consider telling you."

She had never loathed any human being as much as she loathed him at that moment. "Oh, yeah, and thanks for keeping it secret that I'd had a letter from my mom. Were you planning to tell me about that anytime?"

"I should have burned it," he said. "Careless of me. Anything else that comes in the mail for you will go up in smoke—just like our marriage."

"You can sing for the papers in that case. And don't think I'm going to let you see your daughter anymore. You're not safe for a child to be around."

Before she hung up, she heard his mocking laughter down the line. She slammed the receiver so hard that the bank man came to check it wasn't broken before ushering her out.

~

Val was badly shaken by the afternoon's revelations, but she had to calm herself before collecting Nicole from school. As she drove back, she took deep breaths, watching the women in the street outside and wondering if their lives were better than hers. Was that one with the long kaftan and the frizzy red hair happy? How about that plump woman in the too-tight jeans?

She always tried to find something interesting to do with Nicole in the three hours after school before her shift at the office block started, feeling guilty that her little girl had to spend every evening, from Monday to Friday, in such a dull environment. Sometimes they went to a museum, or baked a cake, or visited the library to choose new books. It was their special time. Her hands were shaking and she was still arguing with Tony in her head, but she stretched her lips into a smile and forced her voice to sound cheerful.

"What did you do today?" she asked, and listened to Nicole's long explanation about printing colored patterns on a wall chart with a map of Australia.

There was a travel agent on Darling Street, and Val decided to drop in and ask about the cost of flying to China. Nicole happily flicked through the display of brochures, picking out photos of hotels with turquoise swimming pools and asking, "Can we go here, Mom? Or here? I like this one."

The saleswoman telephoned Qantas, and Val listened to the one-sided conversation with increasing gloom. "Stopover in Singapore . . . then a transfer. Can you fly direct from Singapore to Peking? . . . Uh-huh. And does Harbin have an airport? . . . Uh-huh. . . . Can you give me a ballpark? One woman and a child traveling?"

She hung up the phone and wrote a figure on a slip of paper before handing it to Val. Six hundred and twenty dollars. It might as well have been six thousand. She felt tears pricking her eyelids.

"I see. And how about the cost of going by ship?"

The woman picked up a shipping brochure and skipped through the pages.

"There aren't any tourist sailings from Sydney to China, but merchant ships often take passengers. Let me make a call for you."

Val gripped the edge of her seat, praying under her breath as the travel agent was shunted from one department to another until she found someone who knew what they were talking about. "A hundred and twenty? . . . Sharing a cabin?"

She looked at Val.

"When's the next sailing?" Val asked.

The agent repeated her question, then relayed the reply. "Third of May. Takes three weeks to Tianjin, then you'd have to catch a train to Peking and from there to Harbin. I can book the Harbin train for you. Is that any use?"

It was only two weeks till the third of May. How on earth would she raise the money?

"It could be," she said brightly. "Thanks for finding out. I'll drop by and let you know if I can make that one."

"You'll need visas," the agent told her. "You get them at the consulate."

Somehow I have to manage this, Val thought on the way home. Nicole was holding her hand as she hopped, trying not to land on cracks in the paving stones, and it jerked her arm up and down. It could be my only chance.

She went to apply for their visas the very next day. That was the easy bit. The money for the tickets was going to be much harder to find.

~

The following Saturday evening, Val was washing the dinner dishes around ten when there was a loud knock on the door. She glanced into the bedroom, but Nicole was fast asleep and didn't stir. Who could be calling on her at such a time? It must be a neighbor, because they were on the landing outside rather than down at the street door.

She opened her door a crack and gave a muffled scream as it was shoved so hard that it swung wide and a hand grabbed her hair. Tony's face, scarlet with rage, was inches from hers, his breath stinking of beer. Before she could speak, he drew back his fist and punched her hard on the left side of her face, right on the cheekbone. The force made the back of her head slam off the door frame. Pain knocked her senseless; her cheek was throbbing, and squiggly shapes were exploding inside her eye, but she struggled to push him away.

"Stop!" she begged. "Your daughter's asleep."

Still gripping her hair, Tony started slapping her face: first one side with his palm, then the other with the back of his hand. "You utter bitch. I can't believe I married such a treacherous bloody snake of a woman."

Each slap jerked her head. She could taste blood and her ears were ringing. She was still trying to push him away, but it was futile.

"How did you find me?" she gasped.

He grabbed her throat and began to squeeze. "Your solicitor gave me the address. Nice bloke. We're in the same golf club. He reckoned I should know you're trying to steal my money."

Val grabbed his wrists and tried to pull his hands from her neck, but he was too strong. She began to feel faint but knew she mustn't lose consciousness. If she passed out, he might grab Nicole and she would never see her again. She tried to

kick his shins, but he dodged out of the way, his face ugly
with hatred. Was he going to kill her? He was too much of
a coward. With a criminal conviction, he would get kicked
out of his fancy golf club.

She stopped struggling and Tony loosened his grip slightly,
letting her gasp some air.

"Here's what's going to happen," he said. "You are going to
fetch all the papers you stole from my desk and give them to
me nicely. Any money from that estate is mine, and you will
never get your claws on it. Be quite clear about that."

Val tried to speak, but only a croaky whisper emerged. "Can
we get divorced?"

"Not until I say so," he spat. "You're scum and I don't want
you back. Look at the bloody state of you! Having sex with
you was like having sex with a sack of potatoes. Frigid cow."
He squeezed her throat again, clearly relishing his power over
her. "We'll get divorced if and when I say so, but be very sure
that I will never pay you a cent." He released her and she
rubbed her throat, coughing and straining to inhale. "Now
get the papers."

"What about your daughter?" she croaked. "I know you love
her. And you and I used to love each other too. Remember?"

"Yeah, and then you betrayed me. I want nothing to do
with either of you. The papers!" He shoved her into the flat,
positioning himself in the doorway so she couldn't slam the
door.

Val scooped them quickly into a plastic bag. She just wanted
him gone. So far Nicole had slept through the encounter, but
she couldn't risk him turning on his daughter next.

Tony took the bag and checked the contents quickly. "If
there's anything missing, I'll be back," he warned. "Remember:
I know where you live."

He staggered on his way down the stairs. Val watched him

go. Once he was outside, she rushed down to close the street door behind him and saw that he had forced the flimsy lock.

She hurried back up to the flat and bolted the door from the inside, then went to the bathroom. Her entire face was red and puffy, like a boxer's. The left eye was swollen closed and her lip was cut, dripping blood onto her white T-shirt. Purple fingermarks circled her neck like a macabre tattoo, and her throat felt raw and scratchy. She got some ice from the freezer and wrapped it in a tea towel, then held it to her eye.

She knew Peggy would urge her to call the police. This was the proof of fault she needed to get a divorce—but Val hesitated. There was no phone in the flat, so she would have to run to the phone booth in the next street, and she was scared Tony might still be out there. Besides, he would deny it and there were no witnesses. None of her neighbors had come out to hear what was causing the ruckus. It was a Saturday night; maybe they were out.

What stopped her more than anything was the knowledge that Tony knew where they were. If she called the police, he would be angrier than ever and maybe he would attack Nicole next time. She would have to find another home or he could turn up any night when he'd had a skinful and was looking for a punching bag. She couldn't live in fear of every knock on the door. They would have to move—and soon.

CHAPTER 22

WHEN NICOLE WOKE IN THE MORNING, SHE BURST into tears at the sight of Val's face, which looked worse now than it had the previous evening. Her eye resembled a ripe purple plum and wouldn't open even slightly. The cut on her lip was black and jagged, and her cheeks were swollen like a chipmunk's. She draped a scarf around her neck to hide the fingermarks, but had to invent a story to explain the rest of the injuries to her daughter.

"Your silly mom was tidying the bookshelf when that big fat dictionary fell on top of me," she said.

"Did you cry?" Nicole asked.

"I did a little bit," she said truthfully.

"You should've waked me and I would have kissed it better," Nicole said. She sat down to eat her cereal, but kept eyeing Val as if she were a stranger.

∼

All week Val kept herself to herself, wearing huge Jackie O shades to hide the worst of the swelling and looping colored scarves around her neck. She left home only to ferry Nicole to and from school, to pick up groceries, or to go to her cleaning job in the evening. Her brain was ticking over constantly, trying to decide what to do, weighing up one option after another. Every night she lay awake working out the repercussions and pitfalls of each plan. Tiny noises startled her: was it Tony coming back? She bolted the door and wedged a chair under the handle so it would be hard for him to break down, but still she slept fitfully and wakened at sounds as faint as that of a moth fluttering against the windowpane.

By the end of the week she had made her decision. There was only one route open to her. It was a terrifying prospect, but she had run out of options.

"Shall we visit Aunt Peggy today?" she asked Nicole on the Saturday morning, and Nicole clapped her hands in excitement. She loved playing with Peggy's son, Lenny.

"What the hell happened?" Peggy exclaimed, taking a step back in horror. "Did you get mugged?"

Although Val's appearance was much improved, she still looked as though she had come off worse in a boxing match, and her throat bore the clear imprint of her husband's fingers.

"Was it Tony?" Peggy mouthed, after checking Nicole was out of earshot, and Val nodded.

"He's an animal! You have to go to the police," Peggy's husband, Ken, insisted. "I'll come with you. He can't get away with this."

"I can't." Val shook her head. She had given it a lot of thought. "I'm not brave enough to stand up in court and accuse him. He would hire an expensive solicitor and get off scot-free, then he would come after me. He'd never let it rest." She took a sip of coffee and winced at the sting of hot liquid on her lip. It was still difficult to swallow; the swelling made it feel as though there was a rock stuck in her throat. "No, I've decided that Nicole and I will go to China to see my mom. We'll be gone a couple of months, and on our return I'll find a new flat and a new job. I've started from scratch before, so I can do it again."

Peggy and Ken looked at each other. Ken spoke first. "How will you raise the money? We would help, but—"

"No, it's fine," Val broke in. "But I need you to look after Nicole for me this morning, just for a couple of hours. Is that OK?"

"Of course!" they said in unison. "What are you going to do?" Peggy added, wrinkling her forehead.

"It's better if you don't know," Val told her. She checked the clock. Five to ten. It was time to go.

~

She stopped the car at the end of the street where she had lived for seventeen years and peered down. Tony's car wasn't under the carport. He always played golf on Saturday mornings, and she couldn't imagine he would have changed that routine. She parked in the next street, pulled up the collar of her jacket, and put on her jumbo-sized sunglasses, then walked around the corner, her legs trembling. What if he came back unexpectedly? What if one of the neighbors saw her and came out to say hello, then told Tony she had been there?

She didn't see anyone except some kids playing football, who didn't give her a second glance. She walked up the drive and around to the back of the house, peering in the windows for signs of life. No one there. She took out her old keys and tried them in the back door, but as she had suspected, Tony had changed the locks. Probably did that the week she'd left, knowing him.

Beside the kitchen there was a laundry room with a small window covered by a fine-mesh insect screen. Val never used to close the window over the screen so that the room was aired and didn't smell damp. She was relieved to see Tony hadn't thought to close it either. She had brought a metal nail file with her and slipped it under the edge of the screen, pulling it away from the wooden frame. The aperture was narrow, only two feet tall and slightly narrower in width, but she managed to slide through headfirst and pulled herself over the washing machine to the floor on the other side. As she landed, she knocked over a bag of clothespins and froze, listening. Was anyone else in the house? Maybe Tony had gotten himself a new woman already and she would come rushing down at the noise . . . but there was no sound.

Val's heart was hammering so loudly she thought she might have a heart attack as she crept into the kitchen, where the sink was stacked with dirty dishes. Tony's breakfast plate was on the table, with dozens of ants marching around a spill of marmalade and trudging down the table legs carrying toast crumbs on their backs. You had to keep on top of the ants in that kitchen or they took over in no time.

In the sitting room, there were half a dozen crushed beer cans on the coffee table and dirty clothes slung over the backs of chairs; it didn't look as though he'd been entertaining any women there. She made her way to his study and scanned the room. The plastic bag she'd filled with her father's papers was sitting on his desk, but she couldn't see anything unusual that looked as though it could have come from her father's safe deposit box. She opened each of the desk drawers in turn, then checked inside Tony's briefcase, but it was difficult when she didn't know what she was looking for.

Suddenly there was a noise at the front door. Val ducked down at the side of the desk, making herself as small as possible so she couldn't be seen from the hall. There was a rattle, then a dull thud. It took several seconds before she processed the noises and realized it was the postman delivering the mail. She clutched her face in her hands and breathed deeply before standing up again. It was imperative she get out of there as soon as possible. She couldn't afford to spend any more time searching.

At the back of the usual drawer she found Tony's checkbook and tore a single check from near the end of the book, where its absence wouldn't be noted straightaway. She slid it into her handbag, closed the drawer, had a last look around to check everything was just as it had been, then hurried back to the laundry room. After squeezing out through the window onto the grass, which badly needed cutting, she retrieved a tube of glue from her handbag, dotted it around the edges of the insect screen, and carefully pulled it back into position, smoothing the corners. It would take a miracle for Tony to notice the difference.

Twenty minutes later, she was at Peggy's house accepting another cup of coffee. She could have used a slug of whisky to calm her nerves but knew it would only give her a headache later. Nicole and Lenny were charging around the house in a boisterous game of cowboys and Indians, complete with whooping and pretend gunfire.

~

After taking Nicole to school on Monday morning, Val swung into action. First she went to the bank in Croydon Park, where all the tellers knew her. Vonny, the one with curly red hair, was free, so Val waved and hurried over.

"Tony's only done it again." She smiled. "He forgot to get the housekeeping money on Friday and he's off on a business trip all week, so he wrote me a check for cash." She handed it over. "How was your weekend, Vonny? Lovely weather. Can't believe it's May already."

Vonny picked up the check and glanced at it. Val had forged Tony's signature several times before and knew she could do it better than he did himself.

"My dad had a barbecue," Vonny said. "Usual crowd."

"Are you still seeing that insurance guy? What's his name again?"

"Ian, yeah." Her hand hovered over the stamp and Val willed her to pick it up. She shouldn't really give cash except to the account holder, but she had done this for Val once before.

"He seemed nice," Val said. "Very good-looking." She continued, "Tony went off this morning without any clean socks for the week, even though I'd left them out specially. I pity the man sitting next to him at the conference."

Vonny giggled and stamped the check. "How do you want it?" she asked.

"Tens and twenties," Val said, waving her hand airily as if it was of no consequence.

As soon as she left the bank, she drove to the travel agent on Darling Street.

"Can you still get me on that sailing to China later today?" she asked, out of breath. "I've got cash."

"Strewth! Talk about last-minute! I'll call and check," the agent said. "If not, I'll ask when the next sailing is, shall I?"

The next sailing was no use to Val, and she hopped from foot to foot as the agent spoke on the phone. "Cash," she heard her saying, and that seemed a good sign, then she began talking about the issuing of tickets.

"You're in luck." The woman smiled. "Come back in an hour and I'll have the tickets printed for you. You have to get to the wharf at four, and it sails at five."

Buzzing with a mixture of excitement and nerves—mostly nerves—Val drove to her flat and packed their clothes for the journey into a suitcase, then loaded the rest of their possessions into boxes and drove to Peggy's with them, collecting the tickets on the way. She'd ask Peggy to pick up the furniture, then stick the keys through the mail slot. She hadn't paid the rent for May and the landlord wouldn't be best pleased, but at least she was leaving the place much cleaner than it had been when she arrived.

"So that's what you were up to!" Peggy exclaimed. "You're a dark horse. I'll send Ken for the furniture after work and it will be waiting here for your return. Have a great trip!"

There was no time to hang about: next Val drove to the school to collect Nicole. All the time she kept waiting for something to go wrong. Had Tony discovered the missing check? Would the bank have called to alert him to her cash withdrawal? Had he worked out which school Nicole attended? As she walked into the playground, she kept looking over her shoulder, scared that his hand would land on her shoulder at any moment, followed by his right hook exploding into her cheek.

Nicole came hurrying out with her usual flurry of news, but Val was too distracted to listen. They drove to a Rozelle garage, where she went to the office, ignoring the girlie calendar on the wall, and asked the boiler-suited manager if he would buy her car. She had all the papers with her and crossed her fingers as he came out to inspect it, checking the bodywork, opening the hood, getting into the driver's seat to turn over the engine.

"I'll give you three hundred dollars," he said, and Val spluttered.

"You're kidding me! It's worth at least a thousand." She had seen them advertised new for five thousand, and it was only a couple of years old.

He gave an exaggerated shrug. "Take it or leave it."

"Five hundred," she countered, but he wouldn't budge. She tried to bluff that she would go elsewhere but knew without checking that she was running out of time.

"OK, three hundred it is, if one of your men will drive me and my daughter down to White Bay with our luggage. We're off on holiday."

He looked her up and down. "Fair do's. Come to my office and we'll sign the papers."

She sat there under big-breasted Belinda, May's pinup, certain that she would have gotten at least twice the price if she were male. Nothing could be done about it. She was thankful that at least Tony had put the car papers in her name for insurance purposes so she didn't need his permission to sell it.

Until they reached White Bay, Val hadn't told Nicole that they were going on holiday, but after the mechanic dropped them off with their suitcase, she pointed at their ship, the *Coolabah*, towering like a mountain against the sky.

"Guess what? We're going to China to see your grandma. Won't that be fun?"

"Is it a joke?" Nicole asked, looking from Val to the ship and back again. "How do we get on? Where will we sleep? How long till we get there?"

Val peered back at the approach road. Still she feared that Tony might discover her plans. Perhaps he would manage to bully the information out of Peggy and turn up at the quay, tires screeching, to grab her and stop her leading Nicole up the gangway.

"I'll tell you everything when we're on board," she promised. She showed their tickets to a steward and they found their way to their tiny cabin, two levels below deck. Val didn't dare go out into the open air again until the ship's horn sounded and she could feel them moving out into the harbor. If Tony came now, he'd be too late. She felt the tension begin to melt.

They climbed hand in hand up the metal stairs onto the deck to watch as the ship glided slowly past the Opera House on their right, Taronga Zoo on the left, and out toward the shimmering vastness of the Pacific Ocean.

CHAPTER 23

Petrograd, winter 1921

AFTER MARIA AND PETER LEFT THE FARM IN THE Urals, they headed west in the wagon they had taken from Svetlana and Joe, foraging for food and sleeping huddled under piles of blankets and coats in remote barns. Peter kept a fire going through the night, but still the raw cold ate into their flesh. It was dangerous cold, the type Maria knew could kill. They cocooned the little ones between them, but Maria often woke with excruciating pain in her fingers and toes, shivering convulsively.

Once they were far enough away that Peter felt confident the Cheka—the Bolshevik secret police—would not track them down, he began taking casual work on the new collective farms. Under Lenin's agricultural policy, such farms were only supposed to hire family members but most flouted the rules when they were shorthanded. Peter was a tireless worker with an encyclopedic knowledge of the land. Sometimes a farmer took him on because he had tips about how to rid a crop of pests or to uproot stubborn weeds, or a suggestion for improving the milk yield of a herd. He was the last to leave the field at night, first out in the morning, and he got along with the other workers, careful not to threaten their jobs.

The family never stayed long in one place but moved on, gradually heading toward St. Petersburg, where Peter had heard there were plenty of jobs in the burgeoning new factories. Maria dreamed of simple things: a roof over their heads, running water, a bed. Her past life as a Romanov was like a mirage; whole chunks of time faded from memory.

Once they reached the city, early in 1923, Peter joined long lines of country folk applying for work at labor exchanges: *laptis*, the townsfolk called them disparagingly, after their woven bark shoes. He was eventually assigned to a pig-iron factory, where iron ore, charcoal, and limestone were melted together at high temperatures and black smoke belched from tall chimneys.

With the job came an apartment in a communal block, known as a *kommunalka,* in a new suburb Maria did not know, far from the River Neva. The four of them slept in one room, and they had to share a kitchen and bathroom with nine other families, but it was clean and modern and there was an enclosed courtyard where the children could play.

"How lucky we are!" she exclaimed, looking around—and then she stopped, remembering her slaughtered family and the basement in Ekaterinburg that still haunted her dreams. Luck was only relative.

~

Maria couldn't have explained what made her take the children on the Tsarskoe Selo bus one morning after Peter left for work. She hadn't told him her plan because he would probably have tried to talk her out of it, worried that someone might recognize her there. He was always cautioning her not to stand out from the crowd. She had tied a red scarf around her hair, and wore a wide skirt and a polka-dotted blouse. Over her arm she carried a woven basket, so if challenged she could claim to be collecting wild herbs.

Stepan, now aged four, and Irina, aged two, screeched with excitement and laughed as they were jolted up and down on hard wooden seats when the bus's wheels struck ruts in the road. Tsarskoe Selo had been renamed Detskoye Selo by the Soviet authorities, just as St. Petersburg had been renamed Petrograd. Anything to do with the Church or the monarchy had been obliterated as the Communist authorities tried to reeducate the people. Maria peered out at the fields where workers with hoes were breaking up the winter-hardened ground for planting, and felt immensely grateful that their farming years were over. It was too tough to make a living and the winter months were a struggle for survival.

The bus stopped in town and she led the children up the hill to the Alexander Palace, which had been her family's main home before the Revolution. She'd heard it had been turned into a museum, but it did not appear to be open that day and the gates were locked. She stood and peered through the railings at the long facade of the building with columns in the center and wings on either side. It seemed run-down, as if no one had repainted the exterior since the family left under guard in July 1917. Sunlight blinked off the vacant windows and there wasn't a soul in sight.

Memories came flooding back: tea parties with Alexei and Anastasia in the pavilion on Children's Island; running around the park with their dogs as they chased birds and squirrels; the pet elephant given to them by the King of Siam, which always used to make Maria nervous with its huge stamping feet. And she remembered their days under house arrest, when townspeople jeered at them through these very railings, yet they carried on as normal a life as possible inside the palace walls. Suddenly she yearned to travel back to those days, just to be with her family once more. Had he lived, Alexei would be eighteen now, Olga twenty-seven. Her sisters would no doubt be married, with children of their own. If only she could see them, talk to them, embrace them one more time.

And yet . . . if she did go back, the tiny children who were now tugging impatiently at her skirt would not exist, and she would not have found Peter. It was impossible to imagine ever being truly happy without Peter. He was the magnetic core of her existence. From the evil of the execution in Ekaterinburg had sprung the precious miracle of their love for each other, and she never ceased to be grateful for it.

"Can we go now, Mama?" Stepan demanded in his high-pitched little-boy voice.

She shook herself. "There's another, even more splendid palace just over the hill. Wouldn't you like to see? Come with me."

The Catherine Palace, with its azure-and-white exterior, golden domes, and rococo decorative motifs, was every child's fantasy, set in acres of parkland scattered with lakes, fountains, and grottoes. When they arrived at the brow of the hill, Maria saw the gates were open and there were citizens strolling in the park. She remembered hurrying along the route between the two palaces during the Great War, when she used to visit wounded soldiers who were being nursed there. That was where she had met Kolya Demenkov, the man she'd had a crush on as a fifteen-year-old. It was all so long ago, in a different lifetime; she had been another person then.

She led the children into the grounds, remembering her elder sisters, Olga and Tatiana, in their nurses' uniforms, their hair entirely covered by long white headdresses. They had seemed to flit from girlhood to adulthood overnight as they learned to change bandages and administer injections to the wounded. Tatiana had even assisted at surgical operations, but Olga found they made her queasy.

Suddenly Maria's eye was caught by a tall, slender woman walking down the central pathway toward the lake. Her posture was erect and her gait particularly elegant, and that was what drew Maria's attention first; but then she noticed the pale brown hair set against a swan-like neck and she blinked. It was Tatiana, her beloved sister. A feeling of purest joy spread through her veins.

"Praise God," she whispered, her hand over her mouth, tears springing to her eyes. She was about to set off in pursuit, but Stepan had wandered a little way away, and she had to turn and grab his hand then lift Irina onto her hip before she could start running.

What a coincidence that Tatiana should be there the same day she was visiting! God must have intended them to be reunited. Or perhaps she came here all the time, mourning the family she had lost. It was the most wonderful feeling in the world to see her. Maria couldn't wait to introduce her to her children, to invite her back for dinner that evening to meet Peter. Her heart was exploding with joy.

She paused at a point where two paths crossed and scanned the crowd, then spotted Tatiana, on her own, strolling by the lakeside, a parasol in one hand.

"Quick! Run faster!" she beseeched Stepan, almost pulling his arm out of its socket. There was a clear stretch now and they were gaining. Maria couldn't think what she would say first. Perhaps there would be no need for words.

"Tatiana!" she called, but her voice drifted away on the wind. "Tatiana!" she called again when they were just a few yards away, and the woman turned.

Maria skidded to an abrupt halt, so close now she could

have reached out to touch the woman's coat. She wasn't Tatiana. She was a buxom, coarse-complexioned peasant who looked to be in her forties. It was not a parasol she was carrying, but a long-handled spade. She must be one of the gardeners.

Maria stood with her mouth open, tears spilling down her cheeks.

"Are you all right?" the woman asked, glancing from her down to the children and back again. "Can I help?"

At that, Maria began to sob. After a moment's hesitation, the woman put an arm around her and hugged her like a mother.

"I thought you were someone else," Maria managed to say at last. Little Irina had started to cry too, distressed by her mother's grief.

The woman touched Maria's cheek before she broke away. "I hope you find her," she said, looking deep into her eyes. "I really hope you do."

CHAPTER 24

AFTER THE CHILDREN WERE ASLEEP IN THEIR BEDS that night, Maria told Peter about her mistake, her voice wobbly with emotion. They were sitting at the table, but he pulled his chair closer to put his arm around her and she pressed her leg against his.

"Where do you think Tatiana is now?" she asked. It wasn't the first time they'd had this conversation, but each time she hoped for some new insight.

"After she left Ekaterinburg, I think she would most likely have headed south to the Crimea," Peter said. "And from there she will have gone overseas. She would be unlikely to come here, to St. Petersburg, where she might encounter former palace employees around any corner."

"But surely she will be looking for us?" Maria laid her head on his shoulder. "She would not give up. The newspapers only reported my father killed. I can't believe she would leave Russia without trying to find the rest of us."

"Many families have been displaced by the civil war, not just yours. You can't live with your head in the past. If we ever hear the faintest whisper of your sister's whereabouts, I promise we will go there immediately by any means possible, but in the meantime"—he rubbed his neck and winced slightly—"we have a new generation to care for."

Maria rose and stood behind his chair to massage him. He carried such heavy weights during the day that his shoulders were often tight and painful by bedtime. She rubbed the mass of bunched-up muscle and bent to kiss the back of his neck, then looped her arms around him from behind and kissed the top of his head, breathing in deeply. He never smelled rank, even after hours of hard physical work, but had a faintly musky scent she loved. Whenever she felt anxious, all it took to calm her down was to breathe in his smell.

～

Most days Maria took her children to stand in lines for their rations, armed with the appropriate coupons. There was an office for bread, one for meat, one for vegetables, and sometimes she stood in a line with other wives not even knowing what she was lining up for. Some goods disappeared entirely— it was impossible to get soap anymore—but they were better fed than in the countryside. She'd had no idea how to cook at first, but Peter taught her to rustle up soups and stews with cheap cuts of meat, bulked out with potatoes, carrots, and cabbage. She picked up cooking tips from the women in the food lines or those who shared their communal kitchen, and soon she could turn buckwheat flour, milk, and eggs into tasty pancakes, and make jam from the autumn's crop of berries.

"Didn't your mother teach you to cook?" her neighbor asked, and Maria replied, "No, she wasn't very domestic."

Stepan and Irina developed reserves of patience and learned to entertain themselves as she chatted to the women she met in the endless lines. Many had also lost parents and siblings during the war. When questioned, Maria said her parents had died and she had become separated from her sister. Everyone was in the same boat, it seemed.

There was a woman she particularly liked, by the name of Annushka, who spoke with great sadness of an older brother who had been conscripted into the Red Army in 1918 and had never returned.

"I wish at least I knew the truth. If he is dead, I could visit his grave and have a priest say a *panikhida*. Not knowing is the worst of all worlds."

She was a tall woman with a long, sharp nose and a high, rounded forehead that made her look intellectual. Maria knew she was married and got the impression the marriage was unhappy, because she never mentioned her husband although she doted on her little son.

"Tell me about your brother," Maria said, knowing how much comfort she herself took from talking to Peter about her lost family, describing their traits and relaying memories of events from childhood years.

Annushka smiled. "He's tall, like me, with the family dome of a forehead." She touched two fingers to her own. "And he is as gentle as they come. He has a particular fondness for dogs, and wherever we went he used to stop to pet any dog we encountered. If one looked hungry he would feed it his own lunch . . ." Her voice trailed off.

"What is his name?" Maria asked, careful to use the present tense. She was very sensitive to the use of tense when talking about her own family.

"Fedor Ivanov Lipovsky. If you ever come across him—not that there's any reason why you should—then please tell him I live in the Bolshaya Apartments, number fifty-seven."

When she got home that evening, Maria opened a notebook and wrote down the address, not thinking anything of it ex-

cept that she would like to be better friends with Annushka
and perhaps they might visit each other's homes one day.

~

One autumn day, when the fluffy poplar seeds known as *putch*
were piled in gutters and low sun glinted off the golden domes
of churches, Maria decided to take her children by tram to
the Winter Palace on the banks of the Neva. They did not
care for architecture but she knew they would enjoy watching
the boats plying up- and downriver. As they stood on the
bank, chattering and pointing, she turned to look at the gran-
deur of the peppermint-green–painted palace where her father
used to deal with affairs of state before the war, and where
she had sometimes been allowed to attend dances with her
elder sisters. She could remember every detail of the white lace
dress she had worn, the pearl necklace her mother had lent
her, the white bow she had tied across the top of her head,
and the Frenchman she met one evening who had bowed and
said, "This one is the true beauty of the four"—meaning the
four sisters. She had blushed and stammered, unable to reply,
but hugged the compliment to herself like a secret treasure.

There was a soldier standing on guard outside the palace
who looked somehow familiar, and she took the children's
hands to wander a little closer. He seemed wary as she approached.

"Pray forgive me if I am wrong," she said to him, "but are
you by any chance Fedor Ivanov Lipovsky?"

"Who wants to know?" he demanded.

"You will think me touched, perhaps, but I am a friend of
a woman called Annushka who has lost her brother, and you
seem to me remarkably similar."

He stared, openmouthed. "You know my sister?"

She gave a broad smile. "I was sure it was you. Annushka will be overjoyed to see you again." She gave the address, which had lodged in her memory. "Bolshaya Apartments, number fifty-seven."

"Did you recognize me from the family forehead?" he asked. "We can't be the only people to have these."

Maria shook her head. "Not just the forehead. I like drawing and . . ." She had been about to say that she enjoyed taking photographs, which would instantly have marked her out as a *kulak*, but stopped herself just in time. "I suppose I have a memory for faces," she finished. "I'm glad I could be of use."

Next time she saw Annushka in the bread line, her friend threw her arms around her and almost cried with gratitude. "I will always be in your debt," she said. "Thank you a million, million times."

~

Maria would have thought no more of this chance reunion, but Annushka told some friends about her miraculous eye for faces and she was approached by two other women who had lost family members. They gave her slips of paper with their addresses and asked her to memorize their features just in case she encountered their missing relatives. Maria made quick sketches of each on the back of their papers and promised to keep her eyes peeled, but cautioned them not to have high expectations. Even if their relatives were in the city, it had a population of over a million and new suburbs were springing up every month.

A woman by the name of Raisa came with her husband to stay in the *kommunalka* where Maria and Peter lived. It soon became apparent that she was a gossip who loved nothing better than standing in the hallway discussing the affairs of other neighbors in a way that made Maria uneasy. She did not care to know if the couple on the first floor argued most nights; and when the people on the third floor lost a baby, she would rather respect their privacy and let them mourn in peace. At the same time she did not wish to alienate Raisa, fearing that she herself might become the subject of her gossip, so she listened and changed the subject as soon as it was possible to do so without causing offense. One day she told Raisa of her success in reuniting Annushka and her brother.

"You should go to the block on Tulskaya Ulitsa, just by the bridge," Raisa told her. "My husband and I used to live there and it was full to the brim of displaced people searching for their families, poor things. I think the authorities put them there as a temporary measure in the hope that they will find relatives and not need rehousing after all."

As soon as she mentioned it, the idea took root in Maria's mind: if she heard of such a place, Tatiana might go there to search for her. It was silly, she knew, and she decided not to tell Peter, but to Raisa she said, "I'd love to help if I can. Perhaps you and I could go together and you could introduce me to some of your old neighbors."

Raisa liked the thought of any venture that let her snoop on other people's lives, so one day in the spring of 1924, just after the snow had melted, they went together to the block in question, Stepan and Irina in tow. Raisa knocked on doors, introducing Maria and explaining that she had a talent for reuniting families. Maria had brought a notebook in which she took down their current addresses and drew quick sketches to act as an aide-mémoire. Although she knew it was almost certainly futile, she peered through doorways hoping to catch a glimpse of Tatiana, but with no luck.

One woman brought a boy of around six to her door. "I

have not seen his father since 1918," she said, "but he is the spitting image of this little one. Will you look for him on your travels and ask him to bring me money to raise his son?"

As Maria took down their details, she kept glancing at the woman. There was something about her greenish-hazel eyes that seemed familiar. "Do you by any chance have a sister called Nadezdha?" she asked.

The woman's eyes widened. "How do you know her? When last I heard, she was in Moscow."

"Not anymore." Maria smiled, copying out the address of one of the women she had promised to help. It turned out to be her second successful reunion, and she was proud of that.

When she finally told Peter about her unofficial missing-persons bureau, he was concerned. "Maybe it is not a good idea to draw attention to yourself in this way. The more new people you meet, the more likely you are to be recognized as a Romanov."

Maria shook her head. "No one would recognize me now." Although only twenty-four years old, she had the red-veined cheeks of a countrywoman from the winter nights spent sleeping in barns, and a few tiny lines scored the corners of her eyes; her hands were cracked and calloused, and her hair was short and invariably worn beneath a headscarf. "My only worry is that if Tatiana does pass me in the street, she will no longer know me. I could no more pass for a grand duchess than . . ."

She paused, searching for an apt way to complete her simile. Peter grabbed her and gave her a lingering kiss on the lips. When he broke away, he said, "To me you are still the breath-takingly beautiful girl on the landing in Ekaterinburg whose eyes filled with tears when I told her my father had died in the war. I have never forgotten that moment, and for the rest of my life I never will."

CHAPTER 25

Leningrad, 1925

FOR OVER FOUR YEARS MARIA HAD FOLLOWED SVET-lana's advice on avoiding pregnancies, but as the time approached for Irina to start her education, with Stepan already attending the school nearby, she began to yearn for another baby. When she went for groceries, she couldn't help gazing longingly at the tiny newborns strapped to their mothers' chests, or the older ones beaming gummy grins from perambulators.

"Could we afford another baby?" she asked Peter one night. "Just one more . . ." She slid an arm over his chest and raised herself on an elbow to look him in the eye. "I know we are lucky to have a boy and a girl already, but I can't stop thinking . . ."

He smiled indulgently. "Of course," he said. "If you want another, of course we can."

Katya was born in December, and came out of the womb so pretty that she took Maria's breath away: the darkest blue eyes, golden curls, a pert nose, and elegant fingers that she curved in the air like a fine lady drinking tea from her best china.

"I can't decide who she looks like," Maria sighed. "Perhaps she has an air of Tatiana about her."

"Perhaps," Peter agreed, "but she is also the image of my sister." He looked sad for a moment. "I will write to my mother to tell her of the newcomer to our family and ask one of our factory drivers to post it in Moscow. It is common knowledge that mail deliveries are more reliable from there, so I hope he will not question why."

He could not risk giving a return address; even seven years after the execution of the royal family, it seemed likely that the Cheka would still be looking for the missing Romanov daughter.

~

For those in cities who had jobs, the mid-1920s were a time of relative prosperity. There was free health care and education for workers, and while their accommodation was cramped and wages not lavish, there was enough spare cash for Maria and Peter to take their three young children on vacation in June 1926. Peter did not know the area, so Maria suggested they go to the town of Peterhof on the Gulf of Finland; in the old days her family used to spend the months of May and June there at a grand palace on the water's edge.

They caught a train to Peterhof and booked into a room in a shabby hotel with threadbare carpets and a smell of drains. The children slept in one narrow bed, parents in another, and they ate picnics of pot cheese, baked milk, and black bread for their meals, since they could not afford to go to one of the cafés or restaurants that had sprung up all over town since the government's relaxation of rules regarding private enterprise. They spent the days exploring the green parks and tree-fringed coast of the Gulf. While Maria sat on the pebbly shore with six-month-old Katya, Peter played games with the elder two and taught them new skills that delighted them.

"Pucker your lips as if you are going to kiss me, young Stepan," he challenged. "Now blow." Stepan made a breathy squeaking sound and Peter clapped him on the back. "That's my man! Before the end of this week I will have you whistling like a song thrush."

Stepan soon learned to make tuneful noises but Irina could not manage, so instead Peter taught her to make a squawking sound by blowing through a blade of grass into which he had cut a slit with his thumbnail.

"Like a frog's fart," he told her. "That's what my father used to say."

"Listen, Mama! A frog's fart!" Irina cried, and repeated it all afternoon, overjoyed to have a trick of her own.

Maria rolled her eyes at the coarse language.

Next Peter tried to teach them to skim stones across the surface of the water, but it proved too tricky for little hands. Instead they counted the number of bounces when he threw them, and cheered when he reached eight with an especially smooth pebble.

Maria loved to watch them together. The children were usually asleep when Peter got home from the factory, so this time was important. She wanted them to get to know their father's easygoing temperament and to absorb his wisdom. While she was an anxious personality—she wasn't sure if she had always been that way or if the execution of her family had caused it—Peter never panicked in the face of problems, but pondered calmly until he found a solution. He was less gregarious than her but he saw the best in everyone he met and was always willing to do a favor, so he was well liked by his neighbors and coworkers.

"Shall we catch some fish?" he asked, and sent the children scurrying in the bushes to find long, straight twigs with which to fashion fishing rods.

"What will you use for line and hooks?" Maria called, and he produced a roll of fishing line and some hooks from his jacket pocket with a wink. Trust him to think ahead.

The three of them sat on a rock, each dangling a rod over the water, waiting patiently. Maria got up to stroll along the water's edge, soothing Katya to sleep with a gentle bouncing motion that came as second nature now. It seemed incredible that she had not known how to feed, change, or soothe a baby before Stepan came along, and she hoped he had not suffered from her early mistakes. He was still the serious one of her children. Olga, her eldest sister, had also been serious. Maybe it was the fate of the firstborn.

"Mama, look!" Stepan called. Dangling on the end of his line was a wriggling silver fish, not three inches in length. He was crestfallen when Peter explained that they must throw it back because it was too small to eat.

"We only kill what we can eat," he explained. "If you respect nature, it will give you what you need."

Is that true? Maria wondered, then she looked at the babe in her arms, who had drifted off to sleep so easily. What she had needed after her family was brutally murdered was the love of a good man and a new family to care for, and she had been given both. Whether you believed they had been the gift of nature or of God was a moot point.

She wandered out to a headland and squinted up the coast. It was a perfect day, of the type she remembered from her childhood: warmth in the sun and freshness in the breeze, with a bright blue sky above. Toward the horizon she could see the jetty where they used to moor the royal yacht, the *Shtandart*, and through the trees she thought she could make out the glint of the golden cascade of fountains that led up to the Peterhof palace. Had her father still been Tsar, she might have visited there and let her children play in the park with their nanny, but that cosseted life had no appeal for her now. When she thought back through the men she'd had crushes on, the few foreign princes her parents considered for her spouse, she knew that although Peter was neither aristocratic nor royal, she could not have found a better husband anywhere in the world.

~

The Peterhof vacation was romantic, and a few weeks after their return, Maria found she was pregnant again. Although her fourth pregnancy, this was the first in which she had experienced sickness. She had a constant debilitating nausea that lasted all day, dry-retching when she had not eaten a morsel or drunk a drop of water, and it was difficult to find any foods that she could keep down. Peter brought an herb called black horehound, which he stewed in boiling water to make a tea that offered some relief, but when the sickness continued beyond her third month of pregnancy, he called a doctor to their apartment.

The doctor examined Maria and listened to the baby's heartbeat through a stethoscope, pronouncing himself satisfied that it was strong. He told her to nibble a dry biscuit first thing on awakening, to avoid rich foods, and to keep sipping water so she did not dehydrate.

"What was the date of your last menstrual flow?" he asked, looping the stethoscope around his neck.

"It was in May," Maria told him. "The twentieth or twenty-first."

He took a chart from his medical case and consulted it. "In that case your child is due around the twenty-fourth of February next year," he told her.

She nodded. "Yes, but my babies can be early. My eldest was born on the third of April but I only conceived him in September."

"He must have been small at birth." The doctor frowned.

"No." She shook her head. "He was the same size as the others. I think he just grew faster in the womb."

The doctor smiled, and she sensed an air of condescension. "That is not possible. You must have made a mistake over your dates."

"I'm sure I didn't," she argued, remembering the night when she and Peter first made love by the fire in their mountain hideaway, several weeks after fleeing from Ekaterinburg. He had said it was the third of September.

"Premature babies have trouble feeding," the doctor continued, "and they often have breathing difficulties."

"No, he wasn't like that . . ." Maria faltered.

"Then I doubt he was premature." The doctor began to pack his bag, reiterating his earlier advice about water and dry biscuits. Maria's ears were ringing so loudly she could not take any of it in.

As soon as he left, she lay on her bed, face to the wall, and tried to think. If Stepan was not conceived with Peter in the mountains, the only other possibility—unbearable, repulsive to consider—was that Bolotov had raped her during his attack in the Ekaterinburg bathroom. Her memories of it were hazy. She knew she had been very sore afterward but could only remember him putting his fingers there. They were standing up throughout, so how could he have inserted his seed in her? It was unthinkable.

She had wiped Bolotov's image from her mind, but now she remembered his dark hair and thought of her dark little boy. She and Peter were both light-haired. "No. Please no," she moaned. Katya and Irina resembled members of her or Peter's family, but she could think of no one whom Stepan resembled, no other individual so dark. This was awful.

And then another thought occurred to her. Peter knew the ways of nature; he was aware of the normal length of a pregnancy and must have realized that Stepan had been born two months too soon. She remembered him saying that he came early because she needed him, but that was clearly nonsense. What did Peter believe? She thought back to the scandal after she kissed Ivan Skorokhodov in the hall at the Ekaterinburg house. Perhaps Peter believed Ivan was the father. Perhaps he knew the boy he was raising was not his own son. If so, in five years, he had not once mentioned it. His bond with their eldest was close and unshakable.

What kind of a man could raise another man's son as his own and never once let it show in word, look, or gesture? Maria knew that if anyone could, it was Peter. She determined that she would never mention the topic herself, because poor innocent little Stepan must never know.

CHAPTER 26

O N FEBRUARY 24, EXACTLY AS THE DOCTOR HAD PRE-
dicted, Maria felt the labor pains begin. Peter fetched
the midwife and took the three younger children out for a
walk in the snowy dawn. The baby came easily, after just a
couple of hours, but he was quiet and the midwife had to hold
him upside down and smack him till he breathed. When
Maria held him in her arms and gazed down, she saw a face
that looked like that of an old man, and got goose bumps on
her arms.

"Hello, little one," she whispered. "It's good to meet you."

She let Peter choose the name, and he decided on Pavel,
which meant "small and humble." Unlike her other babies,
this one was difficult to settle and often cried for hours on
end, despite her best efforts to soothe him. The midwife pre-
scribed gripe water, but that made no difference. When she
massaged his little belly with her fingertips, he screamed as
if in agony. At last they decided to call the doctor, and he
examined Pavel, checking his vital signs.

"The cord is not yet healed," he said. "And he has a nasty
bruise on his hip. Did he have a fall?"

"Definitely not," Maria said. "I would know because he hasn't been out of my sight since he was born."

The bruise seemed to have formed where the sling she used to carry him pressed against him, so she tied it differently. When a new dark purple bruise sprang up straightaway, she guessed the truth.

In the back of her mind she had suspected it from the moment Pavel was born: he had the bleeding disorder that had marred the life of her little brother, Alexei. Known as hemophilia, it had been passed on from German relations on her mother's side. As soon as she realized this, she knew that his cries were cries of pain, just as Alexei used to utter. His blood would not clot and the slightest bump could cause agonizing internal bleeding, but there was nothing that could be done except pray.

Her parents had believed in the powers of a spiritual healer called Rasputin, who they thought had brought Alexei back from the brink of death on at least two occasions. Maria knew no such healer—none would have been allowed to practice in this new Bolshevik society—but she prayed for her little boy to be spared suffering.

Peter was ashen when she told him. He had seen how ill Alexei was in the house in Ekaterinburg, and it was heartbreaking to imagine the same fate for their son.

"We will do our best to protect him," he said. "Perhaps the specialists have some new medicines that were not available twenty years ago. I will ask our doctor to find out."

But it was not to be. At the age of just six weeks, Pavel's health deteriorated fast. He could no longer keep milk down, there was blood in his urine, and dark drops trickled from his nose. Maria tended him day and night, speaking in gentle tones, kissing his little face, trying anything she could to distract him from the incessant pain. He no longer had the strength to cry, but whimpered softly and gazed up at her, his eyes begging for help.

One gray morning she woke to find that he had died in the night and was lying beside her, cold and pale, and she knew her prayers had been answered. He would suffer no more.

"Go to my family, little one," she whispered in his ear, because to her mind there was absolutely no doubt that he would be looked after in heaven by her parents and siblings who had died at Ekaterinburg. They would have scooped him up at the moment of death and would already be bathing him in their love, and the love of God.

~

Maria was floored by misery. She couldn't stop thinking about little Pavel and wondering what he would have been like. Artistic, like her? Practical, like Peter? Or his own person entirely? Her breasts ached until the milk dried up, and a useless pouch of flesh hung on her belly, reminding her—if any reminder were needed—of the baby she had lost.

She had halted her search for missing persons during her pregnancy but now she began again, seeking distraction from her sadness. She made a card file, such as her father used to have in his old office at the Alexander Palace, and wrote the name and address of a missing person on each, then stuck on her quick pencil sketches and filed them in alphabetical order. As word spread, strangers came to knock on the street door of her apartment block and ask if she had heard of missing brothers, parents, aunts, uncles, or friends. If their information rang a bell for her, she checked her files and wrote out addresses. The number of successful reunions grew, and some grateful folk brought her gifts in thanks: hand-knitted cardigans for the children, jars of pickled vegetables, or a freshly caught fish.

Peter smiled indulgently and shook his head at his wife's hobby. She was a friendly woman who enjoyed meeting new people, so there was no point trying to stop her. As time went on, the chances of her being recognized grew slimmer. His only concern, he told her, was that she didn't get her hopes up about finding Tatiana.

"No, of course not," she lied. Still, in the back of her mind, she hoped that someday Tatiana would hear of a Leningrad woman who specialized in reuniting families and come to ask for her help. The hope grew fainter over time, but it was her secret fantasy. As a child she had been taught that those who did good would get their reward in heaven, but she hoped God might see fit to send hers sooner. She had lost her family, and then lost a baby; surely it was her turn for some luck.

Both Stepan and Irina were at school now, and when Peter reported that a day care had been established at the pig-iron factory where Katya could be looked after during the day, Maria decided to apply for a job. She had no baby to care for, after all. The extra earnings would help to provide more food and clothes as the children grew. They only had one set of clothing and one pair of shoes each, and it was a struggle to replace them when they wore out.

Before she started, Maria had little idea of what went on at Peter's workplace, and she was taken aback by the rapacious roar of the blast furnaces, the scorching temperatures, the clanging of the huge belts that transported raw materials into the furnaces then conveyed the molten liquid into molds to set. She learned that pig iron got its name because the arrangement of the ingots along a thin runner was said to resemble a litter of piglets suckling at their mother.

At first her job was sweeping the floor rigorously to rid the factory of any contaminants that could affect the quality of the iron, but soon she applied for training in how to mend and maintain the huge traveling belts. It could be dangerous if hair or clothing got caught in these, and she was scrupulously careful about switching off the entire belt before attempting a repair. One woman who worked in the day care had lost a hand because she had not heeded this rule. The remaining flesh of her arm was folded around a stump that acted as a grim reminder to Maria every time she collected Katya from her care.

"Whoever would have thought a grand duchess would carry a spanner and oil in her overalls pocket?" Peter teased her in private. "Amazingly, you even know what to do with them."

In truth, Maria seldom thought of her past now. Life was too full, with her job, her role as a mother and wife, her grief for Pavel, and her sideline in reuniting families. She soon became friends with several of her fellow workers in the factory, and many more came to her with stories of the missing until her card files numbered more than a hundred. One day, however, a wiry man with a salt-and-pepper moustache, whose job it was to stoke the furnaces, approached her pointing a finger of accusation.

"You're the one!' he said. "You told my wife where to find me, and now my mistress has left me as a result. What right do you have to play with people's lives? Did it not occur to you that some folk don't want to be found?"

From then on, Maria only gave out information about people who had asked to be included in her card file. The last thing she wanted was to make enemies.

~

On his eighth birthday, Stepan had joined the Young Octobrists and had been given their five-pointed-star badge with a picture of Lenin on it. He always came home from meetings greatly excited by all he was learning.

"Mama, did you know that the last Tsar was an evil man, like an ogre?"

"Really?" Maria asked, with a straight face. "Why do you say that?"

"Because he and his family bought jewels and expensive cars while the poor people starved," Stepan recited. "They lit cigars with thousand-ruble notes, and if the poor people protested, they shot them."

Maria caught Peter's eye across the table. She wanted to defend her family, to explain that they had been good people simply fulfilling the roles into which they had been born, but a slight shake of Peter's head stopped her.

"I agree that things are much better for working people now," she said. "Society is fairer."

"We must all be prepared if the International Revolution is to succeed," Stepan said, his brow furrowed in concern. "We are proler . . . prolerat . . ." He stumbled over the word. "Aren't we, Papa?"

"Proletariat? Yes, we are, son." Peter nodded.

Maria watched as Stepan played games of "Reds and Whites" with the other boys in the courtyard, reenacting scenes from the civil war, and worried about him growing up with Communism as his ideal. She would have loved to teach her children about religion, but Peter dissuaded her. Although there had been some relaxation of the ban on the Orthodox Church, religion was still seen as backward thinking, and it was better that their kids did not stand out from their contemporaries.

Since working out who must have fathered Stepan, Maria kept a close eye on her eldest, fearful that he might start to show negative character traits, but instead his personality grew increasingly like Peter's: easygoing, calm, and rational. The two often went fishing together on Sunday afternoons, coming home with perch or roach for dinner, and laughing over shared fishing anecdotes: the big one that had nearly pulled Stepan into the river, and the immense trouble Peter took reeling in what turned out to be the wheel of a discarded bicycle.

Stepan's schoolteacher stopped her one day, full of praise. "He is the peacemaker in the class," she said. "If two boys are fighting, he will stand in the middle and urge them to shake hands. And when a girl in his class was bullied by some other children, he somehow made them stop. I asked him what he had said, and he told me, all seriousness: 'There are right things to do in the world and wrong things to do in the world, and we must always choose the right ones.'"

The teacher chuckled at such wisdom from one so young, but Maria got shivers down her spine. Those were the exact words Peter had uttered when she'd asked why he'd rescued her from the forest. Stepan was Peter's son through and through, no matter what had happened before he was born.

～

Raisa stopped Maria on the stairs one day. "You remember I told you that Vladimir from apartment thirty-seven had gone missing and I heard his dog whining through the door?"

"Yes. Is he back yet?" Maria asked.

Raisa shook her head firmly. "He won't be coming back. I heard from Luba, who heard it from her husband, who is in the police, that he was arrested trying to cross the border into Finland."

"Really? I wonder why he wanted to go to Finland?"

"The reason hardly matters, does it? The law is the law and citizens are not allowed to travel overseas without the correct documentation. He has been sent to a labor camp, I hear. The Solovetsky camp in the White Sea."

Maria hated Raisa's self-righteous tone. "What happened to the dog?" she asked. Her children would love a dog, but their living space was too cramped and there were five mouths to feed.

"Someone broke down the door and cut its throat because the whining was stopping people getting any sleep."

Raisa's eyes were cold and she showed no emotion: the dog was making a noise, therefore its throat was cut; Vladimir tried to leave the country so had been sent to a labor camp. Her complete lack of empathy, and her conviction of her own moral rectitude, was chilling.

CHAPTER 27

Leningrad, 1928

MARIA WAS TERRIFIED WHEN SHE FOUND SHE WAS pregnant again. What if this one also had hemophilia? What if he died too? When a boy they called Mikhail was born in March 1928, she watched like a hawk for any signs of bleeding. Every day when she left him in the day care, she feared he would not be breathing when she returned, but he survived his first six months without incident and she began to relax.

She would have preferred to stop working and care for her baby herself, but they needed the money. Nine-year-old Stepan had a voracious appetite, and all the children outgrew their clothes each season, so when General Secretary Stalin asked citizens to volunteer to become "shock workers," who labored longer and harder than everyone else, Peter decided he would apply.

Maria argued against it. "I don't see how you can possibly work harder than you do already. You'll run yourself into the ground."

"My darling Maria, who is never happy unless she has something to worry about," he teased. "Think of it as a promotion: I will have more responsibility and my family will enjoy a better standard of living." He pinched her chin between his finger and thumb and kissed her.

"Ask the boss if you can have more holidays. Tell them your wife insists," she said.

Peter rolled his eyes. "I'll send a telegram to General Secretary Stalin. I'm sure he'll understand."

He was accepted as a shock worker and part of their reward was an apartment with three bedrooms on the second floor of the same block. It felt like a palace: the boys slept in one room, the girls in another, and Peter and Maria in the third, so they had a little more privacy. They received coupons for new winter coats and *valenkie*, the cozy felt boots that were worn under galoshes on snowy days, as well as trousers, skirts, and shirts. Peter worked longer shifts, though; it used to be four days on, one day off, but now it was six days on before the day off. Maria felt his absence keenly, but he reacted with his usual equanimity.

"I'm happy as I am," he said, and she knew it was true. His family was the center of his world and he would have done anything for her or any of their children.

In early 1931, Maria was careless over the dates on which they made love, half thinking she was too old to get pregnant at the age of thirty-one and half wanting another baby. Within a few weeks she knew she was expecting again, a baby who would be her sixth child, the fifth living one. Yelena was a round little dumpling, the biggest of her babies, with chubby cheeks and bracelets of fat at her wrists. There was no question that she was healthy. She greeted each morning with a cheery smile and beamed at strangers in the street. "What a lovely baby," they said, and Maria glowed with pride.

Peter doted on the little one, whispering to her, bringing out the wooden toys he had made for the others, writing another letter to his mother and sister with no return address, but in private he said to Maria, "I think five is enough, sweetheart. Don't you?" and she had to agree.

As she fed Yelena, it came to her in a flash of insight that she had subconsciously re-created the family she had lost: that had consisted of four girls and one boy, whereas she had three and two. Perhaps the idea had been buried in the back of her mind all along.

~

One evening, while Maria was bathing the baby, there was a sharp knock on the door. She wrapped Yelena in a towel and went to open it. One of the local Party bosses and his sidekick—an unpleasant pair if ever there was one—were standing in the hallway.

"Citizen Dubova," the boss said, glancing coldly at the wriggling baby, "we have heard a report that you keep a card index of citizens' private details and we wish to examine it."

"Why?" She was puzzled. "Have you lost a family member?"

"We want to establish your motives for keeping such records. It is the role of the state, not an individual." The boss spoke like a machine, as if reciting some rulebook.

Maria thought hard, but couldn't see any harm in showing them her files. "Come in," she offered, standing back to let them pass. Stepan was hovering in his bedroom doorway and she saw a look of complicity pass between him and the Party boss. That was odd.

She led the men to her room and opened her file, pulling out the first card while balancing a surprisingly patient Yelena on her hip. "You see? I write the name and address on one side, plus the names of the family members they wish to locate. On the other"—she flipped one over to demonstrate—"a quick character sketch to remind me."

"How much do you charge? And who gave you permission?" the boss asked.

She snuggled Yelena to her chest, worried the baby would catch cold if this interrogation continued much longer. "I have never charged a single ruble. It's a very small-scale operation based on my circle of acquaintances. And I didn't realize I needed permission; perhaps you could tell me where I must apply?"

They looked at each other, then the sidekick asked, "Where is your husband this evening? Maybe we should discuss it with him."

Maria glanced at the clock. "My husband is a shock worker and is seldom home by this time. Should I ask him to contact you tomorrow?"

They exchanged glances again, and their attitude transformed. It was the first time Maria fully appreciated the enhanced status Peter had achieved.

"Perhaps we should not disturb him," the boss said. "We will make inquiries and let you know if you are permitted to continue with your enterprise."

"I'm most grateful." Maria bowed her head. "Now if I might dry my baby before she catches a chill . . ." Yelena gurgled at them. She had been trying to talk since the moment she was born but didn't yet have any recognizable words.

After the two men left, Stepan came to stand beside her, looking sheepish. "I'm sorry, Mama," he said. "I told them about your card files at the Pioneers last week."

At the age of ten he had graduated from the Young Octobrists and become a keen Pioneer. "We were asked about any unusual things our parents did and I told because I was proud of you. I didn't realize they would be cross."

Maria smiled at him. "They're not cross. They are just

going to let me know if I need permission. Don't worry about it, son." She ruffled his hair.

When Peter got home later, she followed him to the communal bathroom to help him wash off the grime of the day and told him what had occurred.

He shook his head in disgust. "Children are encouraged to inform on their parents now. And at the factory, I am forced to attend meetings where workers tell tales on coworkers. They are supposed to report if anyone is visiting the lavatory too frequently! Next they will be asking for information on what is done there."

Mària heard no more from the Party boss about her card file, but from then on she and Peter began to be cautious what they said in front of their children. Any sensitive conversations were saved for their private time, in the bathroom or huddled under the covers in bed. They didn't blame Stepan; it was essential for his future prospects that he become an obedient citizen of the Soviet Union.

CHAPTER 28

Leningrad, 1932

PETER CAME HOME ONE NIGHT WITH HAPPY NEWS. "I've been transferred to the sales office," he told Maria. "They want me to negotiate with the merchants who buy our pig iron. It means no more shifting heavy machinery. My back is very grateful." He rubbed his lower spine.

Maria threw her arms around his neck. "What an honor! I'm so glad they appreciate you."

He grinned. "Today my boss took me to the docks to introduce me to some of the foreign merchants we do business with." He glanced around to check none of the older children were in earshot. "Of course it means I'll be under close scrutiny by the secret police."

Her eyes widened. "How do you know?"

"Any Soviet citizen who has contact with foreigners is watched. What's amusing is that they are so obvious." He sat down and unlaced his boots. "I saw several today, sidling close to us in their long coats and fur hats, stamping their feet against the cold, cupping their hands to light a cigarette in the wind. Everyone else has a job to do, but they must stand around freezing all day!" He laughed.

"You won't get into any trouble, will you?"

"Stop worrying, Maria!" He shook his head in amusement. "If you don't have any real problems to worry about, you invent some. This is good news. Let's celebrate tonight."

One of the merchants he dealt with in those early days was a Danish man called Matthias Knudsen, who plied the Baltic in a large, rather rusty steamship. While doing business, the two men chatted about the weather and asked after each other's family, and Peter began to question Matthias about the news that was reported in Denmark, because they heard little of the outside world in Soviet broadcasts.

"Matthias is alarmed about the rise of the fascist leader Adolf Hitler in Germany," he told Maria. "It seems he blames the Jews for Germany's economic woes, but Matthias says every country is suffering a downturn since the American economy collapsed in 1929."

"Perhaps Stalin is not doing such a bad job here," Maria said. Their lifestyle had improved dramatically since he became Party leader.

Peter looked around again to check no one was eavesdropping. "Economic stability isn't everything," he said, pulling a comical face. It was heresy: he was contradicting all the posters that waxed lyrical about industrialization and the Five Year Plan and the shiny Communist utopia.

Maria chuckled. "Will you ask Matthias if he has heard any news of my family?" she asked. The Romanovs were never mentioned in the Russian papers, but she was eager to hear what was reported in the outside world.

"I'll try," he said, his tone wary. She guessed he'd have to do it out of earshot of the foot-stamping secret police.

A few days later, Peter told her that he had broached the subject by asking whether the Danish king, Christian X, was popular among his subjects. "Matthias said his influence has been much reduced and that he is now a symbolic head of state without power. I replied, 'If only our Tsar, Nicholas II, had accepted such a situation, he might be alive today,' then added, 'I don't suppose you read anything about the Romanovs in your newspapers?'"

Maria held her breath as she waited for the answer.

Peter put a hand on her knee. "He told me there is a woman in Berlin who claims to be Anastasia."

Maria gave a little scream and clapped a hand to her mouth.

"But don't get your hopes up," Peter cautioned. "He said the relatives who have visited her think she is an impostor. She doesn't speak any Russian."

"Which relatives have visited? Has my grandmother been?" She would know for sure.

"He mentioned your aunt Olga and aunt Irene." They were her father's and her mother's sisters respectively.

"Olga is Anastasia's godmother. She would definitely know if it is her." Maria shook her head. "But why would anyone pretend to be Anastasia if they are not? I don't understand."

"Perhaps the impostor thinks she can claim the family fortune? I don't know."

Maria was silent for a moment, remembering her lively little sister, the mischievous one of her siblings. "If only we could go to Berlin, I would know in an instant," she said in a voice full of longing. But she might as well have wished to go to the moon.

～

Maria had dozens of questions she wanted Peter to ask Matthias, but he left it several weeks before raising the subject again, so as not to arouse suspicion. This time he returned with some bad news for Maria. "Matthias tells me that your grandmother, Maria Feodorovna, passed away four years ago. I'm sorry. After escaping Russia she lived for a while in London—as we knew—then traveled back to Denmark, where he says she became the figurehead of the Russian émigré community."

"She was old," Maria said. "She must have been eighty. I hope the end came peacefully."

"But your aunt Olga lives on a farm near Copenhagen, where she has raised two sons. Matthias said she enjoys painting watercolors and sometimes exhibits them."

Maria remembered Olga encouraging her drawing when she was younger and felt a wave of longing to see her. Copenhagen was closer than Berlin; they were linked by the same sea. But that made no difference when it was virtually impossible for Soviet citizens to travel.

"If only Matthias could hide us on his ship and take us to Copenhagen," she wished out loud, then looked for Peter's reaction. "Do you think he might, if we paid him with a diamond?"

Peter pondered this. The jewels Maria had sewn into her clothes at the Ekaterinburg house were hidden beneath a floorboard under their bed. They couldn't risk trying to sell them in the Soviet Union, where they would instantly have marked them out as *kulaks*, but Matthias would be able to sell them in Denmark.

"Do you mean for a visit, or to stay there?" he asked.

She turned her head away. She had been thinking perhaps they could all move to Denmark and live with her aunt, but that wouldn't be fair to Peter. It wasn't his family, he didn't speak any language but Russian, and besides, he loved his country. "A visit, certainly, to see how the land lies."

Peter nodded. "I don't think it is practical for us to take all the children and then attempt to return again. The entry requirements at the port are very strict. But perhaps you could visit your aunt. I will see what Matthias says."

Maria panicked. "I couldn't go alone. Who would look after the children?"

"I would manage, with the help of Stepan and Irina."

She did not say so, but she knew she could not get through so much as a day without Peter. She would be heartsick the entire time. He was as necessary to her as air.

"Perhaps I will write first," she decided. "Will Matthias take a letter for us, do you think?"

"I am sure he would," Peter said. "He is an agreeable man."

~

My dearest aunt, Maria wrote. *I have recently been overwhelmed with joy to hear that you are alive and living in Copenhagen. I hope Uncle Nikolai is with you and that your life is full of happiness. I have such wonderful memories of the time you spent with us at Tsarskoe Selo and all the parties you took us to before the Great War.*

She then related in brief what had happened at the Ekaterinburg house in July 1918, and the fact that Tatiana had not been present during the murders. Perhaps Olga knew of Tatiana's whereabouts? If so, she begged that she would let her know. She wrote that she suspected she was the only one who had escaped alive from the basement, and so was curious to learn of the existence of a woman in Berlin who claimed to be Anastasia. *I would love to know your true opinion of this woman. If she is my sister, I must find a way to be reunited with her, and I hoped we might avail ourselves of your hospitality for a time. Sadly, I would not be able to invite her to Leningrad, where my husband and I live the lives of factory workers under assumed names.*

Peter read the letter when she had finished, stumbling over some of the words. His reading had never become fluent. "Were this to fall into the hands of anyone but Matthias, we would be sent to a gulag, but I am sure I can trust him. I'll take it to him tomorrow," he promised.

There was a delay of several weeks before a reply came. Matthias slid the letter between some shipping documents and gave Peter a nod and a pat on the back as he handed them over. A secret policeman hovered unsuspecting as Peter transferred it to an inside pocket of his coat.

Maria recognized Olga's hand on the envelope and tore it open in haste, excited beyond measure to hear from the first family member she had managed to contact since 1918. Her face fell as she read the opening words: *You would not believe how many impostors have contacted me in the last decade to say they are Romanovs. I believe I have heard from three Anastasias, two Alexeis, an Olga, and at least one other apart from you who claims to be Maria. Tatiana is the only sister who does not have an impersonator, or at least I have not yet received any communication from such.*

Maria sat down and read on. *I'm sure you understand how difficult this is for me. My visit to Berlin to meet Anna Tschaikovsky—the one who claims to be Anastasia—was particularly upsetting as the woman is clearly mentally deranged. I suspect she is being manipulated by others for financial gain, but trust me when I tell you she is decidedly not my beloved niece and goddaughter.*

The letter ended: *Forgive me if I seem harsh but I hope you will understand that I cannot invite you to stay in my home without first ascertaining your identity. Should you happen to visit Copenhagen, let me know and I will meet you and make up my own mind.*

Maria felt desperately cast down by this answer. Her own

aunt did not know her, and did not believe any of the others
who had contacted her.

"Write again," Peter urged. "Press your case. There must
be personal stories that only you and she would know."

Maria took his advice: *Do you remember when Joy stole a piece
of cherry cake you had laid on a low table and stood trying to
appear innocent although there were crumbs on the floor between
her paws? Do you remember how hard I cried when my fingers
were trapped in the door of the royal train on the way to Livadia
and only your special bonbons could make me stop? Do you remember the time Anastasia threw a snowball at Tatiana and knocked
her out cold because she had accidentally scooped up a rock inside
the snow? Please know it is me, beloved aunt. Who else would share
these memories?*

Still the reply was not encouraging: *You could have heard
these stories from a member of the royal household. I'm afraid the
only thing that will convince me is to meet you face-to-face and
compare your current appearance with that of the niece I last saw
sixteen years ago.*

Maria showed the letter to Peter. "What if I traveled to
Copenhagen on Matthias's ship and Olga decided I am an
impostor? I was an innocent seventeen-year-old when last she
saw me, and now I am a thirty-three-year-old mother of five
who mends factory conveyor belts. My own mother would not
recognize me."

"I am sure she would know you," Peter soothed. "If you
like, we could pay for the Karl Bulla photographic studio on
Nevsky Prospekt to take your likeness and send that to her."

"If only I had my old camera. Do you remember when I
took your picture?" She smiled, remembering his unease in
front of the lens. "No, I doubt Olga would recognize me from
a photograph, and the experiment would be an expensive one.
Either I go there in person or I do not."

Peter spoke carefully, and she knew he wanted her to make up her own mind. It was her family, after all. "I will support you if you decide to go. My only concern is that once you have left the Soviet Union, it will not be easy to return. Matthias might have to smuggle you in, like contraband."

Maria shuddered. She knew in her heart she was not brave enough to do this without Peter beside her. He was the strong one. She fell silent for a long time, and Peter left her to her thoughts.

Maria could not sleep that night, but lay awake thinking about her life. She had been married to Peter for almost fourteen years and they had five children. Leningrad was where they had made their home, for better or for worse. Maybe it was time for her to stop dreaming of her Romanov past and start appreciating all she had in the present. She lived with a man with whom she never tired of conversing because she always found his views interesting, whose physical presence still gave her a tingle of desire; a man who was tender and loving to her and to all of their children; a man who could always tease her out of her anxiety and make her smile. Her life was here, with him.

After making this decision, she continued to write to Olga, sending greetings at Christmas and Easter, and Olga reciprocated, but as the months went by the gaps between their letters grew longer. Their arrival no longer sparked the thrill Maria had felt when she first made contact with her long-lost aunt.

The fact that Tatiana had not been in touch with Olga persuaded Maria that she must still be in the Soviet Union. One day she must come to Leningrad, and when she did, Maria prayed their paths would cross. Every time she managed to reunite family members who had not seen each other for years, she made a secret wish: please let it be my turn next.

Something strange was happening to their society, though. One day a woman in the factory canteen asked Maria, "Please take my card out of your file and destroy it. I am no longer looking for my father." She would not explain why. Then another woman in the bread line asked that her card be destroyed too.

"They think you are an informer," Annushka whispered. "But don't worry. I know you're not."

"Me!" Maria stuttered in disbelief. "An informer? Who could think that?"

"You would be surprised how many are," Annushka confided, her eyes alighting on a woman three places ahead of them.

"What would I inform about? Their addresses? It's madness," Maria told Peter later.

"It's certainly odd," he agreed with a frown.

Perhaps word had leaked out that she had shown her file to the Party boss and that was why people were nervous. She asked Peter if he thought that could be the case.

"I suppose it could," he said slowly.

She got a sense there was something he was holding back because he didn't want to worry her, but decided not to press him. Sometimes it was better not to know.

CHAPTER 29

Pacific Ocean, May 1974

As soon as they hit open water, Val began to feel nauseous. The ocean wasn't particularly rough, but the slight roll of the ship, the tilt of the horizon, and an odd sense of weightlessness meant her stomach heaved and the taste of vomit was ever-present in her throat. She sat on deck, wrapped in a blanket, trying to focus on a distant point, as one of the sailors advised. Nicole was unaffected, and spent her days socializing with the passengers and crew. Val watched her introduce herself to new groups and marveled at her confidence. She herself would never have been able to do that at five; she still felt shy meeting strangers at thirty-five.

The temperature grew warmer by the day, with blinding sunlight bouncing off the water. Val had been expecting to see lots of South Pacific islands, but apart from a glimpse of one of the Solomon Islands, the only view was interminable ocean and sky. Every nautical mile took her closer to the mother she hadn't seen for twenty-three years, and she thought about her constantly, wondering what to expect, cautioning herself not to set her hopes too high, just in case . . .

One morning there was a kerfuffle. Straight after breakfast, sailors in fancy dress began rounding up passengers who had never crossed the equator before; Val was spared only because of her nausea.

She followed with Nicole as the others were led to an area on deck where a court had been established: King Neptune sitting on a throne in a long white beard, holding a triton; two men in brown bear costumes; a surgeon with a glistening knife; a policeman; and another sailor dressed as a woman, with a mop head for hair. There were nervous giggles as each passenger was summoned in turn while the court assessed their eligibility to become a "shellback"—sailors' slang for someone who had crossed the equator.

"I want to do it!" Nicole cried, and a grinning sailor led her to the front of the pack, whispering something to the surgeon, who passed it along the line.

Neptune rose to his feet and addressed her in a booming voice. "Is it true, Nicole Doyle, that you have not stopped talking since this voyage began? That you are what some would call a chatterbox?"

Nicole looked a little cowed as she replied. "Yes, Mommy says I am."

There were titters in the crowd.

"Is it true that you do not like eggs and have refused to eat them on this voyage even though they are good for you?"

She agreed that was true too.

"A soaking for her!" Neptune cried, and Nicole screamed as she was sprayed with cold water from a hose, which drenched her clothes and hair. Val worried that she might get scared or upset, but instead Nicole laughed out loud as she wrung her wet frock, and beamed with pride when she was awarded a certificate stating that she had passed the Crossing the Line test.

How did she become so brave? Val wondered. Perhaps it was because her confidence had not been beaten out of her by a cold father and a violent husband. Val hated herself for feeling anxious, but she couldn't help worrying about the rest of the journey. How would she locate the train to Harbin when she spoke no Chinese? What if her mother was already dead when they arrived? At the same time, she felt proud of herself for getting so far, and she grinned when she imagined Tony discovering the theft of the check.

One day there was an eerie rumble as a squadron of planes flew overhead, like angry hornets, and Val felt their vibrations rippling through the displaced air.

"American warplanes," a fellow passenger commented. "Heading for Vietnam."

The US was supposed to have withdrawn from the conflict following the Paris Peace Accord but they still had a lot of troops there. Val peered after the planes, wondering how many of their occupants would return home, and how many Vietnamese they would kill. In Sydney, she often saw American soldiers on leave from the fighting. They tended to hang around the bars of the King's Cross district, where there were prostitutes in micro-skirts and white patent go-go boots on every street corner.

Still there was no land in sight as the ship nudged into the East China Sea, until the day they were scheduled to dock, when suddenly a huge industrial port materialized from nowhere. Cranes teetered like long-legged insects above concrete platforms stacked with multicolored shipping containers. The water changed from dark blue to sludgy green as they drew closer, the ship's horn sounding a bleak warning.

Val packed all their belongings ready to disembark. When she asked a sailor how to get to Peking, he told her to take a taxi to Tianjin station and catch a train. They were frequent, he said. Val did not have any Chinese currency, but the ship's purser changed some Australian dollars for her, handing over a stack of colorful notes with Chairman Mao's improbably round face on them.

Her taxi driver spoke no English, but she managed to make herself understood by drawing a picture of a train beside a rectangular building. The journey was short, and at Tianjin station, when she went to a ticket office and repeated "Peking" several times, the woman gave her two tickets and pointed to a platform. As they boarded the train, Val thought: so far, so good.

Everything looked foreign: the passengers wearing colorful cotton jackets and clutching chickens in cages; the workers in fields outside who wore conical hats. These were her mother's compatriots. Val had only the vaguest memory of her mom's appearance: a rope of thick black hair coiled on her head, creamy skin, and a pretty face that lit up when she was happy. Looking around the railway carriage, she wasn't convinced she could have identified her mother were she there. Would she know her on sight? She felt a bubbling of excitement at the thought of introducing her to her granddaughter. Everyone loved Nicole.

An hour later, the train pulled into Peking's main station and all her confidence evaporated. It was a vast hangar, with hundreds of people bustling around beneath a giant noticeboard where all the destinations were written in Chinese characters. She couldn't see a word that looked like "Harbin" and nothing that resembled an information desk. Panic rose like a flutter of moths, but Nicole was unfazed as she peered around.

"Why are they all hurrying, Mommy?"

"Just trying to catch their trains," Val replied, staring at the prebooked tickets she had been given by the Sydney travel agent as if inspiration might lie there.

Suddenly a young Chinese man stopped beside them. "Are you English?" he asked in a halting voice. "May I help you?"

Val showed him their tickets and he nodded and said, "Come with me." She had no option but to trust him as he led them to a platform some distance down the concourse, explaining that he was studying English at university and it was good to have some practice.

"Harbin," he said, indicating that they should board the train. "Have a safe journey."

Val wanted to kiss him. Instead she clasped her hands and bowed her head in thanks, and he bowed too.

The Harbin train set off at exactly the time it said on the tickets, as the big station clock ticked around to the minute. An inspector came by and punched a hole in them, then Val and Nicole sat playing I Spy as they peered out the window: cloud, tree, motorbike, temple, cow. Val was surprised when the first station they stopped at, after an hour of travel, was the exact same one in Tianjin that they had set off from earlier. They could have boarded the Harbin train there; clearly the travel agent back in Sydney had not realized that.

It got darker and Nicole's head sank onto Val's shoulder, then her lap. Val stayed awake peering out at the lights flashing past, followed by long periods of complete blackness. This vast country didn't feel real; was she truly here or was it a complex dream? I'm coming, Mom, she whispered in her head, but her eagerness was tinged with nerves. Something might still go wrong.

Just before dawn, when the sky was gray but with pinkish streaks brushing the horizon, the ticket inspector came past. "Harbin," he announced, pointing out the window at a station that was just coming into view. Nicole was barely awake and Val had to support her with one arm while dragging their suitcase with the other. Outside the station the road was empty. There was nothing that remotely resembled a taxi stand, and the only person in sight was an old man sleeping in a rickshaw decorated with gaudy plastic flowers. Val cleared her throat, but he didn't stir.

"Excuse me?" she said out loud, and he sat up, stretching and yawning. She handed him the letter her mother had sent, on which her address was written in Chinese characters.

The man nodded and said something incomprehensible, then brushed down the plastic-covered passenger seat and indicated that they should climb in. Val lifted Nicole in first, then put their case on the floor and squeezed in after her. The driver mounted the bicycle in front and began to cycle, the contours of his calf muscles standing out.

This is it, Val thought. She was about to be reunited with the woman who had given birth to her.

The driver pulled up outside a single-story shack with weathered wooden walls and a tiled roof. Was this the place? Val wasn't sure, but she climbed down and went to knock on the flimsy door. It was opened straightaway by a stooped older woman. Was this her mother? She didn't think so. The woman seemed to be expecting her, though, and motioned for them to come inside.

Val put down her suitcase as the woman led her toward a back room. There, lying on a mat on the floor, covered only by a sheet, was her mom. Ha Suran was paper-thin and frail-looking, but instantly recognizable.

Val gave a cry and ran to her.

CHAPTER 30

Harbin, June 1974

As they hugged, Val could feel her mother's shoulder blades jutting through her loose nightgown.

"Valerie," Ha Suran whispered into her hair, shaking with emotion. She didn't let go for a long time, and when Val eventually drew back, she saw that her mother's skin and eyes were a bright, unnatural yellow. It must be jaundice. Why did she have jaundice? It seemed too soon to ask what was wrong with her.

"This is your granddaughter." Val beckoned Nicole to join them.

Nicole crouched and whispered, "Hello, Grandma," and Ha Suran touched her arm and smiled but did not seem to have the strength to talk.

Val sat on the floor, holding her mom's hand, and began to describe their journey. Some chickens trotted into the room, pecking at the dirt floor, and Nicole screeched in excitement.

"Look, Mommy! They've got chickens for pets!"

The old woman gave her a handful of seeds, motioning for her to sprinkle them around, and Nicole watched entranced as the chickens squawked and flapped their wings while gobbling them up.

Val looked at the surroundings. She had felt as though she was living on the bread line in Sydney, with a one-bed flat and a cleaning job, but the poverty her mother's family endured was much more fundamental. The walls of the two-room shack were thin, with gaps where the boards didn't quite meet. There were mats arranged along the walls, presumably for sleeping on; she counted six altogether and wondered if two were meant for her and Nicole. A cooking pot hung in a fireplace, but apart from that and the mats, the family seemed to have few possessions.

The old woman was stirring something in the pot, and before long she served them bowls of rice and vegetables, along with some chopsticks. Val could tell there was an egg stirred through the rice but did not mention it to Nicole, who ate with clumsy enthusiasm, using the chopsticks like a spoon. As soon as she finished, the woman gestured for her bowl and refilled it, and Nicole beamed her thanks. They might not have a language in common, but they were becoming friends.

Ha Suran didn't take any food. She closed her eyes and Val couldn't tell if she was asleep or just resting, but she did not want to move from her mother's side. It seemed a miracle that she was here, at last, after all these years, and for now she was prepared to be patient.

~

It grew hotter inside the shack as the morning progressed, and Val used a magazine to fan herself. Nicole and the old woman were playing a game, trying to throw stones into a tin can placed a few feet away and giggling at their successes and failures.

Suddenly Ha Suran opened her eyes and reached for Val, squeezing her hand tight.

"You will stay awhile, won't you?" she begged. "I'm sorry we don't have proper beds . . ."

"This is fine. I'm planning to stay three weeks, so we have plenty of time to catch up. Is that your mother?" She pointed to the old woman.

"My aunt," Ha Suran said. "Your great-aunt, Li Suran." She called across the room to the old woman, who smiled and nodded confirmation.

"Will you have some food, Mom? I can help you to eat." Val could see there was plenty of the rice and vegetables left.

Ha Suran shook her head. "Maybe some water."

Val poured water from a jug she found near the cooking pot, then held the glass to her mother's lips. It still felt odd to call her "Mom." She felt like a stranger, but one for whom Val had a vast amount of affection.

Ha Suran lay back, worn out by the effort of a couple of sips. "You must have so many questions for me, as I have for you. But first I will explain what happened when I left Sydney."

Val shook her head. "Dad said you walked out on us, but that never rang true."

"As if . . ." Ha Suran closed her eyes for a moment, then opened them to look Val in the eye. "You must remember how close you and I were."

Val got a lump in her throat as she thought back to that time, when she had been so sad and lonely and mixed up. "I tried to ask about you, but Dad would never answer my questions. After a while he banned me from mentioning you. He said I was being a nuisance."

Ha Suran spoke in a rush, as if trying to get the words out before her energy was expended. "Your father bought me a ticket home to visit my family in Harbin because I had not seen them since before the war. I thought you were coming with me so you could meet them, but at the last minute he said you couldn't be taken out of school. I nearly didn't board the ship—I had a bad feeling—but I yearned to see my parents. As soon as we set sail, I missed you so badly it was as if my heart had been wrenched from my body. I willed the time to go faster so I could get back to you."

She put a hand over her eyes and there was a long pause, so long that Val wondered if she had fallen asleep, but then she continued. "I caught the train back to Tianjin, found the ship, and tried to board, but they told me my return ticket had been canceled and the money refunded. I argued till I was demented, but they would not relent: there was no ticket. Your father knew I could never raise enough to pay for it myself. You see how my family lives." She gestured at their surroundings, and a tear rolled down her cheek.

Val could imagine the sense of panic, then the terrible anguish. She couldn't carry on living if she lost Nicole and there was no hope of getting her back. She had often thought she would kill herself rather than live without her. "But why did he do it? Was your marriage unhappy?"

"Your father was always an unhappy man. I hoped that family life would lift his spirits, but it was his nature to be miserable and he couldn't change." She paused. "I have thought about this often and I'm still not sure I can answer fully why he got rid of me. I was an obedient wife but I was not the wife he wanted. I think perhaps he was ashamed of me. The Chinese were not popular in Australia at that time."

Val remembered some of the racist comments she had heard her father make over the years, and frowned. "But he married you. He must have loved you once."

"No." Ha Suran shook her head. "I don't think he ever did.

You see, there was another woman he loved. One back in Russia whom he had been forced to leave behind. And to tell the truth, I don't think he ever got over her."

"What was her name?" Val asked. Her father's words in the nursing home came back to her: "I didn't want to kill her." Had the woman he loved died? Had he been suspected of murdering her? Maybe that was why he left Russia, and that was what haunted him right at the end of his life.

Ha Suran closed her eyes. "I don't know. I'm sorry. I must rest now."

~

While her mother slept, Val took Nicole for a walk around the neighborhood in sticky afternoon heat. There was a market where bedding and old clothes were sold alongside rice and vegetables. A toothless stallholder held out a roasted scorpion on a stick, and Nicole screamed and scurried behind Val's back. Everywhere there was a smell of drains and rotting garbage. It was clearly the poor quarter of town.

When they returned, a Chinese doctor was crouched by Ha Suran's bedside. They sat on the floor and waited quietly as he took her pulse and looked into her eyes and mouth. Nicole gasped when he began inserting long needles into her flesh, starting at her feet, between the big toe and the second toe.

"Doesn't that hurt?" she whispered to Val.

Val replied that it was called acupuncture and it was often used to treat illness in Chinese medicine. She didn't think it would hurt.

"Will it make Grandma better?" Nicole asked softly, and Val shrugged and said, "I hope so."

After the doctor left, she asked Ha Suran what he had diagnosed.

"The illness is in my liver." Ha Suran coughed, and winced in pain. "The doctor says it was caused by the misery of being separated from you all these years, but he hopes I might improve a little now we are reunited."

"Have you consulted a Western doctor? Maybe they would have drugs that could help." Val thought of all the medical advances of recent years: chemotherapy and radiotherapy for cancer; artificial hearts and prosthetic limbs: they could do wonders.

"There is a Western clinic in town but it would cost thousands of *yuan*. My doctor works on barter. We give him eggs," Ha Suran explained.

Val only had another fifty dollars' worth of *yuan* to last the remainder of her stay and knew it would not be enough to pay for medical treatment, but she resolved to redouble her efforts to get her father's inheritance once she was back in Australia. He owed Ha Suran after what he had done to her.

Later that afternoon, a cousin came by who spoke a little English. He offered to take Val and Nicole for a ride around town in his open wagon, pulled by a donkey. It was bumpy in the back and they had to cling to the sides, but Nicole squealed in delight. This life of poverty was new and exciting for her.

"Ha Suran seems very ill," Val said to the cousin, whose name was Wang Suran.

"Yes, she is dying," he told her in a matter-of-fact tone.

She had said as much in her letter, but Val was still shocked. "Can't anything be done?"

He shook his head. "No, there is nothing. Our doctor will keep her comfortable until the end."

Val shivered in the afternoon heat. She couldn't accept it; she wouldn't.

They turned onto a busy tree-lined avenue whose buildings

had decorative facades and ornamental motifs. On one corner there was an enormous cathedral with grand frontal archways and multiple domes in green and gold.

"This is the Russian area," her cousin said. "It's called Daoli."

It looked Russian, not that Val was an expert. One shop advertised *stolle* and *piroshki*, both types of pies, and the cars were Ladas and Volgas. The architecture was grand; clearly the people who lived there had money.

The cousin turned his wagon into a side street and pulled on the reins to bring the donkey to a standstill.

"There!" He pointed through a wrought-iron gate toward a mansion set in extensive grounds. "That was your father's house."

Val peered in full of curiosity; she hadn't been expecting that. There were pillars alongside the entrance portico and tall, elegant windows over three floors. A curved driveway was flanked by carefully planted exotic flowers and shrubs, and a shiny racing-green sports car was parked outside.

"Good grief!" she exclaimed. He must have been one of the richest people in town. How had he come to marry her mother, who was one of the poorest? That seemed like an unequal match if ever there was one.

CHAPTER 31

MET HIM IN A PARK," HA SURAN SAID IN ANSWER TO Val's question. "He was sitting on a bench crying. That was in 1925, when I was just sixteen. He spoke only a few words of Chinese while I spoke next to no Russian, but my heart went out to him. I sat down and put my arm around him and he clung to me, sobbing with such misery as I had never heard."

"Why was he sobbing?" Val was mystified. She had never heard her father cry.

"At the time I supposed he was homesick, but later I wondered if he had been crying over that Russian woman, the one he was in love with. Isn't it strange the moments your fate turns upon? I could have walked straight past without stopping; I could have comforted him then hurried on my way; but instead I went home with him that night and became his housekeeper and concubine." She smiled at Val's expression. "You look shocked! I can't explain except to say that he moved me. From the moment I saw him, I wanted to take care of him."

Ha Suran seemed more animated than earlier. Her energy levels clearly fluctuated according to the rhythm of the illness inside her.

"Did he tell you anything about his background?"

"First I had to learn Russian," Ha Suran explained. "That took a while. But in the meantime I worked out a few things for myself. The house was always full of valuable paintings, icons, jewels, fox furs, silver samovars, and other precious items, which were there one day and gone the next. I realized he was selling luxury goods that had been stolen from the abandoned estates of Russian aristocrats. Hundreds of White Russians fled across the border into Manchuria during the civil war. Your father raided their houses then brought the goods to Harbin to sell back to them."

Val was astounded. It had crossed her mind that her father might have made his fortune by criminal means, but she hadn't truly believed it. "Did he ever get caught?" she asked.

Ha Suran nodded. "I know he was a wanted man. He fell foul of the regime in Russia somehow, and by the time I met him he couldn't go back there anymore. There was a sadness deep in his soul—and, fool that I was, I loved him for it."

Val was having trouble reconciling this lovestruck thief with the bullying father she had known. It was as if they were talking about different people.

There was silence between them for a while. Nicole had gone to market with Li Suran, and the only sound was the clucking of chickens in the yard and the buzzing of a persistent bluebottle.

"If he didn't love you, why did he take you to Australia with him?" Val asked.

"Maybe it was easier to get a visa if you were a married couple. Maybe he was lonely." Ha Suran shrugged. "We learned English together from a tutor he hired, who used to come to the house two evenings a week, then we got married in the Orthodox Church. It was all done in a rush, because he did not like the Chinese warlord Zhang Xueliang who took over

Manchuria in 1929. I think he wanted to tax your father's business interests. So he sold the house and car and packed up in a hurry."

"Why Australia? Why not America? Or somewhere in the Far East?"

Again Ha Suran wasn't sure. "I suppose it's the first country that accepted him. I know other Russians from Harbin traveled to Sydney, so it must have been straightforward to get visas."

"What a huge move for you both! And how heartbreaking to leave your family."

Ha Suran didn't sound bitter as she answered, only weary. "I went with my husband because he needed me, and I trusted he would always take care of me. But I was wrong."

~

Later, when Ha Suran was too exhausted to talk anymore, Val sat beside her and described her life in Sydney, trying to glue together past and present.

"Do you remember my schoolfriend Peggy?" she asked. "The one with the freckles?" Ha Suran gave a slight nod. "She's still my best friend today. She helped when I left Tony. In fact, she warned me not to marry him in the first place. I should make a mental note always to listen to Peggy's advice, because she is clearly a better judge of character than me."

She described her marriage, and Ha Suran surprised her by saying, "It sounds as though Tony is an unhappy man, like your father."

Val had never thought of Tony as unhappy, but she saw in a flash that he was. He was forever complaining that someone younger had been promoted over his head at the office, that the golf club had admitted new members who dressed too scruffily, or that their neighbors had a better car than him. His parents were constantly comparing him to his brothers, who according to them were much more successful. That feeling of not being good enough pervaded Tony's character and made him despise Val because she had been needy and desperate enough to marry him. All this came to her in a moment and she blinked in recognition.

She told Ha Suran about the furious rows since she left Tony and the way he had snatched her inheritance, then asked, "I don't suppose you know what Dad kept in his safe deposit box, do you?"

Ha Suran shook her head. "He would never have shared that kind of information with me."

Val remembered the photos that had been in her father's old camera. She'd brought them with her, in a pocket of the suitcase.

"Nicole, darling, could you bring me those old photos?" she asked. Nicole was helping Li Suran to stir dinner in the big cooking pot, but she ran to find the pictures.

Ha Suran flicked through the first four shots without comment.

"I know they're not very clear, but do you think these could be Dad's family?" Val asked.

Ha Suran shook her head. "He never told me anything about his family. I don't know if he had sisters, or who his parents were." She squinted at one shot where the faces were slightly clearer. "I can't see a resemblance."

And then she came to the three young men whose names were written on their pictures—Konstantin Ukraintsev, Peter Vasnetsov, and Ivan Skorokhodov—and stopped at the last one.

"Ivan Skorokhodov. That was your father's Russian name. He changed it by deed poll to Irwin Scott after we arrived in Sydney."

Val was stunned. "Really? Is that *him*?"

The picture was fuzzy, but the subject had dark hair and a slim figure, like her father. Ha Suran strained to lift herself on an elbow so she could hold it to the light filtering through the back door. "I'm not sure. I think your father had a uniform like this—I remember seeing it—but he looks different here. Younger maybe."

Val took the picture to the doorway and examined it in daylight. "It must be him. He wasn't bad-looking as a young man. I wonder if he was still living in Russia when this was taken?"

"He came from Sverdlovsk," Ha Suran said. "It used to be called Ekaterinburg. The town where the Romanovs were killed. He was obsessed with them." She lay down again and continued. "He said he passed the house where they were being held on his way to work in the morning and sometimes caught a glimpse of them in the yard. He used to worry about them because everyone knew they were living on borrowed time."

"Where did he work?"

"Some kind of factory. But the workers were conscripted into the Red Army after the Revolution. They had no choice."

Val tried to imagine her father back then, when he would have been in his late teens. What kind of person was he? What had made him so bitter? She described her visit to the nursing home and her father repeating "I didn't want to kill her" and "There was so much blood." "Do you think he might have been forced to kill some woman while he was in the army?" she asked.

Ha Suran shook her head straightaway. "Your father had many faults," she said, "but I can't imagine him killing a woman." She was quite adamant.

Val felt relief wash over her. It would have been awful to

be the daughter of a killer. At least that was one less thing to worry about.

~

During the mornings, while Ha Suran was resting, Val took Nicole to explore the town of Harbin. She loved the multi-cultural streets where European-style architecture gave way to glittering Chinese temples and extravagant Russian cathedrals. Nicole liked crossing the bridge over the Songhua River to Sun Island, where deer ran wild, tame squirrels ate nuts from the hands of visitors, and a colorful flower garden was planted according to the signs of the zodiac. The weather was humid, not as hot as Sydney in summer but perfect for exploring.

In the afternoon, Nicole played with Li Suran or helped her to prepare the main meal, while Val sat by Ha Suran's bedside. Evenings were spent eating dinner with any members of the extended family who dropped by, making conversation that was stilted because of the language barrier. The mats proved comfortable enough to sleep on, but Val found the hole-in-the-ground toilet and hosepipe shower more challenging.

The days flew past in a blur: one moment they had most of the three weeks in front of them, then somehow it was the final few days.

It was hard to contemplate leaving, but Val comforted herself that Ha Suran seemed better than when she had arrived. The sickly yellow of her skin and eyes was less intense; she could sit up for short periods, and talk for longer without getting tired. Val took photographs of everyone and showed Li Suran how to use the camera so she could take some of the three generations together: mother, daughter, and grand-daughter.

"I'll send you copies as soon as I get back," she promised.

On the last day, she felt like crying every time she looked at Ha Suran. She mourned for all the years they had lost. How different her life would have been if she'd had a mother when she was a teenager.

"Do you remember the song about the two tigers, Mom?" she asked, the memory coming back to her.

Ha Suran began to sing in a pure voice that made her seem twenty years younger, and suddenly Val felt as though she was Nicole's age again. Tears pricked her eyes. All the love Ha Suran had given her as a child was still there. She'd gotten her mom back.

When the song ended, Ha Suran clutched Val's hand. "I wish I could make you happy," she said. "All I ever wanted was for you to be happy, but I can tell you're not."

Val felt choked and couldn't speak for a few moments. "I'll get there," she said at last. "It's going to be a long haul, but I'll get there."

CHAPTER 32

Leningrad, March 1937

PETER'S OFF-DUTY HOURS WERE OFTEN CONSUMED BY MEET-
ings: Communist Party meetings, trade-union meetings,
and—worst of all—Komsomol meetings when workers were
invited to speak out against their coworkers and a commission
decided on their guilt or innocence.

"Grigory Yezhov was summoned today," he told Maria one
evening, after checking that none of the children were in
earshot. "If they can accuse him, none of us are safe."

"What is he accused of?" Maria knew the man and had
always thought him a drearily staunch Communist.

"Yuri Yermilov overheard him saying he doubts we can
achieve the targets in the new Five Year Plan. Now, he might
well have said that; we all know they are absurd. But it's hardly
treason, is it?" He looked gray and exhausted.

"What did the committee decide?"

"He got a reprimand." Peter rubbed his cheek with his
knuckle. "Do you think I should have spoken on his behalf?
I would have if I thought he faced jail."

"It's so petty," Maria sighed. "I don't like the Russian people anymore. This regime brings out the worst in everyone.

But I agree, it's better not to speak up or you could find yourself targeted next."

All over town, portraits of a moustachioed Stalin gazed down at them. His image hung on the outside of shops and factories, on the walls of every office, and in each school classroom. Children sang songs thanking him for the good life he had brought them, and ubiquitous loudspeakers around town blared out his praises, but Maria and Peter were alarmed by the mass arrests under his premiership.

At first it had been the neighbor in their block who tried to cross into Finland, then several factory colleagues disappeared after a purge of the Party in 1933. More recently there had been a purge of any remaining *kulaks*. There was never any warning. Maria arrived in the morning to find coworkers missing and no explanation offered. The woman who'd lost her hand in the conveyor belt disappeared; so did the man who had been angry with Maria for telling his wife where to find him.

The secret police, known as the NKVD, always came in the middle of the night, the brakes of their black vans screeching on the road outside, followed by a loud banging on the door. Maria lay awake listening as a couple on the first floor were arrested one night.

"We've done nothing wrong!" the woman was screaming as they were led away. "We love the Party. We love Stalin."

They must have done something, Maria persuaded herself. We just don't know what it was.

She still kept her card files of people who were looking for missing family members, but was wary when new folk approached her. Every apartment block and workplace had informers who would run to the NKVD at the slightest provocation. They might be jealous because you had a better apartment or a more pleasant job than them; perhaps they thought you had not been effusive enough when greeting them in the street. Maria did her best to be friendly with everyone, as had always been her way, but you never knew who were your true friends and who were secret enemies. As the Komsomol meetings proved, one could turn into the other in the blink of an eye.

~

Stepan turned eighteen in 1937 and left school to study at the Leningrad Institute of Foreign Languages. He chose English as one of his subjects and Maria was able to help him practice. It was the language she and her family had always spoken at home, and she was as fluent in it as she was in Russian. Peter did not speak a word of English, so sometimes they teased him.

"Look who has soup on his face," Maria said to Stepan in English over the dinner table.

He glanced at his father and chuckled to see a thin moustache of soup on his top lip.

"What is it? What are you looking at?" Peter asked, and pulled a comic face, making them laugh even harder.

Stepan was still a serious boy, but Maria's second-eldest, Irina, was a chatty, fun-loving girl who seemed immensely popular with her peers. She was forever meeting groups of friends to walk along Nevsky Prospekt, peering at the goods for sale in luxury shops, or to sit by the canals chatting. She did not yet have a boyfriend but seemed very interested in the opposite sex and acted with girlish coyness if one of Stepan's friends came to collect him on the way to the Institute.

Eleven-year-old Katya reminded Maria of herself. She was stuck between the elder two and the younger two and spent a lot of time on her own, until she struck up a friendship with

Raisa's daughter Galina, who was the same age. Maria was wary of Galina coming to their apartment, since she knew that every last detail of life in their household would be reported back to Raisa, and there was no question in her mind that Raisa was an NKVD informer. She was exactly the type they would target because she would love the self-importance.

Mikhail and Yelena were still young, aged nine and five respectively, and they were bonded at the hip, spending all their time outside school hours in each other's company, endlessly able to invent new games to amuse themselves. They had been the easiest to raise, Maria mused. Perhaps it was because she had become relaxed as a parent.

She often wondered what Pavel would have been like had he lived. His character would have been shaped by the suffering brought by his hemophilia, just as Alexei's had been. Her little brother had developed a stoicism that belied his young years. Maria knew that if she had been nursing Pavel, she would not have been able to work. In fact, she doubted she would have had any more children. Her life would have taken an entirely different path.

～

In the autumn of 1937, workmen arrived to redecorate the apartment block. Walls were to be replastered and painted, creaking floorboards nailed down, and the plumbing and electrics overhauled. At last they would have a bathtub with hot running water; no more staggering to the bathroom with a pot of water boiled on the stove.

Only one thing worried Maria: the workmen were to be allowed access to their apartment while they were at work. She didn't like the thought of strangers poking through her possessions, and she was particularly nervous that the bag of jewels she had sewn into her clothing and brought with her from Ekaterinburg might be discovered in its hiding place beneath the floorboards.

"Do you think we should move it?" she asked Peter.

He knelt to look under their bed and decided there was a chance the workmen might notice that one floorboard was looser than the rest and decide to fix it. "Where else could it go?" he asked, glancing around the room. There weren't many options.

"I am packing away the toys the children no longer play with. I could put the bag inside that wooden train you made for Stepan."

"Are you sure? Perhaps we should throw it in a canal. We have no use for it."

Maria instinctively felt she did not want to lose this last connection with her Romanov past. Things might change. Maybe she would be able to visit her aunt Olga in Copenhagen one day, selling a jewel to pay the fare. Maybe she would hear of Tatiana's whereabouts and need money to travel to her.

"I'll cover the toys with blankets and stack them in a box in the corner with all the other boxes," she suggested. "No one will dig down so far."

Peter chuckled. "I suppose you can't separate a grand duchess from her jewels."

The decorating works commenced and they came home each night to the smell of fresh paint and rooms that looked brand new. The gleaming walls made their curtains and rugs appear shabby in comparison, so Maria took them down and cleaned them, beating the rugs in the outdoor courtyard.

The day the hot tap was connected brought universal excitement, followed, a month later, by shock when they realized how much extra they would have to contribute to the communal electricity bill. A rota was drawn up, allocating set times in the bath to the occupants of each apartment and indicating what proportion of the bill each household would pay.

One October morning, Maria was hanging out laundry in the yard while Yelena and Mikhail played hopscotch. She saw Raisa on the staircase and called a greeting. "The weather's still mild so I hope the washing will dry quickly."

"Just another week till the cold weather," Raisa predicted. "I can feel it in my knees." She looked over her shoulder to check if anyone was listening. "Will you ask Peter to have a word with that young man at number eight? He takes such long baths in the evening that we fall asleep before it's our turn."

"Why not get *your* husband to talk to him?" Maria replied. "Peter is always so tired when he gets home, I don't like to ask him to do anything extra."

"My husband is also tired." Raisa sniffed, an edge to her voice. Her husband had not made the grade as a shock worker and it clearly irked her.

"Yes, of course," Maria agreed. "Perhaps I will talk to him myself. Maybe he does not understand the rota."

Raisa came out to the yard to stand near Maria and lowered her voice to speak in a whisper. "You know his brother was arrested last month. I'm not sure we should be consorting with him. I hope he will lose his apartment before long."

Maria bit her tongue. It was hateful that relatives of those who had been arrested were instantly under suspicion, but that was the way the regime worked. "I'm sure justice will prevail, as it always does," she said. "Meanwhile I'll talk to him about the bath rota."

She picked up her laundry basket and climbed the stairs to the third floor, feeling exhausted. Raisa had that effect on her. As she opened the door, she heard the voices of Katya and Galina inside.

"Hello, Galina," she said. "What are you two playing at?" They were sitting on the floor with something glittering between them.

"Look what we found!" Katya cried. "These were in Stepan's old steam engine. Aren't they pretty?"

Maria's shock must have shown on her face. Her heart started thumping violently, the blood rushed from her head, and she couldn't speak at first. It was as if time stood still while she struggled to compose her features.

"These old rocks!" she exclaimed at last, trying to sound offhand. "I haven't seen them in years. Your father and I found them when we were hiking in the Urals, long before you were born."

She bent and started putting them back in the cloth bag, her hand shaking. There were flawless diamonds, bloodred rubies, dazzling sapphires, and creamy pearls, their colors glowing against the slate gray of the rug.

"Can I have them, Mama?" Katya begged. "If you and Papa don't want them."

"We'll ask him later," Maria said, to buy time. "But for now, please would you girls go down to the yard and keep an eye on the little ones?"

She swept the rest of the jewels into the bag and slipped it in her pocket, not daring to look at Galina, scared of what she might see in her face. Did the girl know that this was enough to identify them as *kulaks*? That their entire family could end up in a gulag?

Katya got to her feet and stretched out a hand to pull her friend up. She was an obedient daughter, a sweet girl. "Can we have something to eat?" she asked, so Maria fetched her tin of homemade *lepeshki* cookies and gave them one each.

When the girls left, she sat down hard in a chair, her chest tight with fear. She prayed Peter would come home on time.

He would know what to do. Please God, don't let him get held up.

~

Maria listened for Peter's footsteps on the stairs, and as soon as she heard them, she rushed out to intercept him. The bathroom was occupied so she led him into the cramped toilet and closed the door, locking it with the hook before telling him what had happened.

"If Galina tells Raisa, she will go to the NKVD. There's nothing surer."

He exhaled a long, slow breath, but didn't say anything at first.

"Maybe we should throw the jewels in a canal tonight," Maria said. "If only I'd listened when you suggested it before."

"Where are they now?" he asked.

"Here." Maria showed him. "In my pocket."

"Give them to me." He held out his hand. "I'll dispose of them. Start dinner without me."

Maria put her arms around him and pressed her body against his, resting her head on his shoulder, breathing in his scent. It was going to be all right.

She opened the toilet door and stepped into the corridor only to see Raisa waiting for her, Galina's hand in hers and an accusing expression on her face.

"Why would two factory workers have a bag of glittering jewels?" Raisa began. "That's the question I've been asking myself, but I can't think of an answer. Perhaps you will enlighten me."

Peter was calm. "Glittering jewels?" He smiled. "Wouldn't that be wonderful! We would not have to worry about electricity bills then, would we? No, I'm afraid there are no jewels—just some old rock samples I picked up in the mountains many years ago. How is your husband, Mrs. Krupicha? I hope he is prospering at the paper mill?"

Raisa was not going to be fobbed off so easily. "What were you two doing in the toilet?" she asked.

Maria spoke. "I was asking Peter to speak to the man in number eight about the length of his baths, just as you requested. He is on his way now. Aren't you, darling?"

Peter took a step toward the stairs. "I'll see what I can do."

Raisa lifted a hand to stop him.

"What about these rocks? Can I see them for myself? Galina was convinced they were jewels, weren't you?" She yanked her daughter's arm.

The girl looked nervous and did not reply.

"Why don't I go to number eight first, then bring them to your apartment later?" Peter suggested, his tone reasonable. "After supper. I don't know about you, but I am ravenous."

"I am here on your floor already," Raisa insisted. "Why not show me now? It will only take two minutes and will save you a journey later." She folded her arms, clearly not about to budge.

Maria felt a tight band constrict her chest. Her brain felt so fuzzy she couldn't think.

"Where did you put them, darling?" Peter asked her, heading to their apartment door. "Are they in the usual place?"

She nodded, unable to speak, sick with fear.

Peter walked to the door and went inside, pushing it closed behind him. Raisa and Maria stood in awkward silence till he emerged again, holding a few of the less remarkable gems in the palm of his hand.

"You see? They are worthless."

The light in the corridor was dim, but still it sparkled on the facets of the stones. Maria held her breath.

"There were more than that," Galina whispered, not addressing the observation to anyone in particular.

"Only a few more," Peter said. "They're all the same." He closed his fingers over the gems. "Now, I'll just go and see the man in number eight."

Raisa put a hand on his arm. "Could I take a couple? I'd like to show my husband."

Peter frowned. "I'm sure he wouldn't be interested."

"All the same." She would not release his arm and held out her other hand, palm upward, waiting.

There was nothing Peter could do without turning it into an argument. He took a couple of the gems and placed them in Raisa's hand. "Don't bother to return them," he said. "Perhaps Galina would like to play with them." He walked down the corridor and turned onto the stairs. "I'll be back soon," he called to Maria over his shoulder, as if he was going for a relaxing stroll.

~

Peter threw most of the jewels into the canal that evening, keeping just the few he had shown Raisa. In bed, he whispered to Maria, "If the police come, say they are mine. As a shock worker I am more likely to be pardoned. We don't want them investigating your past."

"Raisa might not say anything. I hope you convinced her." Maria's voice wobbled.

"If I am arrested, go to my bosses at the factory, and to the Party heads. I think they will speak for me." He sounded uncertain.

"It won't happen. You are too valuable." She could hardly get the words out, her throat was so twisted with anxiety.

Peter always slept well no matter what was going on, but

Maria stayed awake long into the night, listening to his steady breathing, and tensing each time a car passed in the street outside. As dawn began to break, she let herself slide into a light slumber, and that was when it came: a loud banging on the door of their apartment, wooden truncheons hammering on the frame.

"Open the door," a man's voice shouted. "NKVD."

CHAPTER 33

Leningrad, October 1937

Don't answer!" Maria cried. She reached for her husband, but he was already out of bed and pulling on his trousers.

"Pack a small bag," he said. "They might take me for questioning."

"No, don't go with them. Please don't." She had heard that some people who got into the dreaded black vans were never seen again.

He started buttoning his shirt, so she leaped up and clasped her arms around him. Her head was pounding. Please let this not be happening. Please.

The hammering at the door was getting more insistent. Stepan called from the other room. "Shall I answer it, Papa?"

"Maria, please. The bag." Peter gave her a quick kiss, then disengaged himself and bent to pull on his socks and boots.

She busied herself putting a spare shirt and some socks into a brown leather bag. She added his toothbrush, then a tin of *lepeshki* biscuits. Her brain wasn't working properly. How long might he be gone? What else might he need?

She heard Peter open the door and the sound of men's voices: harsh, unfriendly. Peter's tone was measured and polite.

He fetched the cloth bag with the remaining gemstones—of course, that was what they had come about—and took it to them.

"We must search your rooms," barked a thin-faced man in a blue officer's cap. "All the family come here. Stand together."

They huddled in their nightclothes, Maria and Peter in front, the little ones behind, yawning and rubbing their eyes. There were four men. One stood guard while the others searched a room each. Maria heard the crash of her pots being thrown to the floor, drawers being yanked out, mattresses turned over, her card index scattered. They wouldn't find anything else incriminating, she was sure of that, but it felt like a violation that they could see her most personal possessions: her undergarments, the sheets on her bed. She kept her eyes fixed on the ground, gripping Peter's arm and Yelena's hand, sick with fear.

"You must come with us," the officer said to Peter once they had finished. "We have a warrant for your arrest." He pulled a sheet of paper from his jacket pocket.

Peter glanced at it and agreed. "Of course I will."

"No!" Maria screamed, and clung to his arm. "Don't take him. He is a good man. We need him."

Peter turned to Stepan. "Take care of your mother," he said. "You know what to do."

Maria saw Stepan nod and bow his head, grim-faced.

As the officers led Peter away, she had a horrible premonition of disaster and tried to run after him, to drag him back, but Stepan wrapped his arms tightly around her. He was taller than her and much stronger.

"Let me go. Please," she begged, struggling. "They might hurt him." But it was only when they heard the street door slam that Stepan relaxed his grip. Instantly, Maria sprang out of their apartment, still in her nightgown, and hurtled down the stairs, two at a time. She yanked the street door open in time to see the black windowless van roll off.

"No!" she screamed. "Come back!" She started running, barefoot, trying to catch up with it, and got halfway to the main road before Stepan stopped her.

"Come home, Mama," he said gently, and she turned her face to his shoulder and cried, with great racking sobs that shook her entire body.

~

"What did your father mean: that you know what to do?" she asked, once she was seated back in the apartment with a cup of sweet tea. Stepan had draped a blanket around her shoulders because she was shivering and her teeth were chattering. Irina had begun to pick up the belongings that were scattered across the floor and was folding clothes into piles.

He spoke in an even tone, with only a crackle of emotion. "I will make inquiries this morning about where he is being questioned and whether we can present character witnesses. There are many who will speak for him."

Maria was astonished that he could be so calm. "When did you two discuss this?"

"A long time ago," Stepan said. "Papa thought it was inevitable that he would be arrested sometime, because he has a job that brings him into contact with foreigners." He frowned. "What were those stones? Were they really gems?"

Maria shook her head. She couldn't tell him. "We found them in the Ural Mountains, back in 1920. We shouldn't have kept them. It was foolish."

Stepan sucked his teeth. "What's done is done. You must go to work today as if nothing has happened. I will come to the canteen at lunchtime to tell you what I've found out."

The idea of going to work seemed preposterous, but Maria couldn't face staying at home either. The hours would drag. She cut slices of bread for breakfast, careful not to step on the broken plates that littered her floor, and got the younger children ready for school. In answer to their worried questions she told them that their papa had gone for a meeting but would be home soon. As they walked past Raisa's door, she wanted to burst in and scream at her, but restrained herself. She couldn't risk being arrested too.

It was near impossible to work, but she dragged herself around her section at the factory, oiling gears and wiping surfaces clean, her heart pounding as she listened to the radio broadcasts about agriculture targets and the opening of some new canal.

When Stepan came to the canteen at lunchtime, they sat at a corner table and Maria clutched his sleeve as he spoke.

"He's being questioned at Bolshoi Dom," he told her. "I have already spoken to our Party leader and he will go today to testify on his behalf. Could you speak to the factory boss?"

Maria nodded. "I know he'll help."

"I'll ask the children's teachers and the Young Pioneers leaders. The NKVD will soon learn he is one of the most respected men in Leningrad."

Maria felt slight reassurance at this, but only slight. When she got home that evening, Irina and Stepan had finished tidying the apartment but it felt different now. Peter's absence was all around: the empty chair where he normally sat; the rumpled cover on his side of the bed. She tried not to think about what might be happening to him. You heard rumors of torture and beatings, but surely they wouldn't dare with someone as well-thought-of as Peter?

She heard a whimpering noise from one of the bedrooms, as if a wounded animal were sheltering there. She pulled back the covers and found Katya huddled under her bedclothes, shaking with grief. Her daughter's face was swollen and red with crying. "It's my fault Papa has been arrested, isn't it? I showed Galina the stones."

Maria pulled her close, stroking her hair.

"You are a child," she said, "and it was natural you would want to play with them. It is my fault for keeping them. I was being sentimental. Oh God!" She shook her head. "If only I could turn back the clock."

That night she prayed in a way she had not prayed in years. She prayed for all the people she had lost in her life: her family, her baby son, Pavel, and then she prayed hardest of all for Peter. The bed was cold and it was the first night in nineteen years that she was not able to mold her body around him and let his heat warm her. She lay awake till the early hours wondering what kind of bed he was sleeping in. Should she have put a blanket in his bag? A sweater? More food? It felt as though a large oval rock had lodged in her gullet, just behind the ribs. She knew she would never forgive herself if they harmed so much as a hair on his precious head. It would be all her fault.

~

By the end of the following day, Stepan reported that half a dozen friends had been to Bolshoi Dom to testify on Peter's behalf. Maria felt the tension ease a little, but his next words brought her spirits crashing down again.

"The Party leader thinks he will have to plead guilty to some charge. He did have the stones, after all."

"But they were mine!" Maria insisted. "It's not his fault. I wanted to keep them."

Stepan shushed her, looking over his shoulder to check the

others weren't listening. "You mustn't say that. Ever. It would only make things worse." He paused. "Mama, this is going to be hard for you to hear, but we must—all of us—make statements saying that we should have noticed Papa's errant behavior and reported it to the authorities. We must apologize for our lack of vigilance."

Maria was adamant. "Absolutely not! I will not betray him by playing their evil games."

"Papa told me you would say that. We discussed it at length." His eyes didn't leave her face. "It was his wish that if he was arrested, we should all admit to lack of vigilance. It is the only way to stay out of jail ourselves and have a chance of a normal life. Otherwise I will be thrown out of the Institute, we could lose this apartment, and my brother and sisters will never be accepted into further education. Besides, you could be arrested too, and the little ones need at least one of their parents."

Maria shook her head. "I will only do it if Peter asks me himself. I must speak with him. Will they let me visit?"

Stepan sighed, clearly accepting that it would take some effort to persuade her. "I will ask tomorrow. I plan to make my own statement then."

Maria turned away. It wounded her to the core that Stepan would speak against his father, even though she knew it made sense. "If he pleads guilty to some charge, what will happen? Will they let him come home again?"

Stepan didn't speak for a long time, and she couldn't bear to look at his face, fearful of what she might see there. "I don't know," he said at last.

~

After three days without any further news, Maria couldn't bear the suspense any longer. She urged Stepan to let her accompany him to Bolshoi Dom, which was on Liteyny Prospekt. If she was there, on the spot, perhaps they would let her see Peter for a few minutes. She needed to know he hadn't been hurt.

They sat in silence on the tram, arms linked. As they alighted, Stepan said, "Please let me do the talking. I know how to handle this."

"I need to see him," Maria insisted. "Be sure to tell them that."

She paused and gazed up at the modern, pale beige stone building. There were nine stories. Which one was Peter on? Would he sense her presence? Or look out a window and spot her? She couldn't see any faces because light was blinking off the glass.

They walked into a marble entrance hallway and followed directions to the inquiries desk. A silent line stretched all the way back to the lobby. Maria and Stepan waited arm in arm for almost an hour before they reached the desk, where a man with a scowling face was on duty behind a sliding glass partition.

Stepan showed his Party card and asked if it was possible to visit his father, who was being held there.

The officer flicked through a list on the desk in front of him, his expression cold. He found Peter's name, nodded, and opened a drawer. "Fill out this form." He handed it over. "Return tomorrow with the relevant sections completed and we will see."

"If we fill it in now, can we see him today? I'm begging you," Maria asked, clasping her hands together.

He gave her a long stare. "Is this your mother?" he asked Stepan.

"Yes, I—"

"Take her away and tell her to keep her mouth shut in future."

Clutching the form, Stepan led her by the elbow toward the door. Maria stopped at the entrance. Somewhere in that building, Peter was breathing, thinking, his heart beating, and she hoped he could sense she was close by and thinking of him.

They returned the next evening with the form filled out and signed in the correct places, but when they reached the front of the line, the same officer took it and threw it into a filing tray. "Your application will be considered," he said.

Maria had brought a blanket and some fresh clothes for Peter, wrapped up in brown paper and string. "Please, sir, would it be possible to give these to him?" she begged. "He didn't bring warm clothes with him and the nights are drawing in."

"Parcels get handed in over there." He gestured toward an unmanned desk across the room, which had a pile of packages stacked behind it.

"It has his name on it." She showed him. "There. On the top. Will he get it this evening?"

"In due course," he said. "Next!"

"No, please. I am begging you to get my parcel to him tonight. Can you do that?" She had written a note saying that they loved and missed him. It was more important he receive that than anything else.

The man glared at Stepan. "Can you control your mother? Get her out of here."

Maria was bitterly disappointed. She had counted on visiting Peter that evening and giving him the blanket and clothes in person. She hadn't been sure if she would be allowed to hug him, but just to see him and talk to him would have been enough. As soon as they left the building, she began to cry.

"Why are they still holding him? When can I have him

back? Stepan, you don't understand. He's the strong one of the two of us. I can't carry on without him." She clung to her big son and he held her close.

"I'll look after you, Mama," he said, but that only made her cry harder.

CHAPTER 34

A WEEK AFTER PETER'S ARREST, WHEN NOTHING seemed to be helping to get him released, Maria went to visit Annushka, the woman whose brother she had found. Annushka's husband worked for the NKVD. It was a long shot, but perhaps he would help.

When Annushka heard that Peter had been arrested, she was reluctant to invite Maria inside her apartment. She looked terrified, peering along the corridor in case anyone was watching. "I'm sorry for your trouble, but I don't want my husband to find out I know someone who is under suspicion."

"I was hoping I could talk to him for two minutes. Ask his advice. See if there's anything he can do. Please, I'm begging you." Tears were not far away, but she held them back. "Is he due home soon? I don't need to come inside. Please put yourself in my position."

Annushka hesitated, then pulled the door wide. "Of course you must come in and wait. You did so much for me. Please, be my guest."

They sat on a gray wool sofa and Annushka offered tea, which Maria refused. She barely ate or drank these days because the tightness in her chest made it impossible to swallow.

Besides, it wasn't fair that she should eat when Peter might be surviving on prison slops. It didn't bear thinking about. In her positive moments, she planned that she would cook his favorite dishes and make a fuss of him once he was home again. She would make love to him, so tenderly, worshipping every bit of the body she knew as well as her own. In her worst moments, she pictured him being transported to a gulag, forced to haul timber and dig trenches in the bitter cold. She didn't know how she would stand that.

The door opened and Annushka's husband came in, hanging his coat on the rack and looking across with a question in his expression. He was an exceedingly tall, very thin man, and as he came closer, Maria saw that he had a dramatic scar zigzagging down one cheek.

"This is Maria, the woman who found my brother. Remember I told you about her?" Annushka's voice trembled as she spoke. She seemed nervous of him. "Maria, this is my husband, Yuri."

He nodded curtly and said, "Good evening."

Annushka continued. "Maria's husband has found himself in trouble with the NKVD and she begged me to let her ask your advice."

He glowered at her, but came to stand in front of Maria, just a couple of steps away. "Tell me what he is accused of," he ordered.

She told the story about finding the rocks in the mountains and keeping them without thinking any more of it. "They were a souvenir of a happy time. We had just gotten married and were enjoying a hiking holiday. When we moved to Leningrad, they got lost among our possessions and, to be honest, I'd completely forgotten they were there."

"And they are real jewels?" he asked.

She nodded. "It seems so. We had no idea."

"It is hard to believe you did not realize." His tone was not particularly friendly. "I imagine that's what your husband's interrogators are saying."

She clasped her hands, pleading with him. "We are simple people. Neither of us knows anything of jewels."

"And yet you are articulate. You are not a stupid woman."

Maria changed tack. "My husband is a valued shock worker at a pig-iron factory. We have five children who have been brought up loyal Communists. We do good in our community; my husband is always willing to help neighbors mend burst pipes or unblock drains, while I help to find missing relatives, as I did for your wife. What value can it possibly have for my children to lose their father, the factory to lose its worker, and me to lose my husband? I'm begging you—if there is anything you can suggest, I would be forever in your debt." She spoke with passion and determination. This had to work. She couldn't think of anything else.

He appraised her for a while before speaking. "I can see you truly love him. Let me make inquiries. I'll get Annushka to tell you if I have any success."

Tears sprang to Maria's eyes. "Thank you." She bowed her head. "I can't tell you how much that means."

~

Maria allowed herself to feel a shred of hope after the meeting, but a week later, when she spotted Annushka in the bread line, there was no news.

"He hasn't mentioned it," Annushka said. "I'm sorry."

"Will you ask tonight? Please?" Maria begged.

Annushka promised she would, but the following day she said she had not dared to bother him. "He was in a terrible mood," she apologized. "I'll see if he is more amenable tonight."

Maria thought she should at least have asked the question, mood or no mood, but did not say so. Two weeks had passed since Peter was taken away, and it was getting harder to bear with every second that passed. She missed his touch, his smell, the sound of his voice, the space he occupied in a room. She would never feel safe until he was back. Never.

"Let's go to Bolshoi Dom one more time," she pleaded with Stepan.

"Mama, it's not a good idea." He patted her shoulder. "These things take time."

"If you won't come with me, I will go alone," she insisted. Outside the window an early flurry of snow glowed in the light of the street lamps. She pulled on her coat, saying, "Irina, watch the little ones, please."

"Hang on. I'm coming," Stepan agreed wearily. "But let me do the talking. That officer responds better to men. Your persistence irritates him."

The snow was not sticking. The ground in October was too warm from daytime sun. When Peter came back, Maria guessed he would begin sealing the edges of windows and doors so they did not let in drafts during the coldest months.

At Bolshoi Dom there was no line because it was late in the day, but the same unhelpful officer sat behind the inquiries desk. He was expressionless as they approached but slid back the glass partition so they could talk.

Stepan gave his father's name, although the man must surely remember them by now. He picked up his typed list and scanned slowly until he found it. His finger moved across the line, then he looked at them both with a strange expression. Could it be triumph? Satisfaction?

"Prisoner number 5204 has been tried, found guilty, and sentenced to death," he said with a crooked half-smile.

"No!" Maria screamed. It was as if the air had been punched

from her body. "Peter!" Her voice echoed around the high-ceilinged room, bouncing off walls.

"I think you have the wrong person," Stepan said, a tremor in his voice. "Can I see your list?"

The officer handed it over. Stepan checked and double-checked it, then turned to Maria with horror on his face. "It says the sentence was carried out yesterday."

Maria's legs gave way beneath her. The pain was so appalling that she began clawing at her eyes, her face, her neck, drawing blood. "No-o-o!"

"Mama, your face. Stop it!" Stepan pulled at her hands.

But she couldn't stop. She wanted to dig her nails deep into her flesh and carry on gouging holes until she was dead too. That way she wouldn't have to live with this.

Stepan tried to pull her to her feet, but her legs wouldn't take her weight. The officer was grinning now—actually grinning—and she wanted to kill him, but she couldn't get up.

Stepan hoisted her in his arms and carried her toward the door.

"I can't leave without Peter," she cried, trying to struggle free. "We need to take him with us." She would wash his body so tenderly, put the coins on his eyes, lie with him one last time.

"Let's get you home. I'll come for him tomorrow."

Maria began to cry. "But he's on his own. He might be cold. Please . . ."

"Tomorrow. I'll do it first thing tomorrow," Stepan promised.

They were out on the street now and the air was icy with frost, shocking Maria into silence. This couldn't be happening. It couldn't be true. She couldn't carry on living in a world without Peter.

Stepan carried her all the way to the tram stop, just as his father had carried her through the forest back in 1918.

CHAPTER 35

Sydney, September 1974

I T WAS DAUNTING TO ARRIVE BACK IN SYDNEY WITHOUT
a home or a job to go to. Val and Nicole moved into Peggy's
spare room and Val made finding a job her first priority since
her money was all but gone.

"There's work going as a telephone operator at the uni,"
Peggy's friend Sandra told her. "I noticed an ad on the noticeboard when I was waiting for my archeology class last night
and wrote down the number for you." She pulled out a scrap
of paper, and checked before handing it over. "Yeah, that's the
one. My bag's so full of junk, I'm always amazed I can find
anything." She held it open to let them see a jumble of hair-
brush, wallet, makeup, checkbook, pens, and umpteen torn
packs of Juicy Fruit gum.

Val called immediately on Peggy's phone and arranged an
interview the following morning. "I don't have any experience,"
she confessed to Peggy. "I hope I can wing it."

"You need a good speaking voice and a few grains of common sense. You should slip under the wire." Peggy smiled.

Her friend Lynette was also invaluable, providing the number of a woman lawyer who specialized in marital law. Val
tucked it in her wallet. She was determined to find a way of

accessing her inheritance as soon as possible so she could send money to Harbin to pay for her mother's care. If only she could get her to a Western hospital, they might be able to save her.

There was a lot to do, a whole life to reconstruct, but she felt energized by her trip. Even if she had not found answers to all her questions about her father, being reunited with her mother had brought a profound sense of comfort. She felt proud of herself for getting there and back, and knowing how much her mother loved her had boosted her belief in herself. She had returned to friends who were doing their best to help, she had a roof over her head, and Nicole loved staying at Lenny's house because it meant playtime started as soon as she opened her eyes in the morning.

The Saturday after Val's return was unseasonably warm, with temperatures in the low seventies, and Peggy's husband announced he would do the first cookout of the season. He and Peggy invited half a dozen other couples on a potluck basis, where everyone brought a dish and you hoped you didn't end up with ten bowls of potato salad. Val made deviled eggs, with paprika and mustard mixed into the yolks, and wrapped strips of salty bacon around some dates she had wrestled the pits out of.

At six in the evening all the guests were there, beer in one hand and plate of food in the other, children screeching in the sandbox, when there was a loud blaring outside. Someone was pressing their car horn insistently, the sound cutting through the air, stopping everyone midconversation.

Val peered toward the source of the noise and her blood froze. It was Tony's car. He was leaning out the driver's window.

"Where's my slut of a wife?" he yelled. "Watch your wallets, folks. She stole my bloody money and she'll steal yours too if you give her a chance."

Ken walked across the lawn to remonstrate with him, but

Val hesitated. She knew she should go too—he was her husband, after all—but it was as if her legs wouldn't carry her. She was terrified of what he might do. Peggy put a supportive arm around her shoulders. Nicole was playing with the other children, oblivious to the drama.

The sound of the car horn stopped as Tony got out and strode across the lawn to argue with Ken face-to-face. Val couldn't hear the words, but she could see his fists clenched by his sides and knew he was close to losing his temper.

"He might get violent," she warned, and two of the other men put down their beers and hurried over.

Suddenly Tony swung a punch. Ken swayed to avoid it, and the other men grabbed Tony's arms, shouting at him. "What you doing, mate?" Tony struggled to free himself, but they overpowered him easily and marched him to his car, wrestling him inside.

"Don't come back," Val heard one of them yell as he slammed the door.

Tony drove off, waving an emphatic middle finger out the window.

"I'm so sorry," Val apologized to the men when they returned to the party.

"No worries. Bloke's a wanker," one of them said. "You're well out of that."

The barbecue resumed but Val felt uneasy. Now Tony knew she was back, he would be hunting for her. He would never let her get away with stealing from him. No doubt he would have gone to the police and pressed charges if he could.

Let him try, she thought. Let's see how sympathetic the judge is when he hears he isn't paying a cent in child support.

The following afternoon, a brick crashed through Peggy and Ken's sitting-room window, landing just a few feet from where the children were coloring with crayons. By the time

Ken rushed outside, all he could see was a car disappearing around the bend, but he was pretty sure it was the same make and color as Tony's.

As Val and Peggy cleared up the broken glass, Val promised, "I'll get out of here as soon as I possibly can."

Peggy gave her a sympathetic smile, but Val noted that she didn't say "No, stay as long as you like!" Everyone had their limits.

~

Arrangements slid into place over the next week, as if the gods were smiling on Val—for a change, she thought. First she was awarded the job of telephone operator, then the university agreed to give her an advance on her salary to pay the deposit on a flat. She found a tiny apartment in Camperdown, even smaller than the one in Balmain but with an affordable rent. Yet again, she and Nicole would share a bedroom, and the shower was in what amounted to a walk-in closet, but the place had been recently repainted, its floorboards newly stripped and varnished. It was miles more comfortable than her mother's home in Harbin. What was more, there was a primary school down the road from the university, so Val could drop Nicole there on her way to work. After lessons finished, she could play in the university day care for a couple of hours until Val's shift was over, then they could spend their evenings together. It was worlds better than the late-night cleaning job. She wished she could phone her mom in Harbin to tell her; instead she wrote a long letter describing their new life. She hoped Ha Suran would be proud.

When Val took Nicole for her first morning at yet another new school and left her in the care of yet another teacher, she felt a pang of guilt at the way her daughter's life had been disrupted. She was only six, but this was her third school, her third home, in less than a year. Val remembered the intense loneliness she herself had felt when her father made her move at the age of thirteen, and the struggle to make new friends when playground alliances had already been cemented. She hoped Nicole would not have the same trouble, and watched carefully for any signs of anxiety. But after her first day at the new school Nicole asked if someone called Amy could come and play on the weekend, and by the end of the week she was engulfed by a group of girls with white knee-socks and neat hair ribbons as soon as Val led her into the playground.

There wasn't much storage space in the new flat, so many of their possessions had to be left in cardboard boxes stacked in the corner, to be dug out when needed. It was several weeks after moving in when Val came across the old photographs still tucked in a pocket of the suitcase she was using to store winter clothes. She pulled them out to have another look at the ghostly black-and-white images: the girls in their ethereal white dresses, and the one of her father as a young man. Ivan Skorokhodov; the name suited him better than Irwin Scott. He had been Russian to his fingertips.

During her lunch hour the following day, Val went to the university library and found the Russian history section, thinking that she might read about the Revolution and civil war that had forced her father to leave his homeland. She collected a stack of books and sat down to flick through them and decide which was most enticing. There were black-and-white photographs of the Romanov family in one, and she glanced at them, then stopped and flicked through the following pages: four girls and a boy, just as there appeared to be in her father's photographs. What was more, the girls all wore white dresses.

It had to be coincidence. All the same, she checked the book out of the library and took it home.

Holding her photographs against the book, Val realized with creeping amazement that they showed the Romanov family. The first girl she could identify for sure was Tatiana; she had a pixie face with a pronounced bone structure, matching that in one of the images exactly. Maria's face was rounder and prettier, just like the girl in a soft, grainy shot. Alexei had a gaunt face and looked very frail. It appeared they had been photographed in the last house where they were held prisoner, the Ipatiev House: there was the high fence surrounding the yard. But how did her father come to have these pictures? And why was there one of him among them?

Ha Suran said he had been a factory worker. Val assumed cameras were expensive in 1918, and wondered how he could afford one. But after the Revolution, he had made his fortune selling the goods of aristocratic Russians who had fled from the Bolsheviks. She guessed he must have stolen this camera from the Romanovs and then taken photographs of himself and two of his friends on the same film. Why did he never process them? Did he forget they were there?

She looked once more at the images of these people who posed for the camera little suspecting that they were soon to be killed in that very house. Then again, given their haunted expressions, she wondered if perhaps they had an inkling.

She checked in her book but it didn't show any images of the family in the Ipatiev House, where they had spent their final three months. It came to her with a shock that these might even be the last photographs of them alive.

CHAPTER 36

Sydney, October 1974

VAL'S KNOWLEDGE OF THE ROMANOVS WAS SKETCHY, SO SHE borrowed more books from the library and began to read about them. She was surprised to hear that although it was generally assumed they had all been executed, the Bolshevik government had only ever admitted killing Tsar Nicholas, claiming that the others had been moved to a place of safety. Could they still be alive? Alexandra would have been a hundred and two years old, so that seemed unlikely, but the children would be in their seventies. A White Army investigator by the name of Nikolai Sokolov had found some fragments in a forest near Ekaterinburg that he believed showed they were all killed: spectacles, a shoe buckle, a finger, the bones of a small dog. He theorized that their bodies had been dissolved in sulfuric acid and that explained why their remains had never been found. It was a grotesque thought.

Once she felt sure of the basics, Val went to the university's Russian department and showed the photos to one of the lecturers, a tall man called Bill Koskov. He was about her own age, with unruly brown hair, and arms and legs that seemed too long for his body. She told him her theory and he looked thoughtful as he pored over the photographs.

"You might be right," he said. "I know a New York historian who has written about the family, so with your permission I'll fax him. No doubt he'll want to see the pictures, so we should get another set of prints made."

"Which historian?" Val asked, and was thrilled to hear it was a professor whose book she had read. She was even more thrilled the next day when Bill stopped at reception to say the professor wanted to speak to her himself. He was going to ring around twelve noon.

When the call came through, Val described the circumstances of her finding the camera and added, "I read in your book that in the days after the Romanovs were taken from the Ipatiev House, local people wandered in and helped themselves to souvenirs. I wondered if that was how my father got the camera."

"He must have been an early visitor," the professor said. "I'm sure it would have been one of the first items to go."

That evening, she described the conversation to Peggy and her friends. "He spoke to me as if I was a fellow academic. Imagine if he found out that I never even got my high-school diploma!"

"Why don't you do a night-school degree?" Sandra asked. "They accepted me for the archeology class so they can't be fussy about qualifications. It's different when you're what they insultingly call a 'mature student.'"

As soon as the idea was put to her, Val decided to apply. They might not accept her, but if they did, she would prove herself by working harder than any other student. It felt incredible that she might have a chance to use her brain for the first time since school days. She might not be capable of a degree, but there was only one way to find out.

She was bursting to tell her mom about her decision, and wrote as soon as she got home. *I can feel a whole new direction stretching in front of me*, she wrote, *and it's exciting but daunting at the same time. I wish you lived in Sydney. It would be great to share all this with you.*

As yet, there had been no reply to her letters, but she wasn't concerned because she knew the mail from China was very slow.

And then, a few days later, she found a letter with a Chinese postmark in her mailbox. The writing on the outside of the envelope was not in her mother's hand, and when Val opened it, she saw that the letter inside was written in Chinese characters. She turned it over but could not even make out the signature at the end. What did it mean?

In her lunch hour, she took the letter to the Department of Chinese Studies at the university and asked a lecturer to translate. His face grew concerned as he read, and he covered his mouth with his hand.

Once he reached the foot of the page, he said, "I'm terribly sorry. It says your mother has died. Her aunt Li Suran writes that the end was peaceful and that her last words were how happy she was to see you again."

The news hit Val like a body blow. The inheritance money would be too late. Her mom was gone. It was too cruel to find her and then lose her again.

"Thank you," she whispered. She took the letter, then turned and walked downstairs to her post at the telephone exchange, feeling an immense heaviness weighing on her. Although she had been warned that her mom's illness was terminal, she had never accepted it. In her head she'd had visions of them all being together again.

That evening, she explained to Nicole that her grandma had gone to be with the angels.

"It's just as well we visited China," Nicole said in a practical tone, "because now we will recognize each other when we go to the angels too."

~

Over the summer months, Val's new attorney tried repeatedly to get Tony to agree to a legal separation and a financial settlement, but he refused point-blank. He didn't even get a lawyer of his own, but sent back all her letters with obscenities scrawled on them.

"Don't worry," the attorney told Val. "He's playing into our hands."

In July 1975, a new bill was passed by Parliament. Known as the Family Law Act, it allowed for no-fault divorce after twelve months of separation. Since it was well over twelve months since Val had left Tony, she was able to apply straight-away and their case came before a judge.

Her stomach was in knots at the thought of being in the same room as Tony, albeit with court officials present. She dressed in a smart gray suit Peggy had lent her, with sensible low-heeled shoes and neat hair and makeup.

Tony arrived just as proceedings were about to begin. He'd put on a lot of weight, Val noted. She guessed he was living on takeout meat pies. His complexion was florid and his expression cold with hatred. It was impossible to remember what she had ever loved about him.

The judge began by asking whether they had come to any agreement over custody arrangements for Nicole, and Tony burst out, "I don't want any contact with her. To be honest, your honor, I'm not sure she's even mine."

Val was horrified and saddened that he could cast off his own daughter. The day would come when Nicole would want to know why she never saw her daddy, and Val would have to offer an explanation.

The judge ordered that Val have parental responsibility, and ruled that if Tony wanted to see Nicole in future it would have to be with Val's consent. She was happy to agree to that.

Next came the financial settlement. Val's lawyer had requested that she receive half the value of the marital property and two thirds of her father's inheritance as a lump sum, after which she would not ask for any further alimony or child support payments.

Tony argued himself blue in the face over this. The house was his and his alone. He couldn't afford what they were asking. He'd be forced to go bankrupt. Val was a grasping cow who had only ever been after his money.

The judge listened to his arguments, and those of Val's attorney, and within an hour found in Val's favor. Tony swore and was reprimanded by the judge.

"One last thing," the judge said, looking at his notes then addressing Tony. "Your wife requests that you pass to her the contents of her deceased father's safe deposit box. Please make sure it reaches her solicitor's office within two weeks."

Tony looked at Val with a sly expression. "Ah, your honor, I'm not entirely sure where it is at the moment. It might take me a while to find. Besides, it's only sentimental old rubbish."

Val knew he was dragging his feet to wield the last remaining scrap of power he had over her. She had never thought of her father as remotely sentimental and was intrigued to see what the box contained.

"Within two weeks!" the judge ordered. "Or you'll find yourself back in front of me again."

Outside the courtroom, Val hugged her attorney. The money she'd been awarded was enough to buy a decent house in Camperdown and put away a financial cushion. No more cleaning jobs. No more worrying about next month's rent. And what was more, she would never have to see Tony again.

That evening, she explained to Nicole that a judge had decided she did not have to visit her daddy anymore.

"OK." Nicole nodded, quite happy with this. "Will I get a new daddy now? What do we have to do? Should we apply somewhere?"

Val laughed. "I think we'll be fine, just the two of us, without a daddy. Don't you?"

Nicole considered this. "Can we have a rabbit? I'd rather have a rabbit anyway."

Val agreed that this seemed a very good idea. Preferable to a man, certainly.

Peggy and Ken phoned to invite them for a celebration that weekend and Val knew she should be dancing on air. It was a huge relief, certainly. She felt proud that she would be able to give Nicole a secure childhood. If only her mom had been around to hear the news, it would have been perfect.

CHAPTER 37

Leningrad, October 1937

MARIA LAY AWAKE ALL NIGHT, HUGGING A SWEATER of Peter's. She could smell him in the wool, and see the indentation of his head on the pillow next to hers. How was it possible that a person so good and true could simply be gone? What would she tell the children when they woke in the morning? Katya would never forgive herself and the little ones wouldn't understand. How could anyone understand?

She tortured herself imagining his final moments. Did he know he was about to be executed? Did he think of her at the end? She wondered if it had been a firing squad, and if they put a sack over his head so he couldn't see who fired the fatal shot. Or was he gassed? She had heard the NKVD had vans in which they gassed people. She prayed that however he was killed, it had been swift and efficient, unlike the bungling, bloodthirsty executioners who had slaughtered her family. Once she had his body, she would be able to tell from the expression on his face.

The first light of dawn came through the window: a new day that Peter would not see. She murmured the words of the traditional *panikhida* for him but they stuck in her throat. He hadn't believed in God. Did that mean he wouldn't go to heaven? That she wouldn't meet him again on the other side?

She heard the children wakening, Mikhail calling to Yelena. Now was the moment when she must end their childhoods.

Five minutes, she decided. Let them have five more minutes of happiness. Then she would tell them.

~

Stepan helped Maria to comfort his siblings, cuddling Yelena on his lap, answering the endless questions as best he could. "Why is he dead? Why did it happen? When can we see him again?" He had purple shadows beneath his eyes, and Maria could tell he hadn't slept either.

When Irina heard that Stepan was going to Bolshoi Dom to collect their father's body, she insisted on going with him.

How brave she is, Maria thought. None of them should be alone. She had lost her great love, the center of her world, and they had lost their father. The combined loss was unfathomable, like the deepest, widest ocean.

While they were gone, Katya could not stop weeping, but the younger two began to play dominoes. It didn't seem real to them. Only the passage of time, the days and nights when he didn't come back, would make it sink in.

Maria watched out the window, wondering how they would bring him. Would he be in an ambulance? A funeral car? Could she risk finding a priest to conduct an illegal funeral ceremony?

A couple of hours later, she was still watching when Stepan and Irina turned into the street on foot, heads down, not talking. What did that mean? Was Peter being sent later?

She rushed out to meet them on the stairs. Raisa's door closed quickly when she heard their voices.

"Where is he?" she demanded, looking them up and down.

Irina's eyes were red and puffy. Stepan was carrying the brown bag Maria had packed for Peter. He shook his head. "I'm sorry, Mama. We can't have his body. He was buried straightaway, in a communal grave." A sob caught in his throat. "They said that's the way it always happens. They couldn't even tell us which cemetery."

Maria covered her face with her hands. That was it. She would never see him again. She turned, went back to her room, and crawled into bed, pulling the covers over her head.

The pain of losing her family had been unbearable, but this? She knew that as long as she lived she would never recover.

~

Grief flattened Maria, making it impossible for her to get out of bed. She yearned for sleep, because when she was awake the thoughts were too harrowing to endure. Over and over she tried to imagine Peter's last moments, his final thoughts, the realization that he would never see his children growing up. Had he been tortured? Was that why she wasn't allowed to see his body? It was her fault; hers alone.

In the next room Stepan and Irina were caring for their siblings: she could hear the flare of a match as Stepan lit the fire, the clatter of dishes as Irina served a meal. She was their mother; she should be doing that, but she couldn't.

"Your boss at the factory has agreed you can have two weeks off," Stepan reported that evening. He must have been to see him. "You need a rest."

She didn't reply. It was too hard to find words, and her throat had closed so that even if she found them, they wouldn't come out.

On the second day, Raisa came to the door. Maria heard

Irina talking to her and, after some hesitation, deciding to let her in.

Raisa hovered in the doorway to Maria's bedroom, and Maria could tell she was crying: that woman with ice in her heart was finally shedding a tear.

"I can't tell you how sorry I am. I never dreamed this would happen. Peter was a wonderful man. I feel awful. Will you ever forgive me?"

Her voice droned on but Maria couldn't raise her head from the pillow. She simply didn't have the energy. She closed her eyes, and when she opened them again, Raisa had left and the room was empty.

Irina brought food on a tray but she couldn't swallow more than a couple of mouthfuls of soup. At night she slept with her arms around Peter's pillow and her head resting on his old sweater. In the early hours Yelena crept in to share the bed with her. No one asked her; she just slipped between the sheets, with her six-year-old's firm body and steady breathing.

During the next days the children took turns to sit with Maria. Katya was withdrawn. Mikhail was sulky. Stepan was tired. Irina tried to hide her grief but her voice sounded fake and strained. Yelena was the easiest to be with because she gave hugs without trying to talk. All the children were in pain and Maria knew she should be comforting them. She could hear Peter's voice in her head telling her she must be strong, but her body simply wouldn't do it. It was as if she had been run over by a massive truck and none of her muscles worked anymore. Nothing worked except for her imagination, which played ghastly images in her head, like a never-ending horror film.

～

Two weeks passed and Maria forced herself to get up and dress for work. It was terrifying to consider getting out of bed, never mind going out into the world, but she was hoping that if she worked, they would be allowed to keep their apartment. The thought of moving was too much for her.

"I could leave the Institute and take a job at the factory," Stepan offered. "You shouldn't have to work. Not now."

"No," Maria insisted. "Your father was so proud that you were a student. You have to continue, for his sake."

It was agonizing walking into the factory and picking up her tools. She couldn't bear listening to the words of condolence and watching the pity on her fellow workers' faces. She didn't want to cry in front of them; crying was too personal, too painful. It was better to be alone with her grief. All she could manage was to put one foot in front of the other and keep busy.

At home, the older children helped with all the jobs Peter used to do. When the winter storms arrived and the windows rattled in their frames, Stepan found his father's tools and nailed insulation around the edges. He took charge of cleaning the grate and tending the fire, while Irina went to line up for food after she finished school, then helped with the cooking. They were a functioning team, but the heart had gone.

At least no notifications were received asking them to move, although they had only been given the apartment because Peter was a shock worker; perhaps someone had taken pity on them. Maria came straight home after work each day, and refused to answer the door, to see friends, or to help anyone who came to consult her missing persons' register. Irina took over that role, noting down the addresses of the few who stopped by and passing on details of possible matches.

One Sunday in March, when the hours of daylight were

starting to lengthen, Stepan tried to persuade Maria to come on what had been a traditional family outing.

"Remember how Papa used to love watching the ice on the Fontanka cracking? Let's go and stand on the Panteleimon Bridge. We can light candles for him."

Maria hesitated at first. It didn't seem fair to go without Peter, but the children were keen. Yelena tugged on her skirt, crying, "Please, Mama, please."

Maria pulled on her snow boots and warm coat, made sure the little ones were wrapped up warmly, then held Yelena and Mikhail's hands as they trudged to the bridge through streets with gray slush heaped in the gutters.

Fracture lines had formed across the inches-thick ice on the river, and in one section, geometrical chunks were breaking away: parallelograms, triangles, trapezoids. Underneath, the water was dark and impenetrable. Maria leaned on the elegant gilt railing and took the candle Irina handed her. Everywhere there were memories. Peter used to entertain them by imitating the otherworldly cracking sounds the ice made with a strange gurgling noise in his throat. Maria remembered teasing him that he sounded more like a duck.

She fixed her eyes on a spot where there was a hole in the ice, just below the bridge. If she climbed onto the railing and jumped quickly, she would disappear before they could stop her. It was an enticing thought, but she knew she wouldn't do it. Instead she put her arm around Katya and murmured a *panikhida*. The children gathered around, listening to the unfamiliar words, gazing at her face. She shivered when she thought that if it hadn't been for them, there was no question that she would have taken her own life and followed Peter to the grave.

～

When they got back to the apartment, there was a letter slipped under the door with Maria's name on it. She opened it and saw it was a handwritten note; the signature read *Yuri Koshelev*. Annushka's husband.

I'm sorry I was not able to help your husband, it said, *and extend my deepest condolences. There is another matter on which I need to speak with you urgently. I will call on you very soon.*

Maria was baffled by this, and alarmed. Was she about to be arrested and he had come to warn her? She had refused to admit to "lack of vigilance," as her older children had done, even though she knew Peter would have urged her to. Should she pack her bags and flee? She did not have the energy. Whatever happened next, she would just have to endure. Even if it led to her death.

CHAPTER 38

Leningrad, March 1938

WHEN MARIA TURNED INTO HER ROAD ON THE WAY home from the factory one evening and saw a black NKVD van parked outside her apartment block, she considered running in the other direction. But she couldn't; Irina would already be at home with the younger children and she had to protect them.

She walked on, feet dragging, her throat tight with fear. As she neared the van, the front passenger door swung open, and a man's voice said, "Get in. Quickly, before anyone sees you."

She glanced inside and saw Yuri, Annushka's husband. There were no other officers in the front of the van but she couldn't see into the dreaded back section. She was petrified but had no choice. She lowered herself into the seat and pulled the door shut.

Yuri switched on the engine and drove down the road without a word.

"Where are you taking me?" she asked, trying to control the tremor in her voice, clasping her hands in her lap so he wouldn't see them shaking.

"To a quiet street nearby. I thought it best your neighbors don't see me talking to you." He gave her a quick look.

That was strange. Why would he worry what her neighbors thought? They would already assume she had turned informer after Peter's death in order to escape arrest herself. Maybe that was what Yuri wanted to talk to her about; perhaps he was going to ask her to inform on her neighbors or work colleagues. She would refuse; she had long ago decided she would never inform on anyone.

Yuri pulled up in a dark road with a park on one side, warehouses on the other, and lit a cigarette. The name on the packet was Belomorkanal, a brand created to commemorate the construction of a canal linking the White Sea to the Baltic. He offered her one as an afterthought, but she shook her head.

"I wanted to tell you how sorry I was about your husband," he began. "I never met him personally but I know he had a spotless record and I can't understand why the *troika* reached the decision they did."

He drew deeply on his cigarette and Maria turned her head. The harsh smell of smoke in the enclosed space was nauseating.

"I found out that he is buried in the Preobrazhenskoe Cemetery. There is a mass grave in the southeast corner. At least you can go there to pay your respects."

Maria closed her eyes so he wouldn't see how much that information meant to her. "Thank you," she said.

"You must be wondering why I brought you here," he continued, and she waited. "It's not official business. I need your help, as it turns out. Annushka has disappeared with my son and I can't find them. I thought, with your contacts, you might have some idea where she has gone."

Maria frowned. "I haven't seen Annushka since I visited your apartment last October. We used to meet in the bread line but my daughter fetches our bread now. I don't know how I can help."

"And yet . . . with your files of missing people, I thought

perhaps you might find a way. Her parents and her brother say they haven't heard from her, but she must be somewhere."

Maria chose her words carefully. "Did anything happen before she left?"

He shrugged, and wound down the window to throw the cigarette butt into the road. A blast of icy air swirled in. "We had a row, but all couples row. You and Peter must have rowed."

Maria didn't tell him that they never had, not once in nineteen years. When they disagreed, they talked about it until they reached a solution. "I'll ask around and see if I can discover anything," she promised. "But don't get your hopes up. As I said, it's a long time since I've seen her."

Yuri dropped her at the end of her road and she walked home, lost in thought. There was no doubt in her mind that Annushka must have left him and wouldn't want to be found. She would have to handle the situation very carefully so as not to make an enemy of Yuri. Meanwhile, she couldn't wait to go to the Preobrazhenskoe Cemetery and visit Peter's grave. She would disregard all the other people buried in there with him and pretend they were alone once more, just the two of them.

~

The very next day, as soon as she finished work, Maria made her way to the cemetery, picking some early snowdrops from a park since the florists' shops were closed. She hesitated at the entrance gate; the cemetery was divided into Orthodox and Jewish sections, and she assumed Peter's grave must be in the Orthodox side. She walked past grand memorials in ornately carved stone to the southeast corner. There, just inside the boundary wall, she saw a patch of ground where the earth was bare, around twenty feet long by fifteen wide. It was marked with a simple wooden sign: *Enemies of the state*. This must be it. She fell to her knees on the wet grass.

"Peter," she whispered out loud. "I'm sorry it took me so long to find you. They wouldn't tell me . . ." She stopped. He didn't need to know that. She took a deep breath. "I miss you terribly, my love. I still can't believe it." Tears were coming now and she didn't want to cry. She wanted to show him she was being brave. She gulped, staying very still until she had controlled herself, then continued. "The children are fine. Stepan and Irina have grown up a lot. We all miss you. But we are safe. Peter, I tried so hard to save you. I hope you know that."

A woman appeared in the half-light and knelt beside the same grave, a respectful distance away. She bent her head and stayed very still.

Maria did not speak out loud again, but sat silent with her thoughts, hoping Peter could read them, wherever his soul might be. The earth was still hard from winter. His body would have been preserved by the freezing temperatures. She imagined he would still look like himself, strong and sturdy, with his compassionate gray eyes and cowlick hair. If only she could dig him up and kiss him one more time. The yearning was overwhelming.

She became aware of a low keening sound coming from the other woman. She rose, brushing the mud from her skirt, and walked across to lay a hand on her shoulder.

"I suppose we are in the same boat," she said gently. "Is your husband also buried here?"

The woman nodded and squeezed Maria's hand quickly, in a gesture of solidarity. "He was executed in November and now my only son has disappeared and they won't tell me where he is."

Maria sat on the grass beside her. "Was he taken by the NKVD?" she asked.

"I think so, but they will not give me any information. It's been two weeks and nothing."

Maria felt relieved that at least her children were safe. This woman's suffering was worse than hers. She wondered if she might be able to get Yuri to help, since he wanted a favor from her.

"I may have a contact who can make inquiries," she said. "Don't get your hopes up, but I will see what I can find out." She noticed an expression of suspicion flit across the woman's face. "Of course, there's no reason why you should trust me, but what harm can it do to give me your son's name? I will either find out where he is or I won't. It surely can't make things any worse."

The woman considered this for a moment, then told Maria her son's name and the address from which he had been taken.

"I'll return here at this time next week and let you know if I have discovered anything," Maria promised.

~

She had agreed to meet Yuri in the same quiet side road on her way home from work a couple of days hence. As she climbed into the van, she felt a frisson of terror. How many people had been beaten senseless or even killed in the back? What had Peter been thinking as he was driven away in such a van?

"Is there any news?" Yuri asked quickly.

Maria shook her head. "Not yet, but I have made inquiries. You must be patient."

He sighed deeply. "She does not have any money or coupons with her. How can she be feeding our son? I hope . . ." He bit his lip and did not finish the sentence.

"Annushka seemed a good mother. I'm sure your son is safe."

He nodded. "Will you meet me again in a few days? Say Monday? In case there is any word?"

"All right," Maria agreed, steeling herself for what she would ask next. "But I need a favor from you too. Can you find out what is happening to this boy, who has been arrested by the NKVD?" She held out a piece of paper with the name and address written on it. "His mother is distraught because no one will tell her anything. You for one must understand what that feels like."

She caught his eye. He wasn't pleased, but he took the piece of paper, looked at it quickly, and put it in his top pocket.

"I hope when I see you next that we will both have news," he said curtly.

"Me too. Till then." Maria opened the door and got out of the van. She didn't trust Yuri, but as long as he thought she might find his wife and son, he could be useful. It was a dangerous strategy, like dicing with the devil, but she felt it was the right thing to do. Something Peter once said came back to her: "If you can help someone without harming anyone else, then why on earth wouldn't you do it?"

~

Maria took the children to visit their father's grave the following Sunday afternoon. It was a warm day for March. Lone birds were chirruping and the pistachio-green cones of still-furled leaves were sprouting on bare branches. They took bread with potted cheese and cold meats, fruit *pastila*, homemade *kvass* and cups to drink it from, as well as a bunch of colorful spring blooms to lay on the grave. The children were quiet when they arrived, upset to see the lack of respect for the men tossed into this muddy earth. Maria spread a blanket on the grass and laid out the food and drink, all the while talking to Peter in her head.

We're here, she told him. I brought them so you can see they are all right. Look how Mikhail has grown. I think he will be tall one day. And Stepan is turning into a man. Do you see his whiskers? He did not shave this morning.

They sat down and began to eat, and soon they were talking about Peter, sharing memories of him.

"Do you remember the funny noise he made when he sneezed?" Irina asked. "It sounded like a-chi-chi-bo."

Maria smiled at her imitation.

"He could never find his key in the morning," Katya said. "I couldn't understand why he didn't just put it in the same place every evening when he came home."

"He wasn't organized that way," Maria explained. "He came from the countryside where no one locks their doors."

"I have never heard anyone whistle as well as he did," Stepan said. "I tried to learn, but I could never produce a sound so pure and tuneful."

Mikhail whistled a bar of "Slavianka," a tune Peter used to whistle, and for a moment it almost sounded as if he was there with them.

Suddenly Maria realized that Peter hadn't gone. He lived on in these five children, different bits in each. As long as they remembered and talked about him, they would keep his memory alive. It wasn't the same as having him there, and never would be. But if she could come to his grave and talk to him, and keep his children around her, then she would find a way to carry on. She had no choice.

CHAPTER 39

Leningrad, April 1938

MARIA SAW THE WOMAN APPROACHING THROUGH THE dusk, and beckoned her over.

"Do you have news?" the woman asked without any greeting, desperate to learn her son's fate.

"He is alive," Maria began, knowing that was the information she would want to hear first. "But he has been sentenced to five years in a gulag in Kemerovo."

The woman began to wail. "But why? What has he done?"

"I'm so sorry." Maria put a hand on her arm. "I don't know what he was convicted of, but my informant said conditions there are not too bad. The men are mining coal, but they are well fed. And five years is much shorter than the average sentence."

"Mining coal . . ." The woman couldn't stop crying. "He is a clever boy. He had a bright future."

"He still does. Five years will pass, and you can write and send packages. I have the address for you." Maria found a scrap of paper in her bag and handed it over.

The woman read it. "Thank you," she said, sniffing back her tears. "I will write tonight and send some warm clothes.

At least I can do that. But five years . . ." She shook her head. "What kind of state would do this to their young men?"

Maria didn't reply. Criticizing the government to a stranger was a fool's game. She could understand the woman's anger. If she let herself think of the men who had sentenced Peter to death, and the ones who had carried out the sentence, her own fury threatened to overwhelm her, but it could serve no purpose. She couldn't attack the state or their "great leader," Stalin. Best to keep quiet, look after her children, and get on with her own life.

$\sim$

Two days later, when Maria visited Peter's grave, another woman approached. It looked as though she had been waiting for her.

"Are you Maria? My friend told me you can get information about people who have been arrested. I wondered if you could ask about my husband? He was taken by the NKVD a month ago and I've heard nothing since."

Maria was about to say no, she couldn't help, but the woman's eyes were swollen, her face etched with desperation. She imagined Peter listening to their exchange, and replied, "Give me the information and I'll see what I can do."

As she walked home, she pondered the problem. Yuri would not take kindly to her asking another favor when she had nothing to offer in return. Perhaps she should try to locate Annushka, and if she found her, they could concoct a story together.

On her next day off, Maria caught a tram to the Winter Palace and was glad to see that Annushka's brother Fedor was still a guard there.

"How are you?" she greeted him, smiling brightly. "It must be easier to stand here all day now the weather is warmer."

He agreed, but seemed tense.

"Do you work long hours?" she asked. "When do you finish today, for example?"

"I started at eight and finish at six," he told her, glancing around. "I'm not supposed to chat while I'm on duty."

"How is Annushka?" Maria continued. "I haven't seen her in ages."

"I don't know where she is. She's left home. I haven't heard from her." He couldn't meet her eye and she knew he was lying.

"Oh dear, I hope she's all right. Do give her my regards if you see her." Maria smiled and walked past, as if simply going about her business.

At six that evening, she huddled in a doorway of the Admiralty building on the other side of Nevsky Prospekt, waiting to see which way Fedor would head. He crossed to a tram stop heading into town and waited there, stamping his feet against the cold. When she saw a tram approaching, Maria pulled her scarf tight around her head and scampered across the road just in time to jump on the back. She stood behind a large man in workers' overalls as the tram headed out toward the suburban districts.

When Fedor alighted, Maria jumped off too, turning as if to walk in the opposite direction then checking over her shoulder. He didn't look around as he crossed the street and headed into a park. She hurried after him and saw him emerge through a gate on the other side. He stopped by a bread shop, which was closed for the night, and hammered on the door. After a while a woman opened it and handed him a loaf wrapped in paper. He must be a regular.

At last he stopped outside an apartment building. Maria

was on the opposite side of the road so couldn't see which bell he rang, but on the third floor a curtain twitched and she saw a face looking down. It was Annushka. She was sure of it. Fedor entered the building.

Maria crossed the road and waited till someone else opened the street door, then rushed forward to catch it before it slammed. She walked up the concrete stairs, similar to her own, all the way to the third floor, and estimated which door it must be: second along from the main stairs. Thankfully these blocks were built to a uniform pattern.

Fedor opened the door and gawped at her. "What on earth are you doing here?"

"Can I come in?" Maria asked. "I'm here to see Annushka."

He hesitated, then stood back to let her pass. Annushka gasped and clutched her young son to her side as Maria walked into their sitting room.

"How did you find me?" she asked.

"Very easily," Maria told her, looking at Fedor. "And Yuri could do the same anytime. If you want to avoid him, you will have to do better than this." She sat down before explaining that he had asked her to look for them.

Fedor was embarrassed that he had been followed with so little difficulty. "You mustn't tell him where she is," he pleaded.

"Of course I won't," Maria agreed. "But you must tell me the truth."

"I couldn't stay any longer with a man who scares me. You've seen him, Maria." Annushka's eyes were pleading for understanding. "He's moody and unpredictable. He can switch from pleasant to enraged in the blink of an eye. And he's so big, he terrifies me."

"But is it fair to stop him seeing his son?" Maria asked.

"If I let him see the boy, he would never give him back. He would hold him hostage to force me to return."

Fedor looked on, lips pursed, and Maria couldn't tell what he was thinking. Many Russian men had a temper. Yuri was not alone in being volatile.

"Yet here you are a prisoner. You don't dare leave the apartment in case one of Yuri's colleagues sees you on the street. Your son cannot go to school in Leningrad or he will find out." Maria was thinking aloud. "Is there anywhere else you could go? Perhaps to a relative in the countryside? If I tell Yuri that's where you are, but that I don't have the address, perhaps he will give up looking eventually."

"I suppose I could go to my cousin in Moscow." She glanced at Fedor. "For a while at least."

Maria nodded. "Very well. That's what I'll say. Don't tell me your cousin's name, but leave as soon as you can. I will wait another week before telling him."

Annushka ran across and hugged her, kissing her on both cheeks. "Bless you for your kindness to us," she said. "I hope good fortune will be with you."

"With you too," Maria replied, meaning it.

∼

When she met Yuri a week later, Maria waited first to hear what information he had for the woman who had approached her in the cemetery.

"Your friend's husband is being questioned. I think the charges are not serious and that he will be released within a week, if he cooperates." He paused, and Maria knew what he meant: if the man agreed to become an informer.

"Thank you." She hesitated, feeling nervous. If Yuri was as quick-tempered as Annushka claimed, he might lose his temper over what she had to say next. "I have some information for you," she began. "I hear Annushka has gone to stay with a cousin in Moscow. Your son is with her."

Yuri blew out impatiently. "Without telling me. The bitch." He pulled out a Belomorkanal, tapped it on the dashboard, then lit it. "When will she be back?"

"I don't know," Maria ventured. She didn't dare tell him that the answer might be never. "Maybe she needs some time away. All marriages go through difficult patches." She glanced at his face. Was she being too presumptuous? He didn't seem to mind.

"I don't understand what she wants," he complained. "She has a decent home, food, money for clothes, she doesn't have to work . . . What more can I give her?"

Maria never for one moment forgot she was in an NKVD van, talking to an NKVD officer. A single wrong word and she could be summarily arrested. But she decided to tell him part of the truth. "Maybe she wanted to feel loved."

He turned his face away, inhaled deeply on his cigarette. "She never understood the pressure I am under. This is not an easy job."

"I'm sure it's not."

"I see things that . . . well, they haunt you."

Maria dared not ask what. She did not want to imagine. All she wanted was to get out of his van and walk away, back home to her children. She gathered her shopping bag handles, as if to leave.

"Who told you Annushka had gone to her cousin's?" he demanded suddenly.

Maria had been hoping he wouldn't ask. Now she would have to lie. "I asked the women in the baker's shop and they put the word around and news came back. I don't know who found out."

"Who told *you*?" he asked.

"I don't know her name. A blond woman. In a brown coat."

He nodded. "You could point her out to me if we went to the baker's shop together, could you?"

Maria hesitated. "I'm not sure. Possibly not. I've only seen her once."

"But I hear you are very good at remembering faces. That's why you are able to reunite families. Surely you would remember this woman?"

It had turned into an interrogation. Maria was flustered and could feel her cheeks burning.

"Don't ever lie," he said, watching her through narrowed eyes. "You will get found out every time. Your face gives you away."

Maria looked at her lap, clutched her shopping bag closer. What could she say? How could she get out of this?

Before she could answer, he continued, "If you have any other friends who want information, you know where I live."

Maria was astonished. "But you—"

"I have to go now." He flicked his cigarette out the window. "Goodbye, Maria."

She jumped out of the van, slammed the door behind her, and walked quickly down the road. When it rolled past, she did not dare turn around to look.

CHAPTER 40

Sydney, September 1975

A MONTH AFTER HER DIVORCE WENT THROUGH, VAL
got a call from her lawyer to say that finally, after much
argument and following sanctions from the court, Tony had
transferred the money he owed her, and dropped off a box of
items he claimed were from the safe deposit box.

"I'll come by in my lunch hour," Val said straightaway. She
couldn't wait to see what was there.

The attorney's secretary indicated a cardboard box with
"Chiko Roll" printed in diagonal type around the outside. Val
was immediately suspicious. She had never seen her father eat
a Chiko Roll. He served plain food: soup, meat, and potatoes.

She pulled back the top flaps and saw a dark brown leather
traveling bag and a folder of documents with something written in Russian on the cover. They smelled of mold and decay.
At least that seemed authentic. Perhaps the contents were her
father's and Tony had thrown them into a random box.

She carried it back to work but didn't have time to explore
further before she got home that evening. After the evening
meal, while Nicole was watching cartoons on their brand-new
television set, she cleared the kitchen table and opened the
leather bag.

The first thing she pulled out was a sketchbook filled with pretty watercolor close-ups of flowers. The artist was talented, capturing tiny details of stamens and petals in a fine hand. The paper itself was yellowing with age and there were reddish-brown stains on the back pages.

Next she pulled out a leather-bound photograph album, thick as a Bible, with black paper pages. As soon as she began flicking through it, she realized it contained images of the Romanovs. There were the girls in their white dresses and hair ribbons in a pretty garden; little Alexei in a sailor suit; several adults dancing in a circle; the younger ones paddling in the sea, hems held high to stop them getting wet. Far from the formal studio poses Val had seen in books, these were intimate family shots. They all looked younger and happier than in the photos she had found in her father's camera. Perhaps they dated from the years before they were taken captive.

Next she found two Russian Orthodox icons, with gold-haloed figures painted on wood, surrounded by bejeweled frames. She wondered why Tony hadn't taken them. Perhaps he didn't appreciate their value because they looked gaudy, but if they had belonged to the Romanovs, the jewels were almost certainly real.

Finally she turned to the folder with the Russian writing on the front. Inside she found what looked like accountants' ledgers, with columns of figures and dates, none of which she could make out. There were also several sets of identity papers—she counted eight altogether—each with a grainy photograph of her father. He was a young man, but his distinctive brow, pronounced as a window ledge above his dark eyes, was the same as when she knew him.

At the back of the folder there was a leaflet with Russian writing and a blurred photograph printed on it. Val guessed it might be one of the Romanov girls and took out a book to compare it with. Olga had a melancholic look; Tatiana had a pixie face . . . It was Maria, she decided. Her face was plumper and her eyes bigger and rounder than the others'.

As she looked through these objects, Val's mind was jumping around trying to make sense of things. Her father must have stolen them from the Ipatiev House along with the camera. She looked at the bag again: it was a carpet-bag shape with pleats where it was stitched beneath a gold buckle. The base was badly stained with dark blotches. She picked it up by the handles, and as she turned it around, she heard something rattle inside. A few pencils were rolling around the bottom and an object was trapped between the cloth lining and the outer leather.

She found a rip in the inside pocket through which she was able to pull out a rectangular gold-colored box, about half the size of a matchbox. On top there was a yellow stone, one large white one, and a scattering of smaller white ones. She could tell by shaking that there was something inside the box, but she couldn't get it to open no matter how hard she tugged. There was a joint in the metal but it felt as if it had been fused shut. Perhaps the edges were rusted with age.

It felt odd looking through a stranger's belongings, as if she was poking around in someone else's handbag. It didn't tell her anything about her father, except that he must have stolen these items. Why did he not sell them, as he had with all the other White Russian property he stole? He could surely have charged a premium.

Next day, she went back to see Bill Koskov in the Russian department at the university, taking the accounts ledgers, the identity papers, and the leaflet.

"What do you make of this lot?" she asked. "They all came from my father's safe deposit box, and there was a Romanov photo album and a sketchbook with them."

Bill opened one of the accounts books and frowned. Then he read the leaflet and his eyes widened.

"Can you leave them with me?" he asked. "Meet me for lunch in the canteen tomorrow and I'll have the translations for you."

"You speak Russian yourself?" Val asked.

"White Russian parents." He grinned. "I had no choice!"

~

"This is particularly odd," Bill said the next day, pointing at the leaflet with the grainy picture of Maria, the third Romanov daughter. He'd brought his own lunch with him in a Tupperware box: a mountain of cheese sandwiches, which he was devouring in huge bites, as if ravenous.

Val had bought herself a tuna sandwich and a black coffee into which she stirred a sugar cube. "What is?"

Bill swallowed a mouthful. "Whoever wrote it clearly believed that Maria had escaped from Ekaterinburg. It gives her description alongside the photo and offers a reward for information leading to her discovery. It doesn't say she is a Romanov; just that she's a person of great interest."

"Maybe it's not her." Val took the leaflet and had another look.

"I'm pretty sure it is," Bill said. "Especially given the fact that it was found with a Romanov photo album. I've been thinking about it overnight and I've come to the conclusion that the leaflet must have been produced by someone working for the Cheka, the Bolshevik secret police force between 1917 and 1922, and one of their successor organizations thereafter. Just imagine: if one of the Romanovs had escaped, they wouldn't want to publicize it because it would make them look inefficient, but they would have been at great pains to prevent her traveling overseas and telling her story to the outside world."

Val frowned. "Do you think my father was working for the secret police?"

"Either that or he was helping them. One of the accounts books gives the names of people working in different soviets around the country, and there are sums of money as well as dates listed. To me, it looks as though they were on the pay-roll, being bribed to look out for Maria." He caught her eye. "Stop me if I'm being presumptuous. I don't mean to criticize your father."

"No, not at all. Growing up, I assumed he was a White Russian who fled after the Revolution, but the more I learn, the more I realize I didn't know him at all." Val sipped her coffee. Had he been on the Bolshevik side? It was beginning to sound that way.

Bill pulled out another accounts ledger. "This lists letters received at the house of a family called Vasnetsov in Ekaterinburg."

Val recognized the name. "I have a photograph of Peter Vasnetsov. Remember? He was in one of the shots developed from my dad's camera."

"Curious!" Bill smiled at her. "I think we're onto something, don't you? He was clearly under suspicion. Look." He ran his finger down a column. "Here are the dates each letter was received and the places they were posted from. They seem to have come from a village in the Urals, from Perm, from Moscow—never the same place twice."

"So you think Maria was moving around? I suppose she would have done, to evade capture." Val pointed at another ledger. "What's in this book?"

Bill opened the pages. Val noticed that he had long fingers with neat, well-kept nails. It surprised her, since his clothes were scruffy: a beige jacket with saggy pockets, as if he walked around with his hands permanently shoved in them, and faded khaki trousers that bagged at the knees. "It gives the dates of trips from Manchuria into Russia between the years 1920 and 1925. And get this: it ties in with the dates that letters were received at the Vasnetsov house. It looks as though your father traveled to the places each letter was sent from. Perhaps Maria was writing to Peter Vasnetsov and your father hoped to find her by tracking the letters."

"But look at all those trips!" Val realized the ledger covered the years when her father was dealing in stolen White Russian goods. That was why he kept traveling into the country. She didn't want to admit it to Bill, though.

"He was using the different identity papers so as not to arouse suspicion," Bill continued. "But what fascinates me is that he would never have gone to so much trouble if he hadn't had good reason to think Maria was alive. He must have had some evidence."

"Weren't there theories that Anastasia escaped? I'm sure I read that somewhere."

There was a pause while Bill chewed his last bite of sand-wich. "Yeah, there's a woman in America who's been claiming since the early 1920s that she is Anastasia. She seems unde-terred by the fact that no one who actually knew the family believes her."

Bill glanced at Val's uneaten sandwich, and she grinned and pushed it across to him. "Go ahead. I'm not hungry."

"Are you sure? I'm the world's biggest glutton. I can eat my own body weight and still be starving." His eyes were linger-ing on the sandwich, and the minute she said, "I'm sure," he snapped it up, took a bite, then continued. "There were claim-ants for all the Romanov children, but none were ever verified."

The sandwich disappeared in no time. Val wondered how

he could eat so much and still be thin. He didn't have an ounce of excess flesh but at the same time he didn't seem a sporty type. Maybe he burned it off with nervous energy.

"I read a book by a Russian historian a couple of years ago that claimed the Romanovs had been murdered by 'Letts,' or foreigners." He wiped his mouth with a paper napkin. "The Russians still won't take responsibility for it themselves. A classic case of passing the buck."

"Who do you think gave the order?" Val asked. "Did it come from Lenin?"

"There's no paper trail from the top. It seems to have been the men of the Ekaterinburg soviet who made the final decision." He grimaced. "But Lenin had already created the Cheka, and they had the power to order summary executions without trial. You can imagine the sort of men they attracted: power-hungry and unscrupulous . . ." He looked as if he was about to say more, then stopped himself. "I'm sorry. I'm not suggesting your father was like that."

Val screwed up her face. "It's horrible to accept," she said. "But I suppose he might have been."

She agreed that Bill could make copies of the documents and fax them to his colleague in New York. There was no point trying to protect her father's name. If Bill's theory was true, he didn't deserve protection.

~

She took the gold box to Hardy Brothers, an upmarket jeweler near Darling Harbor.

"This is Fabergé," the jeweler said, peering through a loupe at the almost indecipherable engraving on the back. "It has the maker's mark HW. Those are the initials of the man who made it."

Val wasn't surprised to hear it. "Fabergé were jewelers to the Romanovs, weren't they?"

"Among others. They had wealthy customers across Europe. How did it come into your possession?"

"It was my father's," she replied. She couldn't tell this man that she thought it might have belonged to one of the Romanov family without inviting awkward questions.

"Do you know the provenance?" he asked, as if reading her mind.

She shook her head. "I found it among his possessions after he passed away. But I wondered if you know how to open it? There seems to be something inside."

The jeweler peered at the edges. "There's a mechanism sealing it. It's one of their trick boxes, where you have to know the secret." He tried pressing on the jewels, twisting them, but nothing seemed to work. "You would have to contact Fabergé themselves, or find someone who is a Fabergé expert. I could cut it open for you, of course, but that would be a waste."

"Do you know any Fabergé experts in Sydney?" Val asked, but he shook his head.

"Sorry. It's not my area."

Val was intrigued. The box was so small, it couldn't contain anything of major significance, but she imagined there might be something sentimental inside. A baby tooth, perhaps? She kept all Nicole's baby teeth in a little wooden box. She would have to do some research and try to find an expert. It was yet another mystery associated with her father that she was determined to solve.

CHAPTER 41

Leningrad, September 3, 1939

MARIA WAS AT WORK IN THE PIG-IRON FACTORY when there was an announcement over the radio that Britain and France had declared war on Germany. Everyone stopped and looked at each other, eyes wide. Maria felt a knot of anxiety in the pit of her stomach. She remembered visiting soldiers in the hospital in Tsarskoe Selo in 1914, the last time Britain and France went to war with Germany. She could still see those men with bandaged heads and oozing stumps where limbs used to be; men whose minds had wandered because of the horrific sights they had witnessed. Peter's father had been killed during that conflict, and he had told Maria firmly that no good came from war. Not ever.

She had arranged to meet Yuri after work. They saw each other every month, always in his van, always parked in the same quiet street between the park and a warehouse. Maria's reputation for finding information on people arrested by the NKVD had spread, and desperate strangers often accosted her at Peter's graveside and thrust into her hand pieces of paper with names and addresses written on them. They spoke of arrests in the dead of night, no information on charges, no word of where their loved one might be, no help from the authorities, and maddening waits at inquiries desks; all too often the glass partition was slammed shut and the officers went off duty just as they neared the front of the line.

Yuri could usually find some news, but Maria had to act as go-between. The worst times were when he said the individual concerned had been executed. It took her straight back to the moment she was informed of Peter's death. The people she told—usually women—surprised her with their courage. It was as if they had been expecting it. They stooped under the weight of their grief, but generally did not cry out loud.

When Maria and Yuri met on the third of September, she asked him what he thought about the war in Europe. He liked to chat before they got down to business. Annushka had never returned and she could tell he was lonely.

He chewed the inside of his cheek before answering. "Some wars have to be fought. They should never have let Hitler get so powerful, but there was no appetite for another conflict."

"It's lucky we are not involved this time," Maria said. Hitler and Stalin had signed a nonaggression pact just the previous week.

"So far," he said in his enigmatic style, making her stomach flutter with nerves.

"Do you think we might have to fight?" What if Stepan was called up? She couldn't bear that.

He shrugged and didn't answer, and Maria decided not to persist. She was still scared of him. It was impossible to tell what he was thinking.

"Regarding the information you wanted," he said, "there are no executions to report."

That was a relief at least. The killing had been worst in 1937 and 1938, but the rate had slowed now; more men were being sent to gulags in Siberia, with an average sentence of twenty-five years.

He gave her a note of the gulags where the men she was asking about that week had been sent. It must be hard for their families, Maria thought, but at least they could send packages of food, blankets, and clothes, along with letters. She would give anything to be able to write to Peter and read his replies. Almost two years had passed since he had died, and she still cried every day.

~

Two weeks after Britain and France went to war with Germany, Soviet troops invaded eastern Poland and annexed a vast swath of territory there. On the radio the announcers spoke of Polish citizens welcoming the Red Army with open arms, giving them gifts of bread and salt, and Maria wondered if they knew what they were letting themselves in for.

During the winter of 1939–40, Russia went to war with Finland and grabbed yet more land, this time to the north of Leningrad. With each new announcement Maria was terrified that Stepan would be forced to fight. He had almost finished his studies at the Institute and his English was near perfect, while he spoke French and German as well. She hoped he would get work in a university. It would be awful if he were forced to enlist.

As the months rolled on, the news from western Europe was grim: the fall of Belgium, Holland, and then France; the hasty evacuation of British troops at Dunkirk; the bombing of London. Loudspeakers on street corners, in the factory, and outside apartment blocks broadcast the latest developments. Maria saw photographs on the front page of *Pravda* showing ruined buildings, women and children being carried from them on stretchers by men wearing tin helmets while fires burned in the background. It looked like a vision of hell. Thank God the Soviet Union was not involved. Life went on more or less as it had before, far from the tragedy engulfing their western neighbors.

~

On June 22, 1941, a Sunday, Maria was on her way to Peter's grave with the three youngest children. Stepan had gone fishing and Irina was out with her friends. Suddenly a voice boomed from the loudspeakers; she recognized it as that of Vyacheslav Molotov, Commissar of Foreign Affairs.

"Men and women, citizens of the Soviet Union, at four o'clock this morning, without declaration of war and without any claims being made on the Soviet Union, German troops attacked our country."

Around them, everyone in the street came to a standstill. Maria squeezed Yelena's hand so tight she squealed.

"Our cause is good," the voice continued. "Our enemy will be smashed. Victory will be ours."

Maria pulled her children toward her: Yelena now nine, Mikhail thirteen, and Katya fifteen. She wished she could wrap them up in lint.

What shall I do, Peter? she asked in her head when they reached his grave. How shall I keep our children safe? As usual, there was no reply.

That same evening, Stepan announced that he had been to a recruitment office and joined a long line of volunteers to help with civil defense. He told Maria he had been assigned to a team digging antitank trenches several miles out of town and that he must leave the following morning.

"But when will we see you? Will you not be in danger? I don't like this." Maria fretted as she stuffed a bag with fresh clothes, rolls of bandages, and tubes of liniment, and jars of food to supplement his rations.

"I'll be back one day a week. It's only until the city defenses are complete," he told her.

"Others could do that," Maria grumbled. "Digging is back-breaking work and you are an intelligent boy. You should be living off your brains."

Leaflets were distributed urging that all children, old people, and anyone who could not help the war effort should evacuate the city. Maria wrestled with this: she did not want to be parted from her children, but she couldn't leave herself, not while Stepan was still there. Besides, where would they go? Her overriding instinct was to keep the family together, so she ignored the evacuation calls but kept an ear out for every new broadcast in case the situation changed.

"The Red Army has won a great victory, although it was outnumbered four to one by German troops," the announcer Yuri Levitan read in his excitable tones.

"Yes, and I hear Ivan killed five Germans armed only with a spoon," Maria's work colleague whispered to her.

Maria grinned. They were learning not to trust the radio proclamations. Always they spoke of victory, and yet it was clear that the Germans continued to advance.

"Some think Stalin might surrender Leningrad because it is too hard to defend," her colleague continued, then added treacherously, "It might not be altogether a bad thing. I can't imagine Hitler is as bloodthirsty . . ."

That was one good thing about the war: fear of the NKVD appeared to have lessened and people were speaking their minds again, albeit discreetly.

The same colleague told her that a group of children evacuated from the city had been shepherded directly into German lines. "Yet another example of the wonderful efficiency of Soviet bureaucracy," she added with a droll expression.

Maria was glad she had decided to keep her brood around

her. And yet she trembled when the first snub-nosed gray German bombers flew overhead at the end of August. She fitted blackout curtains and hurried down to the block's air-raid shelter when there was a raid on September 8. They were forced to sit opposite Raisa and Galina, but Maria kept her eyes on her children and her thoughts to herself. Where was Stepan? Was he safe? She prayed to God he wouldn't come to any harm.

At work next day, all the talk was that the city was surrounded. It was no longer possible to leave, and overnight German bombs had hit the Badayev warehouses, where the food stores were kept.

"I suppose the Red Army will have to air-drop food for us," said Maria's friend at the factory. "Knowing their prowess, it will land in the middle of Lake Ladoga."

After work, Maria and Irina toured every food store within reach and stood for hours in lines buying whatever was left on the shelves: dried fruits, blanched almonds, even a tin of caviar. Maria also bought a large box of vitamin powder. She had read an article in a magazine claiming that vitamins could prevent diseases like rickets that were caused by a poor diet, so it seemed a good idea.

Rations were reduced in mid-September, but everyone assumed the shortages would only be temporary, until the Red Army started to drop food. Siege was a medieval strategy of war, something the Greeks and Romans had done; Maria couldn't believe it would be maintained for long in the modern age.

CHAPTER 42

Leningrad, September 1941

ALMOST OVERNIGHT, MARIA FOUND HER EVERY WAK-
ing thought was about food. What could she serve for a
meal that evening? Where could she find supplies to top up
their bread ration?

She lay awake in bed remembering what Peter had taught
her about edible plants. There were dandelions and borage,
nettles and cow parsley in the cemetery where he lay. When
she found a crop of white mushrooms there one Sunday it felt
like a gift he had sent from beyond the grave. She decided
she would cook them with wild thyme leaves and serve them
on bread, so their juices were soaked up.

Stepan helped by going fishing whenever he had time off,
so at least once a week they had fish to share. Maria eked out
the last of the potatoes and served the fish baked, with boiled
greens on the side.

There was one more mouth to feed because Stepan had
returned from digging trenches and was now being trained to
operate the big guns on an antiaircraft battery.

"Does that not mean you will be the Germans' first target?"
Maria fretted.

"They're not going to waste a bomb on a few of us when

they can target the docks or the warehouses. Don't worry, Mama," he assured her, with calm rationality.

"But I hear firing during the day. Will their soldiers not try to shoot you?"

"We are well camouflaged," he promised. "I'll make sure no German bullets have my name on them."

At the end of September, just as freezing gusts of rain brought the first sign of winter, the oil and gas supplies to the city were cut. Maria turned on her stove and struck a match but no gas hissed out. She would have to burn wood in the *burzhuika* to heat food. That meant foraging for firewood after she finished work, when she was bone-weary from the day's toil.

The factory switched to production of shell cartridges. They were heavy to carry and the steel shavings cut into the palms of her hands, but she was grateful for the job because it meant her ration was bigger than it would otherwise have been and she got canteen meals at lunchtime. When a vacancy arose, Irina came to work there too, and between them they were able to smuggle home jugs of soup to supplement the family's evening meal and some porridge to heat for their breakfast. It was just as well, because the bread ration was reduced to two slices a day. How could anyone live on that? Especially when you could tell it was made of flour substitute, with an odd texture so that it fell apart when you tried to cut it, and a taste that was bitter and unpleasant.

Meat was a distant memory, and stories circulated of pets being stolen and killed for their flesh. One evening there was a knock on their door and Maria opened it to find a stricken Raisa.

"Have you seen my cat?" she pleaded. "It's been two days. I didn't let him out of the courtyard so I wondered if someone here might . . ." She couldn't finish her sentence.

For the first time since Peter was arrested, Maria felt a twinge of fellow feeling for Raisa. "I'm sorry, I haven't seen him. But I will look out for him, I promise."

She could understand why someone might take a cat. Hunger made otherwise moral people desperate. She had heard of ration cards stolen in the street, of people trading fur coats for a sack of potatoes. Her family were lucky that so far they had not had to resort to desperate measures, but life got tougher as the days passed and the temperature dropped.

The electricity became intermittent, then in November the water supply failed after bombs ripped open the pipelines. Now they had to fetch buckets of water from a fire hydrant at the end of the street, and use a kerosene lamp for light in the evening. Maria gave each child his or her own job: Yelena and Mikhail got the water and Katya collected firewood; Irina brought home the canteen food, and Maria went for the bread and any other food she could forage.

At night, when the planes flew overhead, they sang songs in the shelter to drown out the noise. "The Little Blue Scarf," in which a soldier pined for the girl he loved, was a particular favorite.

It can't last much longer, Maria told herself. Where was the Red Army? Stalin called himself "father of the nation"; now was the time for him to prove it.

~

"My tummy hurts," Mikhail complained one night in November as he slumped over the dinner table. He was thirteen years old and tall for his age. Maria touched the back of her hand to his forehead and noticed that his skin was gray, his eyes dull, and he had a sore at the corner of his lips. She put her arms around him and felt his ribs sticking out. They were all getting thinner, but his weight loss seemed more severe than the others'.

"Have some soup," she told him, ladling a generous portion into a bowl; then she dissolved a teaspoon of vitamin powder in water and told him to swallow it.

"Eat slowly," she cautioned. "Don't make yourself sick. Tomorrow I will try to find extra."

When she picked up her bread the next day, counting out the precious coupons carefully, she asked, "Is there any way to get more for my son? He is unwell."

"Marry a Party boss?" the woman suggested, with a cynical look. "I notice they aren't suffering any hardships."

"Besides that?" Maria shuddered at the thought. She would never marry again. Peter had been the only man for her.

"I hear you get extra rations if you donate blood," the woman said. "But be careful not to weaken yourself. Personally speaking, I need all the blood I've got."

Maria didn't have to be told twice. On her way to work, she stopped at the Hôtel de l'Europe on Nevsky Prospekt, which was being used as a military hospital. Her reward for a pint of blood was coupons for an extra two days' family ration of bread, along with a bag of root vegetables. "Can I come back next week?" she asked, and was disappointed to be told that she could not donate again for another month. At least they ate well that night—a stew of potatoes, onions, carrot, and turnip, with fresh parsley sprinkled on top—and she made sure Mikhail got a bigger portion than his sisters. This deprivation seemed to be harder for men than for women, so she was relieved when Stepan told her that he was receiving army rations at his post on the antiaircraft battery.

～

When the snow came and the rivers iced over, the sense of claustrophobia intensified. There were bombs dropping most nights, gunfire by day, and a cold that felt crueler than in any winter Maria could remember. When Katya couldn't find firewood for their *burzhuika* stove, Maria began to break up items of furniture and rip the baseboards from the walls. It was only December, with at least three more months of winter stretching in front of them. How would they survive? When would the city be relieved? She was beginning to think Stalin had abandoned them. Did he know of their plight? How could he let them starve?

On December 15, a Monday, Maria and Irina were walking to work through the snow. No one had cleared the pavement, so they walked in single file along a track worn by the footsteps of those who had gone before, dodging the rubble from bomb-damaged buildings. At the corner of Ulitsa Pestelya, there was a man lying on his side in the snow. Maria's first thought was that he must have slipped, and she crouched to grasp his elbow and help him up.

"Sir? Are you all right?" she asked. It was then she saw that his eyes were wide open and staring out of a face tinged blue and sparkling with frost.

"He's dead, Mom," Irina said, a sob in her throat. "What should we do?"

Maria had seen dead people before—her family in the basement in Ekaterinburg; her baby Pavel lying in the bed beside her—and she knew straightaway that Irina was right. His body was here, but this man's spirit was long gone. She closed his eyes then searched through his coat pockets until she found a ration card with an address on it. His name was Pavel, like her son, and his apartment block was just around the corner.

"You go ahead to the factory. Tell them I will be half an

hour late," she instructed Irina. "I'll see if any family members are at home."

When she rang the bell of the man's apartment, she could hear a shuffling noise inside, but it was a long time before the door was opened by a gaunt woman who looked to be in her seventies.

"I'm so sorry," Maria said, reaching out to touch her shoulder, "but I have bad news."

The woman nodded when Maria told her and did not seem unduly surprised. She was thin as a pole herself and seemed very frail.

"Do you have children who can help you fetch the body and bury him?" Maria asked.

"My two sons are in the army," the woman told her. There was a tear glinting in her eye, but it was as if she did not have the strength to cry.

"How about a neighbor? Or a friend?"

"Maybe the man at number twelve would help?" She didn't sound too sure.

Maria went to knock on his door, and the man who answered agreed to come with her, although he did not seem too robust himself.

"I heard they are running out of coffins," he told her. "Bodies are being taken to old churches for storage until a funeral can be arranged. Perhaps we should take Pavel to St. Panteleimon's. That's probably the nearest."

He sighed when he saw the body still lying where Maria had found it, covered with a sprinkling of fresh snow. "Poor man. What an end," he said. "A year ago, none of us would have left a dog lying in the snow like this, but now . . ." He left the sentence unfinished.

Between them they lifted the dead man. Maria held his feet while the neighbor clasped his chest, and they staggered slowly to the church, slithering on the icy pavement. In her head, Maria prayed for him, commending his soul to God.

"Will you look after the widow?" she asked before they parted.

"My wife and I will do what we can," the neighbor said. "I wish you and your family strength."

~

A month later, Maria looked back on the day she found Pavel lying in the snow and remembered how little they suspected then of what was to come. By mid-January 1942, it was common to find bodies in the street. Some folk sat down on a wall for a moment's rest and never got up again; others lay in gutters, half buried in snow, their faces blackened and mouths gaping to show lost teeth. Every time she came across a body, Maria searched for a ration card so she could notify a relative, but sometimes it had already been stolen. Coats and shoes were often missing too. There was no longer any respect for the dead, and that felt unbearably sad.

By popular demand, a few Orthodox priests came out of hiding and began to conduct church services. Maria went to St. Vladimir's Cathedral every Sunday and prayed for her own family, for her baby Pavel, for Peter—always for Peter—and for all the souls whose bodies she had found in the streets that week. She no longer visited the cemetery where Peter lay. As her strength ebbed, the walk was too much, and she could not bear to see the piles of corpses waiting for burial. The temperature had dropped to minus thirty and the earth was too hard to dig graves anymore.

All her children were thinner, but Mikhail's pallor had improved since she started finding ways to slip him a little extra food.

"More supplies will be on the way soon," her friend at the factory told her. "The Ice Road has opened at last."

Maria wanted to jump for joy. For some weeks they had been waiting for the ice on Lake Ladoga to freeze to a depth of eight inches, because then it could take the weight of a truck driving over it and their city would once more be connected to the rest of the Soviet Union. She felt proud of her nation's engineers. Germans would never manage such a feat. Only Russians with their long, cold winters knew how to use the elements to their advantage. She remembered the French Emperor Napoleon's defeat in Russia in 1812 because his troops did not know how to survive the cold, and felt a glimmer of confidence that the war would soon be over.

"What food do you think they will bring first?" she asked, and they began to salivate as they talked of succulent beef cooked in a cream sauce, of rich cakes laced with honey, of potatoes baked on the fire and slathered in butter.

She went home that evening to a watery soup made of dandelions and nettles, and half a slice of crumbly, sour-tasting ration bread.

~

Toward the end of January, a neighbor's boy caught whooping cough. The residents of the block sat in the air-raid shelter listening to his painful bouts of coughing followed by the distinctive whooping sound.

"Have you taken him to hospital?" Maria asked his mother. "That sounds nasty."

"They say most children recover in time," she replied, fear in her eyes.

Raisa leaned across to whisper to Maria. "I think we should

tell her not to bring him to the shelter anymore in case he infects the rest of us."

Maria ignored her, but huddled her children close. When they got back upstairs, she gave them a double dose of vitamin powder, just in case.

Over the next three weeks, every time she walked past her neighbor's door, she heard the boy coughing and wheezing, and she said a prayer for him and crossed herself. And then, one morning, the entire block heard howls like those of a wolf echoing around the corridors and across the courtyard. Maria rushed out to the landing in time to hear the mother scream, "God has taken my son. My only son." She hurried down to embrace her, but the woman fought her off. No comfort could be given.

That evening, Maria was thinking of the boy as she wiped the supper dishes clean with a dampened cloth to save water. How lucky we have been, she thought. She felt guilty that she had five living children while her neighbor had lost her only son. Ingenuity in finding food was important in this siege, but survival was also a matter of luck. Maria had suffered incredibly bad luck in losing her parents and siblings, then poor little Pavel and Peter, but now she had another generation to comfort her, and hers were all good children.

She put the plates in her cupboard and wiped the stove clean, ready for the next person to use, before heading back to her apartment. As she stood outside the door, hand poised to turn the handle, she heard coughing and paused. It was Mikhail; she could tell. He coughed hard, as if there was something stuck in his throat, then went silent. Maria waited, scarcely daring to breathe. And then it came: an unmistakable whooping sound. It felt as though a shard of glass had pierced her heart.

CHAPTER 43

Leningrad, January 1942

MARIA WRAPPED MIKHAIL IN HIS THICK COAT AND warm boots, placed a fur hat on his head, and helped him through the dark streets to the Raukhfus children's hospital, grateful that at least there was no bombing that night. Stepan said the Germans' engines froze with the extreme cold so the aircraft couldn't take off. Mikhail's forehead was burning to the touch and the night air brought on fresh bouts of coughing, but Maria hoped that if she could get medicine straightaway, before he grew too weak, he would fare better than her neighbor's son.

There was no heating in the hospital, and frost glazed the insides of windows. The wards were crammed with children as far as the eye could see. Most lay silent, staring into space, but some called out for help, stretching their arms toward her. She wondered if she had made a mistake in bringing Mikhail to this place where there were so many sicker than him, but they joined the line to see a doctor. Right in front of them stood a girl with lice crawling around her blond hair, and Maria leaned away, feeling her own head itch at the sight.

"A fit young man given adequate nourishment should easily recover from whooping cough," the doctor advised after examining Mikhail. "Take him home, keep him warm, and offer as much food as you can."

Maria was horrified. "Are there no medicines? I hoped you could give us something."

The doctor spread his hands. "I have nothing that would help. Bed rest and good food are your best bet. Now, if you don't mind . . ." He gestured to the line. Their turn was over.

Maria's mind was racing on the walk home. She had to do more, but what? Suddenly it was as if she heard Peter's voice in her head, reminding her that he used to use elecampane root to ease the little ones' coughs. Where could she find some? She racked her brain and remembered seeing a small plant in the corner of the graveyard where he was buried. Would the root have survived beneath inches of snow?

Next morning, she rose at dawn and walked all the way to the cemetery. A couple of times she swayed, feeling light-headed, but she was driven by her determination to get back to her ailing son.

When she reached the corner where Peter's grave lay, she stopped briefly to talk to him in her head. We are surviving, she told him, but Mikhail is ill. If you can hear, please tell me what to do.

A gravedigger's spade lying abandoned on the ground nearby caught her eye. She picked it up and walked to the spot where she remembered seeing the wild elecampane. When she brushed the snow away, she saw that the plant had withered back from frost.

She lifted the spade and hit the hard-as-steel ground, vibrations rippling up her arm. "It's not working, Peter," she muttered out loud. She tried using the sharp corner of the spade, leaning her weight into it and seesawing back and forth. Gradually the earth began to chip away. She felt dizzy with the effort, but at last she broke the ground sufficiently to rip up the elecampane's tuberous roots. She wrapped them in a sheet of paper and laid them in the top of her shopping bag, closing her eyes in gratitude. It felt like another gift from Peter, as if he was still trying to help.

On the way home, she began to feel very faint. She sat on a wall with her head between her knees, but the dizziness would not pass. Every time she tried to get up, the world spun. It started to rain and still she couldn't get to her feet without feeling as though she would topple over.

"Can I help you, ma'am?" a voice said, and she looked up to see a young man in army uniform, cap on his head. "Where do you live?"

She told him, but added, "It's quite far."

"No problem," he said, putting an arm around her shoulders and hoisting her to her feet. He was strong, like Peter; she could feel the muscles through his jacket sleeve. It took almost no effort for him to support her as they walked. Maria didn't talk much, conserving her energy for the effort of putting one foot in front of the other, but the soldier chatted about a show he had seen the night before at the Musical Comedy Theatre.

"Can you believe they are still performing? The auditorium was almost full. I don't think I've ever laughed so much," he told her. "I've only got a week's leave and it was too far to go home, but Leningraders have such incredible spirit that I've really enjoyed my stay."

When they reached the street door, Maria fumbled for her keys. "Please," she said. "Come upstairs and let me give you some bread for your trouble."

"I wouldn't dream of it," he exclaimed. "I get army rations. Take care of yourself, ma'am."

Back in the apartment, she chopped the elecampane root and cooked it in a little water. Peter used to mix it with honey, but all she could manage was a few grains of sugar to counter the bitter taste. Mikhail swallowed it then fell back on his pillows exhausted and slept. Maria wanted to say a prayer for the soldier who had helped her, but realized with shame that she hadn't even asked his name.

~

Two days later Katya began coughing and whooping and Maria moved Irina and Yelena into her own bedroom to separate them from the invalids. She made yet another soup from dandelion leaves and split her own bread ration between her sick children so they got an extra slice each. She kept a pot of water boiling in the room where they slept, hoping the steam would ease the congestion in their lungs, and fed them elecampane root several times a day.

Each morning when she opened her eyes she prayed they would have turned the corner, but as she lay listening it wasn't long before she heard the sound of convulsive coughing followed by a gasped whoop.

She took a week off work, and after her boss insisted she return, Irina stayed at home to look after her siblings. When Maria explained to her colleagues why she had been absent, one of them had a suggestion.

"The children's homes on the other side of Lake Ladoga are well run now. It's not like the early days of the war when everything was chaos. My children are in home number 44, and they write that while conditions are not luxurious, they at least get hot meals every day, and there's a school where their education continues. Perhaps you should send your two over there to be nursed back to health?"

Maria yearned with every fiber of her body to keep the family together, but at the same time she knew she would never forgive herself if one or both died of the whooping cough when she'd had it in her power to save them. What would Peter do? If only she could ask him . . .

On her next afternoon off, she walked to Finland Station to ask about reserving a place on an Ice Road crossing, and was aghast at the confusion. Frantic crowds lined up outside evacuation offices, jostling for a slot, pulling their belongings on sleds behind them. Maria was handed a list of regulations: all passengers must have the necessary stamps and paperwork; only sixty pounds of luggage per person; you had to bring a bowl and spoon for the *kasha* and soup that would be served, and enough of your own food to last a few days. Her eye traveled to the bottom of the page, where a warning notice read: *Those with infectious diseases are strictly prohibited.* Her spirits plummeted. That ruled them out. Mikhail and Katya could not stop coughing for long.

She sat on a low wall and buried her head in her hands. She felt weak with hunger and flattened by despair. Each day she worked as hard as she possibly could: when she was not at the factory transporting shell casings, she was lining up for bread, scavenging for the increasingly rare edible plants that grew in parks and open spaces, or at home nursing her children. There was no rest, no free time. She was doing her best but it seemed that wasn't good enough.

A hand pressed her shoulder. "Maria, how are you?" a familiar voice said, and she looked up to see Yuri, the NKVD officer.

Tears filled her eyes and she looked away, annoyed that he'd caught her in a moment of weakness.

He sat on the wall beside her. "How are your children?"

She shook her head. "Two of them have whooping cough. I had hoped to get them across the Ice Road, to receive proper care, but it seems impossible." She waved the leaflet in her hand.

"Perhaps I can help," he said quietly, and she looked up.

"Why would you do that?" The words came out rudely, which was not what she'd intended; her wits did not seem as sharp these days.

"Because you're a good woman. Because you help others despite your own misfortune." His eyes were gentle and looked directly into hers.

Maria shivered and broke away from his gaze. "It says they cannot go on the ice transport if they have an infectious disease. How do I get around that?"

"What if I got them onto a truck ferrying wounded soldiers back from the front line? They would receive good care and the normal rules would not apply." He squeezed her forearm. "I must cross the Ice Road myself tomorrow night and could keep an eye on them. When I return next weekend I will be able to reassure you they are safe."

Maria took a deep breath. "You would do that for us?" She frowned, puzzled. "I would be greatly in your debt."

"There's no need for such formality." He smiled, the shiny pink scar that zigzagged down his cheek stretching. "Perhaps we could attend a concert together on my return," he continued. "I hear the Radio Symphony Orchestra still give performances."

Maria stared at him in astonishment. His experience of the war must be fundamentally different from hers if he could consider spending time and money on anything but food.

He misread her expression. "I'm sorry. I know it is only a little over four years since your husband died, and perhaps you are not ready, but since we are both on our own, I thought perhaps you would like company. I know I would."

Maria felt sick at the thought that he saw this as some kind of romantic overture, but at the same time she yearned to get Mikhail and Katya safely across the lake. She hesitated, not wanting to give him hope yet at the same time keen to take him up on his offer. "I work long hours and am tired when I finish, but perhaps sometime we will be able to listen to music together. It seems like a dream from another life, one I can barely remember."

"I have always loved music," he said. "I couldn't live without it." He smiled again. "So tomorrow, I will collect the children at four o'clock. Have their bags packed and ready."

"Of course I will," she said. "And thank you, from the bottom of my heart."

~

Maria packed with infinite care. Each child had a large bag with sweaters, socks, shoes, nightwear, and a warm blanket, as well as a small satchel that could be slung around their body. In the satchels she packed a bottle of her elecampane mixture, two slices of bread, a precious jar of preserved food from her stock, and a twist of paper with some vitamin powder. She gave each a purse of money, some pencils, paper, and envelopes with stamps so they could write home, and their ration cards, as well as bowls and cutlery. Yuri had said he would take care of the paperwork.

She tried to think of a sentimental keepsake she could send with each, and at the last minute, she slipped in some wooden animals Peter had carved for them when they were little: a waddling duck that could be pulled on a string for Katya, and a roaring tiger for Mikhail. They would chuckle when they unpacked their bags and found them.

"You must look out for each other no matter what," she told them. "Insist you are not to be separated. Write to me when you arrive and ask at the children's home for help in posting your letters. As soon as the siege is lifted, I will come and find you."

"What if we are better before then, Mama? Can't we come home early?" Mikhail asked.

She nodded. "Of course. Come back as soon as you can. But both of you must travel together. Don't forget that rule."

The bell rang at four and Maria gathered her coat and pulled on her boots so she could accompany them to Finland Station. Yuri was driving an NKVD van and motioned for them to climb in the back. There were no windows, just narrow benches to sit on, and it made Maria feel queasy. Peter had been driven off in one of these vans and they'd never seen him again. She shook the thought away. The children were anxious about the journey and it was important that she sound cheerful and positive. Katya's forehead was burning hot; Mikhail's not so bad. Was she doing the right thing sending them off with an NKVD officer? What would Peter think? She hoped he would agree with her decision.

At the station, Yuri bypassed the teeming mass of people, showed his ID papers to a guard, then carried their bags onto a train already standing at the platform. It would take them on a one-hour journey to Osinovets, before they transferred onto the Ice Road. Maria gave both children a last hug, squeezing so tight they could scarcely breathe. "Write as soon as you arrive," she instructed for the hundredth time.

"We will," Mikhail promised, but Katya was too poorly to answer.

Yuri helped them onto the train and Maria stood watching until it pulled away in a pall of smoke.

What am I doing? she panicked. Have I just made the biggest mistake of my life? If so, it was too late to change her mind. She turned and trudged home with dragging feet. The streets echoed to the sound of the metronome that was now broadcast from public loudspeakers in between classical music concerts and news announcements, like the heavily beating heart of the city. Tonight it felt ominous. When would she see them again? Pray God it would be soon.

CHAPTER 44

Leningrad, February 1942

Yuri had said he would return the following weekend and Maria counted the hours. Had he meant Saturday? The day passed without him appearing. Or Sunday? Still no sign. On Sunday evening, she trudged all the way to the Bolshaya Apartments and persuaded a neighbor to let her into the block, then hammered on his door until her knuckles were bruised. Perhaps he had been delayed by work. That must be it.

"How long does it take for a letter to arrive from the other side of the lake?" she quizzed Stepan next morning, after a sleepless night.

He put an arm around her shoulders and gave her a squeeze. "Personal letters are very low priority. The trucks coming back this way are loaded with ammunition and essential supplies. We must have faith that they are fine, and that they will soon be cured. Anything could have happened to Yuri. Maybe he has been arrested. From what you say, he was breaking more than a few rules."

That thought did not comfort Maria. She was desperate for news. If only she knew where to write to Mikhail and Katya; if only they had a telephone. Her family used to have telephones at the Alexander Palace back in 1917; the technology had been available for decades, but most Russians did not have a home telephone, even in 1942. She supposed that if they had, the Germans would have cut the lines.

Worry gnawed at her insides, making it hard to sleep at night, and her work suffered. She knew she was being less efficient in her duties at the factory, but no one complained. All were growing weaker; all had their personal worries.

~

In late February, Galina came to knock on Maria's door, looking like a ghost.

"My mother is sick," she said. "Please will you come?"

Maria hesitated, but her anger with Galina and Raisa for having Peter arrested had long since faded, now that the struggle for survival was paramount. "All right," she said, and followed the girl to their apartment.

All those years they had lived in the same block, Maria had never been inside Raisa's rooms. They were similar to hers, but more sparse. There were holes in the floor where she guessed they had torn up strips of floorboard to burn for heat. Galina led her to the bed, where Raisa lay on her back, eyes closed, mouth wide, skin a ghastly white. Maria knelt to touch her forehead and knew straightaway that she had been dead for some time. All the same, she checked for a pulse and listened with her ear to Raisa's mouth in case she could detect a hint of breath, but there was nothing. Galina was shifting her weight from foot to foot, looking petrified.

"I'm so sorry," Maria said, and the girl wailed a drawn-out "Noooo!"

"Where is your father?" she asked.

"He died in December," Galina stuttered, and Maria felt

ashamed she hadn't noticed. She'd been too busy caring for
her own family.

"What will I do?" Galina cried, hysteria in her voice. "I
can't look after myself."

She was sixteen years old, like Katya. Too young to manage
on her own. But why should Maria take on someone else's
child, a child who had caused her husband to be executed?
She overruled the bitterness in her heart. "You must come and
live with us," she said. "Do you have any food here?"

Galina shook her head.

"I will teach you to forage. If you are to share our food,
you must help to find it. Agreed?"

"Of course." Galina was close to tears. "What shall we do
with Mother?"

Maria knew that no ambulances were sent to collect bodies
anymore, and that they would never find a coffin in which to
bury her. The temperature was twenty degrees below freezing,
so they had time. "Let's leave her in her bed for now. I'll speak
to someone."

Stepan, Irina, and Yelena accepted Galina's presence without question, and Maria was proud of them. Stepan showed
the girl where he had set traps to catch birds and rats and
asked her to check them regularly; Maria taught her the type
of plants to hunt for and where they might be found; and
every day Galina accompanied Irina to collect their rations,
because individuals carrying a brown paper bag of bread were
liable to be mugged before they reached home.

At the factory, the women shared tips on feeding their
families.

"You can scrape the wallpaper paste off the walls and eat
it," one said. "It's flour and water, after all."

"There's some goodness in leather if you boil it long enough
then drink the water," another volunteered.

"I heard some people have turned to cannibalism," an older woman told them, "even murdering their victims in order to eat them."

"Russians would not do such a thing," Maria insisted. But then she remembered that the men who had butchered her family were Russians. If they could do that, perhaps some would consume human flesh.

The bread ration dropped to just one small slice per person per day, and that was bulked out with sawdust so did little to relieve the pain that twisted their guts. The food at the factory canteen was watered down and there was less of it, so it became harder to bring jugs home. Still Maria tried to make the evening meal look appetizing: a taste of green soup, the occasional mushroom or two, a tiny portion of rat, bird, or fish, when available, and the crumbly, bitter-tasting slice of bread. If she ate slowly, and chewed each bite thirty times, she could almost convince herself it was a meal.

~

When Maria's colleague at work received a letter from her children in home number 44, Maria swallowed her jealousy. Mikhail and Katya must be at a different home, a more distant one where it was harder to post letters. She got Stepan to check at Finland Station, since there were no house-to-house deliveries, but each time he reported there was nothing for her.

The wintry weather eased in March and the Ice Road began to melt, meaning that Mikhail and Katya would not have been able to get back to Leningrad even had they been well enough. It would also be more difficult to get letters through. Every couple of weeks Maria visited Yuri's apartment, but there was still no sign of him. She told herself he must have been stationed elsewhere, but felt cross he had not written to let her know. He must realize she would worry. She sent Stepan to inquire at Bolshoi Dom, but he was told they did not give out information about the whereabouts of officers.

Not knowing what had happened to her children was a constant nagging pain. Maria tried to picture them sitting at a long refectory table with lots of other children, eating meat and potatoes, laughing and chatting, but she couldn't hold the image in her mind for long before anxiety returned. She still laid out plates for them at dinnertime before remembering they weren't there. Her family felt diminished. It was too quiet in the apartment. She missed the noise of everyone talking at once, the arguments over the bath, the smell of their hair when she hugged them. It was different from the way she missed Peter, but no less excruciating.

The bombing raids started again with the warmer weather, and still there was no sign of the Red Army coming to relieve them. One Sovinform bulletin said Hitler claimed he would take Leningrad by August and informed citizens that Jews were being rounded up in all the areas his troops had conquered. It seemed there was regular bad news, drip by depressing drip. Even Yuri Levitan couldn't lighten the message.

At least it was easier to find food in the spring. Stepan caught rabbits out by the barricades, and Maria planted a vegetable patch in the courtyard with some seeds distributed as part of a gardening drive. She nurtured herbs there too: ones Peter had taught her had medicinal uses, such as elecampane and yarrow, comfrey and thyme. Irina got a boyfriend who worked at the Krupskaya sweet factory, and she brought home sugary candies and bars of powdery chocolate that had been made without cocoa. Maria could make a single sweet last all evening by holding it in the pouch of her cheek, the flavor oozing out and bringing a temporary contentment. But then the boyfriend slapped Irina, she told him she wouldn't see him anymore, and their brief moments of bliss were over.

Hitler had not arrived in the city by August, but neither was there any sign of the siege breaking. "We can't last another winter," Maria's work colleagues whispered to each other, memories of the bodies in the streets and the unremitting cold still fresh in their minds. Maria remembered Peter telling her that you could predict the severity of a forthcoming winter by the size of the pinecones and the thickness of squirrels' nests, but she could not decide whether they were bigger or smaller than normal.

A universal gloom descended when the first frost came in October, followed closely by a blustery storm. Maria was scared. When she washed herself in the bathroom, she could see that the skin was stretched tight over her bones. Her kneecaps looked huge, and flaps of wrinkled skin hung off her thighs. It hurt to sit on a stool because there was no flesh left on her bottom. She never looked at her face in a mirror, but knew she must be a sight: four teeth had loosened and fallen out while she was eating, and her hair came away in handfuls when she combed it. She was only forty-three years old, but she didn't know if she could survive another winter.

~

On October 31, when Maria set off for work the pavement was glistening like diamonds in the predawn light. Her boots had worn through and the cardboard insoles she'd made provided little insulation, so her feet were frozen numb soon after she left home. Even wrapped in her heavy overcoat and thick wool hat, she never felt warm these days.

It was several weeks since she had managed to visit Peter's grave, and she missed the peacefulness she found there when she talked to him in her head. She resolved to go soon. She'd been putting it off because she didn't feel strong enough, but maybe she would manage if she walked slowly and stopped for lots of rests.

Suddenly she lost her footing on a patch of ice and slipped. She twisted around, scrabbling to catch hold of a railing, and her right leg bent underneath her. There was a sickening crack as she landed on the pavement and she knew straightaway that her thigh was broken. There was no pain at first, just a sensation of deadness, a feeling that her lower half was at the wrong angle. She lay panting, scared to move in case she made it worse. Her first thought was of that nice soldier who had helped her home before. Where was he now? Stepan was at work, and so was Irina. Galina was taking Yelena to line up for bread, but they would go in the opposite direction. It was quiet along the road where she lay, but someone must pass before long.

The sun began to rise but there was no warmth in it, and Maria started to shiver. She heard footsteps approaching from behind and turned to see a woman, stooped and elderly-looking but probably no older than her.

"I've broken my leg," she called. "Please get help."

The woman barely glanced at her as she walked past without stopping. Maria was distraught. What kind of person would do that? The cold was penetrating her bones now and she began to feel sleepy. That was dangerous; a sign of hypothermia. If she gave in, she would never wake again. There was nothing for it but to start dragging herself home.

She reached out with her arms and pulled herself a few inches along the pavement. A jab of excruciating pain made her scream out loud. She paused and tried to shift her weight so that the other leg was closer to the ground, then pulled herself forward again. It was still agony. For a moment she thought she would give up; just lie down and die. It was tempting. But then she pictured her children. Little Yelena was only just eleven and needed her mommy. What would Mikhail and Katya think when they got back to find her gone? And she would be letting Peter down if she did not do all she could to stay alive.

Gritting her teeth, she dragged herself forward once more. When she reached the main road, several people walked around her with eyes averted. She didn't ask for help now, just focused her will on each movement onward.

It must have been over an hour later when she reached the corner of her street. The sun was fully risen and the ice was melting, soaking through her coat. Her leg was throbbing, sending needles of pain up her spinal cord, but the door to her block was in sight.

"Mama!" a voice screamed, and she turned to see Yelena rushing down the road, with Galina close behind carrying a basket. "What happened?"

"I fell on the ice." Maria bit her lip at another spasm of pain. "Can you find someone to help me upstairs? I can't walk."

While Yelena went inside to fetch a neighbor, Maria told Galina the truth, that her leg was broken.

"You should be in hospital," Galina said, but there was no way to get her there.

Yelena returned with a teenage boy who lived on the ground floor, and among the three of them they managed to lift Maria so that her bad leg dangled and she half hopped, was half carried up to the third floor.

There was a table leg from Raisa's apartment in the wood-pile. Maria asked Yelena to bring it to her along with some clean rags, then she peeled back her coat and lifted her skirt to look at her thigh. It was hideously swollen, like an elephant's leg, marked with red and purple blotches, but at least the bone had not penetrated the skin.

"Take my boots off, then leave me alone," she ordered. "I need to be on my own."

Once they left the room, she gripped a pillow between her teeth and felt along her thigh with her fingers, poking through the swelling to see where the bone was cracked and how it should lie. Biting down hard, she pushed it into place, almost passing out with the pain. Tears streamed down her cheeks as she tied the chair leg to her thigh as a splint, pulling hard to tighten the knots. When it was done, she dragged the bedcover over herself, laid her head on the pillow, and lost consciousness.

CHAPTER 45

Leningrad, November 1942

WHEN STEPAN RETURNED, HE WAS SHOCKED BY HIS MOTH-
er's condition. She was shivering with fever and delirious
with pain. He piled on extra blankets and stoked a fire in her
bedroom. Doctors didn't make house calls anymore, and he
had no way of getting her to the hospital. They did not have
so much as an aspirin powder in the house, but he remembered
his father's teaching and made a poultice of comfrey root from
a plant in the courtyard, then wrapped it around her thigh.

Over the next week, Maria drifted in and out of consciousness. She had complicated dreams in which she was running
in the grounds of the Alexander Palace with her brother and
sisters, looking for someone who was missing. She moaned
and murmured, "Tatiana."

"Who is Tatiana?" a voice asked, and she opened her eyes
to see Stepan. Why did he not know?

"Your aunt, of course," she said, gritting her teeth against
a wave of pain before drifting off again.

One night she woke in pitch dark and wondered if she had
already died. She could hear voices in her head. "Let go,
Maria. Come to us. It's your time." It felt as if they were
trying to drag her down a long tunnel. She could sense her

family was there, but not Peter. Why did he not come for her? Maybe that meant they were wrong and it wasn't her time . . . But it must be close. She was too ill. She would not survive this.

Stepan appeared at her bedside with a flickering kerosene lamp. "You were moaning, Mama. Can I get you something?"

She shook her head. It was impossible to swallow now. She knew she didn't have long. But there was one last thing she must do before she died. She must tell Stepan that they were Romanovs, because otherwise the truth about their heritage and an important part of Russian history would be lost forever. He was a sensible soul who would not take the risk of telling others. But where to begin?

"I was born Maria Romanova," she said, her voice faint and husky. "I grew up at the Alexander Palace in Tsarskoe Selo. My father was Tsar Nicholas, my mother Tsarina Alexandra. I had three sisters, Olga, Tatiana, and Anastasia, and a little brother, Alexei." The words flowed once she had started, and he listened carefully, narrowing his eyes in concentration. What if he did not believe her? He must.

When she reached the part about their house arrest and then the brutal execution in the basement, tears filled his eyes. Good. That meant he believed her.

"I opened my eyes where I lay in the back of a truck, facing a fate worse than death at the hands of the men who swarmed all around, and there was your father. Peter." She choked up at the memory. "I asked him to help me and he picked me up and ran into the forest. For three days he ran with me on his back, stopping only to tend my wounds and rest a few hours. He saved my life."

"That's where the jewels came from," Stepan whispered, his eyes glistening in the lamplight. "I understand now."

There was more she had to tell him. "You need to know

that Tatiana did not die in the basement. She had gone to meet her lover, Dmitri Malama, to plan our rescue. I have tried to find her since then but with no luck."

"You have often murmured her name during your illness," Stepan said.

"My aunt Olga lives outside Copenhagen. We have written to each other but it proved impossible to visit. When I die, you must get word to her somehow." She closed her eyes, sad to think she would not see Olga again.

"Mama, you will not die," Stepan insisted. "Stay with us. Please."

She reached for his hand, squeezed it tightly. "I'm trying." She racked her brain. There was something else he had to know. "Your father's real name was Vasnetsov. He had a mother and sister in Ekaterinburg. We have written to them but have not been able to tell them where we are . . ." She paused, too weak to think clearly. Hopefully he would understand.

"Did you know Papa before he rescued you?" Stepan sounded overcome with emotion.

"He was a guard at the house. One of the good ones." She remembered him there: so shy and tongue-tied.

"Were you lovers?" Stepan whispered, stroking her hand.

"No, we were friends." She remembered how awkward he had been when she took his photograph at the top of the stairs. "We didn't become lovers till the end of the summer, when my wounds had healed."

Stepan paused. "But how is that possible when I was born on the third of April? Was I premature?"

Maria was dumbstruck. It hadn't occurred to her he would work that out.

"You must have been lovers before," Stepan persisted.

Maria was tempted to lie to him. The truth was too awful. But she felt sure she would not live through the night, and now was the time for truth. "Your father was another guard in the house, a man who raped me. His name was Anatoly Bolotov. I'm sorry, Stepan."

He pulled his hand away from hers and cried, "No!"

Straightaway Maria hated herself for telling him. She should have lied. If only she'd been thinking straight, she would never have blurted it out. "It made no difference. You were Peter's son in every sense. You are more like him in character than any of your siblings."

Stepan stood up, the lamp swaying. "No!" he whispered again, horror in his voice, and strode toward the door.

"Don't go!" Maria called after him, but he left the room and she heard his bedroom door slam behind him. She had done a terrible, unforgivable thing. Stepan would be devastated and there had been no need for him to know. A tiny lie was all it would have taken. She squeezed her eyes tight shut in shame.

~

She woke the next morning as Irina came into the room carrying a cup of comfrey infusion, its crisp cucumber scent cutting through the smell of woodsmoke and her own sweat.

"Where's Stepan?" she asked straightaway.

"He's gone to work," Irina told her, sitting carefully on the edge of the bed, placing a hand on her mother's forehead.

Maria turned her face away. She yearned to speak to him, to explain.

"I think your fever has broken, Mama," Irina said. "Here. Try to drink."

It was true. Maria felt better, as if she had emerged from a cocoon of fuzziness into the clear light of day. Perhaps sharing her secret had helped—but she had shared too much. Peter would be cross with her. There had been no need.

She heard Stepan return later and called for him. He appeared in the doorway, such a wounded expression on his face that she felt a stab of remorse.

"I just wanted to say that I'm sure you will have questions for me and you may ask me anytime."

He nodded. "I need to think first. But thank you."

Maria fought back tears. "You must understand that Peter was your father by any measure that counts. Your character, your morality, your strength, your humor—all are his."

"Was Anatoly Bolotov dark-haired?" he asked, and Maria nodded, sucking in her lips. "I have often wondered why I am the only dark one in the family. And now I know."

"Please don't blame me," she begged.

"It wasn't your fault my father was a rapist. Don't worry, Mama. I just need time to get used to this news. I'll be all right."

He turned, and she heard the clank of the metal shovel as he began scraping the ashes from the fire in the next room.

~

Maria sat on the edge of her bed and tried to stand up but could not manage. Her broken leg ached with the effort and the other one seemed to have stiffened up and would not bear her weight. She lay down and exercised on the bed: bending her knee then straightening it, sliding her leg out to the side, lifting it off the sheet. It hurt, but she must get some strength back if she was ever to walk again. Twice now she had thought she was about to die and God had given her a reprieve. It was up to her to snatch this chance with both hands.

One evening Stepan came home shouting in excitement. "Everyone! Come and see what I have brought."

He burst into Maria's bedroom carrying a canvas bag from

which he produced a chicken. A whole chicken, complete with head and feathers! It was followed by a bunch of carrots and a round·cabbage, then he held open the top of the bag to show a pile of muddy potatoes. "Our troops have opened a land corridor along the shores of the lake. These supplies arrived this morning and all the gunners got a share."

Maria started to cry. She couldn't help it. "Will the war be over soon?" she asked. "Does this mean we are winning?" If there was a land corridor, surely Mikhail and Katya would return?

"It's a start, Mama. We will beat them back from Russian soil, inch by inch and foot by foot."

Her stomach gurgled at the aroma of the chicken boiling in the pot, and when she sipped the rich, flavorful broth Irina made, she could feel warmth spreading through her bones and strength flooding her veins. It hadn't been her time to die. She had to get used to the idea of living.

"What date is it today?" she asked Yelena, who had come to sit with her.

"The eighteenth of January."

"What year?" she asked, confused. It had been the end of October when she fell on the ice. Had she really been in bed for nearly three months?

"Nineteen forty-three, of course."

Maria set herself goals: by the end of January she would be walking around the apartment; by the end of February she would walk to the park. And in March she would start searching for Mikhail and Katya in earnest. She wanted them back in Leningrad with her and their siblings in time for the summer, and she wouldn't take no for an answer.

CHAPTER 46

Sydney, October 1975

V AL WAS THRILLED WHEN A LETTER ARRIVED TELLING her she had been accepted on the history course at the university, starting the following January, and straightaway she began working through the recommended reading list. She felt self-conscious about the gaps in her knowledge. History had been taught in a piecemeal fashion at her school. She knew about Captain Cook and the convict colony at Botany Bay; she knew about the Federal Constitution declared in 1901 and about all the Australian soldiers who had died at Gallipoli in the First World War. But what had happened in between? And how about the rest of the world?

The course would last three years, and at the end she would have to submit a dissertation. She decided she would like to write about the fate of the Romanovs. It was a subject on which she had firsthand information, and Bill Koskov might be able to help if any documents had to be translated from Russian.

Until the course started, she continued working at the telephone exchange, and he often stopped by to say hello. Bit by bit she learned more about him. He was single and lived with a sheepdog called Bess in a house across the bay at Manly, where he was in easy reach of good surfing beaches. He cycled to the university from the ferry dock every morning and then back in the evening, in all weathers, so he must be sportier than she had thought. And he liked going to the movies. Val had never been to the cinema because Tony didn't fancy sitting still in the dark without a beer in his hand. Bill was aghast when she told him that she hadn't seen *Jaws*, or *Picnic at Hanging Rock*, or *The Rocky Horror Picture Show*.

"These are classics," he exclaimed. "You're missing out on the cultural landmarks of your time."

Val shrugged, with a smile. "Kinda goes with the territory when you have a little one."

"Don't you have a friend who can babysit?" he asked. "Come and see *One Flew Over the Cuckoo's Nest* with me next Saturday. Jack Nicholson's in it and the reviews are ecstatic."

Val was taken by surprise. Did he mean this to be a date? No, it couldn't be. "I'll, erm, ask a friend and let you know," she replied.

She rang Peggy, who was instantly enthusiastic.

"It's about time you went on a date," she gushed. "You're in your prime. All that perfect skin and gorgeous black hair and no one to appreciate them: it's a crime."

Val protested. "There's no way I want a boyfriend. I haven't got time, and Nicole and I are happy on our own."

"Just go!" Peggy chided. "You've got nothing to lose. I'll have Nicole for a sleepover in case you are overcome by lust."

"Lust? What's that?" Val replied. "I've read the term in books but never experienced it."

Peggy laughed, but the fact was, Val thought, it was true.

~

She sat awkwardly in the cinema, careful not to let her elbow touch Bill's on the armrest. They shared a box of popcorn but he ate most of it, scooping up huge handfuls and hoovering them down. The film was excellent: funny and affecting, and Val had to wipe away tears before the lights came up at the end.

Bill insisted on walking her home, wheeling his bike beside him, and they talked about the themes of the movie—mental illness, the use of electroconvulsive therapy—and the great performances by the cast.

At Val's front gate, he carried on talking and she worried that he expected to be invited in. Would he want coffee? Or a beer? Or would he expect to have sex? She tried to remember if she was wearing matching undies. If they did have sex, would it be awkward at work on Monday? Would he think she was an easy lay? She was so busy worrying that she had stopped listening to what he was saying and was jolted back to the present when he remarked, "Do you know, I've never told anyone about that before. You're a great listener."

He leaned over and touched his lips to hers, and she tensed. It wasn't a long kiss. He didn't try to put his tongue in her mouth, which she hated. But it was a kiss that was more intimate than friends would share. And it was nice.

When he broke away, he smiled. "Can we do this again sometime? I need to educate you about cinema, after all."

"OK. Yes, I'd like that," Val replied, feeling like an idiot.

Bill started to wheel his bike down the road. At the corner, he turned and bowed ostentatiously. Val waved.

She lay in bed afterward, curled in a fetal position, her hands pressed between her thighs, nerves all aflutter. What was it that he'd never told anyone before? How could she find out now? Had she kissed him back too much or too little? Should she have invited him in? Did he like her? It certainly seemed that way. What if they started dating and it didn't work out but they had to carry on working in the same place? The mixture of anxiety and excitement kept her awake until the early hours, and she was groggy but smiling ear to ear when she collected Nicole from Peggy's the following morning.

~

Next time they went to a movie Bill suggested dinner first, and it was lovely. Conversation flowed and they laughed easily, but still he seemed happy to leave her with a kiss at her front gate.

Maybe he doesn't fancy me? Val worried. Maybe he's just being friendly.

Then there was another date, and another, and suddenly it was Christmas break.

"Would you and Nicole like to come to Manly for a day over the holidays?" he asked. "I'll make lunch, and I'm near the beach so you could have a splash in the waves."

Val fretted over this. What would she tell Nicole? How would she explain who Bill was? In the end, she said a friend had invited them, and Nicole replied, "Cool!" and didn't ask any questions.

Bill's house was like a summer rental, just a couple of blocks from the beach. When he opened the door, his dog poked its head out to greet them, and Nicole squealed with delight and reached out to pat her.

"She's so soft," she cooed, stroking the silky ears.

"Her name's Bess and she's four years old," Bill told her, but Nicole was so absorbed in the dog that she ignored him.

"Mommy, can we get a dog like this? I *love* her," she trilled.

"I don't know how she would get on with Toffee," Val

cautioned. Toffee was Nicole's pet rabbit, who lived in a hutch in their backyard.

"They'd be best friends," Nicole said airily, the expert on such matters.

Bill led them through to a big kitchen with glass doors opening onto a sunny terrace. On a table he had laid a spread of salads, cold meats, and roast chicken legs.

"I decided to make a self-service picnic in case there's anything you don't like, Nicole," he told her.

She glanced at the table. "Eggs are the only thing I don't like."

"Phew! I didn't do eggs." He grinned.

They ate on the terrace. Bess lay by Nicole's feet, eyes half closed but still alert for any food that might be dropped.

"I think you have a fan," Bill said, and Nicole smiled, pleased with herself.

"I'm good with dogs," she said, although as far as Val was aware, she hadn't known any others.

Val had worried what they might talk about and whether there would be awkward silences, but they chatted about Bess, then about kites, and cycling. Nicole had not yet learned to ride a bike, and when she told Bill, he offered to teach her, then glanced quickly at Val to see if he was overstepping the mark.

"That's very kind," she said, wondering if he had meant to make such a big promise.

When she went to the bathroom, she had a chance to look around the house. It had wooden floors and basic furniture, little in the way of ornament, but it was clean and tidy. A surfboard painted in pink and purple swirls stood against one wall, a bookshelf was built into an alcove, and there was a large TV in the corner. It was a man's house but it looked comfortable. All the time she was collecting information, storing it away. Who was this person? Could she trust him? Would he ever hit her or break her bones? She hadn't known many decent men in her life: there was Peggy's husband, and a few of their friends, but otherwise she'd been let down by every man she had ever come across.

After lunch, they went to the beach. Val was shy taking off her sundress to reveal her figure in a swimsuit, but Bill set her mind at rest by winking in a way that was appreciative without being lascivious. He seemed lankier and more angular in his trunks than with his clothes on—all elbows and knees and skinny torso. He and Nicole ran down the beach with a big psychedelic-patterned kite, shrieking with laughter as it nearly lifted her off the ground.

Val sat on a towel watching, and a sensation of immense peace came over her. Maybe, just maybe, this was going to be all right.

CHAPTER 47

Sydney, January 1976

Bill began to visit val's house on weekends, and good as his word, he taught Nicole to ride a bike. He was so tall it must have strained his back to bend double, holding onto the saddle so she didn't fall, but he persevered until she was confident enough to wobble down the road on her own. Val cooked her best dishes for him and he was appreciative, always insisting on doing the washing up. He left in time to catch the last ferry back to Manly, kissing her on the front step. The kisses lasted longer now, and there was a warm hug to go with them, but he never once asked if he could stay over.

"Maybe he's gay," Peggy suggested.

Val shook her head. "I don't think so."

"Why don't you make the first move? Then you'll find out."

"God, no!" Val shrieked. She was secretly glad there was no pressure to have sex. It would be a whole other area to worry about. She was sure she must be terrible in bed. *Cosmopolitan* and other women's magazines gave tips on how to be a hot lover and she didn't understand half of them, while the rest terrified her. It seemed there was a lot of pressure around sex these days. Bill would probably expect her to be knowledgeable since she'd been married such a long time, and she hated to think she might let him down.

They had been dating for over five months when one night they lost track of the time and Bill realized he had missed the last ferry.

"Stay over," Val insisted. "I can make up a bed on the sofa."

She fetched sheets, a blanket, and two pillows and had begun to arrange them when Bill came up behind her and put his arms around her waist, burying his face in her hair.

"You are lovely." He whispered because Nicole was asleep upstairs.

Val turned in his arms and kissed him. "So are you," she said shyly.

Still she didn't intend to make love with him, but the kiss continued, and she loved the sensation of his hand stroking her back, cupping her head, and then his lips on her neck. They sank onto the sofa together and everything happened naturally, slowly, easily, until he was inside her, moving gently, still kissing her. She raised her hips to meet his and sighed with bliss. Sex had always been painful with Tony, but this sex made her skin tingle all over, and the sensation deep inside was exquisite. His fingers were touching her down there and she wondered what he was doing but it felt so good she couldn't bear him to stop. Suddenly there was a rush of blood and an intense sensation that made her cry out.

Bill kissed her and she could feel he was grinning.

"Was that an orgasm?" she gasped.

"You've never had one before?" He broke away, astounded, to look her in the eye.

She shook her head. "I love it, though."

"Good." He kissed her forehead, her eyelids. "I'll have to give you lots more to make up for lost time."

Later, as they lay in each other's arms, drifting off to sleep, Val asked, "Why did you never try to seduce me before?"

He gave her a tight hug. "I could feel how scared you were and I didn't want to push it before you were ready. I couldn't risk you running away."

Val's eyes filled with tears. It seemed incredible, but perhaps her luck when it came to men had finally changed.

~

Nicole didn't bat an eye when Val and Bill started sleeping in the same bed, either at his place or theirs. She liked him, she liked Bess, and Bess completely ignored Toffee the rabbit, so that wasn't a problem. Peggy and Ken liked him too, and so did Sandra and Lynette. He fitted easily into their social circle and Val liked his friends, both the university bunch and the surfers. It all felt so easy; she kept looking for problems but none arose.

Her course had started at the university, and she loved going to lectures, making copious notes, and discussing topics in tutorials. All the other students were much younger, and that made her more confident about expressing her opinions. Who would have thought it? The timid woman who used to be married to Tony could never have done this. If only she could have told her mother that she was happy at last.

One evening she told Bill about her trip to China to find Ha Suran. Tears filled her eyes as she described hearing about her death in a letter.

"That's tough," he sympathized. "But thank goodness you had time to get to know each other again. It sounds as if it was very important to you."

"Yes, it was," Val agreed. "It changed me. I suppose remembering that there was someone who loved me and believed in me gave me the confidence to build the life I have now."

"Sounds as if you were always strong, but in the years living with your dad and Tony you needed that strength just to survive." He shook his head. "I can't imagine what you went through. My parents were always loving. That's why it came as such a shock when they decided to leave Australia. I took it personally, as if they were leaving me."

"Where do they live now?" she asked.

He frowned. "I told you about them. Remember? Way back on our first date."

Val blushed. "I was so nervous that night I wasn't paying attention. I'm sorry."

He didn't seem to mind her memory lapse. "They were White Russians who fled in 1918 and went first to Paris, then during the 1930s they moved to Sydney. I was born and brought up here but they always pined for the old country. It was difficult for me three years ago when they said they were returning to Moscow. It was the height of the Cold War, Brezhnev was clamping down on dissidents, and I didn't want them to end up in a gulag so I argued myself blue in the face. We fell out badly just before they left."

"You must miss them terribly." Val had a vague memory of him talking about them as they stood at the garden gate that first night. How awful of her not to have listened. "Have you seen them since?"

He shook his head. "No. But I'll get the chance this August. I've been invited to speak at a linguistics conference in Moscow." He stopped and looked at her as if he'd just had a brain wave. "Why don't you and Nicole come along? You should see the country where your father was born."

"Are you serious? I'd love to go to Russia. I can catch up

on any coursework I miss, and I could take Nicole out of school for a while. But isn't it hard to get a visa?" Her mind was galloping ahead.

"I'll ask my hosts to arrange it. I know my parents would love to meet you. We can tag on a trip to Leningrad afterward so you can see the Romanov palaces."

Val could hardly contain her excitement. "What about Ekaterinburg? Could we go there?" She longed to see the Ipatiev House and the town her father came from.

"It's called Sverdlovsk now," he replied, "and it's closed to foreigners. The Soviets are very sensitive about the fate of their erstwhile royal family, so you'd better not mention your research while we're there."

"Mum's the word," she said. But secretly she hoped she would learn more about the Romanovs on this trip, and more about the father she had hardly known. She could take along his Fabergé box and try to find an expert to explain how it worked. Of course, she'd learn more about Bill too: it would be wonderful to travel with this seemingly perfect man who, as far as she was concerned, had yet to put a foot wrong.

CHAPTER 48

Leningrad, January 1944

O N JANUARY 27, 1944, THE SIEGE WAS OFFICIALLY
lifted and Maria and her children joined the crowds of
Leningraders celebrating in the city's parks. They were a sorry
sight, with skeletally thin faces and overcoats that hung off
their shoulders. Even the young ones were stooped and pale,
but the celebrations were heartfelt. No more air raids! No more
gunfire! No more claustrophobic sense of being encircled by
enemies!

Conditions had been improving over the last year, with the
electricity and water supplies reinstated and more food arriving via the land corridor along the lake, but Maria had been
unable to find any information about where Mikhail and
Katya might be. Not a single letter from them had gotten
through. Yuri had not returned to his apartment, which still
lay empty, and she was met with blank looks wherever she
tried to make inquiries. She would have to wait till the authorities brought her children back or they made their own
way home.

In February, groups of children began to arrive at Finland
Station to be reunited with their parents. Maria jumped every

time she heard the street door slam. Katya was eighteen now, Mikhail almost sixteen, and she knew they would be changed. What had they endured during their two years away? Galina had a boyfriend and looked set to marry soon. Might Katya have one too?

The children of her work colleague returned with rosy cheeks, the picture of good health. They complained that they had been forced to help with housework and gardening at their children's home, and had to follow strict rules regarding bedtimes and mealtimes, but they were none the worse for it, she reported, clearly overwhelmed to have them back.

But still no Mikhail and Katya. Maria heard that an office had been set up near the Admiralty building to help reunite families; at last the authorities were trying to do the job she had been doing in her small way ever since she arrived in the city. She rushed there and stood in line for a couple of hours, chatting to her neighbors in the line and hearing their stories of tragedy and loss. It was good to keep her mind occupied as she waited, but her stomach was churning.

When her turn came, she approached the desk and gave Mikhail and Katya's names, their home address, and the date they had been sent across the Ice Road. The woman consulted list after list before shaking her head.

"I'm sorry. They were rather disorganized at the other end. Yours are not the only children we can't find a record of, but it doesn't mean they are lost. I'm sure they will arrive home in due course." She bit her lip, obviously aware how hollow her words sounded.

"How can that be? I sent them in good faith for the state to care for them. And you don't know where they are?" Maria tried to rein in her fury. It wasn't this woman's fault.

"I'm sorry. These things happen in wartime."

Maria clasped her hands to stop them shaking. "Can you give me a list of the homes they might have been sent to so I can look for myself? And the hospitals as well? If you can't find them, I will."

"Of course. Let me get you a copy." The woman hurried to another office and came back with a list several pages long.

"There's one other person I need to find," Maria said. "Could you look for an NKVD officer called Yuri Koshelev? His address was Bolshaya Apartments, but he hasn't returned there."

"I'm sorry." The woman shook her head. "We're not allowed to give out information about the NKVD. You understand, I'm sure . . ."

On the bus home, Maria scanned the list. There were over a hundred homes and hospitals, stretching from Arkhangelsk in the north to Kiev in the south, and west as far as Moscow. It was daunting but she knew she must check them all. Maybe there was a reason the children had not returned. Maybe one was sick and the other had refused to leave without them. She would find them herself, no matter how long it took.

Back in the apartment, she marked each location on a map. She decided to start with the closest ones and gradually extend her search area. She had two days off work every week, so she could stay overnight and travel back the following evening.

Stepan tried to talk her out of it. "They could be anywhere, Mama. Better to send out letters of inquiry and wait for news."

She knew he meant well, but they were not his children. One day he would realize what it was like to be a parent; one day he would feel the visceral tug on your heartstrings when you were apart from any one of them.

~

On her first day of searching, Maria took the train around
Lake Ladoga, then transferred to a local bus. Her broken leg
had set badly and she limped heavily, but that was always
useful for getting seats on buses. She had sketched images of
Katya and Mikhail—good likenesses, if she said so herself—
in case they helped to jog someone's memory, because there
must have been hundreds of children passing through each
institution.

She visited three separate homes that day, and each time
she knocked on the door, a member of the staff looked at her
drawings, checked the names, then shook her head. From what
Maria could see, the homes did not have many comforts: long
corridors, wooden chairs and tables, harsh overhead lights. But
at least the children had food, she comforted herself. At least
they were safe in their beds.

One woman told her they had several younger Leningrad
children whose parents had not responded to letters asking
that they collect them. Maria took a list of names and addresses
from her and promised to hunt for their parents. More likely
than not they had perished during the war years, but if she
could reunite even one family, it was worth the trouble.

When she visited hospitals, she tensed as they checked the
records of children who had died there. She wasn't ready for
that kind of news and knew she never would be, but she had
to explore every possibility.

Each time she approached a new home, she felt a skip of
excitement. Let this be the one, she prayed. Then came the
shake of the head, the sympathetic look that dissolved her
optimism. Not this one; not yet.

When she headed home after the second day of searching,
she was filled with despair. Russia was such a vast country.
Was she kidding herself to think she would just stumble across
them? Yet if she was methodical enough, surely she must?

They had to be somewhere. She put crosses beside the places she had checked, then circled the ones she would travel to next.

"Mama, you're exhausted," Irina exclaimed when she arrived home weary and footsore. "Let me go instead."

But Maria shook her head. They were her children. She would find them.

Her search for relatives of the children abandoned in the homes was largely fruitless. She knocked on doors but got no replies. It seemed they were orphaned and must stay where they were until they were old enough to look after themselves. Only once did she find a young girl's aunt.

"She's alive?" the woman screamed, unable to contain her joy. "I must go to her immediately. Thank you a million times."

When Maria lay in bed at night, she felt bitter anger with the state that had swallowed her children into a vast impenetrable system; with the NKVD officers who had executed Peter for no good reason; and with Stalin, who had coldly abandoned Leningrad to its fate. Her ancient anger for the men who had killed her family still lingered in the background. Sometimes she felt her rage spilling over until she wanted to stand in the street and scream at the top of her voice against the injustice of it all. Instead she took a deep breath and channeled it into her determination to find her children. For her friends and colleagues, life began to return to normal, but for Maria there would be no normal until Mikhail and Katya were home once more.

CHAPTER 49

Leningrad, January 1944

H AVE YOU HEARD ABOUT THE PALACES, MAMA?" STE-
pan demanded when he returned one evening.

Maria looked up at her normally placid son's tone of outrage.
"What about them?"

"The Nazis ransacked and burned them. All that artistry—
up in smoke." He was clearly furious.

"Really? Why would they do that?" It puzzled her, but she
supposed pillage had always been a part of war.

"They must be animals!" Stepan ranted. "They stole the
panels of the Amber Room at the Catherine Palace, the gold
fountains from Peterhof, and any works of art that were not
hidden. What they could not carry, they destroyed. All the
trees were chopped down in the park at Pavlovsk. At Peterhof,
the building itself is partly exploded." He shook his head in
outrage.

Maria felt less concerned at this than she did at the loss of
human life, but decided it was not the time to say so.

"Anyway, I've applied to be part of a team working on the
restoration," he told her. "They think my languages could be
useful if they have to source materials from overseas."

Maria looked at him in surprise, then went to the door to

check that Irina and Yelena were out of range before she spoke. "I can understand you wanting to know more about our imperial heritage, and I'm glad of it—so long as you don't take any risks . . ." She left the implication hanging.

"Your approval means a lot to me," he told her. "And of course I'll be careful."

Within weeks, Stepan had been assigned to the team restoring the Peterhof palace, now known as Petrodvorets. He was to be trained in laying parquet flooring, molding cornices, and applying gold paint to decorative features, as they painstakingly returned the palace room by room to the way it had been in the Romanovs' time.

"Perhaps you can help, Mama," he said to Maria. "You knew it well, I suppose."

Maria nodded, her thoughts slipping back to the years before the First World War when her family used to spend the months of May and June there, strolling in the gardens by the Gulf of Finland. Those innocent days had the shimmery quality of a fairy tale: days before Russians began informing on their neighbors, before the state executed its best men in great purges, before a whole city was left to starve.

～

The summer passed, and another winter came. When arctic storms blew across the land, Maria could not make her trips to search for Mikhail and Katya because the buses were not running. She stared out the window at the horizontal gusts of hail that rattled the panes, fretting about lost time. Soon it would be three years since she packed them off on the Ice Road. Did they think she had forgotten them? They must know that would never happen.

When news came in February that Stalin had met Winston

Churchill and President Roosevelt at Yalta to discuss carving up Europe at the end of the war, Maria seethed that their leader was emerging from the conflict with his prestige boosted. Did the others know that he held his citizens' lives as cheap as dirt? Did foreign newspapers report that Leningraders had dropped dead in the streets in their thousands because he would not send the Red Army to help them? She wanted to spit at his picture in the street but restrained herself.

By March, the thaw had set in and Maria began her search again, traveling further afield now. Always she carried her bulging card file of missing people and added cards for any displaced Leningraders she came across, checking to see if she had details of their relatives. She felt responsible when she saw the hope on their faces, then its gradual fading when she could not find whom they were looking for. She knew the sensation well because it was exactly what she felt with each children's home she approached: hope and then heartbreak.

~

In July 1945, Maria took an overnight train all the way to the town of Yaroslavl to check some children's homes, and during the journey she fell into conversation with a policeman in the same carriage, a man by the name of Leonid. They exchanged stories of their families' fates during the war: his wife had died in an air raid and his mother was helping to raise his infant daughter so he could continue to work.

"What is the work you do?" she asked.

Leonid made a face. "I interview Soviet soldiers who were held prisoner by the Germans. My orders are to make sure that no one with anti-Soviet views comes back into society."

"But the poor men must be traumatized!" Maria cried. "They need support, not interrogation."

He nodded agreement. "Many suffered starvation or disease on forced marches during the last year of the war. Feeding and caring for them was the lowest priority for the German army, so they are in a very poor condition. But I am ordered to question them about whether the Nazis gave them assignments to fulfill on their return, or if Anglo-American intelligence officers brainwashed them. Many can barely speak. It's a horrible job."

Maria was astonished that he should confide in her, a stranger, but everyone spoke more freely in those postwar days. Pulling together to survive the privations of war had created more trust.

"It seems a crime that these men are not allowed home to their families straightaway," she said. "I know firsthand how much they are missed because I run an unofficial missing persons bureau. Look." She opened her bag to show him her index, flicking through a few cards to give him an idea. "Each of these represents a family that has been separated. I do my best to help them."

He smiled warmly. "What a wonderful thing to do!"

"I had many people show me kindness during the war, so it seems only right I should return it," Maria said, and she told him of the soldier who had brought her home the day she felt faint.

"I know what you mean," he replied. "When my apartment building was bombed, my baby daughter was trapped inside. Alerted by her crying, a dozen passersby climbed onto the rubble, despite the danger, and dug down brick by brick to rescue her. I will always be in their debt." He wiped his eyes with his sleeve.

At dinnertime, they shared the food they had brought before lying down on the hard wooden benches to try to get some sleep. When Maria opened her eyes in the dawn, yawning and stiff, Leonid was already awake.

"I've been thinking," he said. "If I give you a list of the Leningrad prisoners of war being held under my jurisdiction, might you be able to let their families know where they are? They are not permitted to write until they have been cleared, but it seems cruel to leave their families in the dark."

"Goodness!" Maria was surprised. "I'd be happy to try."

When the train arrived at Yaroslavl, she accompanied Leonid by tram to the police station where he was to interview some men that afternoon. She waited in the vestibule while he went to fetch the latest list, still marveling that he would trust her with it. How times had changed!

He returned with a sheet of paper with dozens of names, in alphabetical order, along with each serviceman's army number and his last-known address.

"I'll do what I can," she told him, glancing at it. "I wish all the happiness in the world to you and your daughter."

She caught a bus to a children's home nearby, and during the journey she began to scan the list, checking the soldiers' names against her card index, marking with a question mark where there could be a possible match. And then her heart skipped a beat. There, under Dubov, was the name Mikhail Alexandrovich. The same name as her son.

Don't be silly, she told herself. It can't be him. He's too young for the army.

She continued to the children's home, but there was a voice echoing in her head: "What if it *is* him? What if he's here?"

No one at the home had heard of Katya or Mikhail, so she caught the bus back into town and alighted outside the police station, her leg aching badly from all the walking. Leonid was nowhere to be seen, but at the inquiries desk she pointed to her list and asked, "How do I find out where this prisoner of war is being held?"

Memories of the cruelty of the officer at Bolshoi Dom came flooding back, but this one consulted a ledger, then walked through a door behind him to ask a colleague. When he returned, he had a piece of paper in his hand.

"Mikhail Alexandrovich Dubov is at this prison, just across town, awaiting filtration."

"Filtration?"

"Waiting to be assessed." He smiled. "Relative of yours?"

"I don't know. Maybe."

"Go and ask," he suggested. "They might let you see him. Number 46 bus."

As she stood at the bus stop, Maria chided herself. Don't get your hopes up. This is a wild-goose chase. Lots of people have the same name. She spoke to Peter in her head. I have to try every lead, though, because so far nothing is working.

Out the window she saw acres of ruined buildings and piles of broken stone; this town had clearly suffered enemy air raids, just like Leningrad. It was afternoon now and she decided that after visiting the prison she would try the hospital, then look for somewhere to spend the night. There were two more homes to visit in the morning.

The bus driver called out to let her know when they reached the prison. It had a double row of barbed wire around it, some squat brown buildings, and a yard in which a few dozen men in army uniform were milling around. Maria walked to the point where the road ran alongside the yard and peered through the fence, scanning the men one by one. Now that she was here, it seemed a crazy idea.

One of them called to her. "Who are you looking for?"

"Mikhail Alexandrovich Dubov from Leningrad," she replied.

The man yelled into the crowd. "Is Mikhail Alexandrovich

Dubov from Leningrad here?" A couple of others echoed his
call and word was passed around. Suddenly a figure stood up
and came running full pelt toward the fence.

"Mama!" he called, and his voice rose to a scream. "Mama!
Is it you?" He looped his fingers through the fence and began
to sob.

Maria couldn't believe her eyes. He had a long beard, his
hair was matted, and he looked a decade older than his seventeen years, but it was unmistakably Mikhail.

"Get me out of here," he pleaded through his tears.

"I will," she promised, a big lump in her throat. "Hang on,
and I will."

CHAPTER 50

Yaroslavl, July 1945

MARIA WENT TO THE PRISON GATE AND SPOKE TO A
guard. "My son is being held here but there must have
been some mistake. He's only seventeen so he was too young
to fight. Please can I speak to someone?"

She was allowed inside and made to wait over an hour in
a corridor with no chairs before she was led to the governor's
office, where she repeated her story.

"Let's get your son to explain himself," the man said, and
Maria gave a sob of joy.

When Mikhail was led in, she leaped to her feet and embraced him. He was skin and bone, his clothes in tatters—but
he was alive.

"Are you all right? Are you in pain?" she asked first.

He shook his head. "I'm fine."

"How could you be in the army? Is it a mistake? Were you
forced to join up?"

"No." He looked at the floor and spoke in a mumble. "I
was separated from Katya on the Ice Road. I looked everywhere, for months, and couldn't find her."

Maria's throat constricted. She squeezed his hand tight.
"You should have written."

"I was too ashamed at losing her." He gave her a quick glance. "I couldn't get back to Leningrad and I was so angry with the Germans for causing this war that I decided to lie about my age and sign up."

"In 1942?" She was aghast. "You were only fourteen. Who would let you?"

"It was the following year. Just after my fifteenth birthday. I was tall for my age so they didn't question me. I did basic training then was sent out to fight, and within three weeks I had been captured by Germans. I was held in a prisoner-of-war camp until we were released in May and brought here." He looked at the governor. "Now I'm waiting for filtration."

Maria turned to the man. "Surely you can't hold him any longer now you know how young he is? Please can I take him home today?"

"Every prisoner must be interviewed," the governor replied. "There are rules and regulations. I must ask you to leave for now and—"

"No, please." Maria clung to Mikhail, running her fingers through his hair, breathing in the scent of him.

"I'm sorry about Katya," he said quietly. "You made us promise to stick together. Is she home now?"

"Not yet." Maria frowned. "Tell me: how were you separated?" She held her breath as she waited for the reply.

Mikhail closed his eyes. "There was a bombing raid while we were crossing the Ice Road. The truck in front of us was hit and ours turned over, throwing us out. I landed on the ice and lay there stunned until your friend Yuri picked me up and carried me to another truck. He said he was going back for Katya—but he didn't reappear. Our truck started to drive off and I begged them to wait for my sister but they said I would find her at the other side." A tear escaped and rolled down his cheek, and Maria kissed him. "But it was mayhem when we arrived, with so many people and no systems in place. I was taken to hospital and as soon as I was well enough I started looking for Katya, but no one seemed to know anything." He looked at Maria. "What did Yuri say? He must know where she went."

Maria shook her head. "Yuri never came back to Leningrad."

"He didn't?" Mikhail opened his eyes and stared at her in horror. "So where is she? Do you think she . . . Could she be dead?"

"No." Maria spoke firmly. "I have been looking for both of you. Now that I have found you, I will carry on looking until I find Katya. I know she is alive, because if she were dead, I would feel it in my heart. Mothers always know."

Mikhail gave a sigh of relief. He believed her.

Maria pictured the scene on the Ice Road and tried to imagine what had happened. Yuri must have put Katya in a different truck so she was taken to a different home. But where was her little girl now?

~

The day after finding Mikhail, Maria returned to the police station in Yaroslavl and asked for Leonid. When she told him that her seventeen-year-old son was being held awaiting filtration, he rushed across town to interview him personally and had him released by the end of the day.

"Thank you," Maria breathed. "We spoke of kindness on our journey and I will never forget yours."

She bought Mikhail a hot meal before they caught the overnight train to Leningrad.

All the time she couldn't stop gazing at him, drinking in the changes. His voice had deepened, his eyes seemed sunken, and he was taller, much taller.

"Stop staring, Mother." He smiled. "You're making me self-conscious."

She wanted to touch him, to straighten his collar, hold his hand, but she restrained herself. The joy of being with him after all this time was overwhelming.

"The others are fine," she told him. "Stepan is working at the Peterhof palace, helping to restore it; Irina is studying law at university, and Yelena is working hard at school. I can't wait to see their faces when we walk in the door."

Mikhail looked sad for a moment, and she knew he was thinking of Katya.

"Next weekend," she said, "I will carry on the search for your sister. There are still many places to try."

"I'm sorry I didn't write, Mama," he said, his face stricken. "How could I tell you I lost Katya when you had told us we must stick together no matter what?"

"It would have been better to know." He looked so distraught that she quickly added, "But I have you back now and that is all that matters."

As darkness fell outside the train window, she asked him about the prisoner-of-war camp. There was a long pause. "I will tell you sometime," he said eventually. "But not tonight. Not for a while. Do you understand?"

Maria nodded. From the look in his eyes, she could tell it had been bad. She shuddered. It was unthinkable what her children had been through. Life had to get better now. It must.

CHAPTER 51

Leningrad, summer 1945

THE CHILDREN'S HOMES AND HOSPITALS THAT MARIA
had not yet visited were all a long distance away. If the
journey took almost a day, she would have no time to search
before she had to turn and head home again. Reluctantly she
decided she would write to each one instead. The postal
service seemed to be working again, and if she sent a stamped
envelope, she hoped they would reply.

Meanwhile, she began visiting the relatives of Leningrad
men who were being held in Yaroslavl prisons. It was wonderful to share good news, and some families were so delighted
they showered her with gifts of jam, cakes, and sweetmeats.
So much food seemed a miracle after the years of starvation
and she developed a sweet tooth. When there was enough
sugar, she made the almond toffee that had been her favorite
as a young girl.

Please God, she prayed, bring good news for me soon. But
the letters that came back from far-flung children's homes and
hospitals said they had no record of Katya. Maria filed them,
putting a cross beside each name on her list. There were still
many who had not responded, so she clung to hope. She would
never give up, she vowed. Not ever.

Mikhail was quiet for the first few weeks after his return and spent a lot of time in bed. Maria worried that he was brooding, and asked Stepan's opinion.

"He was always quiet," Stepan reminded her. "The women are the chatterboxes in our family, while the men keep their thoughts to themselves."

Maria had to admit that was true. She had always been much more talkative than Peter, and both Irina and Yelena chatted nonstop throughout their waking hours.

"He told me a little," Stepan continued. "He says it was bad in the prison camp but other men looked out for him because of his age. I don't think any lasting harm has been done. He feels terrible about losing Katya, but I reminded him he was so ill with whooping cough that night he could barely walk. There was nothing more he could have done."

"Thank you for talking to him," Maria said. Maybe it was easier for Mikhail to share his experiences with another man than with his mother. She didn't mind so long as he was recovering from his ordeal.

"Would it be all right if I bring a friend for supper on Saturday?" Stepan asked, and there was something about his tone that alerted Maria. He was trying so hard to sound nonchalant that the effect was anything but.

"Of course," she replied. "What's your friend's name?"

"Ludmilla." He blushed, and bent to adjust his shoelace. "She works with me at the palace."

Stepan was twenty-six years old and this was the first girl he had brought home, so Maria was curious. Her eldest son was not particularly handsome, with his heavy-set brow, but she knew the right girl would love him for his gentleness and steadiness—the qualities she had fallen for in Peter.

She was startled on Saturday evening when Ludmilla arrived: an exquisitely pretty girl with pale blond hair, green eyes, fine features, and an intelligent air. She handed Maria a box of chocolates from the Krupskaya sweet factory, tied with a red satin ribbon.

"I'm delighted to meet you," she said. "Stepan speaks of you constantly."

"My goodness, I hope you two have more interesting subjects to discuss," Maria said. "Let me take your coat. Please sit down. Have something to drink." She had laid out a choice of tea, barley water, or *kvass*.

Stepan kept his thoughts to himself while the women chatted. Yelena wanted to know where Ludmilla's coat came from, which led to a discussion of the new clothes shops that had opened in Gostiniy Dvor, then to the thriving black market in clothing coupons, which were easily available under the counter at any street market.

Before the war, they could never have trusted a stranger like this, Maria mused. They would have talked in generalities and certainly never have admitted cheating the system in any way. Of course, there were still informers, there were still purges, and the NKVD still turned up to make arrests in the night, but not nearly as often.

When Maria went to the kitchen to finish preparing the food, Ludmilla followed her.

"Can I help?" she asked, then caught sight of the spread. "Heavens, you've gone to so much trouble!"

Maria had made little side dishes of potatoes, salads, and pickled vegetables to go around the centerpiece of a whole salmon Stepan had caught, cooked with fresh dill from the garden she had cultivated in the courtyard. It did look fetching. "Thank you." She smiled. "I'm very glad to meet you. Stepan has never brought a friend home before."

Ludmilla colored slightly and Maria was pleased. That meant she liked him too. "Tell me about your family," she said as she placed serving spoons onto each dish. "How did they fare in the war?"

"My father was killed at the barricades in 1943," Ludmilla said. "Stepan knew him slightly, and I'm glad of that. He was a good man."

"I'm sorry for your loss. Did your mother survive?"

"She was executed in 1937," Ludmilla said, her tone flat.

Maria gave a sharp intake of breath. Normally no one would admit this.

Ludmilla continued. "She was a devout woman and refused to give up her religious observance even when warned repeatedly by the NKVD. At the time I felt angry that she did not hide it for the sake of her family. But now I think she was extraordinarily brave to stand up for her beliefs."

Maria shook her head. "She must have been torn between her family and her church. What a tragic story!"

Ludmilla nodded. "We all have our sorrows. Stepan told me about your husband. It's such a waste."

"The purges, the war—I feel as though God forsook our country long ago. As if we are paying the price for ancient sins."

Ludmilla reached out and touched Maria's shoulder. "I'm so sorry about your daughter too," she said. "If there is anything I can do to help with your search, you must ask."

All of a sudden, Maria's eyes filled with tears. Silly! She shouldn't cry in front of a stranger, but sometimes her grief welled up unannounced. She turned away, trying to disguise it. Ludmilla slipped an arm around her waist and laid her head on Maria's shoulder in a gesture that was both warm and natural. Maria returned the embrace and the women stood in silence for a minute, holding each other, sharing their sorrow.

Before they broke away, Maria kissed Ludmilla's cheek. "Stepan has good taste," she whispered with a smile.

~

Three weeks later, Ludmilla and Stepan announced their engagement. It would be a civil service, of course, but Maria suggested they keep some traditional elements, such as tying the bride and groom's hands with a *stole*, smashing crystal glasses into shards, and providing a feast for friends and family. They would both wear gold rings, and there would be many toasts to their good health and fertility.

When the day came, Maria missed the solemnity of the church service, with its sacraments, prayers, and vows. She remembered her own wedding to Peter, which she had sobbed all the way through, almost drowning out the priest's words. She cried at Stepan's wedding too, with a mixture of joy and sadness. Joy that he had found such a good woman and that her family was expanding once more; and deep sadness that Peter and Katya, whom she loved more than life itself, could not be there.

CHAPTER 52

Leningrad, 1949

FOR THE FIRST YEARS OF THEIR MARRIED LIFE, STEPAN and Ludmilla lived in Maria's apartment. She rearranged the beds to give them their own room, but in truth they were seldom there. They left early in the morning for the journey by tram and bus to Petrodvorets and were not back till mid-evening.

The other children also spent less time at home. Irina was dating one of Ludmilla's cousins; Mikhail was at college training as a carpenter; and Yelena had finished her school exams and taken work in a dress shop.

Galina had long since married, but she came to visit, and always Maria looked at her and wondered what Katya was like now. They were the same age. Was Katya married? Did she keep her hair long or short? Did she wear makeup? Maria was her mother and should know these things. She often saw her daughter in her dreams, but always in the distance and out of reach, and when she woke, she felt the pangs of loss anew.

One cold but sunny Sunday in November, Ludmilla asked Maria if she and Stepan could accompany her to visit Peter's grave.

"I'd like to pay my respects," she said. "And Stepan and I have something we want to discuss with you."

As they walked, Stepan and Ludmilla chatted about the restoration of the Peterhof palace; both were passionate about the craftsmanship. With Maria's permission, Stepan had told Ludmilla of his mother's Romanov past, which meant they could talk openly when the three of them were together.

"I wish you would visit the palace," Stepan said. "There are many matters I would love to ask your advice about."

He had asked before and Maria always said no. She did not like to be reminded of the opulence of the first eighteen years of her life. It felt fundamentally wrong that at a time when Russia's young men were being blown to pieces in their thousands, she and her siblings had lived in grand palaces. She still felt fury with Stalin and the party apparatchiks who had abandoned the people of Leningrad, and it helped her to understand the anger ordinary Russians had felt for the Romanovs in 1917.

They reached the graveside and Maria set out the picnic she had brought, greeting Peter silently. She liked quiet so she could tell him everything that had happened since her last visit and try to imagine his replies. She knew he was there, somewhere, even though he had not believed in the heaven of her church.

"Mama, Ludmilla and I have some wonderful news," Stepan said, "and we wanted to tell you here, in this special place."

Maria looked at him, clasping her hands to her breast. What could it be?

"We're having a baby." Ludmilla beamed. "It's due in June. Your first grandchild, Maria. You'll be a *babushka*."

She was so choked, she could hardly speak. She hugged Ludmilla, hugged Stepan, wiped her eyes. "Do you hear that, Peter?" she said at last, looking at the grassy mound where he lay among so many others. "We'll be grandparents." She laughed, shook her head. "I couldn't be happier."

"There's something else." Stepan glanced at Ludmilla. "We have decided to move to Petrodvorets before the baby is born and we would like you to come with us. The air is cleaner than in the city, and I will be able to come home at lunchtime and spend plenty of time with my new child."

Maria felt a twinge of jealousy. She had always feared Ludmilla would take her elder son from her, and now it was happening. "I can't leave Leningrad," she replied. "I have three children here, and I need to be home when Katya returns."

"Irina, Mikhail, and Yelena can look after themselves," Stepan argued. "But Ludmilla and I have no experience with babies and will need your help."

That was tempting. Maria loved babies. "I could visit at weekends," she offered. "But I have my job at the factory during the week."

"Mama, you are fifty years old. Don't you think you are rather old to be mending conveyor belts? Why not retire and let your children look after you?" Stepan had clearly given this a lot of thought.

Maria didn't love her job, but she enjoyed the company of the other women there. "I couldn't just stay at home and do nothing," she protested. "I need to be occupied. Anyway, what about my missing persons file?"

Ludmilla had a suggestion. "Why not give your file to the missing persons office in town? They have details of many more people than you, so the chances of them achieving reunions is surely higher."

"They didn't find Mikhail," Maria objected. "They can't find Katya." The truth was, it was simply a job to the women there, while for her it was a mission. If she kept searching,

she hoped that one day she would find Katya and then maybe
Tatiana. But if she gave up, it wouldn't happen.

Ludmilla clutched her hand tightly. "You know I think of
you as the mother I no longer have. Please say you will be
with me for the birth."

"Yes, of course I will," Maria agreed. She wouldn't have
missed that for the world.

~

Stepan and Ludmilla moved into their Petrodvorets apartment
in March 1950, and Maria went to visit soon after. It was a
clean, spacious modern block with communal gardens all
around and pleasant views across town. Ludmilla had put up
some watercolors of flowers that Maria had given them as an
Easter gift and they looked very grand in gilt frames.

"This would be yours," Stepan said, leading her into a large
corner room with windows on two walls that looked out onto
some lime trees.

Maria had to admit it was nice. She could imagine sleeping
there and wakening to see the branches swaying against the
sky and hear the rustling of leaves.

"I'll stay some of the time," she agreed before leaving. "When
you need me. But my home will still be in Leningrad."

Stepan nodded, with a smile. "That's fine, Mama. Let's just
see how it goes."

~

On her next visit, Maria brought vegetable seeds and cultivated
a patch at the back of the garden. She liked gardening. It was
peaceful there, and full of birdsong from rosefinches, siskins,
and nightingales, as well as the squawks of hooded crows.

When Ludmilla reached her eighth month, Maria took over the shopping and cooking to ensure there was a proper meal ready for Stepan when he got home, and that her new grandchild got plenty of good nutrition.

A midwife had been engaged, but it was the middle of the night when Ludmilla went into labor and Maria took charge with utter calm. She sent Stepan to boil water and bring fresh towels and she held Ludmilla's arm, supporting her, as they walked around the room. Ludmilla felt hot, so Maria opened the windows wide and they looked out at the stars in the night sky, feeling the soft breeze on their skin.

"I'm scared," Ludmilla whispered as pain gripped her.

"So was I with my first," Maria replied. "But nature has designed us for this. You'll be fine."

Ludmilla dozed between contractions and Maria sat in a rocking chair by her bed, thinking about her own life: all the births and deaths she had known, all the loss and the happiness too. When dawn began to break, it was one of the most beautiful she had ever seen: orange and pink with streaks of gold, like a religious painting.

Ludmilla awoke with a loud shriek. "The baby's coming! Help me!"

Maria felt her belly, looked between her legs, and realized she was right. There was no time for the midwife now. She would deliver her first grandchild herself.

She wiped the sweat from Ludmilla's brow, gripped her hand, and told her to push, then rest, then push again, and it seemed no time before she could see the top of the head, all white and sticky with mucus. She pulled the baby out and checked the cord was not around the neck. It gave a little mewl, eyes screwed tight against the morning light, and Maria's heart turned over with the weight of her love.

"Is it a boy or a girl?" Ludmilla asked, and Maria shook herself. She hadn't checked.

"A girl," she said.

She cut the cord and began to clean the child, wetting the corner of a towel and wiping her skin with utmost gentleness. Everything was perfect: nose, toes, ears, fingers, knees, every little bit. She felt giddy with joy. Having her own children had been special, but a grandchild . . . Nothing could compare to this.

Suddenly the baby's eyes opened and she squinted up at Maria. There was something about the gaze that reminded her of Katya, though she couldn't have said what.

"I don't know you yet, but I would lay down my life for you," Maria whispered. And as she said it, she knew it was true.

CHAPTER 53

Moscow, summer 1976

WHILE BILL WAS ATTENDING HIS CONFERENCE, VAL
and Nicole were shepherded around the sights of Moscow by a sturdy female guide with bad teeth. Her English was fluent but she spoke in a monotone that made it hard to concentrate, and Nicole was soon bored to distraction.

"Is there nowhere for children, Mommy?" she whispered. "Where do Russian children go?"

Val passed on her question to the guide, who shook her head firmly. They had to stick to the program: Red Square, the Kremlin, lunch, St. Basil's Cathedral, in that order, according to a strict timetable. Val was intrigued to see the gold-domed Cathedral of the Dormition, where Tsar Nicholas and his wife had been crowned in 1896, and the Grand Kremlin Palace, which had been the Romanov family's residence when in Moscow. Compared with the drab gray buildings she saw in surrounding areas, the Kremlin complex was a vivid splash of glitziness.

In their hotel, a stern woman sat at a desk in the corridor outside their room. They were only allocated one towel per person, so when Val wanted to wash her hair, she went to ask for another, miming what she needed it for. The woman reacted with horror and shook her head so emphatically that Val wondered if she had committed some terrible faux pas. Bill had warned her before they arrived that their hotel rooms might be bugged, so they couldn't talk freely.

"All the hotel staff will work for the KGB," he told her. "They report anything suspicious. Whatever you do, don't mention the Romanovs."

Val was surprised. "I thought that was just anti-Soviet propaganda."

"Not at all. They catch foreign businessmen in honey traps with Russian prostitutes and blackmail them for trade secrets. Happens all the time. Don't worry . . ." He grinned, catching the look on Val's face. "I'm not going to fall for it."

The KGB were the modern version of the Cheka, the secret police her father might have worked for when he was searching for Maria Romanova. He had visited Moscow on at least two occasions, according to the ledgers. Where did he go? What was he thinking? Here in his homeland, with Russian speakers all around, he was never far from Val's thoughts, but she felt no closer to understanding him than she had back home in Sydney.

On the day Bill's conference finished, they caught the Metro across town to visit his parents in the southwestern suburb of Novye Cheryomushki. They lived in a concrete four-story block surrounded by trees, not far from the station. Val felt nervous about meeting them, but she needn't have. They seemed overjoyed to see Bill, and to welcome her and Nicole, showering them with compliments: "Look how pretty you are. Such a beautiful dress. You are so kind to visit us old people."

They were ushered straight to a table and served a lavish dinner of Russian specialities: borscht, *pelmeni*, stroganoff, and a multilayered honey cake called *medovik*. Nicole ate three slices of cake, smacking her lips with glee. It was clear that Bill's mother had worked all day to produce this feast, and Val thanked her effusively.

"You don't speak any Russian?" Bill's mother asked. "Why did your father not teach you?"

"I wish he had," Val replied. "I think he wanted me to identify as Australian, although he remained very Russian himself. He went to the Russian church and read only Russian newspapers."

"Of course he did." Bill's father nodded. "Those born in Russia never stop being Russian." He glanced at Bill, and Val watched them. There was affection, but she sensed both were thinking about the bitter argument they'd had when his parents announced they were emigrating.

She was still learning about this man who had unexpectedly become her lover, so it was fascinating to see him with his parents. They were clearly good people and that made her feel more confident that she could trust Bill, that he did not have a hidden propensity for cruelty, as Tony did.

"Which part of the country did your father come from?" Bill's mother asked.

"Ekaterinburg. Sverdlovsk, I believe it's called now."

"Ah, that's mining country. And what was his family business?"

"I don't know anything about his family," Val had to admit. "I was hoping to visit the city during this trip to find out more, but Bill tells me it is impossible."

The old couple looked at each other. "There could be a way," Bill's father said. "But you must not let anyone hear you speak English because it's a closed city and foreigners are not allowed. Also it's a long way; over a day to get there." He looked at Bill. "As a visitor you would not be permitted to buy train tickets, but I could do it for you."

"It would mean a lot to Val," Bill said, "but we don't want to put you at any risk."

"No, no," his father insisted. "We are perfectly safe. Those outside the Soviet Union have an image of it as a police state where people are arrested every day, but I speak my mind here and come to no harm."

"Life is good," his mother added. "We are with our own people and we're happy." She smiled at Val. "I'm glad you have come to visit us in summer when the town is at its best. I wouldn't encourage you to come in winter. But I do hope you will come again."

~

The arrangements the following morning proved complicated. Their Russian minder took Bill, Val, and Nicole by taxi to the dock, where they were scheduled to catch a boat and sail through the canal system to Leningrad. Bill said goodbye and gave the woman a tip, but still she hung around, clearly planning to wait until the boat sailed. They got on board and hid in their cabin, peering surreptitiously through the window until at last she gave up and disappeared into the crowd. Once the coast was clear, they disembarked, dragging their luggage, and caught a taxi to Kazanskaya station, where Bill's father was standing by the Ural Express platform with their tickets.

"You have to change in Kazan," he explained. "Just show the Kazan tickets for now so no one realizes you are planning to go further."

"It's like we're secret agents," Nicole whispered to Val.

She put her finger to her lips. They had to keep quiet anywhere they might be overheard.

At the barrier, a guard eyed them with suspicion. Bill spoke to him in Russian as he checked their tickets, answering the questions that were barked at him without hesitation. Val held her breath until they were waved through. They found seats in a compartment on their own and watched out the window as the train pulled out.

The first part of the journey felt interminable: eight hundred miles of fields, mountains, factories, and drab towns. Val had brought coloring books and board games to entertain Nicole, but soon she was irritable with the sheer tedium.

"I don't like Russia," she said. "It's a country for old people."

"I'm sorry," Bill told her. "I promise you'll like Leningrad. It's full of pretty palaces where princesses used to live."

"Princesses are for kids," Nicole said scornfully, clearly believing that at the age of almost eight she was too grown up for such things.

Eleven and a half hours later, they pulled into Kazan in the late evening. Nicole was sound asleep and had to be wakened as they wandered the station looking for their onward train. There were several sitting at platforms but none had their lights turned on. Bill went to question a guard and came back shaking his head.

"I can't believe it. There are no trains to Ekaterinburg till tomorrow afternoon, but there's a bus outside that leaves in an hour. I suppose we will have to take that."

Val felt a lurch of anxiety. "Is it safe? Should we not give up and go back to Moscow?" She had visions of them all being arrested by the KGB, then interrogated in separate cells.

"Bus is probably safer than train," Bill said. "There is just one driver, and no guards asking for ID. We've come this far, it would be a shame to turn back."

The seats on the bus were cramped and uncushioned, and once the sun rose in the morning, the atmosphere was stifling and airless. On and on they trundled, stopping in small towns along the route. Val and Nicole could not risk speaking even in a whisper so they wrote notes to each other: "I'm thirsty"; "What time is it?"; "How much longer can it be?" Val had a tight knot of anxiety. This was her idea and it had been a crazy one; she hadn't realized quite how long it would take, and how uncomfortable the journey would be, or she would never have suggested it.

They traveled all through that day and into the following night, sleeping only intermittently, before the bus pulled into a town square early the following morning. Bill nodded at Val and stood to get their bags from the rack above. This was Ekaterinburg. Val felt a tingle of excitement, despite the stiffness of her joints, the headache from lack of sleep. This was where the Romanovs had arrived in 1918, and it looked as though little had changed since then. She had been expecting a grim industrial town, but her first impression was of green spaces: parks, tree-lined boulevards, and pretty gardens. This was the view that had greeted Maria and her parents as they arrived, little knowing that they had less than three months to live.

CHAPTER 54

Sverdlovsk, summer 1976

BILL CONSULTED A MAP HE'D BROUGHT AND THEY walked uphill, past some pillared and porticoed buildings, to Vozhnevsky Prospekt. As they climbed higher, there was a clear view across the town and Val could see factory chimneys belching smoke in the distance.

As soon as she spotted the Ipatiev House, she felt goose bumps prickling her skin. It was two stories tall, with decorative cornicing and roof ridges, the bottom floor partly underground because of the way it was set on a slope. The fence that had surrounded it in 1918 was gone, as were the guard posts. Instead, there was a canopied front entrance with a printed sign alongside. Bill translated: "Museum of Revolutionary History."

"Does that mean we can go in?" Val whispered, and Bill nodded. Nicole scuffed her heel back and forth on the pavement and sighed to express her dissatisfaction with this plan.

In the hallway, Bill did the talking as he paid for their tickets and was given a plan of the house. He took Nicole's hand and led them through a door into a dimly lit office, with nothing to distinguish it. "We're supposed to follow the arrows around the ground floor first," he whispered, "although the main rooms where the family lived are on the upper floor."

"We'd better obey," Val replied. "But let's make it quick. There's nothing down here."

They walked through a bewildering succession of rooms full of posters proclaiming the glories of Communism, then out into a yard.

"This is where the Romanovs exercised," Bill said, referring to his plan. The ground sloped steeply and was shadowed by trees, with a climbing rose growing over a pergola. "Over there is the basement," he told Val, "but I don't think we should take Nicole inside. Russians don't tend to sugarcoat grisly details."

Val glanced at the open door and could see a flight of stark stone steps lit by a bare bulb. If she was to write about this as a historian, she should take a look, no matter how much her instincts were warning her not to. It was unlikely she would ever be back there again.

"If I pop down for a moment, will you keep an eye on Nicole?" she asked, and he said, "Sure."

She walked slowly down, her steps echoing. At the bottom, she found herself in a concrete-walled room full of packing cases. A door straight ahead was bolted shut so she took another door on the right and straightaway knew she was in the murder room. Great gashes had been hacked in the plaster of the back wall, exposing the crisscross laths beneath. Piles of rubble lay in front and there were dark patches on the floor that made her shudder. It couldn't be blood, could it? Not so long afterward. All the same, she trod carefully to avoid it.

The walls had been papered in a stripy pattern that had faded now, and they were studded with holes that could only be bullet holes. Loads of them. The killers must have fired and fired and kept firing. For a moment Val felt as if she could smell the gun smoke and hear the family's terrified screams in that enclosed space. The atmosphere crackled with something awful.

Her chest felt tight and her breathing became shallow. Was there enough oxygen? Which was the way out? There were some double doors at the back of the room and she felt momentarily disoriented. Were they the ones she had come in through? Panic took hold until she spun around and saw the other door: it must be that one. The Romanovs couldn't escape that way because their murderers were lined up in front of it.

She hurried into the concrete storeroom, then ran up the steps two by two into the sunlight. At first she couldn't see Bill and Nicole and feared something had happened to them; then she noticed them peering at a wall.

"It's a blue butterfly," Nicole whispered as she got close. "Isn't it pretty?"

"You all right?" Bill asked, noticing the expression on her face.

She grimaced. "No sugarcoating at all."

They made their way back to the main entrance, where the bored receptionist was reading a magazine and barely looked up as they headed for the stairs to the upper floor. On the landing they stopped and listened but there didn't appear to be any other visitors. As they walked into the first room, Bill whispered translations of the words on his plan.

"This was the study of the commandant of the guards, first Avdeyev then Yurovsky," he told Val.

There was faded purple wallpaper with gold palm leaves on which hung a doleful stag's head. Cushions were scattered across a daybed, and on one side there was a large leather-topped desk. Val walked around slowly, drinking in the details and scribbling notes in a spiral-bound notebook.

Next they followed a corridor toward a second set of steps and the lavatory. It was closed to the public but she could see the rope bellpulls the family were supposed to ring when they wanted to use it. They walked through what used to be a kitchen, with a huge iron range, then into a dining room with red and gold wallpaper and a dark-wood sideboard and table. It was eerie to think of the Romanovs eating their meals there, unaware that their days were numbered.

The bedrooms along the far wall of the house were sparsely furnished, with tall south-facing windows—no longer white-washed as they had been in the Romanovs' day. Val could see out across the town. A cathedral was visible in one direction and she imagined that must have been galling for the family, who were disappointed not to be allowed to attend church after they arrived in Ekaterinburg. The rooms were small; it would have been a crush for fourteen to sleep in them. And only one toilet! Did they have a rota?

They walked into the adjoining sitting and drawing rooms next and saw that they were lined with display cabinets of old photographs and newspaper cuttings. Val peered into the first cabinet, pen poised, and Bill translated the captions for her.

"This is Yakov Yurovsky, the commandant in July 1918," Bill said, pointing to the first photograph. The man had a thatch of dark hair, a bushy beard, and a moustache that curled at the sides. Val thought he had mean eyes.

"This one is Peter Ermakov, and the revolver alongside is said to be his."

Val glanced across to where Nicole was examining some needlework lying on a side table. She did not appear to be listening.

"My father had a gun just like that," she said, making a face. "I don't know why."

Bill moved on to a photograph of a handsome young man with dark hair and smiling eyes. "This one is Ivan Skorok-hodov. Hey! Wasn't that your father's name?"

"What?" Val peered at the picture. "It was, but this doesn't look anything like him. But I'm sure this man was in one of the photographs from Dad's camera."

"It says he was a guard here but spent three months in jail in 1918 after getting too close to the Romanov family." Bill looked at her, a question in his expression.

"I know Dad spent some time in jail, so I suppose it's possible, but . . ." She couldn't see any resemblance at all.

The next picture showed a man called Konstantin Ukraintsev. "Here's another one whose picture was in your dad's camera, and it says he was also dismissed for getting too close to the family," Bill told her. "There's a theme here. The Romanovs must have been likeable people if they had to keep changing the guards when they became too friendly."

There were pictures of more guards: Igor Droyadov, Alexander Kotlov, Vassili Petrov, all with short biographies. Val recognized several of the names: they appeared on the fake identity papers her father had used. He must have known these men. But how?

She stopped in front of the next picture and gasped, covering her mouth with her hand. It was unmistakably her father as a young man. He had the same pronounced brow, the same dark eyes. Although he could only be about twenty years old in this picture, she knew without a shadow of a doubt it was him.

"What does this caption say?" she asked, and Bill leaned over.

"Anatoly Bolotov. He was recruited from the Verkh-Isetsk metallurgy plant on the eighth of July 1918 to become a guard here. That's just eight days before the family died."

"He was a guard? Are you sure?" Val felt sick. It meant her father must have been working there when the Romanovs were executed. That would explain why he had the camera and the leather bag with the photo album and sketchbook. Had he stolen them that night? Why had he told her mother his name was Ivan Skorokhodov?

"Are you OK?" Bill asked. "You look a bit pale."

"I think I need some air," Val replied. There was an oppressive atmosphere in the house. Dust motes danced in slants of sunshine, and there was a smell of rotting wood and something else she couldn't put a finger on, something sickly sweet.

"OK, let's go," he said straightaway, putting an arm around her waist. "Shall we find some food? I'm starving."

"You're *always* starving," Nicole giggled.

Val trailed behind them, trying to take in what she had learned. She felt ashamed of her father. He must have known what had happened to the family in the basement; perhaps even witnessed it. Yet still he had seized the opportunity to steal their possessions. It was grotesque. She was embarrassed to be related to him—and terribly worried as to why he had lied about who he was.

CHAPTER 55

Petrodvorets, 1951

L UDMILLA HAD ANOTHER BABY THE YEAR AFTER HER
daughter Anna was born—a little boy called Alexei, who
emerged from the womb with a full head of thick dark hair.
Maria doted on her grandchildren and scarcely spent any time
in Leningrad because she couldn't bear to leave them. What
if Anna started walking or Alexei babbled his first distinct
word when she was not there? While they were apart, her
chest ached with longing for them.

Both little ones adored their *babushka* and loved snuggling
on her lap to listen to stories. She gave them the wooden toys
Peter had carved for his own children and liked to watch them
play—although it was bittersweet because Peter had never
known the joy grandchildren brought, and their auntie Katya
was still missing. None of Maria's letters had yielded any clues
as to where she was, but she still wrote to the few children's
homes that had not yet replied, sending pencil sketches of
Katya and stamped envelopes. One day someone must recognize her.

Maria had given up her factory job but on the rare occasions
when she went back to town, she invited her old colleagues
around for tea and cakes at the apartment. She didn't miss

work. At fifty-three, she was feeling her age. Her lower back ached on cold mornings, and if she crouched to pick up the children's toys she had to grab hold of a piece of furniture to pull herself up again.

When Anna was two and Alexei one, Ludmilla decided to go back to work and Maria became a full-time carer for the little ones. Every day when the weather permitted she took them for walks in the park around the Peterhof palace—she could never learn to call it by the Soviet name of Petrodvorets. She showed them the secret fountains that were designed to soak the unwary, the pretty flower beds, and the different types of bird that alighted there. Always she took a sketchbook because the children clamored for her drawings.

"Draw a giraffe, Babushka," Anna would demand. "And a monkey! Together!"

Sometimes they went inside the palace to visit their mama and papa at work, but Maria felt uncomfortable there, amid the decor dripping with gold. It reminded her of the blinkered child she had once been who took all that Romanov wealth for granted.

~

One morning Stepan told her that he was going on a trip to source some marble and would not be back until late.

"Eat the evening meal without me," he said.

"Take your warm hat," Maria fussed, running after him, and he accepted it from her without a murmur although it was only October and the weather was mild.

She had already gone to bed that night when she heard the sound of Stepan returning home. She glanced at the clock: ten after midnight. It sounded as if Ludmilla was still up, because she could hear the murmur of voices in the kitchen.

The children would wake her around six a.m., so she should go back to sleep, but she wanted to hear about Stepan's trip. She hesitated, then decided that since she was awake anyway, she might as well say goodnight.

The kitchen door was closed as she padded down the corridor, but when she drew near, she heard Ludmilla's voice asking, "Is there absolutely no doubt it was her?"

Something about her tone made Maria stop and wait for the answer.

Stepan sighed heavily. "There was a satchel with a bottle of Mama's elecampane mixture inside and a wooden duck that Papa made for us when we were children."

Maria's heart started thumping so hard she thought it must leap out of her chest. Katya's satchel had been found. But where?

"Perhaps she dropped the satchel that night and it got tangled up with someone else's remains," Ludmilla suggested.

Remains? Maria couldn't stand to hear this. She cupped her face in her hands, fingers over her ears, but did not move from the spot. Her legs had turned to stone.

"The fisherman who pulled her up said the satchel was diagonally across the skeleton." He gave a little sob. "She must have fallen through the ice after the bombing that night. A friend of Mama's also disappeared."

Maria's eyes filled with tears. It was clear now what he was saying.

"I'm so sorry, my love." She heard Ludmilla's voice comforting him, then Stepan gave another sob.

"My beautiful little sister," he croaked before his voice became muffled, and Maria guessed Ludmilla was hugging him.

She should open the door and go into the kitchen so they could mourn together, but something stopped her. Suddenly she realized she had known all these years that Katya was dead. Deep down she had never believed she would find her, just as she did not believe she would ever find Tatiana. They were gone. She hoped Katya had been with Peter in heaven for the ten years since she had died.

"There will have to be a funeral," Stepan said, struggling to control his emotion. "It will be desperately hard for Mama. No parent should have to bury their child."

Maria tried to imagine what a body would look like after all those years in the water. Bones, just bones. That was not her daughter. She believed Katya's soul had left at the precise moment of death. The skeleton was just a relic.

"Does she need to know?" Ludmilla asked. "Maybe it would be easier for her to carry on thinking there is hope."

"Do you think so?" Stepan asked.

Maria considered this. She felt weary. She did not have the energy for grief. Her sorrow for Katya had been spent all those years ago. What if they simply didn't tell her and she pretended she didn't know? Except she *would* know. She had always known.

Treading carefully to avoid creaking floorboards, she turned and tiptoed back to her room and climbed into bed, pulling the covers up to her chin. She said prayers for Katya, imagining her with Peter in heaven. Her Romanov family had not known either of them, but she was sure they would have been welcomed into the fold.

In the morning, if Stepan told her, then she must weep and grieve and arrange a funeral. But if he did not, she would continue to pray for Katya in private, just as she had always done.

Next day, Anna and Alexei woke her at six as usual. Maria pulled on a robe and led them to the kitchen, where she began to warm milk and gave them both a *sukhari* with cinnamon and raisins.

Stepan came into the room and kissed each child on the forehead, then embraced his mother. He had shadows like bruises under his eyes; he always got them when he hadn't slept.

"How was your trip?" she asked, watching his face. Now was the moment of decision. Would he tell her or not?

"I got what I went for," he said. "Everything is fine."

Maria nodded and turned back to watch the pan. She had to make sure the milk did not boil over, which it could do in an instant, and she did not want him to see so much as a glint of a tear in her eye.

CHAPTER 56

Petrodvorets, March 7, 1953

LUDMILLA GOT HOME FROM WORK JUST BEFORE SIX, as Maria was feeding Anna and Alexei their dinner.

"Have you heard the news today?" she asked.

"No. What's happened?" Maria couldn't read Ludmilla's expression: was it good or bad news?

Ludmilla switched on the Mir radio set just in time for the bulletin on the hour. It was read by Yuri Levitan, the man who had been the voice of all those exaggerated wartime broadcasts. He sounded choked with emotion as he read the headline. "The Central Committee of the Communist Party, the Council of Ministers, and the Presidium of the Supreme Soviet of the USSR announce with deep grief to the Party and all workers that on the fifth of March at nine fifty p.m., Josef Vissarionovich Stalin, Secretary of the Communist Party and Chairman of the Council of Ministers, died after a serious illness."

Maria felt a tingling on her scalp. She put down the bowl she was holding in case she dropped it, then sat heavily on a chair. "I should be overjoyed," she commented. "I loathe that man. I blame him for the death of my husband and the disappearance of my daughter. He's the one who engineered a regime in which Russians' lives were worth less than air." She gestured with a flick of her hand. "Yet now that he is dead, I just feel flat."

"He should have answered for his crimes in a court of law," Ludmilla said. "I would like to have seen him get twenty-five years in a gulag."

"There would have been justice in that," Maria agreed. "I wonder what will happen now. Probably life will go on as before and we won't even notice the difference."

When she went out with the children the next morning, church bells were tolling.

"Nice music," Anna said.

"Yes, I like the sound too," Maria said, stopping to tuck a lock of blond hair under her granddaughter's woolly hat and adjust the blanket over Alexei's knees.

~

In the weeks after Stalin's death, new political leaders took over and the rhetoric changed subtly. It was announced that thousands of political prisoners were to be freed from gulags, and as early as Easter, the husband of one of their neighbors in Petrodvorets returned. One day he came out to sit on a wooden bench in the garden while Maria was weeding the vegetable patch and the children were chasing each other and shrieking.

She went over to introduce herself—his name was Viktor—and was horrified to see up close how raddled he looked. His face was beetroot-colored, and she recognized the cause as exposure to the elements rather than the reddish hue some men took on from excessive drinking. He was bone-thin and walked with the aid of a stick although he could only be around forty, perhaps younger. More than that, he looked defeated. There was a hopelessness about him that made Maria wonder what kind of person he had been when he was first sent to the gulag.

It seemed intrusive to ask about his experiences there, so instead she told him the names of her grandchildren and chatted about the vegetables she was growing.

"You have no idea how extraordinary it is simply to sit on a bench doing nothing," he said. "If I'd tried this back in Gdovsky, I would have been beaten half to death and had my rations slashed."

Maria shook her head, lost for words.

"I can't talk to my wife about it. I couldn't bear for her to know how bad it was."

"What work did you do?" Maria asked.

"Felling trees mostly. Logging. Summer and winter, rain and shine." He looked at his hands and Maria saw that his fingers were bent into claws and the knuckles swollen. "I'm lucky I didn't starve to death. Many men did. Others were killed by falling trees or the cold or the beatings."

"I don't think you were lucky," Maria sympathized. "Far from it."

"Do you know what I was sentenced for?" His eyes met hers. "I told a joke about a Party official back in 1937. What an idiot. That was no year for joking."

"My husband was executed that same year for being a *kulak*," Maria told him. "And he couldn't have been less of a *kulak*. He was a shock worker, a Party man through and through."

"At least we can talk about it now," Viktor said. "Times have changed to that extent."

"I'm still cautious when talking to strangers," Maria said. "Things don't change overnight. But you are my neighbor and you have suffered so much that I trust you. If you ever want to talk about your experiences and don't want to distress your wife, you can tell me. I'm an old lady who has lived through many sorrows and I am strong enough to listen to more."

Viktor lifted her hand to his lips and kissed it. "Thank you," he whispered, close to tears. "No one has been kind to me for such a long time that it makes me emotional. Forgive me."

～

That evening, after the children were in bed, Maria told Stepan and Ludmilla of her conversation with Viktor.

"He seems broken," she said. "I don't know if he can ever recover from what he has been through. Sixteen years have been stolen from him: years when he missed his children growing up, when his wife struggled to cope on her own. I don't understand . . ." She turned to Stepan. "You were a good little Bolshevik when you were younger. Did you change your views after what happened to your father?"

"I changed my views long before then," he said, "because of what my father told me about the informers and purges at his work. The ideas behind Communism are sound, but the wrong people got into power."

"Why did the Russian people not rise up in protest?" Maria asked. "They rose to overthrow the Romanovs, but not Stalin. Explain it to me."

Ludmilla replied, "The fear crept up gradually. It was easier to keep quiet while the NKVD were terrorizing someone else's family. When my mother was arrested I couldn't find a single person to testify on her behalf. They said she shouldn't have been so stupid as to make a stand over religion. They thought silence would keep them safe—then they started getting arrested anyway."

"Peter spoke up for other people," Maria said bitterly, "and look where it got him."

She hadn't been to the cemetery for over a month now. She would go that weekend, she decided, so she could tell him that Irina was getting married to Ludmilla's cousin; the wedding was set for spring the following year. Maybe there would be more grandchildren soon. She certainly hoped so. Perhaps Irina could be persuaded to move to Petrodvorets so Maria could look after her little ones alongside Stepan's.

~

One morning in late April, Maria took the children to the palace's Lower Park. The ice on the ponds was thinning and they entertained themselves throwing stones to crack it.

"Stay away from the edge," she called as she sat on a bench to watch. The cold was still bitter and she didn't fancy leaping in to rescue one of them. An image sprang into her head of Katya falling through a hole in the Ice Road. She couldn't bear to think of her struggling and choking in panic in the freezing water. Pray God death had been instantaneous.

Her thoughts turned to her childhood, when Anastasia fell through the ice on one of the ponds at the Catherine Palace. Maria had warned her it might not take her weight, but she insisted it would and stepped out: one foot, then the next. There had been an eerie cracking sound before she fell through, arms in the air, coattails flying, and disappeared underwater. Maria was the only person nearby. She screamed with the full force of her lungs and kept screaming in blind panic. Should she crawl out onto the ice to save her sister? Anastasia's head bobbed up, then disappeared again. Was she going to die?

One of the gardeners came running full pelt along the path and Maria pointed, screaming, "She's in there! She fell!"

The man ripped off his jacket and spread it on the ice, then lay full length along it. He reached into the hole, groping around, then ducked his head underwater. Maria held her breath. It seemed an age but was probably only seconds before he grabbed Anastasia's arm and pulled her up. She gave a loud gasp, spluttering for breath.

Another gardener arrived and between them they managed to ease her carefully across the ice then back onto dry land. Maria was trembling in shock, and she burst into tears as they wrapped Anastasia in their jackets. The second gardener scooped her in his arms and ran with her toward the palace.

"You're OK," the first one told Maria, patting her shoulder. "Don't worry. She'll be fine."

Maria remembered the terrible weight of guilt. "I should have tried to save her," she sobbed.

"Then we'd have been rescuing the two of you." He smiled, and his face was kind. "You did the right thing. Mighty powerful lungs you've got."

Anastasia did not even catch cold after her winter dip, but Maria got a fierce scolding from her mother. "Honestly, I thought you were the sensible one. Why on earth did you not stop her? I'm disappointed in you."

That had been a common refrain in her childhood: she'd been a disappointment. She hoped none of her children felt that way. There was never any need to chastise her grandchildren, who were happy, affectionate creatures. She watched as they hunted for more stones, the air filled with their joyful shrieks. She loved the way their chuckles came from deep in their bellies. It was a sound she never tired of.

In the distance she could see two men and a woman walking arm in arm down the path from the palace. One of them seemed unsteady on his feet and the younger man was helping him. As they passed the Grand Cascade and turned toward her, she recognized Stepan and Irina and waved. What was Irina doing here? Who was the older man, and why were they coming to see her? Something about him seemed familiar, but she couldn't think what.

They kept advancing, and when they were just ten yards away, Maria rose to her feet and blinked hard. The old man looked like Peter. Was her mind playing tricks? Was she going mad? Her heart began racing. His hair was silver, his face had deep grooves like the trunk of an ancient tree, but surely those were his eyes?

"Maria, my love," he said, and it was Peter's voice. But it couldn't be. That wasn't possible.

Maria screamed at the top of her voice, just as hard as she had screamed when Anastasia fell through the ice. She kept screaming, the sound erupting from her lungs in powerful bursts. The little ones were scared and scurried to hide behind their father. Tears began to stream down her cheeks. If this was a trick, it was the cruelest trick ever.

"It's all right, Mama," Irina said, reaching for her arm. "It's him. It's Papa. He's back."

Maria stopped screaming for a moment to stare at him, and that was when Peter stepped forward and pulled her into his arms.

CHAPTER 57

FOR SEVERAL MINUTES THEY STOOD, ARMS WRAPPED around each other. Maria breathed in the old familiar Peter scent, but still her brain kept protesting. *It can't be. This must be a dream. Any minute now I will wake up.*

She pulled back to look at him and saw his cheeks were streaked with tears, like her own.

"You're trembling," he said. "I'm sorry to shock you."

"I d-don't understand," she stammered. "I have been visiting your grave for over fifteen years. In Preobrazhenskoe Cemetery. This can't be."

His hand stroked her cheek and she felt self-conscious about her wrinkles and the hair that had gone white as goose feathers. She was no longer the pretty girl he had married but a plump elderly woman of fifty-three. Since the end of the siege she couldn't stop herself eating. He was thin, so thin. She could feel his ribs through the coarse ragged cloth of his jacket.

"H-how is this possible? They told me you were executed." Could he be a relative of Peter's? No; she was sure it was him. She looked from Stepan to Irina, and they were grinning from ear to ear, her grandchildren puzzled but silent in Stepan's arms.

Peter spoke in a voice that was raw with emotion. "I was sentenced to death by the *troika* and led out to a van thinking I was about to die. But instead of facing a firing squad, I was taken on a journey of several weeks to a gulag in Norilsk, in the Arctic Circle. I was there until recently."

"But why didn't you write? If I'd only known . . ." Maria still couldn't believe it.

"None of us were allowed to contact our relatives. We were sentenced to twenty-five years without communication privileges. I tried many times to get a message to you, but . . ." A shadow passed across his eyes. "It was not possible."

Maria looked at his face and saw a world of suffering there. She wondered what he saw in hers. There was time enough for all that. For now, she took his chin in her hands and pulled his mouth to hers, closing her eyes and sinking into the sensation of his kiss. Her heart was beating so hard she was sure he would feel it. His hands were on her back, holding her close, and she wanted time to stop so that she could savor this moment and live in it forever.

~

"Babushka, who is that man?" a little voice asked.

Maria broke away and smiled. "These are your grandchildren," she told Peter. "Anna and Alexei."

He seemed overwhelmed as he looked at their luminous faces, so full of possibility. "Hello," he said in a croaky voice. They peered at him with curiosity.

"How long have you known?" Maria asked Irina.

"Not long," she said. "He came to the apartment in Leningrad this morning and I brought him straight here. Isn't it *wonderful*?"

Maria still felt stunned. All those conversations she'd had

with Peter in the cemetery; the mushrooms she thought he
had led her to; the times when she could swear he had answered
her. It was too much to take in.

"I must sit down for a while," she said. "I need to think."

"Irina and I will take the children up to the palace," Stepan
offered. "You two need time alone."

They sat on the bench, hand in hand, bodies curved toward
each other. Maria traced the line of a new scar on Peter's brow,
touched the cowlick hair, cupped his chin in her hand. She
felt unbelievably slow-witted.

"Why did they not execute you?" she asked.

"I think they made a mistake," Peter told her. "I was simply
bundled into the wrong van. If I'm right, it means someone
who was intended for a gulag was executed in my place."

Maria thought back to the typed list the Bolshoi Dom
officer had held. "Did you get the package I sent you in jail?
The blanket and the warm clothes?" She remembered the
unattended pile of parcels on the floor.

"No, nothing. But I knew you and Stepan would be doing
all you could, and that comforted me."

Maria tried to respond, but fresh tears came. She leaned
her cheek against his so their tears mingled. "I missed you so
much. I never stopped missing you," she whispered.

"Me too," he replied. "The only thing that kept me alive
was picturing the day I would see you again. And now it's
here, it's more magical than I could ever have imagined."

～

It was too cold to sit outside for long, so they walked slowly
back to the palace. Ludmilla came rushing over to introduce
herself and flung her arms around Peter in tearful greeting.

"Why is everyone crying?" Anna asked.

"Because we're happy," Ludmilla told her.

"That's silly," Anna said with a frown, and the adults laughed.

They set off back to the flat together.

"You're limping. What happened?" Peter asked Maria, gripping her arm.

Stepan answered for her. "When Mama broke her leg during the siege, she set it herself using a table leg."

"You did *what?*"

She shrugged. "What else could I do? Anyway, it worked."

She didn't want to talk of that. She kept thinking of questions she wanted to ask Peter, things she wanted to tell him.

"I suppose Irina told you she is getting married soon," she said.

"I look forward to being at the wedding," he replied, smiling at his daughter.

Maria continued. "Did you see Yelena this morning? She works in a clothes shop; she's crazy about fashion. And Mikhail is a carpenter."

"No one has mentioned Katya, and Irina was vague when I asked," Peter said. "Where does she live now?"

The group fell silent. Maria hesitated before replying. "She went missing after I sent her and Mikhail across the Ice Road during the war," she told him. "I have been searching for years. I'm sure she will find us. It's only a matter of time."

Peter turned to Stepan, and Maria saw a look pass between them that she chose to ignore.

"After all," she continued, "*you* found us, so it proves miracles do happen." She squeezed his hand hard, willing him not to ask any more.

"Tell Papa how you helped all those people whose family members had been arrested by the NKVD," Stepan said, pride in his tone.

"It was nothing." She addressed Peter. "I got to know an officer who was friendlier than most and he helped me track down prisoners who had disappeared in the system, so I could tell their families. He was the one who told me you were buried in Preobrazhenskoe." She shook her head. "I suppose that's what it says in the records."

"I'm glad to hear there was one officer with humanity in that loathsome organization, but your missing persons work was always a bit risky." He smiled fondly. "I suspect if I had been here I'd have tried to talk you out of it."

"I doubt you would have managed," Stepan told him. "I tried."

They arrived at the apartment and the men sat at the kitchen table while Maria, Irina, and Ludmilla bustled around cooking. The children brought their toys to show this man who was their new grandfather, and he smiled to see the wooden ones he had made long ago being enjoyed by a new generation. He tested the wheels of the steam engine against his palm.

"These could use a little oil," he told Alexei. "They are getting stiff. I'll show you how to do it."

Tears came to Maria's eyes again and she knew they would keep doing so for some time to come. It was incredible. She kept touching Peter's shoulder, catching his eye, fussing over him, as if he might disappear again if she stopped.

After they had eaten, she ran a hot bath for him and sat on the edge, soaping his bony back, where the skin was scarred and calloused, the ribs jutting out just as hers used to during the siege.

"Our neighbor Viktor has come back from a gulag," she said. "He told me it is impossible to talk to his wife about it because it would upset her too much. I want you to know that you can tell me anything you like. I am stronger now than I was when you left—"

"You were always strong, Maria," he interrupted. "And I will tell you. But not today. Today is for celebrating. We've been cheated out of sixteen years and now all I want is to make the most of the next sixteen."

It felt odd climbing into bed together, Maria in her voluminous nightdress and Peter in flannel pajamas borrowed from Stepan. She wondered if he would want to make love and whether her old body was still capable of it. Instead he looped his arms around her and fell asleep with his face buried in her neck so she could feel his breath on her skin. She was used to her grandchildren hopping into bed in the morning, their firm, warm flesh smelling faintly of soap, but this was different. Peter felt sharp and angular, but he smelled the same as he always had, and slept just as soundly.

Maria couldn't fall asleep for hours but lay awake looking at the stars through the gap in the curtains and thanking God for this extraordinary miracle.

CHAPTER 58

Leningrad, summer 1976

FOUR DAYS LATER THAN EXPECTED, BILL, VAL, AND Nicole arrived at the boat dock in Moscow for their sailing to Leningrad. Bill lied that he had been suffering from a stomach upset; their tickets were exchanged and a new cabin allocated. It was lovely to be able to sit on deck and watch the countryside go by, and it gave Val time to discuss with Bill what she had discovered in Ekaterinburg. No wonder her father had been secretive about his past if he had been a guard at the Ipatiev House. He was only nineteen when the Romanovs were killed and it must have been harrowing. Something like that could scar you for life.

After 1918, when he was searching for Maria, he had used identity papers in the names of several of his fellow guards. But if the museum was correct—and she assumed it must be—his real name was Anatoly Bolotov. Since seeing that photo at the house, she hadn't been able to get the question out of her head: why had he claimed to be Ivan Skorokhodov? And then changed his name to Irwin Scott? It was as if he was running away from something.

They sailed along canals through farming country, sitting out on deck to catch the sun. The boat edged into Lake Ladoga and Nicole listened in awe when Bill told her that during the Second World War trucks full of people used to drive over the ice.

"Why didn't it break?" she asked.

"They waited until it was eight inches thick and laid down tracks," he replied. "Then it was strong enough."

"Could you skate on it?" She looked at the blue water sparkling in the sunlight.

"I don't think many people tried in the middle of a war," Bill replied, "but in peacetime they probably do."

Val's first impression of Leningrad was of fancy buildings in bold colors decorated with gold trimmings. Every street she glanced along seemed to have its own splendid multi-domed church, and there was a network of canals around the historic district, crisscrossed by bridges flanked with heroic statues.

"It's like living in a museum!" she exclaimed.

"You can certainly see where the Romanovs spent the nation's wealth," Bill agreed.

Their hotel was near the Winter Palace, a mint-green, white and gold building overlooking the River Neva. In every direction there were glorious views.

"I simply can't believe I'm here!" Val gasped, twirling around. "I've read so much about it, but the reality is *miles* better than I expected."

Their official guide, a middle-aged woman with dark hair striped with silver like a badger's, was waiting for them at the hotel. "Tomorrow we start at nine," she said, "with a walking tour of this district. Please wear sensible shoes. In the afternoon we will tour the Hermitage Gallery."

Val glanced at Bill and he replied, "Can't we choose where we go? We only have a few days and are keen to see the palaces."

The guide consulted her schedule. "Thursday is the day we go to Petrodvorets and Friday to Detskoye Selo."

"I appreciate you have your routine," Bill said. "But can't we change it and go to Petrodvorets tomorrow?"

There was a long pause. "You don't want to see the Hermitage? It has a world-class art collection."

"Maybe later in the week," Bill said firmly. "See you at nine."

~

The next morning, the guide arrived at nine on the dot and agreed to take them to Petrodvorets, although she intimated that it had caused her a lot of trouble to change the arrangements. They caught a boat just outside the Winter Palace and motored downriver, past the docks, and out into the Gulf of Finland, where fishermen were casting their nets. They were sitting next to some Russian tourists who tried to teach Nicole a few words in their language. She gamely repeated what they said—"Pree-vee-et," "Spa-seeba"—and didn't mind when they laughed and corrected her pronunciation.

Val was bowled over when their boat docked at a jetty and she looked up toward a mustard, white, and gold building set along a ridge, just visible through the trees.

As they walked toward it, the guide began her talk in a droning voice. "In 1705, Peter the First chose this site for his official summer residence, because the sea is deep enough for ships to dock. Within ten years he had built the original palace and laid out the Upper and Lower Park . . ."

Val tuned out her words and drank in the atmosphere instead: the smell of flowers in the breeze, the tinkling of fountains, the murmuring voices of other visitors.

"Now you must appreciate the Grand Cascade," the guide ordered.

Val glanced at Bill and they shared a smile at her authoritarian tone.

Even Nicole was impressed by the spectacular chain of fountains splashing around shiny gold statues, leading down from the palace. One was designed to soak anyone who tried to take a piece of artificial fruit from a tabletop; another jet of water leaped twenty feet into the air from a lion's mouth. Their guide explained that none of the fountains used pumps; instead they had been designed to operate using the gradient of the site.

Val wondered if the Romanovs had taken these surroundings for granted. Was this simply one of their many homes, or did they appreciate how glorious it was?

"We will look at the Upper Park now and stop for lunch before we enter the palace," the guide said, checking her watch. She led them around to the other side of the building, and Val saw acres of immaculately kept formal gardens with rows of fountains and parterres. There wasn't so much as a leaf on the ground or a dead head on a flower. The gardeners must patrol regularly, checking for decay and correcting every imperfection immediately.

They stopped on a bench to eat a picnic lunch. The guide unpacked slices of stodgy bread, hard-boiled eggs (at which Nicole wrinkled her nose), cold meats, and cheeses. As they ate, Val took the opportunity to show the woman her gold Fabergé box. She had brought it with her because she knew the company had been based in St. Petersburg during the time of the Romanovs and it seemed likely someone there might know about it.

"I'm trying to find how it opens," she said.

The guide narrowed her eyes, peering at the inscription and trying without success to force it. "Perhaps we can ask one of the curators," she said. "I will make inquiries."

When they were eventually ushered inside, at the exact time printed on their tickets, they found the palace interior awash with gold and ornament. It was almost too much, Val thought.

No surface was left undecorated. The overall effect was of fabulous, unlimited wealth, which was probably what the designers intended.

In each room, a guard sat on a chair in the corner, watching that they did not touch any of the priceless items. Their guide spoke in Russian to a woman guarding the Yellow Banqueting Hall, then turned to Val.

"There is a curator here who is a Fabergé expert. We can show him your box. Follow me."

"Nicole and I will stay and explore, if that's OK," Bill said.

The guide was unhappy about leaving them, but agreed with a sniff that she would take Val to meet the curator, then return straightaway.

~

The Fabergé expert, whose name was Stepan Alexandrovich Dubov, smiled when he saw Val's gold box.

"Ah! It's a sun, moon, and stars box," he said, in perfect English, with an accent that was only slightly foreign. "I haven't seen one of those for a while." He looked at the hallmark on the back. "Henrik Wigstrom was the workmaster."

"What is a sun, moon, and stars box?" Val asked.

Stepan pointed to the jewels on the top. "This big diamond represents the Pole Star, the next largest is the moon, while the topaz is the sun and the smaller diamonds are stars. To open it, you hold the box so that the Pole Star is in the north, move the sun from east to west, as it would travel in the course of a day, then as the sun goes down, the moon rises." He moved the jewels as he spoke. There was a distinct click and the box sprang open.

Val leaned forward. Inside there were two rose-gold wedding rings. "Wow!" she exclaimed. "That's what was rattling."

Stepan took out the rings and examined them under a magnifying glass. "They are both engraved with Russian letters," he said. "They're not very clear but one looks like an M and the other an A. Where did you come across the box?"

"My father left it to me," she said. "He was Russian. But my mother's initial was H, so it can't have been her ring."

"Do you think your father brought it with him from Russia?" The man leaned forward with friendly interest. Val warmed to him. He had an honest face and kind eyes.

"I'm not sure where he got it, but I know he was obsessed with the Romanovs. I wondered if it might have belonged to one of them? Could the rings have been Maria's and Anastasia's?"

Stepan raised an eyebrow and looked at the box again. "Many of their possessions were sold on the black market in the years after they disappeared, so it's possible."

"You say they disappeared," Val challenged. "Don't you believe they were executed?"

He shrugged. "I have read the reports of some of the men who claim to have been their executioners, but there are contradictions in the stories. I think no one will ever know for sure unless the bodies are found—and I suspect they never will be. The Sokolov report in the 1920s concluded that they had been dissolved in sulfuric acid."

Val was surprised he was prepared to talk so openly. "I had been warned that the Romanovs were a taboo subject here," she said. "I'm writing a thesis about them so I'm fascinated to learn all I can, but I didn't like to ask our guide."

"I would be happy to answer any of your questions," Stepan said. "It is not such a taboo subject as it was, say, twenty years ago."

"OK," Val asked. "Do you believe any of the Romanovs escaped from Ekaterinburg?"

He looked startled for a moment but quickly regained his composure. "There have been many stories over the years but there is no evidence to back them up."

"What do *you* think?"

He tilted his head to one side. "I think it is possible. But we may never find out, because if any of them did escape, they would have kept a low profile. Even if they were living overseas, there would have been a risk of assassination. A few people who claimed to be Romanovs were killed back in the 1920s."

"So you think the truth might never emerge?" That wasn't what Val wanted to hear.

"I'm convinced it won't. History is not a neat narrative written by Gorky or Chekhov where everything falls into place at the end." He smiled. "But you are a historian. You must agree."

"It's human nature to try to look for patterns in life," Val said, "but I suppose most things are random."

"I think there are patterns in human behavior," he said, "but not in fate." He smiled. "Can I offer you a cup of tea? I am privileged to have a kettle in this office."

While he made the tea, Val fingered the envelope of photographs in her handbag. Bill had told her not to bring them with her to the Soviet Union in case their belongings were searched, but she couldn't resist slipping them into her bag. She felt sure this man, Stepan, was not a government spy because he was far too frank. It would be fascinating to hear what he thought of them.

"No milk, I'm afraid," he said as he put a cup of steaming black liquid in front of her.

"Can I show you something?" she asked, making a spur-of-the-moment decision.

He looked puzzled. "OK."

Val pulled out the prints. "My father had a camera among his possessions. An old Kodak Autographic. There was some film inside that had not been developed, so after he died I got the pictures printed." She passed them across the desk and he began to flick through them. "The quality is not very good," she continued, "but I think it shows the Romanovs in the Ipatiev House."

Stepan did not respond but continued examining the images. He stopped at one and she heard an intake of breath, but she couldn't see which had affected him. He had gone very quiet.

"Do you agree?" she asked.

Stepan looked shaken, as if he'd seen something that disturbed him, and he paused before he spoke. "I wonder if I might borrow these to show a colleague, who is more of an expert than me? If you tell me the name of your hotel, I will return them before you leave."

"Of course you can," she agreed. "I have another set at home, so if your colleague wants to keep them for historical research, that would be fine."

He kept flicking through, shaking his head in astonishment.

"Do you know how your father got this camera?" he asked.

Val bit her lip. Should she trust him? What was the worst that could happen?

"I only found out recently that my father worked at the Ipatiev House," she said. "I think he must have stolen some of the Romanovs' possessions from there. I have a photograph album back in Australia, along with a sketchbook and some icons." She described them, and Stepan listened carefully, occasionally nodding his head.

"You say your father worked at the Ipatiev House. Do you mean he was a guard?"

She nodded, ashamed. "He was a complex man," she said. "Not a great father. He never talked about his early life in

Russia. I think he must have been traumatized by his experiences."

"What was his name?" Stepan asked.

There was utter silence in the room as Val weighed up whether or not to tell him. "Anatoly Bolotov," she muttered at last.

Stepan scraped back his chair on the parquet floor. Val looked up to see that his entire expression had changed.

When he spoke, his voice was frosty. "Bolotov was one of the killers," he told her.

"No!" Val exclaimed. "That's not possible." And then the memory flashed into her mind of her father in the nursing home repeating "I didn't want to kill her" and talking about all the blood.

"Yurovsky, the commandant at the house, named him in his written testimony."

Val clasped her chin in her hands in dismay. "But he was only nineteen!"

"Age was no barrier. One of the other killers was only seventeen." Stepan was staring at her now, his dark eyes boring into her.

"Has Yurovsky's testimony been published anywhere?" she asked. "I'd like to read it for myself."

"It is only available in Soviet archives." His tone was definitely unfriendly; she wasn't imagining it.

"Is it possible to get a copy?"

"No."

Val was stunned. "So you drop this bombshell that my father was a murderer then tell me I can't even read the evidence against him. I just have to live with it?"

"Sometimes that's the only thing we can do," he said, standing up, clearly keen to end their conversation. "Do you want me to return the photographs to you? If so, tell me the name of your hotel."

Val shook her head. "No. Please keep them. Thank you for the tea. I'm sorry."

Stepan didn't offer to shake her hand as she left. She wandered out into the hall to look for Bill and Nicole, not sure what she had apologized for. Because her father had helped to kill their royal family? Sorry didn't even begin to cover it.

CHAPTER 59

BACK IN THEIR HOTEL ROOM, ONCE NICOLE WAS asleep, Val lay on her bed writing in her notebook about all she had seen and heard during the day. She was upset that Stepan had turned so hostile when he found out who her father was, but guessed that he felt a strong sense of loyalty to the erstwhile royal family. She was still reeling at the news that her father had been one of the Romanovs' killers at the age of just nineteen. No wonder her mother found him crying in a park. And no wonder he became such an angry, bitter man in his later years.

There were two single beds in the room and Nicole was tucked up on a folding camp bed. It didn't look particularly comfortable but she had always been able to sleep anywhere.

Bill came out of the bathroom, a speck of toothpaste in the corner of his mouth. "What were you and the curator talking about today?" he asked. "You were in his office for ages."

"First he showed me how the Fabergé box worked." Val had demonstrated it over their meal in the hotel dining room and Nicole had been enchanted, begging to be allowed to take it to school to show her friends when they got home. "And then we chatted about the Romanovs," she continued. "He was surprisingly open about them, saying that if one or more had survived they would probably lie low, even after all this time, because of the assassination risk."

Bill gestured urgently toward the light bulb on the ceiling and she remembered he had told her hotel rooms were often bugged. He beckoned for her to follow him into the bathroom, where he turned the taps on full.

"I warned you not to mention the Romanovs," he hissed, his voice barely audible over the noise of gushing water.

"Don't worry. He was very frank and I knew I could trust him." She was surprised by the horrified expression on Bill's face.

"Did you tell him about us going to Sverdlovsk?"

"No, but I gave him the photographs from my father's camera." Bill gasped and shook his head. She couldn't understand why he was reacting so strongly. "I don't see any harm in it. I've already sent copies to your colleague in New York, so it seemed natural to give them to Stepan. He's going to show them to a Romanov expert here."

"What else did you tell him?" His tone was curt.

"I haven't done anything wrong, Bill. In fact, I had some pretty shattering news and I was hoping for your sympathy." He didn't say anything, so Val continued. "He told me that Anatoly Bolotov was one of the men who killed the Romanovs. Seemingly Yurovsky left a testimony naming him." There was no response, so she stretched out her arms to give him a hug, saying, "I'm sorry if I've upset you."

"You just didn't think," Bill snapped, pulling away. "You don't know this country, but I thought you would respect that I knew what I was talking about when I warned you not to bring those photographs and not to discuss the Romanovs. Did you think I was saying it for fun?"

"No, but I—"

"You didn't give a single thought to how your revelations might affect my parents. My father will be in a whole heap of trouble if it emerges that he bought us train tickets to a closed city. They've spent their life savings moving here, and because of you they could be arrested, lose their apartment, even go to jail."

"No! Surely not!" Val blushed crimson. "How would anyone find out?"

"Once your curator reports us, inquiries will be made and any investigation will mean Mom and Dad being hauled in for questioning."

"Honestly, I'm sure Stepan won't report us," Val insisted. "He wasn't like that."

"And you reckon you're such a good judge of character, do you? Is that why you married a man who broke your wrist?"

Val was shocked. She had never seen this side of Bill before. Where was all his anger coming from? "That's a bit low," she remarked.

"But true. Now tell me exactly what was said. I need to decide whether I have to warn Mom and Dad." He was running his fingers through his hair, looking incredibly stressed.

Val relayed the conversation as best she could, and Bill kept shaking his head. When she had finished, he asked, "How could you be such an idiot?"

"If it was such a big deal," she protested, "why did you let your father buy us the tickets?"

"Because I knew how much it meant to you."

He looked miserable, and Val decided the only thing for it was a full apology. "You're right. It was thoughtless of me to talk to the curator. If there's anything I can do to make things better, just say."

She wished he would give her a hug at least, even if he couldn't forgive her straightaway. Instead he mumbled, "I'm going to bed. We'll see if the guide mentions anything in the morning. That would be a sure sign it's been reported."

There was no goodnight kiss, no invitation to join him in his single bed for some silent lovemaking. Val lay in her own bed feeling bereft. It was the first time they'd argued and she hated the way he had withdrawn from her.

What he'd said in the bathroom was true. She was a poor judge of character. How could she ever hope to have a healthy relationship?

Her misery deepened as she lay awake listening to his regular breathing. She had fallen in love with this man and couldn't bear to lose him. If only there was something she could do to make things better; but for the life of her she couldn't think what.

CHAPTER 60

Leningrad, summer 1976

MARIA WAS IN THE BEDROOM LOOKING FOR A CARdigan when Stepan arrived home from work. She heard him call a greeting to Peter, who was listening to the radio in the kitchen, then he came through to find her and perched on the end of her bed.

"You'll never guess who visited me in the office today, Mama," he said. "I still can't believe it myself."

Maria continued to rifle through her knitwear drawer. The cardigan she wanted was dark blue: not too thick for summer, but not too thin either. She felt the cold more than she used to. "Who?"

"The daughter of Anatoly Bolotov." He paused for effect.

Maria turned to stare at him. "You're not serious! It can't be the same one."

"It is, one and the same. Come and sit down." He motioned her over to the bed. "She gave me some photographs developed from film she found in an old camera after her father died. Look." He pulled out the envelope and, once Maria had shuffled across, handed it to her.

Maria only had to flick through the first few pictures to

realize they were hers. "I took these!" she exclaimed. "Why did Bolotov have my camera?"

"Not just that: he had a photo album of yours, and a sketch-book, some icons, and a Fabergé sun, moon, and stars box containing two wedding rings marked M and A." Stepan put an arm around her. "Are you OK? This must be a shock."

Maria thought back over the years. "They were in the bag I packed when we were told we were leaving the house. It was with me in the basement. Not the wedding rings—I don't know about them—but everything else." She came to the picture of Peter and cried out in joy. "Look how handsome he was! . . . And that's a lovely shot of Tatiana. I'm thrilled to see these."

Although the quality of the prints was poor, her memory filled in the details: where each one had been taken; what was being said as they posed.

"The woman was asking lots of questions about whether I thought any of the Romanovs might have survived. She's a historian writing a thesis about it. I gave her deliberately vague answers."

Maria nodded. "So Bolotov is dead? What age is his daughter?"

"Much younger than me: I'd say late thirties. She was born in Australia. It seems he emigrated there."

"Does she have any brothers or sisters?" She wondered how Stepan felt. It must be peculiar to discover he had a half sister.

"I didn't ask."

"How did she find you?" Maria asked, still watching him.

"She didn't know who I was. Her tour guide brought her to me to ask about the Fabergé box. I didn't enlighten her, but I did tell her that her father was one of the executioners. That shocked her. She hadn't known before."

"Poor woman," Maria said. "It's not her fault. We don't choose our parents."

"I suppose not."

"Did you arrange to meet her again? I would love to see my old sketchbook and photo album, and the Fabergé box Mama gave me."

Stepan shook his head. "I don't want to see her again. She's here on holiday and flying back to Australia soon. But she said I could keep these photos."

"That was kind of her." Maria clutched them to her chest. "Were you polite, Stepan? You don't sound as though you were very pleased to make her acquaintance."

He shrugged. "I made her a cup of tea."

"You didn't feel any kind of bond?"

"Definitely not." He dismissed the idea. "She doesn't look like me. She has black hair, an oriental look. Besides, I have all the family I could possibly want right here in Russia."

Maria smiled and patted his hand. "I'd like to show these pictures to the others," she said. "We can say a tourist brought them to your office, after finding them in an old camera. They don't need to know who that tourist was."

Still, after all these years, she had not told Peter who Stepan's biological father was. He had never asked and she had never seen the need to unburden herself. Some secrets were best kept. As far as she knew, Stepan had not told Ludmilla either. Irina, Mikhail, and Yelena all knew that she had been a Romanov, but her grandchildren had not been told yet, even though the eldest two were in their twenties. Maria had resolved she would never tell any of them that Stepan had a different father than his siblings. It didn't matter anymore; never had.

Stepan helped her up from the bed and took her arm as she hobbled slowly to the kitchen, cardigan forgotten.

"Peter! Turn the radio off!" she called.

He was a little deaf now. She blamed the sixteen years he had spent laboring in a mine in Siberia for all the infirmities he suffered—arthritis, poor hearing, shortness of breath—but he put them down to old age. Mentally he was sharp as a pin. He hadn't been broken by the experience the way her neighbor Viktor had. "It happened but now it is over, and there is no point dwelling on it," he said if she ever raised the subject.

"Peter!" She had to raise her voice to get his attention, even once they were in the kitchen. "I've got something to show you! Guess what?"

~

A few days later, Stepan came home from work and gestured to Maria to follow him to the sitting room.

"I've had a letter from *her*," he whispered, although Peter was the only other person in the flat and he could never have heard what was being said from a different room. "Sent to me at the palace. Here it is."

Maria took the single page, written on stationery from the Astoria Hotel on Bolshaya Morskaya, just a few minutes' walk from the Winter Palace.

Dear Mr. Dubov,

Many thanks for revealing the secrets of my Fabergé box yesterday, and for the cup of tea. Perhaps I am imagining it, but I sensed our meeting ended with some ill feeling. I was certainly stunned to hear that my father was among the Romanovs' executioners. He was a cold man who did some very cruel things in the time I knew him, but I would not have believed him capable of murder. Still, you are the expert and I must accept that you know your subject.

I have fallen out with my partner, who is cross with me for telling you about my background. He seems to think we could get into trouble with the authorities here. I have assured him that you did not seem like a government informer, but he tells me I am naïve and do not understand the Soviet system. Anyway, I am writing to beg you not to take this matter any further. We fly home on Saturday and I hope that will be an end of it.

I thank you again for your time and send all my very best wishes.

Val Scott

Maria looked up at Stepan. "She sounds anxious. Will you reply?"

He shook his head. "No point. They go home tomorrow."

"You could telephone the hotel and leave a neutral message: something like 'Good to meet you, have a safe journey.'" She raised an eyebrow. "It would set her mind at rest."

She watched the conflicting emotions on her son's face. He was fifty-seven years old now. He'd raised his own family, enjoyed a harmonious marriage with Ludmilla, and he loved his work. Over the years he'd become one of the country's leading experts in Fabergé designs, in dinner services made at the old St. Petersburg Imperial Porcelain Works, and in gold- and silverware owned by the Romanovs. Under his supervision, the Petrodvorets palace had been returned to its former glory, with most rooms now open to the public.

He had also known much sadness: the loss of his sister, the sixteen years in which he thought his father was dead, and the knowledge that his biological father had been a rapist. If he chose not to be reminded of that last fact, she could not argue with him.

"I think I'll leave it," he said, then nodded to himself as if satisfied he'd made the right decision.

CHAPTER 61

Leningrad, summer 1976

DURING THEIR LAST FEW DAYS IN RUSSIA, BILL WAS polite but preoccupied and Val was acutely aware of a distance between them. They gawped at the splendors of the Catherine Palace, dripping with gold and set in a magnificent park, with lakes, waterfalls, and grottoes stretching into the distance. They peered through the railings at the old Alexander Palace, now occupied by offices of the Soviet navy, and imagined the Romanovs under house arrest there. And on their last day, they kept their guide happy by wandering around the Hermitage Gallery, set within the glitzy Winter Palace.

Bill joked with Nicole and was civil to Val, but their argument in the hotel bathroom loomed between them like an impermeable barrier. Before that he had been lavish with affection and Val had always felt she could hug or kiss him whenever she felt like it; now neither touched the other and there were no invitations to cross the narrow gap between their single beds.

Was he planning to break up with her? Val wondered. They'd been dating for less than a year but he'd said he loved her. Maybe that was just what you did when you were sleeping with someone. He would probably find himself a new girlfriend within weeks, but she couldn't imagine ever dating again.

They were booked to sit together on the flight home, but perhaps he would tell her as soon as they landed. She felt miserable at the prospect and wished she could telephone Peggy to ask for her advice, but there was too much to explain and the cost of the call would be prohibitive.

She also wished she could tell Peggy what she had found out about her father. It echoed around and around in her head that she was the daughter of a man who had committed murder—and not just any old murder, but that of the last Russian royal family. Even if he was simply obeying orders at a turbulent time in his country's history, it was unforgivable. Had he been right in thinking Maria had escaped that night? If only she could discuss it with Bill—but the subject of the Romanovs had become strictly taboo between them.

On their last night in St. Petersburg, Bill telephoned his parents from the hotel room to say goodbye and Val listened while packing Nicole's case.

"They loved the palaces," he said, "but I think Nicole has seen enough art and architecture to last a lifetime. It was pretty boring for a kid, but she's been amazing . . ."

His voice was warm and loving, and Val wished he would use that tone with her.

"The flight home is thirty-nine hours," he continued. "We're stopping in London, Istanbul, Singapore, and Bali, if you can believe it. Val's brought loads of books and drawing pads for Nicole, but it will be challenging to say the least."

"Hey!" Nicole called in protest. "I was really good on the way here."

"That's true," Bill said, grinning. "I retract my statement. Nicole will manage no problem at all and it's me who will find it challenging."

If only I could retract my conversation with Stepan, Val thought. She had written pleading with him not to report her to the authorities but had not received a reply. Perhaps the letter hadn't reached him. She had no idea how long postal deliveries took in the Soviet Union.

When Bill hung up, she asked, "Are they OK?," trying for a lightness of tone she didn't feel.

"Yeah." He nodded. "They sound fine."

Their eyes met briefly. Bill was the first to look away.

~

It was seven in the morning when they landed at Sydney airport and caught a train into town. The eight-hour time difference meant that, for them, it felt like bedtime the previous evening. Bill explained to Nicole why different countries were on different times and she listened, enthralled.

"So now you need to get back to Sydney time. The best thing is to have a quick snooze this morning, then stay awake until bedtime. Think you can do that?" he asked.

"Definitely. I want to go and see my friends. Can I, Mom? I want to tell them about Russia."

"We'll see," Val said, convinced that Nicole would conk out as soon as they got home. "Are you coming back to mine?" she asked Bill, nerves in her voice.

"Nah, I'd best pick up Bess from the neighbors. I've missed the old girl."

"Come for dinner later?" she pleaded.

He made a face. "I think I need my own bed tonight to catch up on sleep deficit. I'll call you."

Val swallowed. There was no arrangement in place for them to see each other again, just a vague "I'll call you." It didn't sound good. When they hugged goodbye at King's Cross station, she almost burst into tears but held back. Time enough for that later.

~

That afternoon, they went to Peggy's. Nicole rushed to stroke Toffee, who had been staying with them, then she and Lenny disappeared up to his bedroom. Val slumped at the kitchen table and told Peggy the story of their trip and her fear that Bill was about to break up with her. She felt sick with a mixture of sleep deprivation and worry.

Peggy frowned in concentration. "Maybe you should have heeded his warning not to mention the Romanovs, but it's hardly a hanging offense."

"It's as if he stopped loving me, just like that." Val snapped her fingers. "Maybe none of it was real."

Peggy shook her head. "Perhaps it's not about you at all. It's easy to take everything personally in a relationship, but men can be moody critters. They say we're the ones who get PMT, but I swear Ken has it worse than I do. Roughly once a month he turns into a bad-tempered git. I just ignore him and he reverts back soon enough. I'd say hang in there, be cool, just act like everything's normal."

"How can I when he won't even make a date to see me?" Val wailed.

Peggy rolled her eyes. "You're straight off a thirty-nine-hour flight. Give the guy time to catch his breath. In fact, give him time to miss you. Don't call him; let him call you."

Val felt vaguely reassured by her words, but protested, "I don't want to play hard to get. That's not my style."

Peggy shrugged. "You're not playing anything. I imagine you're going to be very busy over the next few days, what with unpacking and laundry. Just get on with your life." She wagged an admonishing finger. "And don't call him!"

~

Bill didn't ring that day or the next, and Val's resolve was beginning to slip, but he called the following morning, sounding reasonably cheerful.

"How's it going?" he asked.

"Oh, busy," Val said breezily, channeling Peggy's advice. "Loads to do."

"Want to have dinner tomorrow night?" he asked. "Either get a sitter or I'll come to yours?"

"You come here," she said immediately. If he was planning to break up with her, she didn't want the ax to fall while they were in a restaurant surrounded by strangers.

"OK. I'll bring Bess in that case."

She roasted a leg of lamb, his favorite, hoping that might change his mind. Wasn't food supposed to be one way to a man's heart? When he arrived at the door, he sniffed the air and said, "Smells good," before giving her a quick hug and a peck on the cheek.

Nicole rushed to fling her arms around Bess.

"Hi there, world traveler." Bill ruffled her hair. "How's the jet lag?"

"I'm OK," Nicole told him. "I've been telling all my friends how amazing Russia is."

Bill raised an eyebrow. "I thought it was a boring country for boring old people."

Val returned to the kitchen, half listening to them from the next room. She was jumpy with nerves. Was he planning to tell her it was over when Nicole went to bed? She would have to keep up her nonchalant act till then.

~

Nicole fell asleep as soon as her head hit the pillow, and Val wandered back to the sitting room clutching a couple of beers. She passed one to Bill, then sat down and waited, an empty feeling in the pit of her stomach despite the meal she had just eaten.

"I've been thinking about your dad," he began, "and I feel sorry for the bloke. He probably didn't have any choice about being part of the execution squad. The Bolsheviks were pretty forceful back in those days. And it clearly haunted him for the rest of his life, which is why he said what he did in the nursing home."

Val was taken aback. This wasn't the conversation she'd been expecting, but she replied, "If *you* had been ordered to shoot five youngsters, you wouldn't have done it, would you?"

"We live in different times," he commented. "The Red Army was brutal. My parents lived through some godawful times during the civil war and the years after. They emigrated when Stalin began his purges in 1933, but had seen some pure evil before then." He took a swig of his beer. "That's why I can't understand them going back. They reckon it's all changed, but look at our experience: we weren't allowed to wander round freely, our hotel rooms were probably bugged, and we had to employ subterfuge to visit Sverdlovsk. A state that's fairly run shouldn't have to resort to such measures."

Val braced herself to bring up their argument. "I'm sorry I could have compromised your parents' situation by talking about the Romanovs. I wasn't thinking."

Bill waved his beer can. "No worries. It doesn't seem as though any harm's been done."

Val looked at him in astonishment. Was that it?

"Sorry I overreacted," he continued. "It freaks me out that Mom and Dad chose to go back there. I still don't understand

their decision so I was a bit preoccupied after seeing them."
He shook his head. "Here they had a lovely bungalow with a
garden, not far from the beach. There they have a concrete
apartment and it's too cold to go out for four months of the
year. It's crazy they retired to a place like that."

Suddenly Val saw that Peggy had been right. Bill had been
upset about his parents' situation and not specifically with her.
A huge weight lifted from her shoulders. He wasn't going to
break up with her. Their argument had just been a hiccup in
an otherwise strong relationship. She realized in a flash that
she had been too insecure to cope with it because she had no
previous experience of healthy relationships.

"There seems to be something about being Russian that
gets into your blood," she said, composing herself. "Even when
they live overseas they continue to celebrate Russian Easter in
Russian churches, to drink Russian vodka and read Russian
books. Maybe you can't understand that magnetic pull if you're
not born and bred there."

"Oh, God, that bloody Orthodox church on Robertson
Road! I spent far too much of my childhood there, watching
an old bloke in a dress swinging incense around." Bill grinned.
"You got off lightly."

"My dad went to the Robertson Road church like clockwork.
The priest used to come to our house sometimes. What was
his name?" She wrinkled her brow.

"Methodius," Bill said. "Father Methodius."

"Of course! The last time I saw him was at Dad's funeral."
She shuddered, thinking back to that bleak day, when Tony
stood by her side probably calculating in his head how much
of a windfall he'd get from the inheritance.

"He actually came to your house?" Bill questioned. "Your
dad must have been close to him. Did you ever think of ask-

ing him what he knows about your dad's early life? Maybe he
could shed some light on it. A priest is the one person a man
can be honest with."

Val stared at him, her mouth hanging open. It was so blind-
ingly obvious, she couldn't believe she hadn't thought of it
before.

CHAPTER 62

Sydney, September 1976

THE SCHOOL TERM BEGAN AND VAL RETURNED TO HER
lectures at the university, so it was the following weekend
before she could seek out Father Methodius. Bill offered to
take Nicole for a walk with Bess, and Val caught a bus across
town to Centennial Park.

The church was set in a nondescript white-walled, red-roofed
building with only a cross on top indicating its purpose. Inside
was another story: the walls were crammed with gold-framed
paintings of saints, while golden chandeliers and gaudy incense
burners hung from the ceiling. It smelled chokingly sweet and
musky. Val looked around, shivering in the unheated interior.
A young man in a white robe approached her.

"I'm looking for Father Methodius," she said.

"You'll find him at the residence down the street," he told
her, giving the address.

She walked along with the park on her left, houses on the
right, until she found the place and rang the bell. It took
several minutes before she heard movement in the hall and
the door was opened by the old man she remembered. He
wore a black cassock but without the embroidered chasuble he
had donned for her father's funeral service. Although he did

not seem overweight, his belly protruded under the loose garment. Straggly gray hair hung loose around his shoulders, and thick black-rimmed spectacles were balanced on his nose.

"Val Scott," he said straightaway, smiling and extending his hand. "Please come in."

"What a great memory you have!" she exclaimed. They had only met a couple of times since she was an adult, and she had looked quite different as a child.

He walked slowly down the hall, leaning on a walking stick, and led her into a small lounge. Venetian blinds let in stripes of light, but the corners of the room were in shadow. He lowered himself into an armchair and gestured for Val to sit on a low sofa.

"I'm delighted to see you," he said. "I've often thought about you and hoped your life was going well."

She made a snap decision not to tell him about her divorce; she didn't want a lecture on the sacrament of marriage. "It's not bad. I'm just back from a trip to the Soviet Union, where I did some digging into Dad's background, but it raised more questions than it answered. I wondered—"

"You wondered if I could help fill in the gaps?" He smiled. "I had a feeling you might come to me one day. Your father led a complicated life and he made many poor decisions, but he was a devout man of great faith. I always welcomed his company."

"Did he tell you much about his past, before he left Russia?"

Father Methodius pushed the spectacles up his nose and they glinted in a beam of sunlight. "I expect you want to know about the Romanovs, don't you?"

Val was startled.

"Let me ask my housekeeper for a pot of tea and I'll tell you all I know."

~

The tea came with a plate of cookies topped with flaked almonds. Val took one and bit into it.

"Mmm. These are good."

Father Methodius smiled. "They're *lepeshki*. It's a Russian recipe, made with sour cream." He took one himself and held it inches from his mouth without taking a bite, as if enjoying the anticipation. "Now, what can I tell you about your father? You probably know that he worked as a guard at the last house where the Romanov family were held?"

Val nodded, her mouth full of *lepeshki*.

"You mustn't judge him for taking the job." The priest put his cookie back on the plate, as if he had decided against eating it. "He had a difficult childhood, growing up in a children's home after his parents died when he was very young. At the age of sixteen, he was sent to work in a factory, where he boarded with other workers in some rather squalid-sounding lodgings. Then one day a man came asking for volunteers for what he described as a very sensitive job. Your father was interviewed about his political beliefs, and although he was not interested in politics, he told the interviewer what he thought he wanted to hear. It was only after he got the job that he learned he was to guard the Romanovs. Imagine how exciting that was for a young man of nineteen who thought he had no prospects!"

"He discussed all this with you?" Val was astonished. Her father had gone to elaborate lengths to cover up his past even from her mother, yet he had confided in this priest.

Father Methodius nodded. "I took his confession over the years and would never breach any confidences from there; but we were friends too, and I think his daughter should know what he did not have a chance to tell you in life. I hope it will help you to look upon him more charitably."

Somehow Val doubted that, and her skepticism must have shown on her face.

"Reserve your judgment, please," the priest continued. His voice was rich, with an accent that seemed neither Australian nor Russian but international. "Let's go back to that young man arriving in a house where the wealthiest people in the world were being held prisoner. The girls were all beautiful, and one of them, Maria, was friendly toward him. He told me that he fell in love with her on the spot."

"In love!" Val echoed.

"I always argued that love at first sight was not true love, but he claimed it was, and he vowed she loved him too."

"Now, that I don't believe," Val retorted. Her father had had neither looks nor charm to recommend him. There was no way a Romanov grand duchess would have fallen for him.

"I also found it hard to believe, but your father told me that certain"—Father Methodius hesitated over the word— "intimacies occurred between them. That's how he knew she felt the same way."

Val's mind was whirring. What kind of intimacies? How was it possible in a heavily guarded house, with the family crammed into such a small space?

"So your father was shocked beyond measure when his commandant summoned the guards to his office and told them the Romanovs were to be executed that very night. He could have excused himself from the execution squad, but instead, on the spur of the moment, he decided to try and rescue Maria. Each man was allocated one of the party to shoot, and he volunteered to shoot Maria, planning that he would deliberately miss, then find a way to rescue her in the aftermath."

The priest stopped to sip his tea, and Val took a moment

to absorb this information. Maria must have been the girl her father had pined for in later life, the one he could never get over. No other woman could measure up to a Romanov daughter—certainly not a poor Manchurian girl.

The priest took a deep breath. "The night of the shooting sounds like pure chaos. Your father said nothing went according to plan. When the band of executioners confronted the family in the basement, he tried to signal to Maria with his eyes that he would save her, but he wasn't sure she understood. Then when the order was given to fire, he discharged his gun into the air and rushed forward to shield her with his body. That was when a bullet grazed his hand."

Val remembered that funny scar, like a slug, between his thumb and index finger. She rubbed the spot on her own hand.

"It must have been sheer hell in that room, with the smoke and the noise of the guns and the screaming. Your father always broke down when he spoke of it. He said he couldn't find Maria at first, and when the smoke cleared he saw that she was badly injured and was lying very still, perhaps dead." He shook his head. "I can still hear his sobs when he told me. There was blood everywhere. He said he was soaked in it."

His words in the nursing home echoed in Val's head. "What did he do?"

"He picked her up and carried her to the van outside, all the while trying to detect signs of life and hoping for an opportunity to run off with her. Other guards were milling around and he would not have got far, but he heard them saying the bodies were being taken to a nearby forest. He decided to steal a horse, follow them there, and snatch Maria. If she was dead, he would bury her with all the proper ceremony and create a shrine to her; if she was alive, he would marry her and take care of her."

Val felt as though she was listening to a story about someone else. This lovestruck teenager bore no resemblance to the father she had known. She looked through the blinds to the street beyond. What a shame he had never told her this himself. Their relationship could have been so different. "I guess his plan didn't succeed," she said.

"No, it did not." Father Methodius put down his cup and crossed his arms across his chest. "When they got to the forest, a guard called Peter Vasnetsov was watching the truck where the bodies lay covered by a tarpaulin. Your father considered overpowering him and snatching Maria, but his shouts would have alerted the other guards, who were eating breakfast. There were loads of people around. Suddenly, as he watched, Peter Vasnetsov grabbed one of the girls from the back of the truck, threw her over his shoulder, and started to run into the forest. Your father hurried after them and saw that it was Maria. He had to think fast—and this is where you should be proud of him . . ." He caught Val's eye and held it. "Instead of trying to stop Vasnetsov, he yelled to the other guards, "They've escaped!" and pointed in the opposite direction, shouting, "They went that way!" The men believed him and rushed off the way he had indicated."

Val frowned, realization dawning. "So he helped them to escape?"

"Indeed." The priest nodded. "Your father waited, and as soon as he could without being observed, he followed Maria and Vasnetsov. He was on horseback and Maria was injured so he should have been able to catch them easily, but he could find no sign. They'd vanished into thin air. He told me that for the next month he kept riding round that area, searching for them, but he never saw a trace. His heart was broken in two. He had two gold wedding rings engraved with an M and an A, so that if he ever found her, he could propose on the spot."

"I've got those," Val interrupted. "He kept them in a Fabergé box."

"Maria's box," the priest said. "I wish you could have seen how hard he sobbed when he showed it to me. Loving Maria was the one good thing in his life, and in my opinion, he never recovered from losing her."

There was silence in the room and Val suddenly became aware of the ticking of a clock, which she hadn't noticed before. When combined with the flickering slats of light and the lilt of the priest's voice, it was hypnotic. If she was to believe his version of events, there was a lot more to her father's character than she had imagined.

CHAPTER 63

THAT EVENING, AFTER TUCKING NICOLE UP IN BED, Val snuggled next to Bill on the sofa and told him all she had heard from the priest. He was a good listener. It was one of his sterling qualities. She always felt he was interested in what she had to say, in stark contrast to her ex-husband.

"You could argue that my father romanticized the facts years after the event to portray himself in a good light," she said. "I'm sure he would have been eager to win the priest's good opinion. But I believe this story because it fits with all the other facts." She listed them on her fingers. "He went back to get Maria's bag from the basement, planning to rescue her and make her his wife, and he kept it all those years hoping to find her. He had wedding rings engraved and kept them in her Fabergé box. And it explains what he said to me in the nursing home before he died."

"What does 'intimacies' mean?" Bill asked. "Do you think the old devil actually had sex with a Romanov girl?"

Val screwed up her nose and shook her head in distaste. "You didn't meet him. I don't think Maria would have gone that far. These girls were grand duchesses, after all. There had been talk of matching them with foreign princes, while my dad was penniless and had nothing to recommend him. But it sounds as though Maria liked him. Remember it said in the museum that they kept having to sack guards because they got too close to the family?"

Bill agreed, but suggested, "It could have been a case of Stockholm syndrome. Remember those hostages in a bank raid in 1973 who ended up testifying on behalf of their captors? Psychologists reckon that forming attachments to captors is a common coping mechanism."

Val thought back to the photos developed from the old camera. "Maria photographed three guards. Maybe she was friendly with them all. But she didn't photograph my father."

"One of them was Peter Vasnetsov, wasn't it? The man who rescued her. And your father's ledgers mentioned letters received by the Vasnetsov family." He narrowed his eyes in concentration. "I wonder what became of Peter. Did he help Maria to escape overseas? Did he even go with her? If he had gone back to his family home, the authorities would have found him. Your dad would have found him."

"You're right." Val nodded. She went to find the packets of photos and pulled out the one of Peter Vasnetsov. He had an honest, unassuming face, she thought.

"Let's have another look," Bill said, and she handed it over. He shook his head. "An unlikely hero. I guess we'll never know what became of him. I wonder why your father didn't process these pictures himself."

"I suppose he wanted to keep things just as they were for when he found Maria," Val guessed.

Bill nodded. "Does Father Methodius think he started working for the secret police straightaway?"

Val shook her head. "He didn't work for them. He stole a uniform and pretended to be a Cheka officer while he spent the next few years of his life looking for Maria and Vasnetsov."

Bill raised an eyebrow. "One day he's just a factory worker turned guard, and the next he's doling out money all over the place to bribe officials? Doesn't make sense, does it?"

Val blushed. "There's part of the story I didn't tell you before, something I learned from my mom." She was embarrassed to tell him her dad had been a criminal, but that was silly; she wasn't responsible for his actions. "During the civil war and right through the early 1920s, he made a living breaking into the houses of the aristocracy and stealing their treasures, then selling them to White Russians living in exile in Harbin. He made a vast amount of money."

Bill laughed. "Good on him! A bit of venture capitalism in the midst of Communist takeover. Times were tough, so no doubt those government officials were happy to cooperate in return for a few extra rubles."

"But then Father Methodius told me he was arrested in Ekaterinburg, charged with impersonating a police officer, and sentenced to death. Aged twenty-six, he sat in a cell waiting to die." Val paused for a moment, trying to imagine what that must have felt like. "By chance, he was able to escape while being led out to a van, and he ran for his life, eventually making it back to Harbin. After that, he didn't dare return to Russia. He had to accept that he would never find the woman he loved. He married my mother because she took good care of him, but she never stood a chance of winning his heart because he had already given it to another."

"It must make you look on him quite differently," Bill said.

"The one thing I can't forgive him for is sending Mom back to Harbin when I was thirteen." Val remembered the heartbroken months after her mother left, when the house was silent and she sobbed herself to sleep every night; then she thought of the terrible suffering her mother endured, which the Chinese doctor believed was the cause of her premature death. "Father Methodius says he was very depressed at the time, but that's no excuse."

Bill put his arms around her. "What's done is done. I think it's great you understand more now so you can think of him as a sad, troubled man rather than a monster."

Val turned to kiss him. It was still new and extraordinary for her to be with someone who was interested in her past, who realized it affected who she was in the present. Tony wouldn't have given a damn. Part of her still felt unworthy of Bill's love, but she was determined to enjoy it all the same.

She ran her hands over his chest and shoulders, then down his torso. She loved his shape, with the long thighs, the lean waist, the shoulders that her head rested so comfortably against. As they removed each other's clothes and began to make love, Bess raised her head to watch for a bit, then lay down and went back to sleep on her mat in the corner.

~

Later, when they were getting ready for bed, Val ventured a question that had been on her mind since she spoke to Father Methodius.

"I was thinking of writing to that curator in Petrodvorets to tell him what I've discovered, but I won't if you have any objection. I don't want to jeopardize your parents' safety." She turned to watch his expression, wary that it might revive the old argument—still the only one they'd had.

Bill looked her in the eye. "Sweetheart, you do what you want. I'm sorry I made such an issue of things when we were in Leningrad. I was just worried about Mom and Dad. You understood that, didn't you?"

"Eventually." She smiled.

"But why do you care what that curator thinks? If you want

to make your dad's story public, we could tell my colleague in New York and let him publish it. Or you could write about it yourself." He kissed her shoulder. "It could be the first of many publications in your career as a world-class historian."

Val laughed. "You're jumping the gun somewhat; I'm only a few months into my degree. But about Stepan—I really warmed to him. I felt as if I knew him. All the other Russians we met seemed authoritarian and cold, but he was familiar, like someone I could be friends with. I suppose his opinion mattered to me."

"You write to him if you want, darling. It's entirely your decision."

He switched off the bedside light and pulled the covers up to her chin, making sure she was snug. Spring was on the way, but it still got chilly in the darkest hours of the night.

CHAPTER 64

Leningrad, November 1976

STEPAN BROUGHT THE LETTER HOME FROM WORK AND handed it to Maria where she sat at her sewing machine by the window. Mikhail's teenage daughter had bought some purple velvet in a market and brought it to her *babushka*, asking her to make a fashionable maxi skirt. The style was similar to skirts she and her sisters wore in the old days, although much more fitting.

"What's this?" she asked, squinting at the pages, which were written in English.

"It's from the Australian woman who brought me those photos in the summer." Stepan glanced around at Peter, who was bent over a newspaper, spectacles perched on his nose. "I think you'll find it interesting."

Maria began to read and cried out when she came to the second paragraph. Val wrote that her father, Anatoly Bolotov, had been in love with Maria and believed his affections had been reciprocated.

She stared at Stepan, openmouthed. How *could* he? Was it true, or a story he had concocted in retrospect to excuse his actions? Could he possibly have mistaken her friendly politeness in the house for romantic encouragement?

"Are you all right, dear?" Peter asked.

She shook her head in disbelief. "Do you remember Anatoly Bolotov, that guard at the Ipatiev House? This letter is from his daughter. Stepan met her in the summer. She seems to think Bolotov was in love with me."

Peter put down his newspaper and smiled. "We were *all* in love with you."

Maria's flesh crawled. Had Bolotov believed when he raped her that she was a willing participant? She hadn't struggled or screamed, but that was because of her fear of someone hearing them. She felt sick to think of it, even now.

She turned back to the letter and read the next paragraph before reporting its contents to Peter. "It says that each man in the execution squad was allocated one member of the family to kill, and that Bolotov volunteered to shoot at me. But when the order was given, he deliberately missed. He hoped he could rescue me but others stepped in and shot and stabbed me instead."

"Perhaps you owe him your life," Peter suggested. "If he had shot you at close range, he would have killed you."

Maria glanced at Stepan, whose face reflected his conflicting emotions. He had always loathed the man who fathered him and seemed reluctant to revise that opinion.

She read on, then told Peter, "Bolotov was watching when you lifted me off the truck. He was on horseback and could easily have caught us, but instead he shouted to the rest of the men that we had fled in the opposite direction. He did it to save us."

"Did he now?" Peter gave a low whistle. "I always thought it odd they didn't catch us. I didn't even spot any signs of pursuit. We owe him a debt of gratitude."

Stepan walked over to gaze out the window, so Maria couldn't see his expression anymore.

"It says he hunted for us for years and spent the rest of his life pining for me." Maria wrinkled her nose. According to the letter, he'd even bought wedding rings for the two of them. "That's ridiculous. He only knew me for what—a week?"

"You had a powerful effect on all the young men there," Peter said, with a twinkle. "I wonder what became of Ivan Skorokhodov? I bet *he* never forgot you."

Maria knew what he was thinking: that Ivan had been Stepan's father. Should she tell him the truth now? What would be the point?

"I always felt guilty that Ivan went to jail because of me. I was probably a little too flirtatious with him."

Stepan turned to her, a question in his eyes, while Peter grinned. These two men, who were so alike, both believed a different version of the past and it didn't matter one iota.

"What will you reply to the Australian woman?" she asked Stepan. "You should at least thank her for her letter."

"I don't know." He shrugged. "I'll think about it."

It was what he always said when delaying a decision: if one of his children asked if they could vacation by the seaside, or if Ludmilla wanted to redecorate the apartment. It usually meant he would do nothing at all.

CHAPTER 65

Leningrad, June 1979

Maria was working in her garden, sowing carrots and runner beans, when Stepan rushed around the corner of the building and hurried across to her. She looked up, surprised, because it was midday and he should have been at work.

"Mama, there's something I have to tell you," he said, breathing heavily as if he had run all the way. "Please come and sit down."

Maria's blood chilled. Someone had died. Who was it? Please let it not be one of her children or grandchildren, because she couldn't bear that. She glanced around to where Peter was sitting on a bench, enjoying the warmth of the sunshine.

Stepan took her arm and led her to the bench, helping her to sit beside Peter, then closed his eyes before beginning to speak, as if choosing his words with care.

"It looks as if they have found the grave of your family in Ekaterinburg," he said.

Maria clutched her hands to her face and felt goose bumps prick her skin. She had long wished for this news, but at the same time it was hard to hear. Tears came and Peter put his arm around her and pulled her close.

Stepan continued. "A colleague of mine called Geli Ryabov visited the children of Comrade Yurovsky last year, and they showed him some notes their father made about the murders. Using these, and with the help of local geologists and chemistry experts, he found a spot where there are a number of skeletons."

Maria's tears were flowing freely now as an ancient grief was resurrected.

"He took three of the skulls to Moscow for tests and he's convinced one is your father's, but he says no ministry wants to get involved. It's still too politically sensitive."

Maria couldn't bear to think of them as "skeletons" with "skulls." "I hope they are being treated with respect," she cried.

"Ryabov assures me that he got a local priest to say a *panikhida* for them," Stepan said.

Maria thought of Tatiana. Was she still alive? Would she hear this news? She would be eighty-two years old that month. Maria's first instinct was to travel to Ekaterinburg and ensure that the bodies were reburied with religious honor and ceremony. She knew Tatiana would wish the same. Perhaps they would bump into each other there.

"Do you think I would be allowed to bury them, if I tell the authorities who I am?" She asked the question with longing, but knew the answer before Stepan responded. She had no evidence to prove her identity now and would simply become one in a long list of Romanov claimants stretching back to the 1920s. Her aunt Olga had died almost twenty years earlier and there was no one left who could personally identify her. Besides, although it was more than sixty years since the Revolution, it could still be risky to reveal herself. Soviet president Leonid Brezhnev tended to have those whose political views differed from his own committed to mental asylums, and rumor had it the conditions weren't much better than in the gulags. She felt sure Tatiana would make the same calculation. If she was overseas, she would not risk returning.

"The authorities want to brush this under the carpet," Stepan told her. "The news will not be announced in the press and no official ceremonies are planned. I think they might leave the bodies where they are."

"We can hold a private ceremony for them here," Peter suggested, and Maria laid her head on his shoulder in gratitude. He had never believed in her religion but he knew how much comfort it gave her.

She decided she would gather her entire family and ask a local priest to conduct a memorial service. They would have flowers and candles, and she would say goodbye properly, even if she could not lay their corporeal remains to rest.

It had all been such a waste. Stepan and Peter hugged her, one on either side, as she wept for the future her family had been denied, and for the children and grandchildren they never had a chance to bear.

~

In the weeks after the bodies were discovered, Maria started having vivid dreams about her childhood: playing quoits with the sailors on the deck of the *Shtandart*; that Frenchman at a ball who called her "the true beauty of the four"; the excited barking of Jemmy, Joy, and Ortipo when they chased squirrels in the park. Sometimes she woke in a sweat when the dream changed and her siblings were transformed into hideous skeletons, their flesh dissolved in sulfuric acid.

"Your siblings stayed forever young," Peter said. "Their skin never wrinkled and their hair never thinned."

That was true, at least. When she washed Peter's back in the bath, she felt sad to see the folds of skin hanging off his limbs where there used to be solid muscle. He had black moles on his torso, varicose veins on his legs, and liver spots on his hands. His silver hair had thinned at the crown, but he still had his cowlick, perched above the weathered skin of his face. So many little imperfections, but she loved the soul of him.

What must he see when he watched her naked at her toilette? She had become the fat little bow-wow her sisters used to tease her for being. Six pregnancies, plus the appetite for sweet foods she developed after the siege, had left her with an apron of flesh hanging from her belly. Her breasts, which Peter used to love, drooped low and flat when not encased in a brassiere, and she chose not to imagine what her bottom looked like. Yet still he felt desire for her and she for him. Their lovemaking was slower and more careful than in their youth. She had a bad back and a weak leg, while Peter did not have the strength to rest his weight on his elbows in the missionary position, but they found ways to keep their passion alive that were both comfortable and intimate.

～

During the remainder of that year, Maria felt herself slowing down. She often fell asleep after lunch and dozed for part of the afternoon. Peter sat beside her pretending to read his paper, but when she opened her eyes she usually found he was snoring gently, mouth open and spectacles slipped down his nose. She felt the cold more than ever, and her fingers stiffened so that sewing became difficult. Sometimes she forgot the names of her grandchildren, confusing one with the other, or accidentally calling them "Katya" or "Pavel." "Silly me." She frowned, recognizing her mistakes.

No matter. They were lucky, she and Peter. They were survivors. Their neighbor Viktor had died in his fifties from a heart attack, and his wife blamed the gulag. Peter was made of stronger stuff and his overall health seemed good as he entered his eightieth year. They had met sixty-one years ago, spent nineteen years together, sixteen years apart, and now it was twenty-six years since the day he came back to her in the Peterhof palace garden. Still she smiled when she remembered that moment: the shock, the incredulity, and the dawning realization that God had wrought a miracle for her.

In their last twenty-six years Peter had become close to his eight grandchildren and passed on his natural wisdom and equanimity, lessons no school could ever teach. They worshipped him, visiting often and bringing fish they had caught or rabbits they had trapped using his methods.

Autumn came, and both Peter and Maria succumbed to a nasty cold and cough. It was nice to have an excuse not to get out of bed as the skies outside darkened and the temperature dropped. Ludmilla brought hot soup, and made Peter's elecampane infusion under his careful instruction. When both developed fevers, she called a doctor, but there was little he could recommend except bed rest and plenty of fluids.

As they lay side by side, Peter and Maria whispered reminiscences: of Stepan's birth in a barn; of their coworkers at the pig-iron factory; of the sentimental song "The Little Blue Scarf" that everyone used to sing in wartime, both in Leningrad and in the Norilsk gulag. Trivia, really.

Sometimes Maria watched Peter while he slept, his complexion pale and his breathing labored, and wondered which of them would die first. She wasn't sure she would survive the news of his death a second time. To attend his funeral knowing that she would never see him again on this earth would be intolerable. Yet at the same time she did not want him to have the pain of losing her. She would rather spare him that sorrow.

The doctor came again and listened to Maria's breathing first, then to Peter's, before pronouncing them much improved. Their lungs were not so congested, he said. There was no reason they should not get up soon, although he recommended they stay indoors for the remainder of the week.

That night, Maria slept with Peter's arm around her. She loved to feel the weight of it resting across her waist. His face was so close she could smell the sourness of his breath and hear a tiny rattle in his throat. She roused slightly in pitch blackness and noticed his breaths were faint, with long gaps between. He was in the fathomless depths of sleep.

"I love you," she whispered, not thinking he would hear, but she felt a tiny movement of his finger where it rested against her back and knew that he had. She shifted her head a little to kiss him on the lips, then let herself slide back into the seductive darkness of sleep.

When Stepan came with tea in the morning, he found them pale and stiff, their skin cool to the touch. Both had passed away gently in the night. Their expressions were calm and their lips still touching.

EPILOGUE

Peterhof, 2007

ONE EVENING STEPAN SWITCHED ON THE TELEVISION news just in time to hear the young blond newsreader announce that two more graves thought to belong to Romanovs had been found near Ekaterinburg.

"One of the bodies is said to be Alexei and the other is either Maria or Anastasia," she said. "That means all the family are now accounted for."

"Rubbish!" Stepan shouted at the set. Ludmilla was in the kitchen talking to their daughter Anna, now in her fifties, and their granddaughter Eva, aged thirty-two, who were cooking the evening meal.

He had kept up to date with the research on the graves over the years and was scathing about the amount of misinformation the reports contained. These scientists with their fancy computers and DNA technology knew nothing at all. The bones had been separated, manhandled, and sent to laboratories across Russia, the UK, and America, in the process becoming so contaminated that they could have belonged to Stalin, Hitler, or Genghis Khan, for that matter.

Stepan had often discussed their Romanov heritage with his children and grandchildren. If any of them decided they wanted to reveal their ancestry, he would not try to stop them, but he warned it would be an uphill struggle to make anyone believe them, despite all the fuss about DNA. So far all had decided not to bother.

That Australian woman Val had written a thesis in the 1980s suggesting that Maria had escaped from Ekaterinburg. Stepan had come across it through a footnote in an American author's book, and his grandson Misha had downloaded a copy from the Internet. He had read it with interest, not least because it contained more information about the strange life of Anatoly Bolotov, including extracts from ledgers he had kept, detailing his efforts to find Maria over the years. He had traveled all over Russia, and had monitored the letters received by Peter's family; Stepan realized he had clearly been a man obsessed.

Val's thesis had attracted only minimal interest from Romanov scholars, although she was a professor of history at Sydney University. The truth did not sound plausible, Stepan mused. Experts wanted a neat ending with all the royal family in one place. To his knowledge, no books or theses had been published that so much as hinted at the fate of Tatiana. No one would ever know what happened to her after she left the Ipatiev House on July 15, 1918.

One summer he had gone to Sverdlovsk with Ludmilla to try looking for the Vasnetsov family, but they had also disappeared into thin air. He had applied for information on Yuri Koshelev, the NKVD officer who had taken Mikhail and Katya on the Ice Road, but his file simply said that he died in 1942. Some people could never be found.

He began thinking about Val and wondering how she would receive the news of this latest Romanov find. He knew he had been rude in not replying when she wrote to him in a spirit of friendship. So many years had passed that she might be dead by now, although he reckoned she had been a good twenty years younger than him. That meant she was only in her late sixties; he himself had reached the grand old age of eighty-eight and was still amazed to think he had made it into the twenty-first century. He'd always assumed he'd be dead by then.

Over dinner that evening, he asked his grandson, "If I wanted to track down a woman who used to work at Sydney University, would that be easy to do?"

"What's her name?" Misha asked, picking up his smart-phone.

"Val Scott. She was a professor of history."

Within seconds, Misha had found her. "Scott was her maiden name. Her married name is Koskov. Do you want to email her?"

Ludmilla gave Stepan an amused look. "After all this time?"

Stepan gave a shrug. "I don't know. Not email. No." If she lived in the Leningrad area, he would have asked her for a cup of coffee, but there was too much to say to put it in an email.

"We could ask if she wants to do a Skype call," Misha suggested. Stepan looked puzzled, so he continued, "It's a video telephone call where you can see each other on the computer screen."

Stepan muttered, "What will they think of next?" Why was he even considering contacting her after all this time? Perhaps he felt he owed her an apology for his brusqueness and for not replying to her letters. He could tell her he had read her thesis, and they could laugh at all the experts who'd gotten it wrong over the Romanov graves.

"Sydney is eight hours ahead," Misha said, having found that information on his phone. "If you call in the morning our time, it will be evening for her."

"She probably won't want to speak to me," Stepan said.

Anyway, what would he say to her? He couldn't tell her that their father had been a rapist. There was no need for her to know.

"I'll email and ask her if she would like to Skype," Misha said, typing away with impressive speed.

"Remind her that we met in the Peterhof palace in 1976 when she brought in a sun, moon, and stars box," Stepan said.

"Done!" Misha replied.

Stepan pursed his lips. What would be would be.

He didn't have long to wait. When he arrived at breakfast the next morning, Misha grinned. "Your lady friend in Sydney says yes, she would love to talk to you. She's sent her Skype address. Want to do it this morning?"

"I don't know . . ." Stepan had never been a man who suffered from anxiety, but he felt a knot in his stomach when he thought about this conversation. He had decided in bed the night before how he would begin.

"I'm around today so I can set it up for you," Misha persisted. "Shall I say eleven our time?"

An hour to go. Was he really going to do this? "All right," Stepan agreed, and sat down to his cup of coffee.

An hour later, he perched upright in the chair in front of the screen while Misha typed in the address and they waited for a connection. There was a buzzing sound as one computer tried to talk to another on the opposite side of the world, and Stepan marveled at that. He jumped when Val's face appeared full-size on the screen. It was slightly blurred but obviously the same woman he had met. She was smiling, her eyes merry.

"Hi there!" she said, her voice as clear as if she was in the next room. "What a surprise to hear from you!"

Stepan took a deep breath before he spoke. "Hello, little sister," he said. "I think I owe you an explanation."

ACKNOWLEDGMENTS

I'm hugely grateful to my legendary agent, Vivien Green at Sheil Land, and my foreign rights agent, Gaia Banks; thanks to them, my books have now been sold in a staggering twenty countries. The crack team at my US publisher—Lucia Macro, Asanté Simons, Jennifer Hart, Amelia Wood, Danielle Bartlett, and Jean Marie Kelly—are a force of nature, positively bursting with energy and enthusiasm, and I feel very fortunate to be published by them.

Some brilliant advisors helped with this novel. Dave Yorath explained to me in detail how old cameras worked, in particular the Kodak Autographic, and he showed me what 1918 film developed in the 1970s might look like. Paula Grainger suggested the herbal remedies that Peter might have used, checking Russian sources to make sure they were available in the season and the part of the country that my plot required. Gerrie Fletcher, a longtime Sydney resident, checked the details of Val's life there, as well as the Australian characters' dialogue. Ben Balliger, an attorney and graduate in Russian history from the School of Slavonic and Eastern European Studies at University College London, checked the Russian sections. I'm incredibly grateful for their help but must emphasize that if any errors have crept in, they are mine alone.

My first readers were the incredible Karen Sullivan and Lor Bingham. Both have a huge amount going on in their lives so I was touched to the core that they took the time and trouble to give me their invaluable thoughts and suggestions. I'm also grateful to Scott Whitmont of Lindfield Books in Sydney for reading an advance copy and sending back a lovely review and a correction! And Jane Selley did a marvelous job of copy-editing; it's the second time we've worked together and she truly is the greatest, most forensic copy editor ever.

With each novel, I am blown away by the generous support of the book blogging community. I'd like to thank in particular the bloggers who chose *Another Woman's Husband* for their "favorite books of 2017" lists: Anne Williams, Karen Cocking, Anne Cater, Kaisha Holloway, Victoria Goldman, Nicola Smith, Lor Bingham, and Caryl, aka Mrs. Bloggs. And thanks to all bloggers who host blog tours: I know it can be very demanding and really appreciate the effort you put in.

Love and thanks to my fabulous sister, Fiona Williams, who now has a dedicated bookcase for my novels; to my aunt Anne Nicholson for regular encouragement over the years; to the never-miss-a-party crew of Tina, Martyn, Peggy, Lee, Katie, Nev, et al; to author friends Sue Reid Sexton, Louise Beech, Marnie Riches, Liz Trenow, Kirsty Crawford, Tracy Rees, Tammy Perry, Lesley Downer, Hazel Gaynor, David Boyle, and Kerry Fisher for writerly support; and to Karel for being my own personal Peter Vasnetsov.

About the author

About the book

Insights,
Interviews
& More . . .

Meet Gill Paul

Christina Jansen

GILL PAUL is an author of historical fiction, specializing in relatively recent history. She has written two novels about the last Russian royal family: *The Secret Wife*, published in 2016, which tells the story of cavalry officer Dmitri Malama and Grand Duchess Tatiana, the second daughter of Russia's last Tsar; and *The Lost Daughter,* published in August 2019, the story of Grand Duchess Maria, Tsar Nicolas II's third daughter.

Gill's other novels include *Another Woman's Husband*, about links you may not have been aware of between Wallis Simpson, later Duchess of Windsor, and Diana, Princess of Wales; *Women and Children First,* about a young steward who works on the *Titanic*; *The Affair,* set in Rome in 1961–62 as Elizabeth Taylor and Richard Burton fall in love while making *Cleopatra*; and *No Place for a Lady,* about two Victorian sisters who travel to the Crimean Peninsula during the war there in 1854–56 and face challenges beyond anything they could have imagined.

Gill also writes historical nonfiction. Her titles include *A History of Medicine in 50 Objects* and the Love Stories series, which contains tales of real-life couples. Published around the world, the series includes *Royal Love Stories, World War I Love Stories,* and *Titanic Love Stories.*

Gill was born in Glasgow and grew up there, apart from an eventful year at school in the United States when she was ten. She studied medicine at Glasgow University, then English literature and history. (She was a student for a long time.)

She now lives in London, where as well as writing full-time, she swims year-round in an outdoor pond, complete with a heron, a variety of ducks, and a family of kingfishers. ∾

A Deleted Scene from *The Lost Daughter*

Ekaterinburg, June 19, 1918

ONE MORNING, just after the family's scripture reading, Ivan Kharitonov, the cook, put his head around the door of the sitting room and said in a low voice, "Excuse me, Miss Maria. Might I have a word?"

She frowned. What could he want? Putting down her sketchbook, she rose and followed him out to the passageway that led to the kitchen.

He looked over his shoulder before fishing an envelope from the pocket of his white chef's apron. "This came an hour ago. It was in the wooden box in which the nuns deliver our food, hidden beneath the butter."

Maria took the rather dog-eared envelope and saw her name written in English on the outside, along with the words *Strictly private and personal.* How very odd!

"Thank you, Ivan." She smiled. "I appreciate your discretion."

She considered taking it back into the sitting room, but then she would have to pass it around for all to read. Since she had no idea who could have written it or what it might say, she decided to open it on her own in the girls' bedroom.

There were two pages covered in neat handwriting she did not recognize so she searched for the signature at the end: *Dickie*. It was her cousin, Prince Louis of Battenberg. They had been close playmates as children, when their families spent summer holidays together in Germany or in Russia. His mother, Princess Victoria, was the sister of her own mother, making them first cousins. The last time she had seen him was in 1913 when he joined them on the *Shtandart* for a Baltic cruise. Why was he writing to her? She sat on her bed to read.

My dearest Maria, he began. *News filters through to me of the appalling way your family are being treated. It's simply ghastly. I wish I could come straight to Russia and whisk you all to safety but I am currently serving in the Royal Navy. I must not tell you where, or which ship I am on, but it is one of the most powerful dreadnoughts and we are achieving considerable success against the Hun.*

Maria mused how difficult this war must be for him. Both his parents were German-born—like her mother—yet he was fighting for Britain, the country in which he had been raised.

As soon as we are victorious, which I believe will not be much longer, I will come to Russia to help overthrow this evil dictator Lenin, so your family can be restored to its rightful position. I cannot divulge them here, but trust me when I say that plans are afoot.

Maria was overjoyed. For too long there had been no news from the outside world so it felt as though they had been forgotten by their European relatives. But it seemed they were not. Allied troops were coming. Dickie was coming.

During the long months at sea, he continued, *I have had time to think about my future once all this is over and I have come to a very important decision—perhaps the most important a man can make. You must know that I have always had a soft spot for you, my beautiful, darling cousin. I have never met a girl like you, no matter where in the world I have traveled.* Maria's face blanched and her heart began to pound as she guessed what was coming. *It would make me the happiest man in the world if you would agree to be my wife.*

Maria put the letter down, her stomach churning. My ▶

goodness! It was all so unexpected. As children, she and Dickie had played tennis together, had swum in the sea, and had played hide and seek—but marry? She had simply never thought of him that way. He was handsome enough, with sleek dark hair above a high forehead, a long, thin nose, and penetrating eyes. He had already been tall, with distinguished bearing, when last she saw him, despite being just thirteen years of age. But *marry*?

Suddenly she remembered an incident during that visit. They had been strolling on an island in the Gulf of Finland, and she had run ahead and ducked behind a tree, planning to leap out and surprise him. But when she jumped out he was closer than she'd thought, right beside the tree, and she bumped into him. He extended a hand to steady her and his palm brushed against her breast. It was insignificant, over in a moment, and yet that encounter stuck in her mind because she could remember the exact expression on his face. He appeared embarrassed, but there was something else in his eyes: a hungry look that puzzled her at the time. She realized now it must have been desire.

Her cheeks felt hot as she read the remainder of the letter. Dickie suggested that they should set up home near Portsmouth, as he planned to continue his naval career after the war, but he promised they would visit her family as often as she wanted. He wrote that he hoped to have children and he knew Maria would make an excellent mother—*the very best kind*. He praised her complexion, her eyes, her hair, her gentleness, in terms that made her blush even more deeply.

To protect those who have helped me, I will not tell you how I contrived to get this letter to you, he said, *but I would be eternally grateful if you could respond tomorrow morning, putting your reply in the exact same place this was discovered. I'm sorry to rush you but it must be tomorrow or else your letter could fall into the wrong hands. If you are unable to make up your mind so fast, please at least tell me whether I might have hope.*

Maria was giddy with the swirl of emotions that engulfed her. Foremost was astonishment that Dickie felt that way about her.

She had known he liked her, but not enough to propose marriage, not *that* kind of liking. She felt flattered, because there was no doubt he was a good catch. He was a prince, a great-grandson of Queen Victoria, with connections throughout European royalty. How extraordinary that he should propose to her rather than to one of her elder sisters! She felt worried that she might hurt his feelings if she did not consent, yet how could she? She had known him only as a playfellow. He was good company but she scarcely knew anything of his character as an adult.

Maria's mother had been just twelve years old when she met her father at the wedding of her elder sister Ella to a Russian nobleman, but she said they fell in love straightaway. Both knew their own minds from the very start. Maria had felt great passion for the officer Kolya Demenkov, whom she met in 1914. She used to toss and turn in bed at night, her skin tingling as she pictured him kissing her and holding her in his arms. But she had never imagined kissing Dickie and wasn't sure she could. She didn't think of him that way; he was more like a brother. Did that matter? Could you learn to love someone over time?

She knew she must tell her mother of this proposal but she hesitated. When Olga came into the bedroom to retrieve her shawl, Maria slid the letter between the pages of a book. She wanted to think it through so she could know her own mind—but there was little time to spare if she must respond by next morning.

~

"Oh, but that's wonderful news!" her mother cried as she read the letter that evening.

"Victoria will be delighted. We discussed the possibility of a match when she was here just before the war, and both agreed you and Dickie were very compatible."

"You did?" Maria was stunned. "Why did you not tell me?"

Her mother shrugged. "It's better for young people to find out for themselves. I would never force any of my children to marry someone they did not love." ▸

A Deleted Scene from *The Lost Daughter* *(continued)*

"But how can I know if I would love him? We were children when we last met. Besides, he's younger than I."

"Only a year. That's nothing." Alexandra peered at her over the top of the pages.

"There's another thing you might consider: if you were to become engaged to a member of the British royal family, they would have to redouble their efforts to get us out of here. It could only work in our favor."

Maria was alarmed. "So you think I should accept him for that reason? Even though I don't love him?"

Her mother frowned. "Not accept, necessarily, but it would be kind to give him hope, surely? Then after we are rescued from here, you can spend all the time you like getting to know each other. I think it's a charming letter, Mashka. What do you have to lose?"

Maria considered this. "Can we keep it secret from the others? They will tease me and I'm not sure . . ." Her voice trailed off. "Besides, Olga and Tatiana might be jealous if I get engaged before them."

"I'll tell your father, of course, but the others don't need to know. Now, let's get to work on your letter. I imagine it will be collected by someone who works for Thomas Preston, the British consul in Ekaterinburg. Victoria met him when she was here just before the war. Perhaps he will be able to put it in a diplomatic pouch going back to Britain." She opened her Moroccan-leather writing set and pulled out a sheet of notepaper with the Romanov mauve-and-cream crest, a quill pen, and a silver inkwell with a gold filigree lid.

There was no table in the bedroom, so Maria balanced the leather case on her lap as she wrote *My dear Dickie*. She stopped and looked at Alexandra for guidance.

You can't imagine how surprised I was to receive your letter, her mother dictated, *and how delighted.*

Maria wrote as she was told. She had always been the most obedient of the five children.

Next morning, an hour before breakfast, she took her letter to the kitchen, where Ivan Kharitonov was baking bread.

"Will you slip this in the exact same place as you found the last one?" she asked.

"Of course I will, Miss Maria." He nodded, taking it from her with a discreet smile.

She wandered back to the bedroom, feeling the weight of the world on her shoulders. When would the letter reach Dickie? What would he think?

Her reply felt dishonest. She had given him hope when really there should be none. She had deliberately misled him. But what choice did she have when the safety of her family was at stake? She hoped fervently that before they met again, he would have fallen in love with some other girl and would not hold her to any implied commitment. Of all possible outcomes, she decided that would be the best.

Historical Note

During the war, anti-German sentiment in the UK persuaded the Battenbergs to change their name to Mountbatten. Lord Louis Mountbatten went on to have a long and distinguished career in the Royal Navy, oversaw the transition to Indian independence in 1947–48, became First Sea Lord in 1955, and served as Chief of the Defence Staff in the early 1960s. He married an English heiress, Edwina Ashley, in 1922 and they had three children. He was particularly close to Prince Charles, to whom he was a great-uncle. In 1979 he was assassinated when the Irish Republican Army blew up his fishing boat off the coast of County Sligo. Until the day he died, he kept a photograph of Maria Romanova on a mantelpiece in his bedroom. ᔡ

Historical Afterword

WHEN THE ROMANOV royal family were placed under house arrest following the February 1917 revolution, few could have believed the Tsar and Tsarina would be executed less than seventeen months later, along with their five children. After all, they were the wealthiest family in the world and closely interconnected with several European royal dynasties.

The initial plan was for them to be exiled to Britain, but arrangements were complicated by the war in Europe, and King George V dragged his heels. As Russia lurched toward civil war during the summer of 1917, the Romanovs were transported to Tobolsk, Siberia, in a move that was said to be for their own safety. Attitudes toward them hardened after Lenin seized power in the October Revolution, and in April 1918, Maria and her parents were escorted to the smaller, more heavily guarded Ipatiev House in Ekaterinburg, which is where *The Lost Daughter* begins.

My depiction of the character of Maria is based on facts we know about her. She did

Grand Duchess Maria Nikolaevna of Russia. Library of Congress Prints and Photographs Division Washington, D.C., Bain Collection

not feel secure in her parents' affections, and once wrote to her mother saying she considered herself unloved. She was plump as a child, earning her the nickname "fat little bow-wow," but many considered her the most beautiful of the four girls, with her huge eyes "like saucers." She was physically the strongest of the four, able to lift and carry thirteen-year-old Alexei on her own. And although she was not academically gifted, she was artistic, enjoying drawing, painting, and photography.

Around men, Maria appears to have been naturally but innocently flirtatious. One guard, Alexander Stretokin, wrote that she was "a girl who loved to have fun." Commandant Yurovsky wrote that she had a "sincere, modest character" that made her very popular with his men. He said that she "spent most time with the sentries" and he remembered her showing them her photograph albums.

It is well documented that a guard called Ivan Skorokhodov smuggled a cake into the house on Maria's birthday in June 1918, then the pair of them disappeared together and were caught in what were described as "compromising circumstances." No one knows exactly what happened, but Ivan was jailed for three months and thereafter disappears from the history books.

Maria was clearly a friendly, outgoing kind of girl with a healthy interest in the opposite sex. If the guards were going to save any one of the girls in the house, surely it would have been her? And if she did escape, her physical strength would have helped her to survive. That was my thinking when I began to shape the story of *The Lost Daughter*.

~

I have stuck closely to the known facts about the Romanovs' stay in Ekaterinburg. Konstantin Ukraintsev, Avdeyev, and Yurovsky are all real people, but the characters of Peter Vasnetsov and Anatoly Bolotov are my inventions. The men who executed the Romanovs were recruited from the militant Verkh-Isetsk metallurgy works and the meeting I describe in the prologue of this novel did take place. My depiction of the events of July 16–17, 1918, is derived from accounts left by Yurovsky and others who were present. In the days following the mass execution, members of the public were able to wander into the Ipatiev House and help themselves to souvenirs, and the place later became an unofficial pilgrimage site. It was destroyed under Leonid Brezhnev's premiership in 1977, just a year after my fictional Australian character Val visited it. ▶

Two days after the execution in 1918, it was announced in Russian newspapers that Tsar Nicholas had been killed but that the rest of the family were being held in a safe location. This location was never divulged and the uncertainty led to dozens of Romanov impostors emerging over the subsequent decade, most famously Anna Tschaikovsky (later Anderson), who claimed to be Anastasia and was only proved posthumously to have been a Polish factory worker. Some Maria impostors came forward but none of the stories were credible.

A report by a White Army inspector, Nikolai Sokolov, first published in 1924, gave a strong hint as to the fate of the Romanovs. It detailed some grisly objects he had found near an abandoned mine shaft in the Ekaterinburg area, including belt buckles, shoes, dentures, and bone fragments, though he did not discover the family's graves. Under Stalin's authoritarian rule, speculation on the fate of the erstwhile royals was discouraged and the subject was seldom raised in the Soviet Union. During the mid-1970s, when my character Val began investigating the Romanov possessions she found in her late father's house and safe deposit box, the fate of Russia's royal family was still not entirely certain.

Some amateur archeologists found the main grave site in 1979, but the news was not publicly announced until 1991, after the collapse of Communism. The bodies were then exhumed and sent to labs in Russia, the UK, and the US for DNA analysis. It was discovered that the remains of Alexei and one of the younger girls—either Maria or Anastasia—were missing. Their grave was not found until 2007.

The mainstream view is that the Tsar and Tsarina, their five children, and the four retainers—Dr. Botkin, Anna Demidova, Alexei Trupp, and Ivan Kharitonov—were shot and bayoneted to death in the Ipatiev House during the night of July 16–17. A few historians, however, still claim that there could have been mistakes in the identification of the remains due to contamination of the bone samples, and that one or more of the Romanovs could have escaped the slaughter in Ekaterinburg.

The Lost Daughter follows Maria through the Russian civil war and the Bolshevik economic experiments that led to the famine of 1921–22, in which a staggering five million Russians died. There was a mass movement of peasants to the cities thereafter and the population of St. Petersburg grew rapidly. Citizens lived in communal apartments, often sharing a single room with other families and sleeping in curtained-off areas. Several families used the same bathroom and cooking facilities, leading inevitably to conflicts between neighbors, but I decided to make Peter a shock worker and give his family an apartment of their own.

The Cheka was formed by Lenin in December 1917 as a secret police force to root out enemies of Bolshevism. It had the power to conduct its own nonjudicial trials and executions, and to torture suspects. In 1922 the Cheka was reorganized and eventually the NKVD, the dreaded police force of Stalin's regime, took over. Hundreds of thousands of Russians were convicted by NKVD *troikas* and either executed or sent to gulags. There were waves of purges through various professions—the army, doctors, *kulaks*—and against any perceived enemies of the state. Between 1936 and 1938, in what became known as the Great Terror, over a million people may have died in front of firing squads or in the notorious gas vans. Those whose family members had been jailed or executed came under suspicion themselves, and becoming an informer was one way to avoid arrest.

The siege of Leningrad was one of the most avoidable tragedies in twentieth-century history. Stalin completely misread Hitler's intentions when he signed a nonaggression pact with him in 1939, and the Soviet army was totally unprepared for invasion, not least because many of its top commanders had been purged in the preceding years. Once the siege began, Stalin seemed to write off the beleaguered city as indefensible and failed to prioritize getting supplies through. Between September 1941 and January 1944, around a quarter to a third of the prewar population of Leningrad died—700,000 to 800,000 people. In the brutally cold January and February of 1942, around 100,000 were dying per ▶

month. For years afterward, the siege was rarely spoken about, either inside or outside the Soviet Union. There were references to "hardships" suffered in wartime, but it was only after the collapse of Communism that the true scale of the horror came to light in the form of survivors' memories and diaries. I've used many details from these in my descriptions of conditions.

∼

In the years during and after the Russian civil war, between 100,000 and 200,000 White Russians fled across the country's eastern border into Harbin, Manchuria. There was already an established Russian community there, with their own Orthodox churches and Russian businesses. Some were waiting in the hope that the Bolsheviks would be overthrown and they could return to their homeland without fear of retribution for being *kulaks*, or intellectuals, or Whites. But during the 1920s, Soviet influence grew stronger in the town and life must have felt more precarious. Some people emigrated back into the Soviet Union, others to Japan and South America, but a sizeable number sailed south to Australia, as I have Val's father doing in my novel.

Some Russian political exiles had already arrived in Sydney after the February 1917 revolution, and another wave followed in the 1920s. A club known as the Russian House was founded as an organization to help new arrivals find work and a meeting place in which to celebrate Russian festivals. In 1933, Father Methodius Shlemin began to hold Orthodox services there, and in 1942 the church I describe in the novel was founded on Robertson Road, Centennial Park. Sydney retains a strong Russian community to this day.

∼

This is my second novel about the Romanovs. The first, *The Secret Wife*, concerns the romance between the second-eldest daughter, Tatiana, and a cavalry officer called Dmitri Malama. I have alluded to their story in *The Lost Daughter*. But the family's fate is so shocking and haunting that I couldn't resist returning to it in 2018, the centenary of their murders. I feel as moved by it now as I did when I first read the story as a teenager.

For a regime to execute a monarch and his wife was not unheard of, but to execute their five children as well, the youngest just thirteen years old, was barbarous in the extreme. If only Nicholas's first cousin, George V, had let them flee to safety in England. If only one of the many rescue attempts had succeeded. There is no paper trail connecting Lenin to the murders, but he could certainly have saved them had he tried.

The slaughter happened in the twentieth century, to a family who often filmed themselves with movie cameras, so you can find them on YouTube prancing through the gardens of their palaces, paddling in the sea, and playing with the sailors on their royal yacht. The girls are beautiful and utterly innocent of anything except being born into the wrong family at the wrong time. They could have been mothers and grandmothers, wives and lovers, farmers or artists or authors. In my novels, they are.

The Romanov Family. From the left: Grand Duchess Olga, Grand Duchess Maria, Tsar Nicholas II, Tsarina Alexandra, Grand Duchess Anastasia, Tsarevitch Alexei, and Grand Duchess Tatiana. *Portrait by the Levitsky Studio, Livadiya*

Sources

HELEN RAPPAPORT'S THREE BOOKS on the Romanovs are compelling and beautifully written. I highly recommend *Four Sisters* for an in-depth look at the characters of the girls, *Ekaterinburg* for a chilling countdown of the final days of their lives, and *The Race to Save the Romanovs* for a gripping account of the attempts to rescue them. Greg King and Penny Wilson's *The Fate of the Romanovs* contains a wealth of detail that I found invaluable. It was fascinating to read the diaries and letters of the family, which have been translated into English by Helen Azar. And I also valued Robert K. Massie's *The Romanovs: The Final Chapter* and Andrew Cook's *The Murder of the Romanovs*.

Treasure of the Tsars, a 2017 exhibition at the Hermitage in Amsterdam, had many poignant exhibits, including drawings by the children, clothes, and letters. I was also able to use my own memories of a visit to St. Petersburg in 2016, when I fell in love with the glitzy palaces and the exquisite Fabergé Museum.

While researching the period after the Revolution, I began with Orlando Figes's brilliant and comprehensive book *A People's Tragedy*. The exhibitions *Revolution: Russian Art 1917–1932* at London's Royal Academy in 2017 and *Russian Revolution: Hope, Tragedy, Myths* at the British Library in the same year were both invaluable. Actually seeing ration cards and photographs of factory life and communal living, then reading stories of individuals executed by the NKVD, made the era seem all the more real.

If you want to know about life in Stalinist Russia, the starting point has got to be Orlando Figes's extraordinary book *The Whisperers*, which collects personal testimonies from survivors throughout the Soviet Union. I also found some compelling stories online, and there was useful information in the memoir *My Life in Stalinist Russia* by an American woman called Mary M. Leder.

Anna Reid's masterful *Leningrad: Tragedy of a City Under Siege* is the best account I found of that period. She quotes liberally from diaries and personal accounts and provides the kind of detail that is a gift for a novelist. Alexis Peri's *The War Within: Diaries from the Siege of Leningrad* was also very useful, and I found several other accounts online.

Finally, while researching Sydney in the 1970s, I used a 1973 guide to the city entitled *Ruth Park's Sydney*. I also had a wonderful reader in Sydney resident Gerrie Fletcher, and was helped by my own happy memories of a six-week stay in the city in the 1990s.

The Love Lives of the Romanov Daughters

GRAND DUCHESSES OLGA, Tatiana, Maria, and Anastasia were born in an era when royals still needed to marry other royals, or else the marriage would be declared morganatic and their offspring would not inherit their titles. But Nicholas and Alexandra had married for love and wanted the same for their beloved daughters. They trawled through the pool of eligible European royals and considered candidates from the Balkan countries, as well as the sons of their first cousins in Germany and Great Britain, but no great romances ensued and the outbreak of war in 1914 put the search on hold.

The Romanov girls had led cloistered lives, rarely socializing except with direct family members, and as a result they were young for their ages. Most evenings were spent at home sewing, reading, and playing card games such as bezique and board games such as halma. Before 1914 their main contact with the opposite sex had been with sailors on the royal yacht *Shtandart* or members of the imperial guard, whom they would rope in to games of tennis or croquet. Olga had crushes on a couple of them, writing breathlessly in her diary in February 1913, "Sat with AKSH [Alexander Konstantinovich Shvedov] . . . and strongly fell in love with him." But she was fickle; by June 10 that year she was writing of Pavel Voronov, an officer on the *Shtandart*: "He is so *affectionate* . . . I love him *so much!*"

The outbreak of war in 1914 brought many potential new beaus into their sphere when the Catherine Palace at Tsarskoe Selo was turned into a makeshift military hospital, and Olga, then aged eighteen, and Tatiana, seventeen, trained as nurses. It was by far the most exciting thing that had ever happened to them.

Soon Olga met the man who would be the great love of her life: Dmitri Shakh-Bagov, known to all as Mitya, a soldier she nursed in 1914. They corresponded after he went back to the front, and a sister at the hospital wrote in her 1916 diary, "A letter came from Shakh-Bagov. Olga . . . threw all her things around from delight— she felt feverish and she jumped around, saying: 'Can one have a stroke at 20 years old? I think I am having a stroke!'"

The whole family knew of Olga's romance, conducted by letter and in fevered meetings when Mitya was back in Tsarskoe Selo. They could easily have married after the war; he came from an aristocratic family and Nicholas's sister had married an aristocrat, so it was not unprecedented. But the last time they saw each other was on December 27, 1916, two months before the Russian Revolution, when Mitya spent an evening with the family before heading back to his Yerevan Regiment.

There is no evidence that he wrote to Olga once the family were under house arrest but she got word of him in April 1918, writing in her diary, "Kupov wrote a letter. He saw Mitya in Petrograd. He sent us regards." We can only imagine her dejection that he only sent "regards"! It doesn't sound very loving. Olga suffered from depression during the family's sixteen months in captivity and perhaps his coldness was one cause.

We are not sure what happened to Mitya after 1918: he may have fought with the White Army who were trying to overthrow the Bolsheviks; he may have ended up in a Soviet labor camp; or he could have escaped into exile. But I bet he never expected to be remembered a hundred years later for his romance with a Romanov grand duchess.

Tatiana also had a favorite among the officers at the hospital— Dmitri Malama. In the first week of the war he was wounded in the leg while rescuing a fellow officer under fire and was awarded for gallantry. She soon became very attached to him, writing in her diary, "After dinner Malama came over . . . I was terribly glad to see him, he was very sweet." He clearly liked her too, because he bought her a gift of a French bulldog, whom she called Ortipo, the same name as his cavalry horse. Alexandra invited him to lunch at the palace in 1915 and later wrote to Nicholas, "I have to admit, he would make an excellent son-in-law. Why are foreign princes not like him?"

Malama, who is the subject of my novel *The Secret Wife* ▶

(spoiler alert if you haven't read it), did his best to save his country from the Bolsheviks, fighting valiantly with the White Army. He died at the battle of Tsaritsyn in June 1919, by which time he probably suspected that his sweetheart, Tatiana, might be dead, although he could not have known for sure.

Maria, who was fifteen at the outbreak of war, had a crush on an officer in the Guards Equipage called Nikolai Demenkov, known to all as Kolya. He was slightly chubby, as was she, and her sisters teased her by calling him "Fat Kolya." In her diary she referred to herself as "Mrs. Demenkov" so she clearly had strong feelings for him, but she was not to see him again after a meeting in March 1916. We know that she corresponded with him while the family was under house arrest. In one postcard sent from Tobolsk on November 22, 1917, she writes, "May you have all the best in life. So sad that we have not heard from you in so long . . . We reminisce about the happy times, the games . . . May God keep you." Demenkov managed to escape from Soviet Russia in 1920, going first to Constantinople and then to Paris, where he lived until 1950 and was of great help to Romanov family historians.

Anastasia was only fifteen when the family was placed under house arrest. She was a tomboy, a boisterous child, so there is no documented love affair, but she was fond of her friend Katya's brother, Viktor Zborovsky, who was nursed at Tsarskoe Selo after being wounded in the war. In one letter to Katya in June 1917 Anastasia reminisced about a time when they had water fights with Viktor in their garden. Could her feelings for him have developed into something deeper had she lived?

All the girls' romances were innocent, giddy crushes that never had the chance to blossom, but they are poignant for the insights they give into these very normal girls with their keenly felt passions.

There's one more poignant thought: had Olga or Tatiana been engaged or married to a European royal before 1917, surely the country concerned would have been honor-bound to rescue the

Romanovs from their Bolshevik captors? I imagined a proposal from Prince Louis of Battenberg in the "deleted scene" on page 4 of this PS section but, while there is evidence he liked Maria, no such letter existed. Perhaps if the Romanovs had not held out for love matches but had opted for traditional arranged marriages with members of other royal dynasties, they could all have survived. ᕒᕐᕒᕐ

Reading Group Questions

1. Do you think a marriage could work between a couple with such opposite backgrounds as Maria and Peter? They came from different social classes, in an era when that meant a whole lot more than it does now; he was far less educated than she in the academic sense; he did not believe in the religion that meant so much to her; and his political beliefs were at odds with her family's heritage. Did the relationship convince you in the novel?

2. Both Maria and Val believed that they grew stronger over the years. Do you think their characters developed through the course of the novel? Or did they just learn to cope with adversity through necessity?

3. Val's experience of a violent marriage is quite common: many domestic abuse survivors say that the worst violence occurred in the early days, and after that they were scared and did all they could to avoid confrontation. Why do so many women stay in such marriages and only leave in order to protect their children? Is it to do with low self-esteem? Lack of money? Because they still love the men despite everything?

4. Is Tony simply a monster or do you get a sense of why he is violent and controlling? Can you understand why Val married him?

5. There are many different locations in this book. Which one was the most vivid for you?

6. Was there enough explanation of Russian history for those who did not know much about it before? Some readers Google as they go along, and that's fine, but ideally the book should stand alone without any additional explanation.

7. The siege of Leningrad was one of the most harrowing aspects of the Second World War, yet little was written about it for several decades afterward. The Soviet government discouraged discussion, simply saying, "Life was hard for Leningraders," and it is only recently that historians have collected and published oral testimonies from those who lived through it. Did you feel you got a sense of the developing tragedy from the novel?

8. Did the novel make you consider how you would survive in a police state? Would you inform on your neighbors and/or work colleagues to protect your children, for example?

9. We get only glimpses of the complex character of Val's father, and most of these are damning. Did the priest's words make you reevaluate him?

10. One theme of the novel is fatherhood: What it means to be a good or a bad father. What do you think makes a good father? How does it affect children if they have a bad father?

11. Stepan resembles Peter in his character and his moral outlook although he is not his biological son. Would he have been a different person if he had been raised by Anatoly? In other words, is nurture more important than nature? ▶

12. Why do you think so many people claimed to be Romanovs after the family's disappearance? Were they doing it for attention? In the hope of claiming the family fortune? Or were they deranged and actually believed it themselves?

13. If one of the Romanov children had survived, would we ever find out?

14. Did you read *The Secret Wife* before this? If so, compare the two books. Which do you prefer, and why? ∿

Discover great authors, exclusive offers, and more at hc.com.